LAYOVER

LAYOVER

DAVID BELL

BERKLEY
NEW YORK

BERKLEY
An imprint of Penguin Random House LLC
1745 Broadway, New York, NY 10019

Copyright © 2019 by David J. Bell

Library of Congress Cataloging-in-Publication Data

Names: Bell, David, 1969 November 17– author.
Title: Layover / David Bell.
Description: New York : Berkley, 2019.
Identifiers: LCCN 2018053560| ISBN 9780440000860 (hardback) |
ISBN 9780440000884 (ebook)
Subjects: | BISAC: FICTION / Suspense. | FICTION / Contemporary Women. |
GSAFD: Suspense fiction.
Classification: LCC PS3602.E64544 L39 2019 | DDC 813/.6—dc23
LC record available at https://lccn.loc.gov/2018053560

First Edition: July 2019

Printed in the United States of America
1   3   5   7   9   10   8   6   4   2

Jacket art: woman by Raul Belinchon/Gallery Stock; airplane by Genja/Shutterstock Images;
airfield by Hospach/Shutterstock Images
Jacket design by Emily Osborne
Title page art: woman leaving airport by Rob Wilson/Shutterstock Images
Book design by Kristin del Rosario

In memory of Mary Ellen Miller
Teacher, poet, friend

LAYOVER

Prologue

The nurse opened the curtain around my bed and said there was somebody who wanted to see me.

I tried to read the look on her face. She cut her eyes away from mine, busying herself with the chart that hung on the wall and then asking me to lean forward so she could examine the back of my head. She wore a colorful smock decorated with Disney characters, and when she came close I caught a whiff of cigarette smoke clinging to her clothes. It almost made me gag.

"Everything looks good," she said, her voice flat. Her shoes squeaked against the floor. "How's the pain?"

"Throbbing mostly," I said.

"That's not surprising," she said. "You have a mild concussion. You're lucky it wasn't worse. Most people who get hit the way you were end up with staples in their scalp."

"Who wants to see me?" I asked. Each word required effort, like I was pushing it out of my mouth.

I pieced together the previous few hours from the fragments of my concussed memory. The amusement park. My face in the rich, damp earth. A cop standing over me, shining a light in my eyes, snapping his fingers as if I were a fighter down for the count. And then the ambulance ride to the hospital, winding through the county roads, nausea rising with each turn and bump.

I knew I was in Wyckoff, Kentucky, the little college town ninety minutes northwest of Nashville. And I knew what I'd come there for.

And *who* I'd come there for.

And I knew no one else in town, so if someone wanted to see me . . .

Could it be . . . Morgan? Coming to check on me?

The nurse slipped out through the privacy curtain. I heard the sounds of the emergency room around me. The chatter of doctors and nurses. A machine beeping nearby, tracking the rhythm of someone's beating heart.

On the other side of the curtain, a man's hoarse voice muttered in response to a doctor's questions. "No, sir. No, sir. I wasn't drinking. No, sir."

The lights above me were bright, making me squint. I needed to use the bathroom, the pressure in my bladder increasing. And a wave of nausea swept through me again, roiling my stomach like a rising tide.

Then a woman pushed aside the curtain the nurse had just exited through. She wore a business suit—tan pants and jacket, a white shirt. She held an iPhone, and the overhead lights flashed off the gold badge clipped to her belt. The glinting hurt my eyes, and I turned away, wishing I could bury my face in the stiff pillow that supported my head.

"Mr. Fields?" she asked. "Joshua Fields?"

"That's me," I said, eyes squeezed shut. It felt like a strange statement, announcing my own identity to a stranger. But did I really know who I was anymore?

"How are you feeling?" she asked. She cocked her head, one

corner of her mouth lifting. She had a friendly face with big, sympathetic eyes, but her voice was strong, each word landing with certainty and force.

"My head hurts." I looked down. The blanket came up to my chest, and I appeared to be wearing a flimsy hospital gown with a strange geometric pattern on it. I wasn't sure if I still had my boxers on. "And I don't know where my clothes are."

"They'll give those back when the time comes," she said. "I'm Detective Kimberly Givens with the Laurel Falls police. We spoke on the phone earlier. You remember that, right? I need to ask you some questions, and they're fairly urgent. Do you think you're up for that right now?"

It didn't sound like a question. My heart started to race at a rate that matched the thumping in my head. If I'd been hooked up to one of those machines that monitored my pulse, I suspect it would have beeped like a video game. Detective Givens lifted one eyebrow, and that gesture served as a repetition of her question.

Was I up for that right now?

Did I have a choice?

"Can you dim the lights?" I asked. "Maybe this overhead one can be turned off."

The detective looked around on the wall for a moment and flicked a switch with her index finger.

Instant relief. The lower-wattage recessed lights in the room provided gentler illumination. I breathed easier, stopped squinting.

"Better?" she asked.

"Yes." My mouth felt like I'd been chewing felt. I looked around for a drink but saw none. No way that nurse was coming back while the detective was with me.

"Do you know how you ended up here?" Givens asked. "Do you remember where we found you?"

I closed my eyes again, saw a replay of the same images. The amusement park . . . my face in the dirt . . . the cop shining a flashlight in my face . . . the ambulance ride . . .

Hey, buddy. Hey, buddy. Are you with us? Can you hear me?

"Somebody hit me," I said. "I think."

"You weren't alone out there, were you?" she asked.

"No."

"There was another man on the ground near you. Someone had hit him. Likely more than once. Do you remember that?"

I looked down. Even in the dimmed light, I could see my right hand resting on the white blanket. My knuckles were scraped and raw like they'd been dragged across concrete. I felt an ache like I'd punched a rock. I didn't try to slide my hand under the covers. Givens followed my gaze, staring right at the scraped knuckles, and her eyebrows rose again.

"Is he okay?" I asked.

Givens held my gaze for a moment, and then she said, "Who else was out there with you?"

My lips were as cracked as crumbling plaster. I ran my tongue over them, trying to generate some moisture.

"Mr. Fields? Who else was out there with you?"

I returned her gaze and didn't blink. "You must know who."

"Tell me where she went," she said.

"I don't know."

"Here's what happened," she said. "The police arrive at the scene. We find two unconscious men. Both with hands that look like they've been in a fight. Oh, and did I mention . . ." She paused so long I thought she was finished speaking. She drew out the moment, holding her words back, letting me stew. But then she said, "You know, we found other evidence out there as well. Very interesting evidence."

"What kind of evidence?" I asked, my voice cracking like my lips.

She chose not to tell me. "So, what can we conclude, Joshua? You're the only one left to explain it all."

For the first time in my life, I wondered if I needed a lawyer.

So I remained quiet.

"Tell me, Joshua. It's time."

The machine kept beeping. A siren rose and fell in the distance.

"You're not going to tell me how that man is doing?" I asked.

"I really don't know. But if you start to answer my questions, I can see what I can find out." She took a step closer to the bed. "See, I bet you're the kind of guy who cares how that man is doing. Especially if you're the one who hurt him. You're a nice guy, right? Not the kind who gets involved in crimes like this. Right?"

The pain at the back of my head came back in a rush. Even with the lights dimmed, I felt the need to squint. But I couldn't pull the covers over my head and I couldn't walk out, not with a detective standing over me. Not without any clothes. I had no idea where my car was. I was very far from home.

And alone.

I was in over my head. And the hole was likely getting deeper.

"Morgan Reynolds, Joshua," Givens said. "Tell me how you met her. Tell me the whole story."

I sighed. I was tired. And I hurt.

"It began at the airport, during a layover. . . ."

PART ONE

1

We ended up next to each other in the airport gift shop.

Fate. Chance. Randomness.

I passed through Atlanta at least once a week, almost every week, heading for another city to take care of the same customers I'd been working with for five years. I arrived and left on the same flights, always the same times. One week I might fly to St. Louis, the next to Dallas or Little Rock.

On that Tuesday I was headed to Tampa.

I traveled all over the eastern third of the country. There was a never-ending blandness and sterility to the concourses and planes. On more than one occasion, I'd found myself in an airport, walking briskly through the terminal, and couldn't recall exactly which city I was in or where I was heading. I slept better in hotels than in my own apartment.

But that Tuesday, the day I met Morgan, something different happened. That day something put the two of us right next to each other.

I'd been working in commercial real estate development for five years, ever since I graduated from college. My life felt like an endless merry-go-round. I'd hopped on when my dad helped me get the job, and the carousel had been spinning since then. Everything around me had blurred.

My apartment.

My friends.

My life.

I passed through airport gates across the country, handed over my boarding passes, thanked the flight attendants and pilots. I didn't notice faces anymore. I didn't connect with the people I passed in my travels. We transacted things. Business. Commerce. Money. I bounced along with the rest of them like cattle in a chute.

My dad always told me to keep my cards close to the vest when negotiating. I'd taken that advice too much to heart. I'd started doing it everywhere.

But then she ended up in line next to me in the gift shop.

I wouldn't have noticed except she almost dropped her purse.

Something rustled and shuffled behind me. When I turned to look, she made a sudden movement, lunging to catch the leather bag before it fell, but her iPhone tumbled to the floor, bouncing and ending up next to my shoe. Since she was clutching the bag with both hands, I bent down and picked the phone up.

"Good thing you have a case," I said.

Her left hand shook as she took the phone back.

Nervous flier?

But she didn't thank me. I couldn't say I blamed her, since I'd been tuning my fellow travelers out for years. I'd adopted a glassy-eyed stare, a cold, determined look that warded off conversation.

But when she took her phone back, I really noticed her. The shaking hand—the vulnerability—somehow slipped past my defenses.

I looked right at her.

She wore her dark brown hair in a loose ponytail that hung

below a tan bucket hat with a red band. Her eyes and a good portion of her face were covered by oversized sunglasses I knew she had to have taken off before she got through security.

She was almost as tall as I am—a couple of inches under six feet—and wore black leggings, black running shoes, and a gray Lycra hoodie. She had a carry-on over one shoulder and clutched the purse against her body. Her flushed cheeks looked delicate, the skin nearly flawless. We appeared to be the same age, mid-twenties.

She looked away from me as I studied her. At least she seemed to be looking away from me, as much as I could tell with the sunglasses on.

Some holdup occurred ahead of us, drawing my attention to the front of the line. An elderly man wearing clunky shoes with his pants hiked up almost to his chest started arguing about the price he was charged for his newspaper. He felt like he'd been asked to pay five cents too many. The cashier listened with a strained look on her face.

I almost reached into my pocket to get the nickel, but I hadn't carried loose change with me since I was a kid.

So I turned to the woman behind me again. The one who had dropped her phone and taken it back without thanking me. The one with the shaking hand. The one who had managed to pierce the stoic determination I adopted when I traveled. It actually felt good to sense that small opening, to have the façade of cold impersonality cracked ever so slightly. That was a surprise.

"We might be here a while," I said, nodding toward the elderly man in front of us.

The woman ignored me again. She opened her purse and started rooting around inside of it. Her movements seemed frantic, as though she thought she'd lost something.

"I don't think anything else fell out," I said, trying to be helpful.

She whipped her head up toward me. "What did you say?"

Her voice came out sharp and possibly louder than she intended.

"I'm sorry," I said. "I was just saying . . . you look like you thought you lost something. When the purse fell."

She considered me for a moment from behind the glasses. Her mouth was small, the lips plump. A tiny beauty mark sat on her left cheek. A silly thought crossed my mind: *She's a celebrity. After all, we are in Atlanta, and they film a lot of movies here. I occasionally spot celebrities in the airport, actors I recognize from TV shows. That explains the sunglasses. That's why she's so pretty.*

It looked as though she was going to say something, but then she tucked her purse against her body, tossed a pack of gum she was holding back onto the display, and, grunting with exasperation, turned and walked away.

2

That should have been it.

I should have gone on with my Tuesday layover routine—paid for the paperback thriller I'd picked up off the rack, stopped in the bathroom and swallowed another Xanax, headed to the bar for my preflight drink and maybe something to eat.

But it didn't work out that way.

I did buy the book. It bore an embossed foil cover and the black, shadowy outline of a man who carried a gun and appeared to be running away, turning slightly to look over his shoulder. And I did head toward the bathroom near my gate. My flight boarded in ninety minutes, so I had plenty of time to kill. I moved through the crowds on the concourse, dodging my fellow travelers and their heavy bags, their recalcitrant kids, the beeping courtesy carts ferrying the elderly and slow from one terminal to the other.

It was all the same. Everywhere I went, always the same . . .

Except . . .

I found myself thinking about *her* as I walked. Her face—those full lips, those delicate cheeks. The beauty mark, the brown hair. Her shaking hand. Her apparent shock when I spoke. Her coldness toward me before she walked away. What did she think she'd lost that made her so frantic?

My love life had been floundering recently. Six months earlier, I'd broken up with Renee, who'd been my girlfriend for almost a year. I liked her quite a bit, although I'm not sure I loved her. We broke up because of that. And because I traveled so much and worked so many hours, leaving little time or energy for anything else.

Renee and I had been talking off and on again, had even slept together one night two weeks earlier. But neither one of us seemed ready to jump into a full-on reconciliation. At least not yet. But the thought of being with Renee back in Chicago had started to become more and more appealing to me. I was tired of being on the road, of sleeping in hotels and using tiny soaps and shampoos. I'd eaten too much room service, knew the names of none of my neighbors in my apartment building. The thought of being home seven nights a week, of having someone to come home to, of sharing a meal and conversation about the day just past or the week to come, made my heart swell with anticipation.

And then Renee texted me as I walked to the bathroom:

Hey, guy, have a great trip!

Was that all marriage was? A lifetime spent with someone who cared about whether you had a good flight? Someone who'd notice if you didn't come home or check in when you were supposed to? Would that same person make sure you took your pills in old age? Would she make sure you didn't eat foods that disagreed with you and bring you an antacid if you did?

It was starting to sound pretty good.

I stopped outside the bathroom door, tucked the book under my arm, and started to write back. An announcement came over the PA, telling someone they'd left their passport at the main security gate. The odor of baking cinnamon rolls and brewing coffee reached me from one of the restaurants, stirring a faint rumble in my stomach. I hadn't eaten before I left home that morning for my first flight, from Chicago to Atlanta.

Thanks! At the airport but

Then *she* came out of the bathroom. The woman from the gift shop.

She still wore the hat and sunglasses, had the carry-on over one shoulder, the purse in her left hand. And she froze in her tracks when she saw me. I stopped midtext. It felt like our gazes locked, but I couldn't be certain because I couldn't see her eyes. But I saw the brown hair and the beauty mark and the long, athletic body as our fellow travelers moved past us and around us, their suitcase wheels squeaking, their conversations creating an endless hum of human chatter.

And what must she have thought of me? I wore a sport coat and a button-down shirt. Khaki pants and lace-up oxford shoes. I looked like any other young shmuck going off to some boring, uninspiring job. Airports and planes and offices were full of them. A dime a dozen. What made me stand out? My kindness in picking up her phone? My gentle mocking of the elderly man and his five cents?

She took two steps toward me, and her lips parted as though she was about to speak. But she didn't. I put the phone away, sliding it into my inside jacket pocket. I'd get back to Renee later.

For a brief moment, I wondered if the woman before me couldn't hear well or was wearing headphones I couldn't see. It would explain why the only thing she'd said to me in the gift shop had been "What did you say?"

Rather than scare her off again, I waited, making what I hoped was something close to eye contact.

Finally she spoke.

She said, "I'm sorry about before. I . . ."

Again, I waited, hoping she'd finish the thought. But she didn't.

"What about before?" I asked.

"I was distracted. My mind was somewhere else. So when you spoke to me, I was lost in my own head."

Her voice carried a tinge of hoarseness, as well as the trace of a Southern accent.

I nodded, relieved to see she could hear me and that she didn't seem to think I was a total creep who harassed strange women in airport gift shops.

"I get it," I said. "I get lost in my thoughts sometimes too. Especially before noon and especially in airports. About the only thing to do is think."

She nodded as though she understood.

I relaxed. We'd connected, even if only to a small degree.

We could have gone our separate ways then, having reached an understanding and knowing that the hiccup in the gift shop line was nothing to worry about.

Then I saw something in her hand, something that hadn't been there before.

"That's a good one," I said, pointing to it.

"What's that?" She looked down, saw the book in her hand as though she'd forgotten it was there. "Oh, this. Yeah, I was looking for something to pass the time."

"I read it last week while I was flying." Some of the details about the story came back to me. A woman who used to be a spy was being pressed into service after a terrorist attack in Europe. "It moved really fast."

"Good. That's what I need. Distraction."

She stopped speaking but didn't move. She didn't rush off or head for a gate.

And I wanted to know what was behind those sunglasses. I really did.

Maybe I wasn't aware back then of how desperate I was to connect with someone, to share something on a deep level. To be surprised by what someone else was thinking or doing. Or feeling.

In the gift shop, the door had opened a crack. I wanted to kick it open farther. I needed the fresh air, the bright light.

"I'm sorry to interrupt," she said. "You were texting someone—"

"It's early," I said, ignoring her comment, "but I always get a drink before my flight or when I have a layover. Would you like to join me?"

I pointed behind her in the direction of a little airport bar, something called the Keg 'n Craft. I'd stopped there many times for a beer or a sandwich or to watch a football game. I'd started thinking about a career change when one of the bartenders recognized me and began calling me by name.

Again, I thought I'd overstepped. I'd pushed harder than I should.

She looked behind her and then glanced down at the Fitbit Surge on her wrist, checking the time. "My flight . . . I've got . . ."

"If you're in a hurry—"

"You know what?" she said. "I shouldn't, but I could really use a drink today, more than any other day." She nodded, confirming her decision. "Let's do it."

3

I went to take a seat at the front of the Keg 'n Craft, on the side closest to the concourse. It happened to be the most crowded side at that time of the morning, and sitting there afforded an easy view of the flight boards and a better chance to hear the announcements.

But when I pulled a barstool out, she kept walking. She didn't say anything or look back as she went to the side of the bar where no one else sat. The stools there offered a view of the parked planes, and you could sit and watch runway workers driving back and forth in their little carts, their giant hearing-protection headsets guarding against the noise.

I followed her.

She hopped up on a barstool, and I slid onto the one next to her. She put the carry-on bag on the bar in front of her and then placed her purse next to it. She seemed to want to keep those things close to her at all times, even though no one was sitting nearby and it didn't matter whether she took up a lot of space.

Although we'd connected briefly on the concourse and she'd agreed to the drink, she seemed to have regressed. She was acting the same way she had in the gift shop. When I sat down, she kept her face straight ahead, as though I wasn't there. And she still wore the sunglasses.

The bartender made drinks for a couple of travelers near the front, giving us a few moments to sit next to each other without any distraction except the muted TV above the bar. A daytime talk show played on the screen, with a panel of women gesturing back and forth at one another, apparently arguing over something the president had said on Twitter.

My phone dinged in my pocket. Twice in quick succession.

"You better get that," she said without looking at me. "Someone really wants to talk to you."

I knew it was Renee. I reached into my pocket and pulled the phone out.

> Did you get this?

> Just worried your flight was delayed and you'll miss your connection.

I wrote back quickly, finishing the thought from earlier.

> Thanks! Made it to Atlanta. Going to eat during layover.
> More later.

I silenced the ringer.

"Sorry," I said, putting the phone away.

"It's okay," she said, still looking ahead. But her voice became lighter, almost flirtatious, when she said, "Somebody cares about you."

Could she tell by the way the phone chimed that a woman was writing to me?

Emboldened by the new tone in her voice, I decided to seize the moment. "I'm Joshua," I said. "Joshua Fields."

I held my hand out.

She nodded but still didn't look at me. "Right," she said. "We're going to have to do this, aren't we?"

"Do what?" I asked.

She turned, the sunglasses still on. She reached out and took my hand, her skin soft against mine even though her grip was firm. "I'm . . . Morgan. Nice to meet you."

"Where are you headed?" I asked, ignoring the strange pause before she told me her name.

Again, a pause. She reached up and took her sunglasses off, revealing eyes that were a cool blue and tired-looking. At just after ten a.m., a number of the travelers in the airport probably had sad, weary eyes, including me.

"You're awfully curious for so early in the morning," Morgan said.

"It's either ask about you or watch the television. And there's no sound. Actually I was kind of worried you couldn't hear me back there in the gift shop."

She smiled just a little, and some of the weariness left her eyes. "Oh, yeah. That. Well, it's been a long few days. I've been dealing with some . . . let's say family complications." She paused for a moment, looking me over. "But now I'm going to a friendlier place."

"And where would that be?" I asked.

She paused again, her tongue working around inside her cheek. "Where I went to college. In Kentucky. About an hour and a half from Nashville. Have you heard of it? Henry Clay University? It's in a little college town called Wyckoff."

I had heard of it, so I nodded. "I live in Chicago now, but I grew up in Indiana. I got brochures from Henry Clay when I was looking at colleges. And I learned about him in school. What did they call him—?"

"'The Great Compromiser.' Yes, I know all about it."

"Right. Exactly."

"I grew up in Wyckoff," she said. "It was easy for me to decide to go there." She pressed her lips together, tapped her fingers against the top of the bar. "Yeah, that's home, more or less. A lot of memories."

"Are you going for a reunion or something?" I asked. It was early October, the time of year for homecoming weekends and football games. "Getting together with college friends?"

"I wish it were that simple. Sure." She smiled without showing her teeth, and beneath the smile I detected a strain. She seemed eager to turn the question back on me. "What about you? This is work travel for you?"

"Is it that obvious I'm not going to have any fun?" I asked.

She nodded at me. "The clothes kind of tipped me off."

I held my arms out wide. "How do you know this isn't my beachwear?"

"Not quite," she said with a little laugh. "Not even close."

"Okay, you got it. I'm traveling for work. Again. I'm in the air about two hundred thousand miles a year. Multiple times a week."

Her eyebrows rose, and her mouth opened. It was the most animation she'd shown since I'd seen her in the gift shop. "Wow. Now, that's exciting. I'd love to travel that much."

"It's not as glamorous as it sounds," I said. "It's all for work, and my job is pretty dull. Like you said, the idea of traveling sounds really exciting, but in reality all I see are airports and planes and hotels and conference rooms. It's just the same, over and over again. I'm not seeing the sights, eating good food, going hiking or scuba diving." I leaned forward. "Sometimes I look in the mirror, and I feel like I'm turning into my dad."

"Is that a bad thing?" she asked.

"No, not really. He's a good man. But maybe . . . Here." I reached into my pants pocket. I brought out a small, round plastic case and held it in my palm. "Do you want to know a secret?"

She moved ever so slightly toward me. "I'd love to. Everybody has a secret. And here in an airport bar is the perfect place to spill it. Everything here is temporary, isn't it? We're all just passing through on the way to somewhere else."

Her words brought me up short. "Yes, that's exactly how I feel. Like I'm a tourist, except the thing I'm observing is my own life. This is my life, right? And I'm just kind of buzzing through it without absorbing anything."

"That's pretty existential for the Keg 'n Craft," she said, with a real smile this time. "So, what's that in your hand?"

"Oh. Right." I twisted off the lid of the pill case and revealed its contents. "Do you know what that is?"

"Viagra?"

"Really?"

"Just having fun. It looks like it might be Xanax."

"Exactly. I hate to fly. I absolutely despise it. Lots of nights, including last night, I have nightmares about a plane crashing and being trapped on board. Do you know why I take one of these and then head to the bar? It's the only way I can get on a plane every time I have to fly. That's how much I hate flying. In fact, I took one this morning to get on my first flight. And now that I'm on my layover, I'm going to take another so I can get on the next flight."

"And yet you do it that much?" she asked. "You're afraid that much of the time?"

Hearing someone else say it made it seem even more absurd. "Yeah. Crazy, right?"

"Then why do you do it?" she asked. She didn't seem to be asking the question rhetorically. She seemed genuinely curious about my answer, as though some great mystery would be revealed when I spoke.

I answered honestly. "Because that's what my job requires. I make good money doing it." I paused. "And I really don't like any of the work I do, but I keep doing it. It's not exactly what I envisioned for myself when I was in college. I thought . . . I thought it would all be more exciting, you know?"

Morgan nodded as if she understood. But then she surprised me with what she said. "Can I be honest with you? I feel for you. I do. But I'd trade my problems for yours any day."

I started to ask what she meant, but the bartender finally showed up and asked what we wanted. Before she placed her order, Morgan slipped her sunglasses back on.

4

After the drinks came—a Bloody Mary for her, a bourbon on the rocks for me—I asked her about the sunglasses, which she still wore.

"Why did you put them back on before you ordered?"

She pinched her straw between her thumb and index finger and jabbed it into the drink a few times. The ice rattled against the side of the glass.

She turned and looked at me when she answered. "Why do you work a job that makes you miserable? Why do you think you're turning into your dad?"

First things first: I noted how she evaded my question. I also felt disarmed by the directness of her response. On a couple of occasions, I'd tried to talk to Renee about my job, about feeling unfulfilled. Once we sat at the kitchen table of my small but very nicely furnished apartment, long after our dinner was over, discussing the problem over more and more drinks, and no matter how hard I tried to explain my dissatisfaction, I couldn't seem to make it clear to Renee. Maybe the failure lay with me and my inability to articulate my unhappiness.

Or maybe she just couldn't hear me. Really hear me.

Renee was practical. She could plan. She could see challenges coming down the road, anticipate them, and adjust. Maybe we were too much alike in that way.

"Everyone feels this way in their twenties," Renee told me. "You have a good job. Lots of people would kill for a job like yours. Who knows where it will lead?"

I couldn't argue with her. I knew how fortunate I was. I knew most people didn't have a dad like mine who set me up with a sales territory and greased the wheels for me to start working as soon as I walked off the campus of Indiana University with a diploma in my hand. And Renee was focused on her career too. She worked for an architectural design firm, taking on bigger and bigger projects as the months went by. We were perfect for each other in every way . . . except the way that mattered most.

Morgan was still staring at me, and I saw the faint outline of my head reflected in her sunglasses.

"I'd like to quit," I said. "But that's tough. Especially when your dad gets you the job. And he's the boss. My dad made a lot of sacrifices for me when I was growing up. He worked his butt off raising me and building a business. So it's not easy to walk away."

"I quit my job." She turned back around, facing forward. She leaned down and took a long pull through her straw, her cheeks sucking in as she did so. "But I understand what you're saying about things not going the way you planned."

"How so?"

"I guess I thought working would be different. That my coworkers would be more mature, more thoughtful, more courageous than the kids I went to college with. I thought there'd be a higher purpose, something more meaningful. But I learned pretty quickly that people in the workforce are just like the college kids I knew. Scared. Impulsive. Deceitful."

She sounded cynical, jaded. Almost bitter.

I understood, even though I tried very hard to avoid giving in to those feelings.

"Maybe not all places are like that," I said. "Maybe we just haven't found the right place yet."

"Maybe. It's a complicated situation, but my mother is sick too. Very sick with cancer."

I let out a small, involuntary gasp when she said that. I simply hated to hear it.

"I'm sorry," I said.

"Thank you." She seemed to be fighting off the beginning of a quiver in her chin. She looked genuinely touched, almost moved by my words. Her response seemed out of proportion with the blandness of my statement. I meant it, but I wished I'd found something more original or meaningful to say. "It's okay. Really. But she needs someone to care for her. To just be with her, you know, as things get closer to the end. That's part of why I quit my job. Not all of it, but some. I had to decide what mattered the most. I had to make a choice." She seemed to be thinking of something else. "It was an easy decision really."

Things grew quiet between us for a moment, but I kept my eyes on her, realizing I hadn't taken my second Xanax yet. I'd made the mistake once of getting on a flight without it, thinking that I'd been taking it and flying for so many years my body might not notice the difference. But by the time the plane landed, my shirt was soaked with sweat, and my heart pounded in my ears louder than the jet's engines.

I needed it. But I also didn't want my senses to be dulled any more in that moment. The alcohol, draining its way into my empty stomach, provided a pleasant buzz. And the directness of Morgan's words, the unvarnished bluntness of a stranger I'd likely never see again, made the hairs on my arms stand up. A possibility opened up before me. I had the sense that the conversation could be going anywhere and could touch on anything. How different it was from the prescribed work conversations I always had, the same sales pitch and negotiation I went through over and over again.

Morgan was right about the airport—it was all temporary. Maybe that freed me too. Or maybe I just liked her, felt something for her, a spark or a flash I hadn't experienced in a while. My guard dropped further. My force field weakened. Those cards I'd always clutched so tight were about to be spread on the table.

"My mother left me when I was seven," I said as I turned away from her. I hadn't planned the words. They came out of their own free will. "I've seen her maybe three times since then. She didn't want anything to do with me or my dad after that. Not really."

"I'm sorry," she said.

"Thanks. My dad handled both roles. The older I get, the more I realize how tough it was for him. And how well he did it all."

Silence lingered again. Two older couples at the front of the bar laughed and toasted, clinking their glasses against each other and saying, "Here's to Vegas!"

"You know what I think?" Morgan said, drawing my attention back to her.

"What?"

She smiled a broad, genuine smile. The spark I'd felt grew hotter, the embers flaring.

"I think I need another drink. And so do you."

5

I usually stuck to one drink before each flight. That and the Xanax did the trick, allowing me to doze off—sometimes even before the plane left the ground—but kept me from being so far out of commission that I couldn't work once I reached my destination.

But Morgan left little room for argument or discussion. And I'd spent the past few years wishing fervently that something different, something surprising, would occur in the middle of my daily work life, so it would have been absurd for me not to embrace it. A beautiful woman wanted to have another drink with me, so when Morgan called the bartender over I ordered a refill.

"You're hard to say no to," I said when the glass of bourbon was placed in front of me. "Are you like this with everyone? Or am I just lucky?"

She seemed to take my question seriously and considered her answer before she spoke. "You're special," she said. "I can tell."

"Am I? You can sense that after one round?"

"I can."

"How?"

"You're trying to figure things out. Most people don't even

bother to ask these questions." Morgan took a long drink, then said, "What would you do if you quit your job? What do you dream of being?"

Again, her question was so direct, so simple, it took me off guard. I stared into the amber liquid in my glass and gave the question some thought. "Promise not to laugh."

"Do I seem like the kind of person to laugh at another person's dreams?"

"I guess not." The liquor had warmed the inside of my body. I felt any remaining inhibitions coming down—and quickly. Morgan smiled while I formed my answer. Her teeth were perfectly straight and white.

"I've always thought about being an illustrator." It felt strange to give voice to my dreams. I hadn't mentioned them to anyone in a long time. "I like to draw. I took a few classes in college."

"Why didn't you take more?" she asked.

"I had to be practical. My mom left us the same year my dad started his business. I guess trouble had been building between them for a long time."

"Crazy."

"Yeah. So there were some tough times for my dad and me. But we also adopted a 'you and me against the world' mentality. We were going to make it no matter what."

"Sure."

"And my mom leaving taught me a lesson. I just didn't want to be . . . unprepared for the world. I wanted to know where I was going. I wanted certainty. Or I thought I did."

"I hear you," she said. "Economics, having to make money, parents . . . It's complicated."

"It must be for you, if your mom is sick. Is your dad—?"

She started to answer but then held her index finger up in the air. "Can you hold that thought? I have to run to the bathroom."

"Sure."

She took another long sip through the straw, then gathered up her purse and carry-on.

"I can watch—"

"It's okay," she said. And then she left, walking around the bar and out to the concourse.

Once she was gone, I looked at my phone again. I saw a text from my dad. I was meeting him in Tampa that afternoon to see a couple of properties for new developments. We didn't always work side by side, but he saw a great deal of potential in this new project he was developing—a small upscale strip mall in an up-and-coming neighborhood. He hoped to get a couple of restaurants and maybe a craft brewery to go in there, and he thought he needed me along to offer the "young person's perspective." He was more than capable of handling everything on his own, as he'd been doing for years. I suspected he wanted me there because he was grooming me to take over the business. He'd been working on that particular project for the past three months, and his text message was typically short and didactic:

> See you at 2. Don't be late. Remember, don't oversell
> these properties. They speak for themselves.

I wanted to write back and remind him how long I'd been working for him and how many deals I'd handled on my own. But I kept my response to myself.

When I put the phone away and looked up, I expected to see Morgan returning from the bathroom. It was just across the concourse—where she and I had spoken the second time—but she wasn't there.

I did see two airport police officers walking past the Keg 'n Craft, their thumbs tucked into their belts, their leather boots thumping as they moved. It came back to me then that just a week earlier, on a day when I wasn't flying through Atlanta, there'd been a security scare. A foreign exchange student had left a suitcase—which contained a laptop, iPad, and chargers and cords—unattended on the concourse, prompting an evacuation. The FBI and the bomb squad arrived, shutting down the airport for several hours and delaying hundreds of flights.

It ended up being nothing, but I'd seen the story trending on Twitter while I was in Pennsylvania, and when it was my turn to fly home, I tossed back two Xanax and an extra bourbon in order to work up the courage to get on the plane. It unnerved me to think of all the things that could go wrong during a flight—bombs, terrorists, mechanical failures, pilot error, weather.

The increased police presence didn't necessarily reassure me. In fact, the swaggering cops only served as a reminder of how much I disliked flying. They continued out of sight, and I returned the phone to my pocket.

And Morgan still hadn't come back.

An unreasonable fear set in. Maybe she'd walked off, left me at the bar while she boarded her plane. We owed nothing to each other, and if she wanted to fade from my life as quickly and quietly as possible, she could. I'd have no way to find her.

But I realized how silly that was. Sometimes people took a long time in the bathroom. Or maybe she'd stopped to make a phone call, reaching out to her own version of Renee in some faraway city. *I'll be there soon. . . . I can't wait to see you. . . . I miss you. . . .*

And as I thought about that, an unreasonable jealousy crept through me. What did I care if she had someone else? What claim did I have on someone I'd known for just an hour?

The truth was that her life, despite the problems she'd told me about, sounded better than mine. I was trapped by work and obligation. She was going somewhere she associated with happy memories. Her travels sounded uncomplicated and easy.

But then she was there, walking toward me with her two bags. And still wearing the sunglasses. If I wasn't mistaken, her cheeks looked a little flushed, almost like she'd been running. Or maybe it was the effects of the alcohol.

She came close to touching me but kept standing. "I have to go now."

The corners of her mouth dropped, but I doubted her sadness was about saying good-bye to me. I wanted to ask if something had happened, if she'd received some news that had unnerved her. But I didn't.

"I thought you had more time," I said, looking at my watch. "And you still have a drink." I tried to sound light and carefree, but I really felt desperate. I didn't want her to go yet. I wanted to stay wrapped in the moment we'd been in for the last hour. It was possible to imagine the time we shared at that bar would stretch out forever, that the bubble would never pop.

But here she was wielding a giant pin, ending our time together and sending me back to my mundane life. Florida. Real estate. Dad.

She put her bags on the bar, and my heart lifted. She was going to stay. I very much wanted her to stay. I wanted to talk more. I didn't want to get cheated out of however many minutes we had left.

But she ignored the drink and took off her sunglasses, putting them on the bar as well. She moved in so close to me that her body slid between my legs. She placed her arms around the back of my neck and leaned in. Her soft skin brushed against mine, cheek against cheek. I couldn't believe it was happening, even though I'd known all along this was where we were heading.

"I've got to go," she said. "Really."

"Are you sure?"

"I wish I could stay, but I can't."

"I don't even know your last name."

I smelled the tangy Bloody Mary on her breath as she leaned against me, felt her hair against my face.

She didn't speak right away. We stayed frozen like that for a drawn-out moment before she said anything.

"My name's Morgan." She paused. "Morgan Reynolds."

And then her mouth brushed across my cheek and pressed, soft and smooth, against my lips. But it wasn't just a quick peck. She increased the pressure, our lips sliding and working against each other, and then she gently but firmly darted her tongue into my mouth.

I lost myself in the kiss. I gave in, slipping away from the airport as everything around us disappeared.

Long seconds passed, and I placed my hands on her hips and started to slide them around, feeling the Lycra against my skin. My hands started to move up—

But then she abruptly pulled back.

She wasn't angry. She was smiling, and I didn't want to let her go.

She stayed close.

"I like you. I really do. And I loved that kiss."

"You know, you don't have to—"

But she was shaking her head, her eyes weary again.

"I do," she said. "I really, really have to go. And I mean I *have to.*" She pulled away from me and picked up her bags and her sunglasses, which she slid back onto her face. "And you know what else?"

"What?"

"I'm sorry," she said. "But we're never going to see each other again."

6

Kimberly Givens was running late.

As always.

She ran from her bedroom down the steps of her town house, carrying her laptop bag in one hand, her gun and badge in the other. Her hair was still damp from the shower, and she looked down quickly just to make sure her shoes matched. She'd gone to work once wearing one black and one brown and didn't feel like making that mistake again. She breathed a sigh of relief when she saw they were the same color.

Kimberly had no time to waste that Tuesday since her daughter, Maria, was already waiting just inside the back door, her soccer gear in her hand, her face scrunched by the kind of searing impatience and irritation only a twelve-year-old could muster. The Laurel Falls, Kentucky, city sedan with municipal plates sat right outside in the carport, and as Maria opened the back door, Kimberly deftly found the key fob, hitting the button without dropping her gun or her computer.

"There, it's open," she said to Maria. "Go on."

She checked the clock above the stove: 9:55. Nope. She wouldn't have time to eat anything. She couldn't be late. She was meeting with the mayor of Laurel Falls at eleven. She had to deliver an update on the case.

The case. The case.

If only she had something good to tell her . . . But it had landed in Kimberly's lap just the day before, Monday, when a prominent local businessman named Giles Caldwell hadn't shown up for work after not being seen or heard from all weekend. She'd had less than twenty-four hours to make any progress.

Maria stepped outside and tossed her things—cleats, shin guards, goalie gloves, backpack—into the backseat of the car and then slid into the passenger seat.

Kimberly locked the town house and put her things in the back of the car, then climbed in and jabbed the "Start" button with her index finger. The vehicle hummed to life.

"We're going to be late," Maria said, the first words she'd spoken that morning.

"We'll be fine," Kimberly said. "It's practice, not a game. And it's fall break. Plus, I'm allowed to speed."

"Don't," Maria said in her best sullen-preteen voice. "Everyone will look at us."

"I was kidding," Kimberly said as she backed out of the driveway and into the street, heading toward the soccer field. She rolled her window down, hoping to let the pleasant October air dry her hair naturally. "I'll get you there in time. I was up late last night reading some reports for a big meeting I have today, so I was slow to get moving. Unfortunately, I just happen to have given birth to the most punctual tween in America."

They rode in silence for several blocks. Maria tapped her fingers against the passenger-side door, her breath going in and out through her nostrils like a cartoon bull's. Kimberly rolled her eyes internally, recognizing behavior her daughter had gotten from her ex-husband and Maria's father, Peter. Maria had always fumed and stomped when things didn't go her way, even as a toddler, and when

Kimberly and Peter were married, Kimberly called her "Peter Junior," jokingly hoping to establish the narrative that the girl had inherited her negative qualities from her dad. Kimberly knew it wasn't true, knew nothing was ever that black-and-white, but she allowed herself to think it was on certain occasions when she grew most frazzled by work and co-parenting.

"You've got all your stuff?" Kimberly asked.

"Yes."

"Did you make eggs?"

"Yes. And toast." She paused. "I would have made you some, but you were still in the shower."

"That's fine. I'll get something later. After my meeting with the mayor."

"Okay."

Maria showed no interest in her mother's meeting with the highest elected official in Laurel Falls. Tough crowd.

"Are you going to miss me all day?" Kimberly asked.

"Mom."

"Okay, okay. I'll stop. But I'm not going to see you tonight, so I want to know how you're doing."

Maria's head snapped toward her mother. "What do you mean you won't see me tonight? It's fall break. We were going to . . . Oh, forget it."

"I'm working late," Kimberly said, feeling the guilt rising like high tide in her chest. "I told you that could happen this week. Dad's picking you up after soccer and bringing you to his place. He works for himself, so he can do that."

"So we're not . . ."

"Shit, yes. I mean, no. We'll watch the movie another night. I promise."

Maria let out a sigh to end all sighs.

"We still have the rest of the week."

"Is it the same stupid case you got yesterday messing up fall break?"

"Yes, it is. We don't usually solve them in a day. If you think we can, you should run for mayor."

"This is the missing old guy?"

"He's not that old. He's fifty." Then she felt the need to provide reassurance. "You know, this is unusual. It's safe here in Laurel Falls. People don't just disappear."

"This old guy did. What's his name? Miles?"

"Giles."

"How long has he been gone?"

"We found out yesterday. But it's possible no one's seen him since Thursday afternoon. That's when he last showed up at work. We don't know."

"So he's dead," Maria said.

"Why would you say that?"

"I know the first forty-eight hours matter the most. You always say that."

"Just to make myself feel better, I'm going to revise that and say the first forty-eight hours since I found out matter the most. And we're at about eighteen right now." She hoped Maria wouldn't be afraid, hoped her friends and her friends' parents wouldn't overreact and worry. After all, it wasn't a kid who'd gone missing, not even a teenager. She tried to change the subject. For Maria's sake, yes, but also for her own. She didn't want to dwell on how little she knew about what had happened to Giles Caldwell. "You'll have plenty of things to do with Dad, I'm sure. He has Netflix and HBO."

"Ugh. Who cares? Jennifer will be there."

"Oh, her." Thanks to the new case, Kimberly had managed not to think about Peter's new girlfriend, Jennifer, but Maria's words conjured the younger, more attractive woman in her mind. She felt angry with herself more than anything else. She and Peter had been divorced for three years, and she didn't want him back, so why did she care that he'd started living with someone? Because Maria would see them cohabiting before marriage? No, she didn't worry about that. Because Jennifer was younger and prettier than she was? *You're getting warm.* . . . "I thought she seemed . . . nice. I thought you liked her okay."

"She has a stupid laugh."

"Do you want me to run her in? I think there's a state law against stupid laughs."

"Mom, you're not helping."

"You know my job can be unpredictable. But Dad and I will switch a day next week to make up for it. You'll be back in school then, but we'll manage."

No response. Maria was looking out the window, apparently fascinated by the passing trees, the other cars, the buildings and houses of Laurel Falls, Kentucky. Anything but actual conversation with her mother.

"You know," Kimberly said, as if she were just thinking out loud and not expecting any response, "if I get promoted, my work hours will be more regular."

"You said you were going to get promoted a couple of years ago, and they gave it to that other guy. The really old one."

"I know. But that job is available again."

"Did the old guy die?"

"He's retiring. And he's my boss, not some old guy. Show some respect. He's a police lieutenant. And he's a good man."

And I have to see him this morning and tell him we don't have any solid leads almost a day into the town's biggest case in years. He'll be thrilled.

"You said they don't promote women," Maria said.

"I might have said that, yes. But I don't want you to worry about that. You can do anything you want, anything a man can do."

"I know, Mom. You tell me this all the time. So does Dad."

"Does he?"

"Yes."

Kimberly placed a mental check in Peter's "good" column. His encouragement of Maria more than canceled out the effects of Jennifer. Her unnaturally bright hair, her yoga-toned body. Even, yes, her stupid laugh.

"Well, I'm going to go for the promotion again. This case I'm working on now might make it happen." *If I can solve it . . .* She gripped the wheel tighter as the field came into view. She saw Maria's friends milling around in their shorts and cleats, their smiles vivid, their gestures exaggerated. They all ran so hot and cold, so bright and dark. The sharp voices of the girls reached her through the open window, but she ignored them. "We're waiting on a detailed crime scene report. I'm hoping there's something in there since the mayor is breathing down my neck. It looks like this guy just disappeared into thin air. Or maybe he ran away. None of it makes sense yet. We need to catch a break."

"You know you're just talking to yourself," Maria said.

"I thought I was talking to you."

"Kind of." Then Maria sat up straighter. "Pull over. Right here."

"I know the drill," Kimberly said. "You don't want me to get too close. I'd think most of these kids would find it fascinating that your mom is a detective working on a big case. It's going to be all over the local news today. And I got interviewed for TV and the paper." She stopped the car and waited patiently while Maria went around to the back and dragged her things out. Her task complete, she came by Kimberly's window.

"So Dad's picking me up after practice?" she asked.

"He is. I texted him last night."

She sighed again. "How long before you find out what happened with this missing man?"

Kimberly didn't believe in lying to her daughter or giving her false hope. Those things accomplished nothing, either at home or at work.

"I don't know, pumpkin. When people disappear like this . . . I just don't know. We're only now starting to piece things together. It's slow work."

Maria shivered, and the corner of her mouth lifted in discomfort. "A man really disappeared? A grown man?"

"He did."

"But grown men don't disappear, do they?" she asked, suddenly interested. "You always say women are vulnerable. And kids. But a man. Someone that old. I mean . . . who would want to take him?"

"We don't know that anyone took him. He might just be . . . out of town or on a trip. Or something. Maybe he went away and forgot to tell anyone. He might have other problems. He's a businessman, so you never know what he could be tied up in."

"Like, he owes money to the mob?" Maria asked in a dramatic voice.

"We don't have that here."

"Yes, we do. I read about it online. The Dixie Mafia. They're all over Kentucky."

"I don't think he's mixed up with the Dixie Mafia, honey." But then Kimberly wondered. . . . How did she know what he was mixed up with? "Whatever it is, you don't have to worry about it. Your school is safe. The soccer field is safe. The coaches are here."

"Do you think he's dead?" Maria asked, clearly curious but trying to sound casual.

"I have no evidence of that. I just know that he's missing, and his brother is worried."

"Will you have to see a dead body or something? What if it's decaying and smells? You know, on *True Detective*—"

"Let's not get ahead of ourselves," Kimberly said. "Wait a minute. When did you watch *True Detective*?"

"At Dad's house. With Jennifer. You just said I should watch HBO there."

"That's a TV show, not reality," Kimberly said, grunting. "We'll talk about this later. Remember, Dad is picking you up."

"You *are* coming to my match tomorrow night, right? It's the first time I'm starting in goal."

"I wouldn't miss it. My calendar's highlighted. In bold letters."

"Okay." Maria sighed again. "Bye."

She walked away, cutting off Kimberly's farewell.

"Bye-bye. I love you."

7

After Morgan was gone, I finished my drink.

The taste of her mouth, the feel of her lips against mine, the touch of my hands running over her hips—all of those sensations lingered, like waking up from a vivid dream. The desire she'd stirred was both an ache that stabbed at the center of my body and an emptiness, something I feared would never be filled.

The drink didn't help. I finished it, but it just made me wish she were there even more. Hunger, real hunger, gnawed in my gut as well. My head swirled with the effects of the alcohol and the intoxication of being so close to Morgan, of holding her and kissing her so intensely for those brief moments. Except for her abandoned drink on the bar next to me and the taste of her on my lips, I might have believed she'd never been there at all, that my mind had conjured her like a vision caused by a fever.

The bartender came my way, a slender, middle-aged woman with long braids. She acted nonchalant, wiping up an invisible spill nearby, but she looked over at me from the corner of her eye.

"Did you want another one?" she asked.

"I have to stop," I said.

"What about your . . . friend?"

I looked at the half-finished Bloody Mary, saw a faint mark left on the tip of the straw by Morgan's mouth. Lipstick.

"She left," I said. "She had to get to her flight."

I read the bartender's name tag: JANICE. She took our glasses away, and then she handed me an ice water. She lingered, still holding the rag and searching for another spill to clean. I felt the curiosity coming off of her body in waves.

"Thanks," I said.

"You two seemed to be having an intense conversation," Janice said, her voice free of judgment. She must have seen and heard a fair amount in the bland anonymity of the Keg 'n Craft.

"That was one of the strangest things that's ever happened to me," I said, figuring I could at least spill my guts to a bartender. Janice served as the secular priest of the anonymous airport, possibly offering advice or even benediction as the case called for. "I just met her in the gift shop. We started talking about our lives, and then she just kissed me like that."

Janice nodded, her eyes large and sympathetic. "Not your average Tuesday morning, is it?"

"No. Not even close."

"Hell, I wish someone would talk to me like she did. Or kiss me that way."

"I'm a little shocked myself."

"Are you okay?" she asked. "Do you want something to eat? You look a little pale."

I knew I needed to eat. I needed to slow the swirling in my head, even if I wasn't sure it was caused only by the two drinks on an empty stomach. I asked Janice if she could bring me a club sandwich, and she winked at me before wandering off to place the order.

I checked my phone again. My dad had written two more times, his messages growing increasingly prescriptive. He told me what to wear, even though I always wore the same clothes to these meetings, the clothes he'd told me to wear when I started working for him five years earlier. And then he reminded me not to have a drink before I boarded my flight, to make sure I didn't show up smelling like alcohol.

I know you insist on doing that before you fly. Take the pills if you must but forget the booze.

Too late.

My dad could summon little sympathy for weaknesses or phobias of any kind. He thought I let my fear of flying control my life more than it should. *Control it?* I flew all the time despite it, but I couldn't tell the old man that. *Close to the vest. Keep it close to the vest.*

I started thinking of what was to come. A series of images paraded through my brain. The long, tense flight to Florida. The cramped seat, the enclosed space. The rental car pickup, the bored, indifferent clerk. The sterility of the highways, the never-ending stream of fast food restaurants, gas stations, and toll plazas. All of it leading to a meeting with my dad and a few strangers, men in clothes just like mine who wanted to talk about zoning ordinances and profit and loss.

A cold sweat broke out on my forehead. I felt like a guy staring down a long, narrow tunnel with the light at the end flickering.

Nashville . . .

Janice was out of sight. I reached for my wallet and found a fifty. For good measure, I threw another twenty down with it. I figured that should cover the four drinks as well as the sandwich that hadn't yet come.

I grabbed my carry-on and headed for the concourse.

8

I checked the board as I left the Keg 'n Craft. I found the flight—the only one in that terminal—departing for Nashville. My heart was thumping against my rib cage, and when I saw the word "boarding," it started to pound with more force.

I caught the gate number—I knew from experience it was half-way up the terminal—and started moving. Enough time had passed since my arrival in Atlanta that the concourse had grown more crowded. As I headed toward the gate, I encountered every manner of clueless and slow traveler. An elderly couple with canes shuffled across my path, forcing me to swerve to the left to avoid hitting them. A woman holding a baby, her other hand attached to a screaming child, studied another departure board, and I sidestepped around them.

Then I saw the same two cops who had strolled by the Keg 'n Craft while I'd waited for Morgan to return from the bathroom. They were across the concourse from me, moving in the opposite direction and watching everything. As I dashed past them, their heads swiveled and I half expected to be tackled from behind and wrestled to the ground at any moment.

But I managed to reach the Nashville gate without incident. A line of people moved slowly into the retractable jet bridge, their feet shuffling as they held out their boarding passes to a smiling airline employee in a blue suit. I looked for Morgan. A brief fantasy came to my mind. She'd see me. She'd smile. She'd beckon me to her. Or maybe she'd get out of line and come to see me.

But I saw no sign of her.

She must have already boarded. Or maybe she was on a different flight.

That thought brought me to a stop. What if Morgan wasn't even on that plane?

I took a step back, looked at the departure board again. I scanned through the list of cities. Baltimore, Dallas, Las Vegas, Nashville . . .

Still only one flight for Nashville.

Unless she'd lied . . .

"Can I help you, sir?"

A middle-aged man with thick glasses and thinning hair stood behind the counter. He wore a short-sleeved shirt and a dark blue tie.

"Is this the only flight to Nashville?" I asked.

"The only one we have right now." He looked down at his computer screen. "There's another scheduled in two hours."

"Can I get on this one? I had a change of plans."

"I can check," he said, although he didn't look very happy about it. "It's pretty full. Might be overbooked."

My heart sank. But still he asked for my boarding pass and started tapping away. He pounded at the keyboard as if it had offended him. And while he did, I looked out at the plane, the long silver tube that probably—likely—held Morgan.

Then I realized I had a problem: I hadn't taken my second Xanax yet.

"Shit," I said.

"What's that?" the man asked.

"Nothing. How's it looking?"

"We don't have anything."

The pent-up air I'd been holding in escaped my lungs. It wasn't meant to be.

But then the man went on. "Nothing in coach at least. I can get you in first class." He looked over at the line to the jet bridge. "The last group is boarding."

I didn't hesitate. Not then. Not the way I felt. Not with the memory of the kiss and the conversation and everything else. I had to gamble. Chips to the center of the table, cards faceup.

"I'll take it."

"There's a fee, plus the seat upgrade—"

"Just do it. I'm a member. I have tons of miles."

The man looked at the screen again and nodded. "I guess you do. You travel with us a lot, Mr. Fields. And we appreciate your business."

"And I appreciate you getting me on that plane."

"Oh, wait," the man said. He started shaking his head. "Our computers have been glitchy all morning."

I looked over and the entire line of people had passed through the jet bridge. The woman who'd been collecting tickets moved toward the door and started to swing it shut.

"Am I on or not?" I asked.

"Hold on—"

"They're closing the door."

The man kept tapping away, and then he looked over his shoulder to the gate. "Just a minute, Gwen."

He sounded too casual, too relaxed. Didn't he know I was dancing on the edge of a knife? That I was changing the course of my life based on a brief but intense conversation in a bar?

And a kiss. I could not, would not, forget that kiss.

"Ah," he said. "Got it."

Then something started printing—my boarding pass. It came out, and the man handed it to me.

"There you go."

"Thanks."

"And, sir?"

I looked back for the briefest second. "Yes?"

"Have a safe flight."

I thanked him again and darted for the door to the jet bridge.

9

I hustled down the jet bridge alone, my carry-on banging against my side.

An image of my dad flashed in my mind. I wouldn't ever be able to explain this to him, wouldn't even know how to try. But I also felt a secret rush that I was doing something I knew would piss him off. It was a juvenile way to think, of course, but I couldn't help myself. There'd be hell to pay, but I'd face it later.

The flight attendant smiled at me and checked my boarding pass as I entered the plane. I was in the third row, aisle seat, right at the front. Everyone in first class was seated, and I looked past them, through the passageway to the coach section, where a few stragglers were blocking the aisle, stowing their bags overhead. I scanned the faces quickly, of those sitting and standing, but I couldn't see her.

The flight attendant came along beside me, gently placing her hand on my shoulder. "We have room for your bag right here." She took it and lifted it into an overhead bin across the aisle from my seat. "If you'd just settle in now, sir."

"I have to go back there. I have to see someone."

As if on cue, another flight attendant appeared from coach, stepped through the passageway, and pulled the curtain shut behind her.

"We're close to takeoff, sir," the attendant by my side said. "We need everyone to buckle in."

"It won't take long—"

"You'll be able to do that once we're in the air," she said, straining to remain patient. "Once the captain decides it's safe to turn off the 'Fasten Seat Belt' sign."

I stood frozen in place. I contemplated ignoring the flight attendant's wishes and just going back there to find Morgan. *If she was even there.* I took one step in that direction, but I knew it would be pointless. They wouldn't let me. And for all I knew they'd throw me off the plane if I tried.

How long until that seat belt sign went off?

Fifteen minutes? Twenty?

I hated to wait. But I had no choice.

"Okay, okay," I said and finally sat down.

I saw the relief on her face, the belief that she'd avoided finding herself in one of those viral videos of an unruly passenger being dragged from a plane. I buckled up and pulled out my phone, hoping to take advantage of the few minutes before electronics had to be shut off.

I texted my dad, trying to tell him . . . but I didn't know what to say.

On the jet bridge, just minutes before, I'd experienced the thrill of doing something I knew was going to irritate my father to no end. Sitting on the plane, as the flight attendants gave their instructions and the plane rolled back from the gate with the soft hum of the tires against the tarmac, I started to dread the fallout from my impulsive choice. I didn't regret it. Not at all. But I knew how unpleasant it would be with my dad. And even though I was a grown man, I hated to disappoint him.

I'd rarely acted out as a teenager. I'd sensed intuitively how overwhelmed he was playing the role of single father while also trying to run a business. Once, when I was fifteen, I drank too much and vomited all over the bathroom floor. He chewed me out, his voice piercing my brain with greater sharpness than the hangover. And then, when I was sixteen, I reached out to my mother without telling him, asking her if I could come and visit that summer. He was madder about that than he'd been about the drinking, and he proceeded to give me a long, detailed lecture about the many ways my mother had failed us.

My mother never responded to me. And I never saw her again.

But mostly my dad and I got along. I respected him for the work he did—both as a father and as a businessman. I knew the sacrifices he'd made, the hours he'd devoted to building his company, the opportunities he'd afforded me. It made it basically impossible to contemplate telling him I wanted to quit and do something else.

So I wrote quickly, trying not to overthink.

> Dad, long story. Problem with flight. I won't make the meeting on time. Call you later.

And then the flight attendant was next to me, asking me to turn the phone off. Only then did it sink in that we were taxiing down the runway, the pilot's tinny voice over the speaker telling the crew to prepare for takeoff.

The Xanax rattled in my pocket like dice. Too late to help.

I gripped my armrests as tightly as I could and wished for one more drink.

We sped down the runway, the plane accelerating almost as fast as my anxiety, the tires rumbling against the pavement, and then my stomach dropped as we lifted into the air.

10

Kimberly ate a sandwich at her desk, tuna on wheat from the shop across the square. She knew it would serve as breakfast *and* lunch and maybe dinner, so she tried to chew it slowly and enjoy the experience of eating rather than just shove food down her throat to satisfy a late-morning biological need. But she lost herself in the process of reading a report about Giles Caldwell's business dealings, and before she knew it, the sandwich was gone, having disappeared and leaving her no real memory of eating it.

"I did it again," she said out loud. "I need to slow down."

She'd also bought a homemade chocolate chip cookie so big it looked like a small saucer. She unwrapped the cellophane, the gooey chips sticking to it, and took a large first bite, savoring it in her mouth in a way she hadn't with the tuna.

"That's good," she said to the half-empty office. Phones had been ringing with greater frequency and her coworkers had been moving with more speed and urgency for the past day, ever since Giles Caldwell had been reported missing.

The meeting with the mayor that morning had been short and decidedly unsweet. Elena Robbins was in her second term, hoping for a third. She was in her mid-sixties and had spent thirty years becoming a millionaire selling tires to trucking companies. Then she decided her second act would be as mayor of Laurel Falls, Kentucky.

In the meeting, Mayor Robbins spoke and the cops listened. She enumerated Giles Caldwell's contributions to the town, both in business and in philanthropy. She reminded the police they had a funding measure on the ballot the next month, one that could be used to hire more officers and upgrade their equipment.

"Voters won't vote for it if you can't find a grown man in a town of sixty thousand people," Mayor Robbins told them. "They won't vote for you if they don't feel safe in a town this size. It's almost a day since this was reported. Maybe more since he's been gone."

Kimberly wanted to say, *Maybe he doesn't want to be found,* but she held her tongue. The cops were in the room to listen. To get their marching orders from the mayor.

Find Giles Caldwell. *Soon.*

Kimberly knew finding him meant more time away from Maria. The chance at the promotion . . . or the chance to fail spectacularly in the biggest case in years. Laurel Falls had a few homicides every year, almost always solved quickly. Unexplained and unsolved disappearances were even rarer. How long would this take?

So the guilt flooded back. She and Maria liked to split one of the cookies for dessert, both of them rolling their eyes with exaggerated pleasure as they ate.

Kimberly told the voices in her head to knock it off. She did this from time to time, whenever she started to contemplate all the other careers that would have allowed her more time with her rapidly aging and changing daughter. Nurse? Maybe. Teacher? Perhaps. Accountant, computer programmer, blackjack dealer, surgeon. Nope, nope, nope, nope. There'd only ever been one job for her, one career she wanted. And she had it.

She'd spend time with Maria that weekend . . . or the next

week. Once Giles Caldwell was found. Alive, she hoped. Peter, for all his faults, was an excellent father, and he'd see that Maria ate right and brushed her teeth and finished her homework. The girl was in good hands.

And even Jennifer, shiny-haired Jennifer, didn't bother her. That much. The *True Detective* thing they would have to work on. . . .

Just do your job, she told herself. *Wrap this up as soon as you can, but do it right.*

Her spirits lifted when she saw Brandon Ehrlich, one of her fellow detectives. He'd promised to come see her as soon as he heard from the state crime lab. She finished chewing the piece of cookie, swallowed, and wiped her face with the back of her hand, a decidedly unladylike gesture, but who was she trying to impress?

"Brandon," she said, "tell me something good. Let's avoid another ass chewing."

Brandon Ehrlich was thirty, ten years younger than Kimberly. He was already losing his hair and seemed to be compensating with a rigorous workout schedule that saw him run close to fifty miles a week. He and his wife had a newborn son at home, and just the thought of a newborn made Kimberly feel tired. Even more tired than dealing with an intensely driven, smarter-than-average preteen.

"I've got the report."

"And you're going to tell me the key to Giles Caldwell's disappearance is in there, right? That all of our questions will be answered by that report."

Brandon stared at her for a moment. "All of our questions will be answered by this report."

"Seriously?" Kimberly asked, her hopes rising.

"No," Brandon said.

"Shit." She reached over and broke off another piece of cookie. She offered it to Brandon, who refused because he hadn't eaten refined sugar in six months or something ridiculous like that. It was no way to live, no way at all. "Okay, tell me what we've got. Any hits on fingerprints?"

Brandon shook his head. "There were a lot of prints in the house. Giles Caldwell might have had money, but you saw he didn't clean much. Lots of prints. Everywhere."

"I figured he'd have a cleaning person."

"Nope. Whatever usable prints they found, they ran through all the databases. Nothing."

"Figures. What about blood? Any traces we couldn't see?" Kimberly asked.

"Nothing. They're still working on the hair and fiber analysis, but we need a suspect to match it to. That's about all we've got."

"Great. I won't buy any lottery tickets today either."

"What about Giles's ex-wife? Anything there?"

"I just got off the phone with her half an hour ago," Kimberly said. "Nothing useful. They divorced years ago. She walked away with a tidy sum, and it doesn't even look like they speak to each other. She lives in Idaho."

"Kids?"

"None."

"And we've talked to his lovely brother, Simon. He was a piece of work."

"Yeah," Kimberly said, "like we really needed his theories on what happened to Giles. What were they? Central American gangs? The neighbor who complained because Giles left his trash cans out too long once?"

"Don't forget a neighborhood kid selling candy. Have we had a rash of Girl Scouts murdering grown men?"

"Not that I'm aware of," Kimberly said. "He's worse than the nuts who send us notes with the letters they cut out of magazines.

That's why I didn't give him my cell number. He can call me here if he wants to talk. I don't need his heat with no light."

Brandon tapped the report against his knee, making a low thwacking noise. "By the way, what was he doing this past weekend when his brother supposedly disappeared?"

"We're piecing it all together," Kimberly said. "He says he went to a lecture on campus one night. A poker game with friends another. He lives alone too, so he has a lot of time unaccounted for."

"Hmm," Brandon said.

"Yeah. Yesterday, he comes in here and pitches a fit about his brother missing. But something seems off about the guy. Don't you think?"

"He's pushy. And he has the two assaults on his record."

"He seemed more concerned about chewing us out than his brother's welfare. Did you notice that? He didn't show any real emotion over the fact his brother might be in danger."

"Sure. That could just be his way. Some people respond to grief with anger."

"Or maybe he protests too much. I told him we'll call when we know anything. I'm hoping he backs off a little, but I'm not ruling anything out about him."

A phone rang and rang on another desk, and a uniformed officer picked it up. A door near the front of the room opened and closed, slamming shut loudly, but Kimberly ignored it. She heard the same noise hundreds of times a day and had given up wondering why the maintenance crew failed to fix it.

"It doesn't look like Giles has a lot of friends," Kimberly said, eyeing the rest of the cookie. "He just works a lot. He's focused on the job. His business partner is out of the country but is flying back soon."

"Nothing at the office?"

"We've started talking to the employees. It's one of those hippy-dippy places. Ping-Pong in the cafeteria. People bringing their dogs to work. Everyone seems to show up whenever they want, so we've only talked to some of them." Kimberly rolled her eyes as she took in the lack of amenities surrounding her. Burned coffee. Broken door. Peanut butter crackers in the vending machine. "So far we've got nothing. The employees I've talked to are giving the impression that Giles was distant, hands-off. A little odd, a little cold. He founded the company, but the other guy, his partner . . ."

"Steven Hatfield," Brandon said.

"He handles the people side of things. He's the guy who's always on the local news touting the company's achievements, giving big checks to charity. It doesn't sound like Giles's thing, although a lot of it is Giles's money. That's why the mayor cares so much. Giles donated to her campaign. Big-time."

"Money makes the world go round."

"It does."

"And Hatfield's out of town?" Brandon asked.

"Coming back late tonight or tomorrow. He cut his vacation short."

"And the only thing missing is the engagement ring. Giles's mother's engagement ring."

"No electronics," Kimberly said. "TV's there. Computers."

"His car too. A meth head or junkie would have taken something else."

"Hmm. It's odd. The place was ransacked, but only the ring was missing."

"But the ransacking . . . ," Brandon said.

"Yes?"

"Is it possible for ransacking to be half-hearted? Stuff was thrown around, but some drawers were untouched. Like you said, there was stuff that should have been stolen. But it wasn't. Like the thief barely looked."

"What are you getting at?"

"It almost looked . . . fake. Like staged ransacking to make it look like a robbery. Like someone went through the house and threw some things around but didn't really want to trash the place. Could Giles Caldwell have wanted to disappear and make it look like a robbery? Or did he just pack in a hurry and toss some clothes around as he filled his suitcases?"

"Maybe our crook got interrupted. Someone drove down the street, the headlights spooked him."

"I don't know," Brandon said. "It's all very odd."

"We're actually wondering if it's possible Giles Caldwell staged his own disappearance? We haven't found any reason for him to do something like that."

"I'm thinking out loud. About everything."

"And the ring was sitting out in that creepy display dedicated to his mother. It didn't take much effort to find, and there wasn't any other expensive stuff around. Giles didn't buy a lot of finer things. So we have a criminal who only takes antique jewelry and ransacks half-heartedly. I'll say this—it's original."

Brandon tapped the file folder against his knee a few more times. "What do you want to do now? I've got another report to finish, then court this afternoon, but I can stay late tonight."

Kimberly reached out and took the file. "You should go home to your wife and baby. That's what you should do tonight."

"What about you? You have a daughter to go home to."

"She's spending the night with her dad, a benefit of being divorced," Kimberly said.

"Aren't the schools on break?"

"They are. All week. Why couldn't Giles Caldwell disappear

when I didn't have plans to bond with my daughter? I'm going to look this over in more detail and then make more calls. But you have other work to do. There's more happening than just Giles Caldwell."

"That's not how the mayor feels."

"We've got plenty of eyes on this. And the State Bureau of Investigation is sending people down. Aren't you trying to wrap up that assault? And wasn't there a drug bust in the projects on the east side?"

"There was. I'm finishing all of that."

"I'll let you know if I need you."

Brandon stayed in his seat.

"What?" Kimberly asked.

"I hope you get promoted to lieutenant. I really do."

"Thanks, Brandon. I hope so too."

"You're sure you don't want me to stay late?" he asked.

"I'm sure," Kimberly said. "We've got two other detectives helping. And that little blob of a baby you have at home? Before you know it, he'll be a moody teen. And then he'll be in college. Enjoy it while you can."

She watched Brandon go and opened the manila folder.

11

My hands remained locked on the armrests until we reached our cruising altitude and the seat belt sign dinged off. My joints ached from squeezing the seat so hard, and I hadn't even bothered to open the book I'd purchased in the gift shop, the one meant to take my mind off flying. But as soon as that sign went off, I breathed a little easier. We were up high, above the clouds, unable to see land. Like being in the airport, being in the air felt like a moment of suspension, a temporary break from whatever rules governed behavior on the ground. Real-world problems receded out of sight.

I kept my phone turned off because I didn't want to hear back from Dad. Whatever he had to say—and it wouldn't be good—could wait until I was on the ground again. Back in the real world of consequences.

The thought of landing gave me pause—what exactly did I think was going to happen once we arrived in Nashville? I had no business there, no friends, no family.

So what did I think was going to happen when she saw me? Were we going to fall into each other's arms and then run off together? I pushed all of those thoughts aside, since they were several steps ahead of me. After all, I didn't know yet if Morgan was even on the damn plane. Maybe I'd bought a ticket and boarded the wrong flight, fouling up my day and things with my dad for nothing.

I unbuckled, the metal clasp clinking against the armrest I'd gripped so tight, and stood up. A couple of other first-class passengers also rose, stretching and taking things out of the overhead bins. The curtain to the rest of the plane had been opened, affording me a view of coach, but several people were up and milling around back there as well, so I still couldn't see much.

A low hum of conversation filled the confined space. My ears had popped on the way up, so everything sounded like we were underwater. The recirculated air cycled through the plane with a dull rush, and the fuselage rocked gently as we knifed through the soft, puffy clouds. Little could be seen outside but blue and white. The sun was in the distance, a bright yellow disk on the far horizon.

I started back, excusing myself around my fellow travelers. As soon as I passed the curtain to coach, I scanned the seats, looking for the telltale hat and glasses. If she'd taken them off, would I even be able to recognize her?

Some people looked up as I moved by. Others were lost in their own worlds. They wore headphones, read books and magazines, whispered gently to their partners or children. Two flight attendants pushed a drink cart my way, the ice and beverage cans rattling as they moved. I thought I'd have to turn around and go back, wait for them to clear out, and I felt like a man swimming against the tide. My patience waned as I contemplated a further delay in my plans.

But then I saw Morgan, sitting on my left near the rear of the plane, the bucket hat and sunglasses appearing among the sea of faces.

The flight attendant's cart still blocked my way. But I caught a break. The aisle seat next to the cart was unoccupied, so I stepped into it, then squeezed around the cart, drawing an irritated look from the attendant. Then I rushed down the aisle the rest of the way to where Morgan sat.

I thought she'd sense me coming, that she'd automatically look up and see me moving down the aisle, but she kept her head down as though reading something. My mouth went dry, and I tried to think of what I was going to say when she did see me standing there like a beggar.

Before I could formulate anything brilliant, I was next to her, standing over her and looking down.

She stared at her iPad, headphones in her ears. She still hadn't noticed me. So I reached out slowly with my right hand and tapped her shoulder.

Her head whipped up as quickly as it had spun toward me in the gift shop. She moved so fast, it startled me, and I took a step back, then held my hand up, palm forward, in a gesture of peace. The plane hit a pocket of rough air, which caused it to shift, and I lost my balance for a moment, stumbling back one step before re-gaining my footing.

Not the most graceful approach.

"It's me," I said. "I didn't mean to startle you."

I again saw myself reflected in her sunglasses. She kept them directed my way for what felt like a long time, her facial expression below the hat and the shades not changing, even though her cheeks flushed.

She kept in the earbuds she was wearing, and I pointed at my ears so she would remove them. She did, but her face showed no joy or surprise at seeing me. She simply looked put out, as if I were a complete stranger interrupting her private reverie.

"I changed my flight," I said in a rush. "I'm in first class. That's all they had left. I know this is nuts. . . ."

Morgan still hadn't spoken, but a couple of the people around her—the gray-haired woman in the middle seat, the college student right in front of her—stopped what they were doing and stared up at me, not even trying to hide their fascination with our one-sided conversation. Behind me and up the aisle, I heard the flight attendants offering my fellow passengers drinks, their polite questions punctuated by the fizzing of newly opened soda cans and the tearing of peanut and cookie wrappers.

Morgan said nothing, so I looked around, desperate for my next move. A guy about my age, wearing a flannel shirt and eating a fast food hamburger, sat across the aisle from Morgan. He too had turned his head our way, his face impassive as he chewed his food and took in our little drama.

"Do you want to sit in first class?" I asked him. "We could trade seats so I can sit by her."

The guy looked confused. The stubble on his face was patchy, and a bright red pimple grew on the left side of his nose. He looked eager to sit in first class, but when he glanced Morgan's way, his face grew uncertain.

"Hold it," Morgan said. "Don't do this. I don't want to sit by you."

The guy turned his head away, focusing on his hamburger as though it held all the secrets of the world between its buns.

I felt my mouth drop open. I wasn't even sure what to say. If I'd been standing out on the wing with the wind and the clouds buffeting me, I couldn't have been more exposed.

I sensed more sets of eyes turn to me. I was quickly becoming the hottest thing to watch at thirty thousand feet.

I leaned toward Morgan, speaking in a lower voice, although I was certain everyone around us could still hear me. Let's face it—there isn't much privacy to be found in the cabin of a 737 with everyone wedged on top of one another like strangers in a flying elevator.

"I know this is crazy, me changing my flight. I didn't think I'd ever do something like this. And I didn't even know for sure if you were on board when I did it. But we had a real connection back there, at the bar, and I just . . . I couldn't stand the thought of never seeing you again. When you said that, Morgan, that we'd never see each other—"

"I don't know what you're talking about," she said in the coldest voice I'd ever heard. "I've never seen you before in my life. That's not even my name."

"But—"

"You don't even know me."

The woman next to Morgan gasped, then pursed her lips, staring at me in disapproval. She held an architecture magazine in her hand, which caused my mind to flash to Renee back in Chicago, and the woman looked like she wanted to throw it at me. And then I noticed the same disapproving look rippling across the faces of our other fellow passengers. With those few words, Morgan had transformed me into an aggressive creep, a stalker, a weirdo, and there was no coming back from something like that.

I couldn't understand her behavior.

Why speak so intimately, why kiss me that way in the bar, if she wanted to send me away?

"Morgan, I don't—"

But instead of listening, she stuck her hand straight up and hit the "Call" button, summoning a flight attendant.

The woman next to her leaned over and said, "You're fine, honey. We won't let him bother you this way."

My mind raced, searching for what I could say to change the

direction of the encounter, but I pressed my lips tight. None of this was going the way I pictured. In no scenario did I imagine Morgan would pretend not to know me, never to have met me.

A flight attendant materialized out of nowhere behind me. Her hair was streaked with blond highlights, and the red of her lipstick matched the pimple on the face of the guy across the aisle. Her perfume tickled my nose. She ignored me and asked what Morgan needed.

"This man," Morgan said, nodding my way as though I were a road sign or a pile of trash. "This man thinks I'm someone else. He's bothering me and won't return to his seat."

The woman with the magazine joined her, all too eager to participate in my execution. If there'd been a guillotine, she would have gladly let the blade fall. "She's right. He's being very insistent and rude. He tried to make that gentleman move so he could sit down."

"Where is your seat, sir?" the flight attendant asked me. She wore her hair in a tight bun and had a thick layer of makeup on her face. Her nails were immaculately painted and a gold ring on her left hand caught the faint light through the window.

"First class," I said.

"Would you like to go back and sit down? You can get a beverage up there and something to eat." She sounded firm and calm, like an animal trainer.

I looked down at Morgan, at her soft lips, her sunglasses and hat. I saw the indifference on her face. Her jaw was set firm, the muscles working under the skin.

The flight attendant placed her hand on my shoulder, gently guiding me away and to my seat.

But I resisted, turning back. "She's wrong," I said loudly, trying to explain the injustice of it all to a preoccupied jury. For some reason, I held my hands out as if I really thought I could convince them. "I do know her. She's wrong."

The flight attendant spoke low enough so that only I could hear, her face close to mine. "Sir, I don't want to have to get the pilot involved."

I knew it was no idle threat. And I didn't need to get arrested on top of everything else. I didn't need a scene, so I dropped my arms and let the flight attendant lead me away. Everyone was staring at me as I went up the aisle. But before I passed the curtain to first class, I stopped.

This was my last chance. I could slip past the flight attendant and dash down the aisle, back to the only person who'd made me feel alive in months, maybe even years.

Or I could do what was expected of me, return to my thousand-dollar first-class seat and sit quietly for the rest of the flight.

So I took one look back at Morgan, her blank, stoic face, and walked to the front of the plane.

12

I stayed in my seat the rest of the way to Nashville.

The image of Morgan—if that was even her name—reaching for the "Call" button, the memory of the flight attendant providing the subtle threat of summoning the pilot, the realization that everyone thought I was a stalker . . . It all brought a flush of embarrassment to my cheeks. It had been a long time since I'd misread a situation so badly.

I knew I'd *never* made a fool of myself like that, in front of a plane full of people. It reminded me there was a reason I didn't do impulsive things like jumping on an airplane to be near a woman I'd kissed once in the Keg 'n Craft.

I wasn't good at it.

And I returned to my dad's lifelong advice—play things close to the vest.

Maybe he was right. Maybe nothing good came from laying it all on the line.

It was an hour-long flight, but the time in the air dragged interminably. I tried to read the book with the running man on the cover. I learned about his drinking problem brought on by the loss of his wife and child in a tragic accident. And how that tragedy turned the man into a loner who killed for hire. But only criminals who deserved it. Soon enough, I found myself reading the same lines over and over again and put the book aside.

The woman next to me, who looked to be in her seventies, paged through a photo album. From the corner of my eye, I caught scattered glimpses of smiling grandchildren of all ages. Kids with bright eyes and missing teeth, kids in front of a Christmas tree, kids in a dance recital. I envied her—she seemed to have a safe, fulfilling life, one full of shining memories. She looked over and smiled at me, and I nodded back. But we didn't speak.

When the plane rolled to a stop and reached the gate, I grabbed my bag as fast as I could and shouldered my way past the other first-class passengers to get out as soon as possible. If I never saw Morgan, the flight attendants, or the passengers around her again, it would be too soon. Surely they'd all go home and tell the story about the weird guy creeping after the beautiful woman on the plane. I was so embarrassed I vowed never to fly to Nashville again unless I did it in disguise.

I needed a new plan. I knew that when I turned my phone back on, a blast of texts and voice mails from my dad would be waiting. I couldn't make the meeting in Tampa, no way, but I could try to get there by early evening. He'd likely scheduled a dinner with the other developers, and I could swoop in and turn up the charm, present the united front of father and son working side by side. I could never mention that I'd been chasing a woman in the wrong direction, and I knew if I did he'd shake his head, his eyebrows lifting in bafflement as if to ask himself what kind of idiot child he had raised.

I beelined to the nearest ticket counter and asked about flights to Tampa. As the fates would have it, one was leaving, direct, in two hours. And it still had room for me. I said I desperately needed to get on that flight, so the ticket agent, a middle-aged woman with a pencil stuck in her hair, started tapping away to make it happen.

The effects of the alcohol were abating. I'd swallowed a Coke and some salty potato chips during the flight, and I was starting to feel more like myself. Feet on the ground. Plans to be made.

And mercifully out of the sky for a short time.

I leaned against the counter, trying not to look at the passengers from the Atlanta flight as they deplaned. I knew Morgan would be among them, near the very back of the crowd. She'd have to walk right past me.

Don't look. Don't look for the hat and glasses. Just let her go.

The ticket agent worked everything out and booked my seat. She printed a boarding pass, my third of the day.

"Thanks," I said.

I lingered for a moment. I tried to think of something else to say to the agent, some silly question that would keep me occupied as Morgan walked by.

But I suddenly changed my mind. I decided I did want to see her, so I spun around and scanned the people exiting the jet bridge. Would it be so wrong to take one last look?

At first, I saw no one familiar. Maybe she'd already gone past me or maybe she'd walked another way. But then I saw the familiar bucket hat, the bobbing brown ponytail, the large sunglasses. She walked with purpose, her head never turning.

I watched her go, holding back the impulse to approach or say anything else. I didn't need to have a long conversation with her. I just wanted to ask: *Why? What the hell's going on?*

Is there something wrong?

But I squashed the desire. And she passed me and left my life forever.

With two hours to kill, I headed for the nearest bar.

13

I skipped the alcohol and opted for water and a sandwich, something to prepare me for what was sure to be an onslaught of texts and voice mails from Dad. I knew I couldn't avoid them forever—although I figured a scolding from the old man wouldn't be nearly as humiliating as the events on the plane.

So I held the phone up to my ear and listened.

But people can surprise you. Morgan did. More than once.

And so did my dad.

His familiar, permanently raspy voice came through.

"Hey, kid, what's going on? Did something happen? Are you in trouble? Now I'm worried about you. Give me a call when you get this, okay? Love you."

My eyes burned with tears. I needed a moment to collect myself. Somehow he knew exactly what I needed and when I needed it. A pick-me-up, a show of support. Yes, people can surprise you in all kinds of ways.

I called him and he answered right away.

"Are you okay, Joshua?"

"I'm okay. Don't worry."

"What's the story?" he asked.

"It's a long one, Dad. Maybe I should tell you later."

"But are you really okay? That's all I want to know. You've never been late, you've never missed a meeting."

"I know. I got sidetracked."

"Are you stuck in Atlanta?"

"A little north of there."

"What's north of Atlanta? Anything?"

"Nashville."

"Nashville? Oh, God. What are you doing there?"

"I've booked a flight to Tampa for later this afternoon. I can catch you for dinner, okay? We won't miss a beat."

"That's fine." He'd adopted the soothing voice he used in crises, the one he'd brought out when I pierced my skin with a fish hook at age nine, the one he'd used when I accidentally scraped the entire side of the car against the garage when I was seventeen. Being a single parent, he'd learned to play every angle, to be both good cop and bad cop, disciplinarian and softie. "I don't care about the deal. The deal will happen. I want to know what's going on with you."

"I told you, I'm good."

"Look," he said, "we don't have to talk about this now, but I can tell things aren't right. I can tell you aren't happy with the job."

"Dad, it's okay—"

"Why don't we make sure we talk when you get to Tampa? We can find the time. Hell, we never get to talk for real. We used to sometimes, back when you were in high school. Remember?"

"I do. I know."

"And I've always tried to give you your space, to not smother you. Even when you were a moody teenager. You were responsible, and you liked to be left alone to do your own thing. Like me."

I thought of all the work we had to do, all the deals in progress. I thought of Dad staying up late into the night after I'd gone to bed as a kid, doing paperwork and studying reports. He never stopped charging forward. He gave me everything. If it meant I had to put up with the occasional gruff text or short-tempered call, I could handle it. It seemed like a small price to pay to have financial security and someone I could always count on.

"Dad, I just . . . I've been a little lost lately, a little distracted. But I'm back on board. I am. I'll see you in Tampa."

"Is it Renee?" he asked, gently probing. "Lord knows I don't know anything about women or relationships, so I can't help you there. But she always seemed like a nice girl. She's levelheaded, has a good job. She's crazy about you. I never could understand why the two of you couldn't get on the same page."

"It's not Renee, Dad," I said. "In fact, Renee looks better and better every moment."

"Oh." He sounded surprised. "Well, all right. So I guess that means I gave you good advice for a change."

"You usually do. I've got to go, Dad," I said, even though I had nowhere to be for two hours. I just didn't want to keep dodging his questions.

"Travel safe, kid. Love you."

I hadn't paid any attention to the TV screen above the bar until that moment, but my eye caught a flash of something there. A face.

A woman's face, a still photograph.

And it looked like Morgan.

But then it was gone. And I told myself that my mind had been warped by her touch, by the kiss, by the alcohol and the Xanax. I thought I was seeing her everywhere.

"Did you hear me?" Dad asked.

"What?"

"I said, 'I love you.'"

"Yes, of course. I love you too."

"Talk soon."

I felt better once I was off the phone.

My food came, and it tasted delicious, more satisfying than the junk I'd eaten on the plane. I brought out my computer and started looking over the files relevant to the trip to Tampa, just to make sure I really knew everything I needed to.

I also texted Renee, leaving out where I was and why. She certainly didn't need to know that. But I told her I was doing fine and we could talk that night when I got to my hotel.

She wrote back right away, telling me she looked forward to hearing my voice. Were we actually getting back together? It kind of sounded like we might be heading that way.

I finished my food and went back to the files. But I couldn't really concentrate and curiosity grabbed ahold of me. I took out my phone, opened my Facebook app, and typed in a name: "Morgan Reynolds."

I scrolled through the results until I saw her face. Without sunglasses. It was unmistakably her. I hesitated before opening her page. What did I think I would see there? Pictures of a boyfriend or a fiancé? Or . . . even a husband?

Something that would explain her behavior?

Did I need to know any of it?

But, despite my best intentions, I couldn't set the phone aside. It was the same impulse that drove me to change my flight and board a plane to Nashville. I couldn't stop myself from looking. So I clicked through.

When the page came up, her profile picture filled my screen. Yes, she looked beautiful. And natural. And happy. And more relaxed. She stood on a trail in a wooded area, wearing hiking clothes, her smile bright and full.

Then I checked out the cover photo behind her profile picture. Morgan in a group of people at what looked like an office holiday party, with reindeer antlers on her head and an ugly Christmas sweater.

And, I realized with surprise, it looked like her name really was Morgan Reynolds. Why she said it wasn't on the plane, I had no idea.

I thought I'd seen enough. She was a regular person with a regular life. Like millions of other people, she worked a job and hiked for fun. We'd brushed up against each other like two swirling atoms, and then we'd parted. And that was that. I had no idea why she'd blown me off, but maybe it was just that simple. Maybe she'd wanted just a brief encounter, a moment we'd never forget.

Still, I couldn't close the page, couldn't look away. I took a quick scroll through her timeline, and what I saw there almost sent me tumbling back off the barstool.

HAVE YOU SEEN MORGAN? Missing Person. Believed Endangered.

MORGAN REYNOLDS Age 25

14

My mind locked. I didn't understand what I was reading.

I stared at the words on the screen, not entirely processing them.

HAVE YOU SEEN MORGAN?

The question might as well have been in a foreign language. It looked like one of those word jumbles in the newspaper, the kind I never had the patience to figure out.

HAVE YOU SEEN MORGAN?

When I shook myself loose, the gears in my mind finally unlocking and moving forward again, I scrolled through the rest of her timeline. I saw the same announcement posted five times.

HAVE YOU SEEN MORGAN?

I caught a few details as the words and images went past. *Hasn't been seen in several days . . . not answering her phone . . . not at her apartment . . . everyone is worried . . .*

It required a great deal of effort to remain on the barstool. I had to concentrate to stay there. My body felt weak and loose, composed of nothing but air and water. No bone or muscle, nothing that would provide strength and stability. I repositioned my feet, making sure I didn't slide off.

It explained so many things. The sunglasses, the hat. Her refusal to speak to me on the plane. Her cryptic farewell delivered with such bedrock certainty: *We're never going to see each other again.*

Had that been her face on the TV? On the local news there in Nashville, reporting her disappearance?

It all led to the question: *Why?*

I regained some sense of balance. My body felt steadier, more solid. Could I very well travel to Tampa and continue with my day if I'd just seen a missing person?

And then it hit me—maybe she hadn't even left the airport yet.

I picked up my bag and made my way back to the concourse, feeling a strong sense of purpose. I had to find the airport police. I went up to the ticket agent, the one with the pencil in her hair.

"Excuse me," I said.

She didn't seem to recognize me. She seemed distracted, her eyes remaining on her computer screen. "How can I help you, sir?"

"I need the police. How do I find them?"

The woman's face fell. She looked like *she* was in trouble. "Is something wrong? Is this an emergency?"

"I'm not sure," I said. How exactly should I explain the situation? "I think I just need to talk to them."

The woman picked up a phone and pressed a few buttons. She said something, but I didn't pay attention. Scenarios ran through my mind. Morgan was being chased. She was running to something or away from someone. She owed money or had defaulted on a loan. A relationship had ended poorly, causing her to flee her life. I couldn't even conceive of it all.

I lost track of time. I stood off to the side, staring out the huge windows at the arriving and departing planes, the sun glancing off their wings and windows. The next thing I knew, two police officers in dark uniforms, their gold badges flashing under the lights, came up to me. They asked what the nature of my emergency was, and I told them I wasn't sure if I had one or not. I reported what I'd seen. But as I heard myself saying the words, standing on the concourse with the business of commerce and travel going on around me, I realized how far-fetched and just insane my story sounded. I gave them the bare-bones outline: I met a stranger in Atlanta and changed all my plans to follow her to Nashville. And now I thought she was a missing person.

When I finished speaking, they both studied me, their eyes opaque.

"Why don't you come with us, sir?" one of them said.

15

While we walked, they said nothing to me, so I kept my mouth shut too. They were on either side of me, as if they expected me to bolt at any second. The two officers used their key cards to open electronic locks on several heavy steel doors we passed through.

The station occupied a small space on a lower level of the airport, and only when they had me seated in somebody's office, a utilitarian space with a couple of desks and an American flag in the corner, did they start to ask me questions. I directed them to Morgan's Facebook page and waited while they called it up on an oversize desktop computer. They both studied it, their brows furrowed.

"It says she lives in Nashville," one said. He was older, likely in his fifties, with gray hair and large glasses that reflected the bright light. His name was Officer Travis. "So if she flew here, maybe she was heading home? Maybe she's rethinking whatever led her to leave town and be considered missing?"

"I guess that's possible. Yes."

"But she told you she was going up to Wyckoff, Kentucky? To Henry Clay?"

"Yes, sir."

"Still about ninety minutes from here to Wyckoff. Across the state line into Kentucky."

"She said she grew up and went to college there," I said.

"This is social media stuff from friends. Has she been officially reported to the police?"

"I think it was on TV," I said. "The local news. I thought I saw her face on the screen out of the corner of my eye."

"Really. Why don't you give Metro Nashville a call and see what's going on there?" Travis said to his partner, who was about my age, a broad-chested man with dark hair cut in a military-style buzz. His cheeks were red like he'd just come in from the cold, although to me the station felt excessively warm. His name tag said JANSEN.

Jansen left the room while Travis studied the computer screen. I couldn't be certain if he was trying to make me grow nervous or if he was genuinely curious about what people were saying about Morgan.

"I don't remember seeing an alert about this, but if it's new . . ." He picked up the phone and pressed a few buttons. "I'm going to need to look at a passenger list. And the CCTV footage from Concourse B, near gate thirteen." He provided the flight number and the airline, then hung up but kept his eyes on the screen. "When's your flight out of here?"

"A couple of hours."

Travis shook his head, indicating they might not be finished with me by then.

"It's work," I said. "I have to get down to Florida."

"So you just met this woman in the line at the gift shop in Atlanta? And then decided to change your plans and follow her here to Nashville?"

"Yeah. I know it sounds crazy. You know how sometimes you just connect with someone right away?"

Travis turned away from the screen and looked at me, the

reflection in his glasses obscuring his eyes, but I could clearly see he was skeptical. Apparently his uniform didn't conceal the beating heart of a romantic.

"What was she wearing?" he asked.

I described everything I remembered, including the sunglasses and hat.

"So you didn't really see her face?" Travis asked.

"She took the glasses off. Once. Briefly."

"Why?"

I hesitated. But then I figured the cops had heard it all. "We kissed. At the bar. She took her glasses off before we kissed."

"A real kiss?" he asked.

"Excuse me?"

"Was it a real kiss? Not just a peck on the cheek, but . . ." He searched for the correct words. "You know, something romantic. Something . . . full-on."

"Yes," I said somewhat reluctantly. "I guess you could say 'full-on.' And then she left." I filled him in on the rest—changing flights, the seat in first class. Approaching her at the rear of the plane.

"She said her name wasn't Morgan?" he asked, his brow furrowing with even more skepticism. "And she didn't know you?"

"That's right."

"Was she the same person?" he asked. "You only saw her briefly without the hat and sunglasses."

"It was her. I know it was. Same hat. Same beauty mark. But I don't know why she said she wasn't Morgan. Or why she acted like she didn't know me. She called the flight attendant."

"Maybe she's married and regretted getting you all stirred up," he said, his face serious.

"She didn't have a ring on."

"Some people don't wear rings. Even if they're married."

I pointed at his computer. "I don't know much. I don't have all the answers. But, look, she's clearly in trouble. People are worried about her. It's right there. I didn't make this up. If someone is in danger, then we have to help, don't we? Isn't that your job?"

"Easy, chief," he said, leaning back. "By the way, do you have ID on you?"

I handed my license over and he stared at it, then entered something into the computer. While he did that, I thought about the things he'd been asking me. I even started to doubt myself. She'd said her name was Morgan Reynolds, but that didn't mean it was. I didn't see any official documentation.

And I'd seen her face only briefly, so maybe the woman on the Facebook page wasn't the same woman I'd met. Maybe she wasn't the same woman who'd kissed me and then abruptly left with the most mysterious parting words ever. Maybe I just wanted to believe something else was going on, something that would explain her bizarre behavior.

But none of that was right. I knew what had happened. I'd seen Morgan's face as close as anyone could see a face. It was imprinted on my brain. I tried, sitting there in the underground police station, to summon the taste of her kiss again, and I thought I could, bringing forth the tang of the Bloody Mary like it had just happened.

I knew who I saw. I knew what had happened.

Officer Travis handed back my license. I was clean. I'd never received so much as a ticket for a moving violation in my life.

Jansen came back into the room and nodded at Travis. Apparently they were able to communicate that way, because Travis asked me to leave the room and wait in an outer office, which I did. I sat in an uncomfortable chair while other cops came and went, ignoring my presence.

I took the opportunity to call up Morgan's Facebook page again.

I scrolled through the posts. I just saw her last week. Does anybody know what's happening? What are the police saying?

The airport cops made me wait longer than I expected. I thought about calling my dad, but what exactly would I say to him at that point?

About twenty minutes passed, and then Jansen opened the door and summoned me back with a quick wave of his hand. His face was a mask of indifference, as though I'd just shown up to pay a parking ticket and not to report a missing person.

"Have a seat there, Joshua," Travis said. I did what he asked, and he sat behind the desk with his hands steepled together under his chin.

"We talked to the Metro Nashville Police Department," he said, "and it does appear that this Morgan Reynolds from Facebook was reported as a missing person just yesterday. That's why she was probably showing up on the local news, and that's why her friends are concerned. Nobody's heard from her for a few days, so the word is getting out on social media and in the press. She's not answering calls or texts. I looked it up and saw the alert."

"Maybe she has relatives in Nashville. Did they talk to any?"

"Metro Nashville is looking into all of that."

A chill ran up my back, oppressive and clammy.

"She is an adult," Travis said, "and if she doesn't want to answer her phone or talk to her friends, she really doesn't have to. But she should check in so they can stop worrying. There's no evidence of a crime. Yet."

"But something is preventing her from talking to people and letting them know she's okay."

"It could be a misunderstanding. Like I said, maybe she's heading home from a trip and forgot to tell people. I looked more carefully and—" He paused and shifted in his seat. His mouth twisted in a way that indicated displeasure. "This kind of thing happens on social media, you know? Somebody doesn't show up where they're supposed to once or twice, and everybody goes crazy with the announcements. Then someone goes to the cops. Like I said, adults have the right to not let people know where they are. And the police can only do so much if that's the case."

"But the police think she is missing."

"Sure. But you say you just saw her. So maybe she's back."

"Yeah, but— So we do nothing? The police do nothing?"

"Nashville PD are on it. She's in their system, and you saw her on the news. They're taking care of *that* missing persons case."

I didn't like the way Travis sounded. He suddenly possessed the demeanor of a guy who wanted to wash his hands of the problem on his desk.

"That case?" I asked. "Why are you saying 'that case'? Isn't it the same case? I met Morgan Reynolds in the airport. She's missing."

"We've looked at the CCTV footage," Travis said, continuing. "We saw a woman matching the description you gave getting off that flight at the time you indicated. Heck, we saw her walk right past you without even turning her head to look your way."

I felt a little needle stick me in the heart when he told me that. I was glad they didn't feel the need to show me the scene in slow motion. I'd been there. I knew what had happened.

"Okay," I said, "but you have to admit she's acting strange. She's wearing a hat and sunglasses. It's like she's hiding."

"There's no law against dressing that way," Jansen said. "And it's not that weird. This is Nashville. Everybody thinks they're a star."

"So, what does all this mean?" I asked. "Are you just saying I'm crazy?"

Travis paused. He looked over at his partner and then his eyes settled on me.

"Here's the thing about your involvement, and what you think you saw."

"I did see it. Her."

"Well, we checked the passenger list," he said. "Ordinarily, we can't access it, but because of the situation, we got authorization. I'm not sure who you saw, but there was no one named Morgan Reynolds on that flight. According to the airline, she was never on that plane."

16

I have to give those airport police officers credit—they were patient with me. Maybe it was a slow day at work. Or maybe they were just nice, sympathetic guys who felt bad for me because I might have been led up the garden path by the Keg 'n Craft's version of a femme fatale. In any case, they put up with me for another fifteen minutes as I threw a variety of alternate and progressively less believable theories at them to explain Morgan's behavior.

But when I suggested maybe she was suffering from amnesia or had had some kind of psychotic break, they decided we all needed to get on with the rest of our lives.

Travis stood up from behind his desk, hitching his pants as he did. He gave me a patient look, one that was almost fatherly and served only to remind me of the clock ticking against my flight to Tampa.

"Look, Joshua," Travis said, coming around and sitting on the edge of the desk. His black shoes were polished to a military shine, reflecting the light like a dark mirror. "We don't know what's going on with this woman any more than you do. I have no doubt you met someone in the Atlanta airport and spent time with her. I'm sure you kissed her and followed her here. Why she chose to blow you off or say she didn't know who you were . . . Well, I think you just need to chalk this one up to a strange, brief encounter."

"But if she's missing—"

"Like I said, Nashville PD is searching," he said. "And we're going to file a report right here as well."

"Was there anyone named Morgan on the plane? Anything like that?"

Travis sighed. "I can't just pull everybody with a certain first name off a flight. And even if there was another Morgan, and I really only looked at last names, then she probably isn't your Morgan. Maybe this woman on the plane just gave you a fake name to throw you off her trail. Maybe she had heard of Morgan Reynolds the missing person and decided to say that's who she was. It's kind of the equivalent of a woman handing out a fake phone number in a bar when she doesn't want a guy to call her. Maybe you just ran into a jumpy, fickle girl. We've all been there, right?"

He looked at Jansen, who nodded in agreement. And then he looked back at me. I was supposed to nod too, and then we could all laugh and say things like, *Women. Can't live with them, can't shoot them.*

But his words failed to make me feel any better. In fact, they made me feel worse, since his tone of voice and paternal manner suggested I'd been misled, making me the amiable stooge who'd fallen for the whimsical games of a manipulative woman.

I hated to be taken for a fool, in business or in love.

Cards close to the vest.

I hated even more that Travis might be right.

But I did know one thing with certainty—it made no sense to continue to talk to Travis and Jansen. They were finished with me.

I stood up and shook both of the officers' hands. We nodded to each other solemnly before I gathered up my bag, and then they walked me back to the concourse. Again, we walked in silence, the only sound the clicking of their heavy shoes against the floor, but when we reached the public area, Travis pointed at the large digital clock hanging from the ceiling, its red numerals impossible to miss.

"Looks like this worked out for you," he said. "You can still make that flight to Tampa. You can get back to your life. And if we need anything else, we'll give you a call."

They slipped away before I could argue, and I trudged down the concourse toward my gate with thirty minutes left. I avoided the bar, avoided anyplace that might sell alcohol. My shoulders felt heavy and weighted, my feet like lead. I'd never had a day like that one before. I vowed never to have another one like it.

I found a quiet place near my gate but away from the other passengers. I didn't read the book I'd bought or scroll through my phone. I sat out of the way, staring into space, ignoring the comings and goings and noise of the terminal.

None of it made sense. And I had to accept that it never would. Maybe the cop Travis was right in his own paternal way—I'd run into a strange, unpredictable woman, and she'd taken me for a ride. Why did people get pleasure out of doing such things? Who knew? But those people existed. Maybe Morgan liked the attention. Maybe she was laughing at me right then.

Except . . .

Why had she left town in a way that alarmed so many of her friends and caused someone to go to the police? It was the only piece that didn't fit with what Travis said, unless she simply wanted to take everyone for a ride. Everyone she knew, everyone she encountered on social media, and even a random guy she met in the airport. Me.

I wasn't sure how many times the PA announcer called my name before I heard it. I'd disappeared so far into my own thoughts that the sound of my own name seemed to reach me as though it were coming through a distant fog. Like a bell tolling in the distance, signaling . . . hope? Or danger?

When I finally heard it, I shivered. It had to be the cops. Travis and Jansen, they wanted something else from me. Maybe they'd learned another key piece of information. Or maybe they'd learned news that would provide some much-needed clarity.

I wondered if I could just board my flight and pretend I'd never heard the page. What could the airport police in Nashville do once I was on my flight and heading for Tampa?

But I was too curious. And shaken. If they needed something from me, I'd provide it, no matter how painful and embarrassing. I saw myself as a good boy, someone who followed the rules and tried to help the authorities when they needed it.

I asked the first ticket agent I saw where the courtesy phone was. She pointed me in the right direction. As I walked across the concourse, I mused over the phone's continued existence. It seemed like a relic of a bygone era, a time when people needed to be called on landlines instead of being texted or contacted by cell. When I picked it up, I expected to hear nothing, the dead air of an outdated instrument. But an operator waited, and when I gave my name, she told me to hold one moment. I heard a couple of clicks and remembered that I'd given the police my phone number when they'd first approached me. If they'd wanted to reach me, they could have called my cell, so . . .

"Hello?" I said.

"It's me." The voice on the other end was unmistakable. "Don't hang up."

It was Morgan.

17

I looked around the concourse before I said anything. No one was paying any attention to me. People shuffled past on their way to and from their flights. An airport employee pushed a dolly loaded with bottled water, the wheels squeaking and rattling. He hummed along to some music only he could hear, a contented smile on his face.

"Are you calling to tell me what's going on with you?" I asked. "Or did you want to dick me around some more?"

"I'm not dicking you around."

"It sure feels like it. It's been a long time since I've been dicked around this hard. Maybe never. But I'm pretty sure this is what it feels like."

"I don't have much time," she said.

"Why? Are you afraid someone will trace the call?"

"Who would do that?" she asked.

"I don't know," I said, shaking my head even though she couldn't see me. "I have no idea what's going on with you."

In the background, I could hear the steady whoosh of what sounded like passing cars. I guessed she was at a pay phone. If anyone cared to trace the call, they'd learn only that she stopped by the side of the road somewhere and slid quarters into a slot, probably using the last remaining pay phone in the city of Nashville.

"Look," I said, "your friends think you've disappeared. They're worried. The police are looking for you. I think I saw you on TV."

Morgan sighed. "I know all about that. I'll take care of it as soon as I can. Some things are beyond my control right now. And I have other things to deal with."

"So what did you call me for?" I asked.

"I called because I wanted to apologize. I know I acted like . . . I don't know what. A total weirdo. A freak."

"A lunatic," I said. "A nut job. A psychopath."

"Whatever word you want to use, I guess. There's a reason why I did that, blew you off that way on the plane and then walked past you in the airport. I told you we'd never see each other again. I had every intention of honoring that."

"My plane's leaving soon," I said. "My plane to Tampa for the meeting I already missed because of you. If you have something more to say, you should spit it out."

"That's just it," she said. "Your job, all the things we talked about at the bar. I'm glad we said those things about having a larger purpose in life. I've been struggling with that a lot lately. And it was good to find someone else who felt the same way I feel."

I kept my mouth shut. I agreed with her—it *had* felt good to connect, to talk about those things. But I wasn't ready to say so. Not yet. "Go on."

"I don't know what else there is to say. I needed a little lift, and you gave it to me. That's why I kissed you. That's why . . . I'll always remember you. And that moment."

My defenses weakened. Something shifted inside me. The ice had cracked. It was floating away as it melted. Her voice—the barely there Southern flavor, the soothing tone. The unvarnished honesty. No one talked to me like that. No one.

"Why are you traveling under another name?" I asked. "Why are you hiding behind the hat and the sunglasses? Are you in trouble?"

"How do you know about the name? Oh, I get it. You've been to the cops, haven't you?"

"I had to. I saw everything online about you being missing. But I don't even know if the cops in the airport believe it was you."

"Shit," she said. "Word spreads fast."

"People tend to take it seriously when someone disappears."

"Okay, then. I have to get moving."

A horn honked in the background. Was she alone? Was that just a car driving past? Or was someone with her, waiting, summoning her to go?

"Where are you?" I asked. "Are you really going to Wyckoff?"

"Look, just remember what we talked about. Don't go to that stupid meeting in Tampa if you don't want to. I know it's with your dad, and that makes it complicated. But, believe me, it can all get much more complicated if you stay involved with something that isn't working. I know all about that."

"That's easy for you to say. You quit your job. You're free."

She laughed, and I sensed a combination of frustration and humor. "Look, if you have to take Xanax in order to do your job, maybe it isn't the right one."

"You should call your friends," I said. "Let them know you're okay."

"Yeah. I don't know. I'm trying . . ."

"Morgan, if you're in trouble . . . if you need someone to help you, let me do it. I can go back to the cops, I can call someone."

"I meant what I said about never seeing you again. That can't happen."

"Why? Because you're in danger?"

"Forget that job, Joshua," she said. "Have a good life. A meaningful one."

"Morgan?"

But the line was dead. She was gone.

Again.

18

Kimberly spent ninety minutes at the possible crime scene, Giles Caldwell's house. She met the crime scene tech there, and together they walked through the premises, making sure all the evidence had been cataloged properly and accurately. Kimberly held out hope they'd stumble across something they'd missed, something that would provide the much-needed breakthrough. A blood spatter. A note. A shell casing.

But she knew she was dreaming.

If one of those things had been there to discover, it would have already been found.

"What do you think about the way this place is ransacked?" she asked the tech, echoing Brandon's theory.

The tech wore a blue Windbreaker and pushed her large glasses up on her nose. "Incomplete," the tech said.

"Meaning?"

"Not thorough."

"Staged?"

The tech scrunched her face. "I don't know. Maybe. It's odd nothing is missing but that ring."

"Yeah."

After Kimberly finished with the crime scene tech, she joined the other detectives and uniformed officers as they fanned out through the neighborhood, going house by house again in case they missed something or someone the first time. The early autumn sun was hot on Kimberly's neck, and she felt her frustration grow with each dead end. It didn't help that the mayor called her twice for updates, forcing Kimberly to put the brightest shine possible on their lack of progress. The second time she spoke to the mayor, the call ended with a long sigh from Elena Robbins, who then hung up without saying good-bye.

Kimberly felt helpless. It had been twenty-four hours since Giles Caldwell had been reported missing by his brother, Simon. Twenty-four hours and nothing to go on.

When she returned to the station, she saw that three hours had slipped away. Hunger started to gnaw at her gut, and she wished she hadn't polished off the whole cookie at lunch. She checked the landline on her desk and saw five calls from Simon Caldwell.

"What now?" she said out loud. "Did he see Jack the Ripper fleeing his brother's house?"

Then she received a text from Peter.

> You're going to be at the soccer match tomorrow night, right?

Kimberly wrote back, feigning a confidence that was starting to slip away, Of course. See you there.

> Jennifer's coming. Is that okay?

A sudden and sharp anger rose inside her. Why did he think he needed to ask her?

She started to type. I'm not a shrinking violet. I know you're fucking someone else—

But she stopped herself. No need to text in anger. And she tried to adjust her thinking, give Peter the benefit of the doubt for being considerate. Who had the hair-trigger temper now?

So she wrote back, No worries. Maria is excited to be a starter for a change.

"Ugh."

She gripped the phone so tight her fingertips ached. She never thought she'd end up divorced, never expected to have an ex-husband. But who did? No one walked down the aisle thinking, *I can't wait until we split up.*

Let it go, she told herself. *Think about Maria. Think about the great child the two of you managed to create.* That was her world, and if she lacked any excitement in her love life—and she lacked it, she sorely lacked it—she took solace in having a great kid and a job she loved. Even if the job was pushing her to the edge.

She missed the kid—she did—and wished she could punch the clock at four thirty or five and head home like everybody else. She wished for a night of watching mindless TV and double-checking Maria's latest paper on the history of American Indian tribes in western Kentucky or stretching her brain as she helped her review fractions.

But how many people had it easy in this life? Everyone struggled, and everyone wished for more. She remembered riding in the car with her parents as a kid, her mom singing along to the radio. *I beg your pardon, I never promised you a rose garden. . . .*

Who got the rose garden? Anyone?

Kimberly knew her nights wouldn't return to normal until the case was cleared, until they knew exactly what had happened to

Giles Caldwell. She wished they had just one decent, working theory. He'd run off with a woman. He'd fallen victim to a random, violent break-in. He owed a mobster money. His brother killed him in a fit of rage. . . .

You never knew what family members would do to one another.

She'd already told Peter to prepare for more nights with Maria, more unpredictability. They worked better as a divorced couple than they ever had when they were married. Maybe that was her rose garden—a healthy, functional divorce.

Her cell phone rang. She rolled her eyes when she saw the name on the caller ID.

She gave serious thought to ignoring it. She had too much going on and didn't have time to fend off yet another mindless request for a date from a fellow officer. She might have been alone, but she wasn't desperate.

But something compelled her to answer. Maybe deep down she liked the flattery of being pursued. Maybe she wanted something to distract her from the open case, some excuse not to continue to bang her head against the wall.

Some excuse to believe the mayor hadn't taken up residence in her mind.

"Hey, Nelson," she said. "To what do I owe the pleasure?"

"Kimberly, doesn't the sound of my voice make your day?"

"More than you'll ever know," she said, not hiding her disdain.

Detective Ben Nelson worked for the Nashville Police Department, an hour away from Laurel Falls. They'd met on a handful of occasions, hanging out at local conferences and working regional cases the departments collaborated on. Nelson wasn't bad-looking for a guy in his late forties, even though he wore clothes that were twenty years out of date and somehow always managed to have black dirt under his fingernails as though he'd been digging in the backyard in his free time. He was divorced with three kids, all older than Maria, and asked every unmarried woman he came across to dinner. And kept asking. Kimberly felt thankful for the sixty-mile buffer between them.

"Well, I suspect you're expecting an invitation to dinner, aren't you?" Nelson asked.

"I'd hate for you to disappoint me. I like saying no for the ninety-ninth time."

"Then prepare to be disappointed," he said, his voice buoyant.

Kimberly's mind started to wind up, wondering what else he could be calling about. "Okay. I'm listening."

"I mean, I could still ask you out at the end of the call," he said, "but what I have to tell you might be more important."

"What are you calling about, Nelson?" Kimberly asked. "Please?"

His voice changed. It grew more professional, more subdued. "Okay, I've got a friend who works for the airport police here in Nashville. He's been there for years, name's Travis. A good guy. We used to bowl together."

In her mind's eye, Kimberly saw Nelson bowling, his grimy nails against a ball adorned with swirled colors.

"So I was talking to Travis a little while ago about another case. No big deal. We had a guy run out on bail down here, and they grabbed him getting on a plane. It happens. But in the course of our talk, he tells me about this thing that just happened at the airport."

Kimberly felt her mind wander. She looked back at her desk, back at the file Brandon had dropped off earlier. She expected Nelson to share some diverting story about a terrorist scare or someone smuggling something bizarre—drugs or an exotic lizard—in a strange orifice. She listened with one ear and half of her mind. . . .

"Meets this woman on a plane . . . shares a kiss with her . . . then she ignores him when they're up in the air. . . . He finds her on

Facebook. . . . He finds out she's missing. . . . Turns out she used to live in Laurel Falls. . . ."

Kimberly pulled her eyes away from the file. "What was that?"

"She used to live in Laurel Falls. Up until a few months ago. My friend Travis, he looked her up on social media. She lived and worked in Laurel Falls until she moved down here to Nashville a few months ago."

"So where is she missing from?" Kimberly asked.

"That's just it—no one really knows what's going on. A friend filed a police report, and there's a lot of chatter on her Facebook page. Travis and his guys at the airport took all the information down and let the man who smooched her go on his way. There wasn't much else they could do at that point, right? And they're not even sure if he saw this woman or if he was just kind of lovestruck. She didn't show up on the passenger list."

"Sure, okay. So you're calling me because this woman lived in Laurel Falls at one time?" Kimberly asked. "Are you saying you want me to do some legwork for you? Because I'm kind of buried right now."

"I know you're buried. You've got a missing adult up there in little Laurel Falls. Prominent businessman, friend of the mayor. Clock's ticking, right?"

"Even as we speak."

"I'm not calling about him," he said. "Not exactly." His voice brimmed with excitement, like that of a salesman building up to the revelation of the amazing deal he'd been holding back. "When Travis told me about it, I checked out this woman's Facebook page too. Just curious, you know? And I won't lie: It's a little slow here today."

Kimberly tried to organize her thoughts. What did this guy kissing a woman in the airport have to do with her? Why had she even answered the phone?

"What did you see?" she asked, trying to speed things along.

"I just sent you the link," he said. "It should be in your inbox. I figured I'd let you check it out for yourself. Travis will probably call you soon, but I wanted to be the first to share the news. You can thank me later."

And then he hung up.

Kimberly sighed as she closed windows in an attempt to access her e-mail. The message from Nelson wasn't there yet, and while she waited, whistling softly to herself, she felt a strange anticipation growing in her chest, a thrumming, tingling adrenaline.

Slow down, she thought. Had she grown so desperate for a break that she allowed herself to think a guy like Nelson could deliver one via e-mail? Knowing him, it was more likely to be a bad joke or a stupid cartoon. Maybe a video of a guy getting hit in the nuts by a soccer ball.

But then the message popped up, accompanied by the irritating new-mail chime.

She clicked on the link, which took her to the Facebook page for someone named Morgan Reynolds, who was apparently the woman in the Nashville airport who had been reported missing. Kimberly scanned the woman's page. She saw pictures of her hiking, pictures with friends. Pictures with a dog and pictures of her drinking a pink cocktail on what looked like New Year's Eve. A pretty girl, no doubt about that. Athletic, slender. Beautiful eyes.

But why had Nelson sent it to her? What did it have to do with her life besides being a reminder of how much younger everyone else looked and how much fun they all seemed to be having?

She glanced at Nelson's message again and read what he'd written above the link.

Check out where she worked.

Kimberly did, clicking the "About" button on Morgan's page.

The name of the company where the woman had been most recently employed popped up.

She read it once. And then twice.

It took three times for it to really sink in.

"Holy crap," she said, even though no one was listening.

19

I went as far as standing in line with the other passengers, getting ready to board the flight to Tampa. I held my boarding pass in my hand, my feet doing the slow walk to the jet bridge and the gate agent, which I considered the point of no return for getting on a plane.

But as I shuffled along, pressed against the bodies of those around me, hearing their conversations, their chiming phones, the repeated "Thank yous" and "Enjoy your flights" from the airline employee in her blue clothes, I kept thinking about Morgan. An undercurrent of desperation had run beneath her words when we spoke on the courtesy phone. She'd sounded like a person who wanted to say more, *needed* to say more, but couldn't.

The rush to get away from me, the failure to explain it all.

The alias, the sunglasses.

How could I just stand by and do nothing?

I couldn't go back to the airport police. They weren't even convinced I'd seen Morgan on that plane. And I was wondering exactly who I had seen. . . .

And wasn't it possible involving the police would make things more difficult for Morgan? Was she in some situation the police couldn't help her out of, at least not yet?

I stopped four people back from the jet bridge, the boarding pass getting wet as my palms started to sweat. I faced the prospect of squeezing into a long metal tube with only a free Coke and a bag of peanuts to look forward to.

Or I could turn around, rent a roomy car, and try to help someone who really needed help.

What choice did I have?

I headed for the rental car counter, where I acquired a large sedan, something more comfortable even than the car I drove back home. Once my carry-on and my computer bag were stowed in the trunk, I started out. The tires hummed pleasantly over the interstate, the dashboard-mounted GPS pointing me north on I-65 toward the Tennessee-Kentucky border. Traffic was just light enough ahead of rush hour to allow me to make good time.

I left downtown Nashville in the rearview, the receding football stadium, the tall buildings. The racing cars and spaghetti snarl of converging interstates.

I quickly found myself past the outer suburbs, with more room, more lanes, less traffic. I saw bunches of trees, a sea of mostly green. The leaves were just thinking about changing, and I knew the coming weeks would show full-on autumn, a blast of colors that would nearly hurt the eyes. I suddenly felt like I could breathe more easily. I was seventy-eight minutes from Wyckoff and kind of looking forward to what I hoped would be a calming drive.

Then I remembered my dad. "Shit."

What would I tell him about this excursion to Wyckoff?

I checked the clock on the dash: 4:33. He wouldn't expect me until dinnertime, probably not until seven or so. That gave me some cushion. I decided to get to Wyckoff and look around. Based on what I was able to learn I could decide what to tell Dad. I hoped to know something quickly, and then I could give him as much information as possible. He'd still think I was nuts, but at least I could provide the whole story.

I wasn't sure what I expected. Before I started my drive, I asked Siri for information about Wyckoff and learned it had about seven thousand permanent residents and close to fifteen thousand students. That seemed manageable, right?

As soon as I had that thought, I felt foolish. Even with a population of just one thousand people, how would I find a single person who clearly didn't want to be found? And how did I know she'd even gone to Wyckoff after she'd bobbed and weaved around so many other facts?

But what did I have to lose? If I went there and struck out—the most likely scenario—then I could return to my life knowing I'd done everything I could to help Morgan. If I'd taken the plane to Tampa, swallowed the peanuts and the Coke, and then faked it through a series of work meetings and dinners, I'd always wonder.

I didn't want to wonder.

I crossed the state line from Tennessee into Kentucky, and then the GPS took me off the interstate at a town called Deep Creek, sending me northwest toward Wyckoff on a two-lane state road. At first I passed a series of strip malls and fast food restaurants with everything crowded and jumbled together. Traffic flowed heavy in both directions, and I missed being on the interstate with no one close by.

A trace of a sickly sweet smell filled the car as I left the town limits. A giant hill rose on my right, the grass green and lush, flocks of birds circling at the top. Massive trucks motored over a makeshift road. A landfill, a garbage dump, and the gross stench overwhelmed the car. I breathed through my mouth for a few miles until I saw a sign that said Wyckoff was only forty-two miles away. The outlined route on the GPS looked winding and slow, a two-lane with few places to pass. I took a chance on breathing again and discovered the dump smell was gone, receding with its image in the rearview. I cracked the window, letting the fresh air wash over me.

Then my phone rang. I saw the caller's name on the car's display. Renee.

"Double shit," I said.

But I answered.

"Hey."

"Hey, guy. Are you in Florida yet?"

I thought about lying. *Well, a little north of there.* But that felt just plain wrong, not to mention foolish. I might not have been in love with Renee, *really in love*, but I didn't want to lie to her.

"A change of plans," I said. "I'm not going to Florida."

"Oh," she said. "Does your dad have you doing something else?"

"No, I'm doing something on my own," I said.

"You are? What do you mean? Your own deal?"

The farther I went, the more peaceful the scenery looked. Open fields, white farmhouses. Scattered cows and horses and even sheep. It reminded me of growing up in Indiana, the miles and miles of flat land, the unimpeded view of the horizon. I'd lived in Chicago for five years, but it never felt as much like home as a place surrounded by neat rows of corn and soybeans.

"It's not work," I said.

And then I took a chance—a big chance—and told her the CliffsNotes version of the story. Meeting Morgan in the gift shop. The drinks at the bar. The Facebook posts about her disappearance.

I left out the kiss. Of course. And I left out the awkward exchange on the flight to Nashville, the one that ended when the flight attendant threatened to summon the pilot.

But Renee was smart. She could figure out that I wouldn't be following a woman across state lines unless I felt something for her.

Something strong.

Renee remained silent while I talked. Very silent. And maybe I was an idiot for telling her the truth, but I didn't feel like lying. I didn't feel like living a life I didn't want to live anymore.

When I was finished, she stayed quiet. The kind of quiet that makes a person wonder if the call dropped.

"Are you there, Renee?"

"That's quite a story."

"You understand, right, that I can't just turn my back on someone who might be in trouble?"

The question sounded foolish even as I asked it.

"Someone in trouble who happens to be a woman," she said. "Joshua, you could be getting in really deep here. What if she's dangerous? What if it's some scam? What if there are other people involved, people who might hurt you? You're smarter than that. Let the police handle it. She could be a crazy person, and you're running off to chase her like you're some chivalrous knight."

"It's not like that, Renee. It's about . . ."

But I couldn't finish the sentence. It *was* about her being a woman. A beautiful woman. And it was about that kiss. It was about how connected I already felt to her.

It was about all of it.

"I've been patient, Joshua," Renee said. "I thought we were moving toward something. Isn't that why we hooked up again a couple of weeks ago?"

"Maybe, but neither one of us said that out loud."

"Oh, God." She laughed, the sound coming through the speaker like a spit. "Do you think I'm so pathetic that I just want some promise from you? A ring or something stupid like that?"

"I didn't say—"

"It's fine, Joshua. Go on and do what you have to do. You're a good guy—I know you are. And I'd see that sometimes, especially the first six months we dated. But I swear, though, Joshua, the last six months or so we dated I couldn't get you to tell me the most basic thing about your life. Getting you to tell me how your day went felt like pulling teeth. I'd ask you how the food tasted, and you'd barely manage to get out the word 'fine.' Every time. And God forbid I ever asked you about your mother. Who knows? But this stranger . . . You were able to talk to a stranger in a bar? Wow. Maybe all of this running around will bring you some clarity."

"I . . ." But she was right. I did want clarity. Not really about Renee. More about myself, my life. About everything. "I hope so too."

"Good," she said. "But when you get back, don't expect to find me waiting again. Because we are as over as over can be."

20

I entered Wyckoff, Kentucky, the college town Morgan said she was heading to, and drove along the edge of the campus. It had taken me nearly ninety minutes to get there from Nashville, and the sun was just fading, the sky a darkening blue with skittering black birds lifting off and sweeping across the colors.

College kids, students at Henry Clay University, shuffled along the sidewalks in packs, joking and laughing. Afternoon classes were winding down, and the students would be heading back to the residence halls for dinner, then on to homework or bullshitting, fraternity and sorority meetings, intramural games. Later, perhaps, encounters with romantic partners, either long-term loves or short-term flings, the kinds of relationships that caused hormones and emotions to rocket and then crash to earth.

Nostalgia sank its hooks into me. I existed at a strange intersection in my life. Far enough away from college to remember it with fondness, close enough to believe I could easily go back. For a moment, as I passed by the redbrick Georgian buildings, the kiosks covered with flyers fluttering in the light breeze, the sunshine bouncing off the windows, I allowed myself to wonder how I would do things differently if that mythical time machine existed.

Would I major in illustration as I'd always wanted? Would I spend more time having fun instead of following the narrowly prescribed path that led to the life I lived?

Would I find the guts to say no to my dad when he offered me the chance to start a career in his company? It hurt in a sweetly painful way to think about, like a tongue probing a cold sore. I pushed the thoughts away, tried to accept a past that couldn't be changed. I'd read something in a fortune cookie once or maybe on a cocktail napkin: *The unlived life is not worth examining.*

I followed the state road around the north end of campus and took it into the small downtown, the main drag populated by independent businesses. The streets were cobblestone, which made the car jink and bounce like an airplane as I passed dive bars advertising cheap beer, T-shirt shops selling college gear, and sandwich places with overly hip names. More students milled on the sidewalks there, and I scanned the faces, looking for Morgan. Futility landed on me like a heavy cloak. Needle in a haystack much?

I made several circuits of the downtown and then went through the middle of campus twice. I felt like a goldfish in a bowl, bumping up against the same glass over and over. I needed to make a more coherent plan, so when I ended up in the downtown again, I pulled over in front of a coin-operated laundry and looked up hotels on my phone. Would Morgan even be staying in a hotel? Or was she crashing with a friend or a lover or a family member? But I had to start somewhere, and there weren't too many hotels to search, considering the size of the town. Some were obviously fleabags, based on their locations—far outside of town—or their names. I strongly suspected a place called the Tropical Court and Hideaway wasn't going to be high-class in Wyckoff, Kentucky. There were also listings for a couple of expensive-sounding bed-and-breakfasts. And why would you go to a bed-and-breakfast if you were trying to hide? At a bed-and-breakfast, everyone knew your business.

Two of the moderately priced hotels sat within a block of each other—a Best Western and a Hampton Inn. Perfect. They were in a commercial area just south of campus, so I headed that way, cutting across town and then driving past a row of fraternity houses where a group of shirtless guys threw a Frisbee around. The marching band practiced in an open field a block farther along, the thumping of the drums and bleating of the tubas coming through the open windows above the rush of the wind.

I found the side-by-side hotels across the street from a giant Walmart and next to an Indian restaurant, which sent the pungent odor of curry into the car. The sun continued to slide, the hotels' bright signs illuminating the early evening like beacons. I pulled into the Best Western lot and circled the building, hoping . . . what exactly? That I'd find Morgan standing outside, one hand on her hip, eagerly awaiting my arrival, wishing I'd save her skin?

When my initial search proved fruitless, I took another turn around the building, more out of desperation than because I had a plan. I knew I couldn't just walk in and ask if someone—especially a woman—was staying there. And if Morgan had purchased her plane ticket under an assumed name, why would she stay in the hotel using her real one?

So I guided the car over to the Hampton Inn, where I saw an elderly couple unloading luggage in the parking lot but no one else. I circled once and then one more time, and that was when I caught a break. A hotel employee, a young guy, college age, pushed a large bin of trash out the back door, heading for the Dumpster. I pulled my car alongside him and climbed out. Either he was trying to ignore me or he was so focused on his work that he didn't react until I cleared my throat. He finally turned and looked at me.

"Help you with something, sir?" He sounded unconcerned, as if asking the question out of reflex. He was thin and wiry with floppy hair that fell over his forehead, requiring him to constantly brush it off his face. His name tag read BILLY.

"I'm looking for someone."

"A hotel guest?"

"Possibly."

"You can ask at the front desk," he said. "But they aren't at liberty to give much information out."

"That's what I thought." I brought out my phone and showed him the picture of Morgan from her Facebook page. "Have you seen her?"

Billy finished dumping the trash and then pushed his hair away again. He leaned over, studying the picture. "I don't know, man. I don't interact with the guests much."

"This lot is pretty empty, which means the hotel is pretty empty too, right? Couldn't you maybe just go in and wander around and look? Or ask someone at the desk if they've seen someone who looks like her? You must know the people who work the desk, right?"

He stared at me. His hair tumbled down again, but this time he ignored it.

I reached into my pocket and brought out two twenties. "She's a friend of mine. I'm not going to hurt her. I'm here to help her. Just let me know if she's here."

Billy studied the two bills in my hand. The wind blew, shaking them like leaves. I thought he was going to walk away and leave me hanging, but then he reached out, took them, and tucked the bills into his shirt pocket right behind his name tag.

"You've got to give me a minute, okay?" he said. "I need to take this back in and dump another load."

"Sure."

He shrugged and pushed the bin toward the building. I got back into my rental car, pulled into an empty spot, and waited.

21

It took fifteen minutes for the security guard to come out the same door Billy had gone in with his trash bin, his floppy hair, and my forty bucks. The guard made a beeline for my car, a large walkie-talkie in his right hand.

"Thanks, Billy, you little bastard," I said to myself. Apparently forty bucks wasn't the going rate for buying off a garbage boy in a college-town hotel.

I should have driven away, but the guard was next to the car so quickly I couldn't unless I wanted to run him over. He bent down by the hood, studying the plate, then came along the driver's-side window.

"Are you looking for someone, sir?" he asked, his voice higher pitched than I would have expected.

He had a shaved head that could have been used as a battering ram and wore a dark suit two sizes too big. Up close I saw he wasn't much older than Billy, but he believed in his mission a lot more. He chewed a wad of gum with teeth stained yellow from either neglect or smoking, and he looked on the verge of breathing fire into my car.

"Just a friend," I said. "She told me she'd be here."

"But she didn't tell you her room number?"

"I guess we miscommunicated. Maybe I have the wrong hotel. Maybe I'm in the wrong state."

"The police might like to know that you're here bribing hotel employees for information about one of our guests." He said the word "guests" in a weirdly proprietary way, like a cult leader speaking of his flock.

"They might," I said. "But I didn't really think of it as a bribe. I thought of it more as a donation to his college fund. You know, helping a working kid out."

"You need to leave, sir," the guard said, unmoved by my positive spin on bribery and snooping. "And I've taken down the plate number on your car. If I see you back, I will call the police."

"Sure, sure. I prefer the Marriott anyway."

He didn't smile. If he had, his face might have cracked.

I pulled out of the space under his watchful, almost predatory, eye. I flipped my headlights on to cut through the encroaching evening and looked back once. He was still in place, staring after me as I drove away. I decided it wouldn't do me any good to go to the Best Western right then either, since the security guard might call over and alert them to my presence. So I left.

I didn't know where to go except to some of the dive hotels. I hated to think of Morgan staying in one of those, but it sounded more pleasant to be in the Tropical Court than the Hampton Inn just then. At the Tropical Court, forty dollars would likely secure a room for the night and all the information I needed.

Three blocks from the Hampton Inn and Best Western, I saw a figure trudging along the side of the street, his hands tucked in his pockets. I recognized his floppy hair and the sickly green uniform he wore. I pulled over, powering down the passenger-side window. He must have heard the engine, because he turned to look at me.

"Thanks for ratting me out."

Billy looked both ways up and down the street, then stepped over to my car. "I didn't rat you out. Sean overheard me talking to the desk clerk. He creeps around all over that place, listening to everybody." He dug in his pocket, bringing out the two twenties. "You can have this back if you want."

"It's okay," I said. "I didn't mean to get you in trouble. You didn't get fired or anything, did you?"

"No, I'm off now. The last thing I do is take the trash out."

"Do you need a ride?" I asked.

"I'm cool. My girlfriend lives up here." He nodded toward the next block.

His words struck a chord. They sounded so simple and so uncomplicated. A quick stroll up the street, a warm greeting from a beautiful young woman. A night together. The possibilities seemed endless.

"Well, have fun. Okay?" I said. "Enjoy it while you can."

First Billy looked puzzled, then like he wanted to say more. He leaned down, casting his eyes both ways before resting his hands on the windowsill.

"What's up?" I asked.

"My friend Bridget, who works the desk. Did you see her? Sometimes she works at the hotel next door too. The Best Western. We all get moved back and forth between the two places if they need us. They're both owned by the same people. An Indian family."

"Okay," I said. "Go on."

"She was over there earlier today, helping out. She says a lady like the one you showed me checked in there. She might be the one you're looking for."

"Are you shitting me?" I asked.

"No. I was hoping I'd see you, but I had to sneak out before Sean busted me. Don't worry. He didn't call the cops, but he did take your license plate down. He'll call them if you go back, that's for sure. He's kind of crazy. He once hit a guy with his flashlight."

"The clerk thinks this woman who checked in was my friend? The one I'm looking for?"

"Might be," he said. "She couldn't remember the exact room number, but it's on the third floor. Three ten? Three fourteen? Three eighteen? Something like that."

"Okay." I felt better. At least I had something. "Thanks. That's great."

"She remembered her because she was so pretty, like that picture you showed me," he said. "And she seemed kind of jumpy."

"Jumpy? Really?"

"Yeah, and she was crying. Crying the whole time she checked in."

22

I walked through the lobby of the Best Western like I belonged there. The desk clerk, who was busy talking on the phone, nodding as she listened intently to the caller, barely looked my way as I breezed past. I hopped on the elevator and pressed 3, anxious until the doors closed.

It had to be her.

But what happens when I get to her room? Would she be alone? Why was she holed up in this hotel? Why was she crying?

The doors opened and I stepped onto the third floor. The carpet matched Billy's uniform, a dark puke green. Bright bulbs in gold sconces guided the way, illuminating ugly tan wallpaper. A musty smell reached my nose, as though there had been a leak that had not been properly dried.

The room numbers Billy had mentioned were to the left, so I went that way. From behind a closed door, I heard a loud TV, and some kind of sad Muzak leaked through unseen speakers overhead. Aside from that, the atmosphere felt hushed and sterile, like I was in a nursing home for wayward travelers.

Room 310 came in sight, the first possibility Billy had given me. I stopped in front of the door, listening, but heard nothing. I drew a deep breath, and then I knocked.

It took a minute, and then the door opened, revealing a massive guy who wore only a white towel and had a garishly colored eagle tattooed on his hairless chest. He had a Fu Manchu mustache and looked at me like I was a bug he wanted to step on.

"I'm sorry," I said. "I'm looking for Morgan."

"You're barking up the wrong tree, bud."

"Yeah, maybe I am." But I still looked past him into the room. I saw a neatly made bed, a discarded pair of jeans, and work boots with a thick coating of mud on the soles. The TV played a liberal cable news program. I wanted to see if Morgan was in there, somehow being protected by the middle linebacker in front of me.

"Need something else?" he asked. He didn't sound like a patient man. And he'd stopped calling me "bud," which meant we weren't as good friends as we had been just seconds before.

"Not really—"

He closed the door in my face, generating a gust of wind so strong it brushed my hair back. So I went to the next room Billy mentioned, hoping for either better results or a less massive occupant. I knocked but no one answered, so I knocked again. No answer. I worried that at some point someone might complain to the front desk about me stopping at every door asking questions. It was possible the guy with the eagle tattoo already had, although he seemed like the type to solve his own problems without relying on others.

I moved on and knocked on yet another door without receiving an answer. And then I came to room 306. With sore knuckles and fading hopes, I knocked.

A light glowed from behind the peephole, and then something blocked it for a moment, meaning someone was looking out. But the door didn't open, and no one said anything. The person remained at the peephole a long time, longer than it should take to see who was outside and make a decision about opening the door.

For all I knew, the person was calling the front desk right then, summoning Sean, his overworked gum, and his deadly flashlight.

I knocked one more time.

"Hello?" I said.

I took a step back, ready to give up, and that's when I heard the lock being undone from the other side with a series of rattles and clacks. The door came open, and it was her. Morgan. No hat, no sunglasses, but wearing the same clothes she'd worn in the airport. The hallway light struck her face, catching her eyes, and the breath stuck in my throat. *Damn,* I thought.

She was as beautiful as I remembered.

Her face was as blank as the hotel's walls. She stared at me, her lips pressed together. She didn't speak, and I understood she must have regarded me like one would an unexpected package that might explode. Her eyes darted to either side of me, up the hallway and down. When they settled on me again, they narrowed.

"Shit," she said. "What in the name of God are you doing here?"

"I followed you," I said. "I was worried."

She let out a long sigh, the sound of a punctured tire rapidly losing air. Her shoulders slumped. She shook her head, taking in the human form of a perpetually returning bad penny.

"Get in here," she said, waving me into the room.

I went in, and she bolted the door shut behind me. I looked around the room. Two beds, the carry-on bag next to the hat and sunglasses on one of them. The TV played a black-and-white movie with the volume muted, a Henry Fonda Western I'd once watched with my dad. Wyatt Earp had just married a beautiful schoolmarm, and the two of them danced with joy while the crowd clapped. A world apart from the way Morgan had greeted me.

"Are you alone?" I asked. The minifridge cycled on and then off with a rattle.

"Of course I'm alone." She came closer but didn't sit down. "You shouldn't be here. You really, really should leave. Go back to wherever you have to go."

"You told me to quit my job," I said.

"Fine. Go do that. But you can't do it here. Really, Joshua, this isn't good for you."

"Is it good for you?" I asked. "You're using another name, traveling in disguise. Your friends think you've disappeared."

"Those are my problems. Not yours."

"You agreed to have a drink with me. You kissed me, and then you called me at the airport."

"And told you to leave me alone," she said, making a dismissive gesture with her hand.

"I couldn't," I said. "Not when it seems like you're in danger. Not . . . not when we connected the way we did."

"Oh, God . . ."

"If you tell me everything is okay, I'll turn around and go. But I don't think you can tell me that. I think there's something going on, something bad, and you seem to be dealing with it alone."

"And what does that make you? The second coming of Sir Galahad?"

That made two times that day a woman had compared me to a knight on a quest. I wished for such a sharp, clear purpose.

She continued to stare at me. Her eyes were red and raw. I saw a box of tissues on the nightstand, and some crumpled ones littered the floor. She looked very alone and very anxious.

"Are you going to throw me out?" I asked.

She took a deep breath. "Not yet."

I felt a small measure of relief.

"So why don't you tell me what's going on?" I asked.

She turned away, paced to the door, and then came back, her hand lifted to her mouth. She was shaking her head, her hair bouncing across her shoulders.

"You don't want to know," she said, but she sounded softer, less determined to dismiss me.

"I do, Morgan. Look how far I've come."

"You're an idiot, then."

"Thanks a lot."

"You'll be implicated. Do you know that?"

"Implicated? In what?"

"I'm not trying to be cruel. . . . I just . . ."

"Look, try me. Okay? Just try me."

"Okay," she said after a long pause. "I haven't told anybody, so I might as well tell you." She pointed to the minifridge. "I bought a six-pack. And you might need one if you want to hear it all."

I grabbed a beer for myself and one for her, the bottles cold and slick against my palms. I opened them both and handed one over. We sat across from each other on opposite beds, and I waited for her to begin.

23

She didn't drink her beer, but her grip on the bottle was tight. I saw the pressure being exerted by her knuckles against the glass.

"Do you know anything about the way women can be treated in tech companies?" she asked.

"I've heard stories," I said. I waited for her to say more, but she didn't. She stared at the ugly green carpet, her feet planted on the floor. "Is that what happened to you? Were you . . . harassed or something?"

She shook her head. "No, nothing like that. I'm talking about the way women get taken advantage of in terms of their work. We get shut out and overlooked. Or ignored."

I told her I understood. She might not have been drinking her beer, but I drank mine. Even though I felt dehydrated from being in the air and in the car all day, the beer tasted good. It kept me calm, made me patient.

"Remember this morning, how we talked about making a difference?" she asked. "How we come out of college all idealistic and hoping to make a difference?"

"Sure."

"That's what I thought I was doing." She paused. "I went to work for this tech company called TechGreen. All one word.

TechGreen. They make apps and do Web design. The kind of stuff that's really been taking off over the last few years."

"Where was this?" I asked.

"In Laurel Falls, Kentucky. A midsize town about thirty minutes east of here and an hour north of Nashville."

"I saw it on the map," I said. "I didn't go through it, but I took a state road that went west of there."

"That makes sense. I got the job at TechGreen a year after I finished college here at Henry Clay. I moved to Laurel Falls just knowing a few people. But it sounded like a good place to work. They were trying to help the environment through tech, and they said they treated their employees differently. You know, healthy, catered lunches in the break room. Massages or yoga on special days. That kind of thing."

I compared her experience to working for my dad. We had no real office outside of our homes. I spent most of my time cramped in airplanes or hunched over a laptop at my dining room table. Dad didn't know what yoga was, and the closest thing I came to a catered meal was when he took me to his favorite diner for greasy eggs or a patty melt and regaled me with stories of his early days in business. To be honest, I liked hearing the old man talk about his past. I learned more about him at those breakfasts than at any other time.

"I've heard of companies like that," I said.

"It was great. I met people I liked. We all wanted to create technology that helped the planet. Things that reduced our impact on the environment." She met my eye. "Like I said, idealism. Making a difference."

"Right."

She looked at the beer bottle as though she hadn't realized it was in her hand. She studied the label and then took a long drink.

Her throat bobbed, and when she was finished, she smacked her lips with satisfaction.

"That's good. Better than that crappy Bloody Mary in the airport."

"No surprise."

"Thanks for paying for that, by the way. I know I stuck you with the tab."

"I'll write it off on my taxes."

She let out a small laugh. "So, I'm working for TechGreen. And everything is going well. I get involved in some fulfilling projects, make some decent money. I feel like I'm moving along the way I'm supposed to. Then it was time for me to take a step forward. It was time for me to take the lead on an app instead of just following along and helping other people in the company."

"That sounds like progress."

"Moving on up. Becoming a big girl."

She sounded cynical and disappointed. Maybe we'd both seen what was behind the curtain of adulthood and found it wanting. But what was the alternative to going to school, getting a real job and your own place to live? Dad wouldn't have let me sleep in my childhood bedroom with the Peyton Manning poster and the GI Joes forever.

She drank from the beer again, then said, "I came up with an idea for an app, something the company could really get behind, something they could take and run with. It was simple, so simple it was brilliant."

"The best ideas usually are," I said.

"Right. It was an app that allowed you to enter products you found in the store—clothes, food, cleaning supplies, whatever— and then the app would tell you the product's environmental impact. You know, are there poisons in the product? Or was pollution generated as it was made? Were workers being mistreated somewhere in the world?" She shook her head as she thought about it.

"We called it LifeShoppe with an 'e' on the end, and, damn, it was good."

"I'm sure they were happy," I said.

"Oh, yeah, they were. It's a small company, founded and run by just a couple of guys. A really good app like that, a really good idea, could make the place take off like you wouldn't believe." Her face suddenly became less animated, taking on the same lost, distant look it had earlier. "They were desperate for an idea that would set them apart and make everything they did stand out. It's a crowded field."

"That all sounds good," I said. "I sense there's a 'but' coming. . . ."

"Oh, there is," she said, taking another drink of her beer and suppressing a small burp. "There most definitely is."

24

I finished my beer but stayed on the bed, not wanting to throw off her train of thought. I remained still, waiting for her to go on.

"You can see where this story is going, can't you?" she asked.

I had a pretty good guess at the most likely outcome.

"LifeShoppe was a huge smash," I said. "Everybody loved it."

She was nodding before I even finished my sentence. Then she tilted her head back and finished her beer.

"Do you want another?" I asked.

"Please."

I went to the minifridge and brought out two more, the bottles clinking against each other as I held them in one hand. I carried an opener on my key chain, so I popped the two tops and handed one to her. Our fingers brushed as she took the bottle from me, and then our eyes met briefly.

I didn't say anything, but I damn sure remembered that kiss in the airport . . . which seemed like it had happened about a month earlier. I moved my tongue around in my mouth, trying to find some remnant of that Bloody Mary flavor from her lips, but too much alcohol and time had passed for me to summon it again. Had we really met only that morning at ten o'clock? I checked the large red numbers on the bedside clock: 7:21. It was getting late, too late. I had to call Dad soon.

Dad. *Shit.* I couldn't avoid him forever.

I took my seat again, and Morgan kicked her running shoes off and scooted back on her bed, folding her long, slender legs under her body. I became acutely aware of the silly work clothes I still wore—my button-down shirt, my jacket, my dress shoes. We looked like we existed in two different worlds.

"The app was a smash," she said. "It sold and sold. And got written up in a few industry magazines. It did better than anything else TechGreen had ever done. By far. It was . . . really just great. I mean, I felt like not only had I come up with an idea and worked on something that actually made the world a better place, as cheesy as that sounds, but I'd also done something to help the company. It was a win-win for everybody."

"A rising tide lifts all boats," I said.

"Yeah." She took a drink of her beer. And then another. "God, this tastes really good. I mean, really. I've been craving this ever since I left Nashville but didn't know it."

Morgan started picking at the label on her beer bottle. She used her thumbnail, which was covered with chipped pink nail polish. She performed the act aggressively, almost as if she were taking something out on the label. And she seemed to have forgotten I was in the room, even though I was watching her from just a few feet away.

I waited as long as I could, not wanting to interrupt her private reverie. But a deadline loomed—the call to my dad—and I wanted the story to resume if there was more. And I strongly suspected there was.

"So, the app was a smash," I said, trying to jar her back to reality. "What happened after that?"

She kept picking away, her nail making a small pinging sound against the bottle. I thought she hadn't heard me, but she said, "You're a business guy. Clearly. You must know that when you sign on to work for a company like that, whatever you design or create for them becomes their intellectual property. Right?"

"Sounds pretty standard," I said.

She stopped picking and nodded. "I knew that. I may have been young and idealistic when I started working there, but I wasn't stupid. Or naïve. I wasn't a dumb kid. I knew how the world worked. I knew that if the app did well I could go find a job somewhere else and make more money. Or get a raise. Or start my own company. Hell, I knew what I could do."

"So what went wrong?" I asked.

She heaved a big sigh, her shoulders moving up and down. Out in the hallway, I heard cubes tumbling through the ice machine and hammering a plastic bucket. An all-too-familiar noise considering how many nights I'd sat in a hotel room and listened to its percussive rhythm.

"They'd had successful apps before," Morgan said. "Not quite this big, but things that had done well. Every time—*every time*—the owner of the company would give the person or team who came up with the idea a nice bonus. I never knew exactly how much they got, but I heard rumors. It was a healthy piece of compensation for work well done. Nothing like what the company made, but enough to say that the company valued what those people had accomplished."

"Seems normal," I said. "Bonuses always help morale."

Morgan became quiet again. I watched her intently, choosing not to say anything to speed her along because of the troubled look that had just come over her face. Tears formed there, filling her eyes. She reached up with her free hand, the one not holding the beer, and brushed them away. Then she sniffled.

"I'm sorry," I said.

"This is way more than you bargained for, isn't it?" she asked. "You probably knocked on my door hoping for a quick lay, right?"

"This is a long way to go for a quick lay," I said. "I'm supposed to be in Florida right now. Remember? I could have gone there and found a seventy-five-year-old widow at the hotel bar if I'd wanted a quick lay."

She laughed but wiped more tears away. "Shit. I don't want to be crying."

"We can stop talking if—"

"No," she said. "I want to tell you. It actually feels good to have someone listening."

"Okay. I'm a captive audience."

She drank from her bottle. "You can guess, right? I didn't get the damn bonus. Nothing." She shook her head. "And here's the kicker. Those other developers, the ones who had received bonuses when their apps did well? They were all men. I was the first woman to make them this much money, and when it came time to get the bonus, there was nothing for me. Nothing at all."

25

Morgan scooted across the bed, holding her beer away from her body so nothing spilled, and stood up. She rushed to the bathroom without saying anything, closed the door behind her, and locked it.

I walked over, my steps cautious. But I heard running water and then coughing. I couldn't be sure if she was getting sick or crying. I knocked gently.

"Are you okay?" I asked. "Do you need anything?"

"Just leave me alone," she said.

A pretty clear answer. I checked the time again and saw I needed to call Dad. I didn't want to. I had no idea what I could say to him. But I couldn't leave him high and dry, wondering where I was.

"I'm going to step out and make a phone call," I said through the closed door, hoping Morgan heard me. She made no response, but the water still ran. So I undid the locks and went out.

I took the stairs at the end of the hall down to the first floor, my steps echoing like drumbeats in the closed space, and found a sitting area in the lobby. No one was there, which meant I'd have a little privacy. I sat at a small table in the corner and took a deep breath. Then I called.

When Dad answered, he sounded cheery. His tone told me the afternoon meetings had gone well.

"Hey. Did you just land? Was the plane late?"

"I haven't landed."

A pause. "Joshua, what's going on?"

"Well, I'm not coming to Tampa."

"Okay . . ."

His voice sounded gravelly and low, uncertainty bordering on disapproval bleeding through the phone. He was going to give me the benefit of the doubt . . . but for only about twenty more seconds.

"Dad, a friend of mine is going through a personal crisis right now."

"A friend? What friend? A friend from home?"

"No. It's a long story, and I don't have time to tell it now. But what matters is I'm not going to make it to Tampa tonight. I have to be here. It's the best thing, and I know you can handle what's going on down there."

"I don't like this, Joshua. First you tell me one thing and then you decide to do something else. Are you in some kind of trouble?"

"No, I'm not." But I wasn't sure. I remembered the word Morgan had used. *Implicated.* Not a pretty word, not at all. "Dad, remember earlier today when we talked, and you said you could sense that I was a little dissatisfied?"

"Sure. We said we'd talk about it when you got here."

"I know. And I appreciate that. But you were right, so I'm trying to take care of something, with this friend, because it seems more important at the moment than work does. Does that make sense?"

A man in khaki pants and a sweatshirt came through the swooshing automatic doors and into the lobby. He looked around, nodded at me, and then went to the desk. I couldn't say why, but I wondered if he was looking for Morgan. It seemed like an irrational thought, not backed up by anything he'd done, but given her clandestine movements across the country, it didn't seem far-fetched. Might someone be looking for her? She sure acted like it.

"Is this *friend* a woman?" Dad asked, placing an arch emphasis on the word "friend."

What could I say? Did it matter if I lied?

"Yes, she is."

"Oh, Joshua," he said. "A woman?" He let out a rough sigh. "Look, Joshua, I know what it's like to be on the road. Hell, your mother left me so many years ago. . . . I understand the temptations. The hotels and the bars and the late nights. And I'd be lying if I said I hadn't indulged myself from time to time over the years."

"Dad, I really don't need—"

"But you need to be smart here," he went on. "You need to know how to do this without getting attached and letting it interfere with your life."

"It's not like that, Dad. It's not. It's not some . . . one-night stand or whatever."

"Then what is it?" he asked.

I started to speak but couldn't find the words. Wasn't I doing exactly what my dad had just accused me of? What did I have with Morgan beyond a—potential—one-night stand? All started by that kiss in the airport bar.

Was I thinking with anything more than the lower regions of my body?

The man at the counter seemed unhappy with whatever he and the clerk were discussing. He shook his head disgustedly. Either he didn't care for the out-of-date décor, or else Sean had threatened him with the flashlight treatment. The man finally stepped back from the counter and looked around the lobby. His eyes passed over me and then came back. He stared for a moment and then walked down the hall toward the opposite wing of the building from where Morgan was staying. He continued to shake his head.

"If I'm making a mistake, Dad, then I'm making a mistake. I'm not sure what else to say at this point. I'll call you tomorrow and give you an update."

"Okay, okay."

I heard the impatience in his voice, his desire to be finished with a conversation that wasn't moving in the direction he wanted. I'd heard that tone more than once in my life.

"What's this woman's name?" he asked. "And where are you? Are you actually in Nashville? At least tell me that. If something goes wrong, I want to know where you are and who you're with."

"Dad, I'm not—"

"Come on. Just tell me. Somebody needs to know."

I hesitated. I wasn't a little kid. I didn't need to check in with my father . . . especially if I wanted to spend time with a woman.

But I knew so little about her. . . .

"I'm in Kentucky," I said.

"Kentucky? Sheesh. I thought you were flying to Nashville."

"You fly to Nashville to get to southern Kentucky. The town I'm in is called Wyckoff. Ninety minutes northwest of Nashville. And her name is Morgan Reynolds."

Dad muttered to himself as he wrote the information down.

"We'll talk tomorrow," he said. "I have more work to do tonight. But if you wake up in the bathtub missing a kidney, don't say I didn't warn you."

26

I knocked on Morgan's door. A "Do Not Disturb" sign hung from the knob, and I tried to remember if it had been there before. I didn't think it had. I waited and knocked again, increasing the force, but still received no response. I'd gone to the car and retrieved my bags, and their weight on my shoulder tilted me to one side.

I leaned in close, pressing my ear against the varnished wood as I tried to pick up any noises. I thought I heard the sound of running water and maybe more coughing. But the humming of the ice machine, the whirring of the air-conditioning system, made it hard to hear. My mind might have been playing auditory tricks on me, telling me Morgan was still inside the room when she wasn't.

I looked up the hall, one way and then the other. If she refused to answer the door, what could I do? I wasn't a registered guest, and I had no real claim to speak to her. If she wanted to ignore me and hope I would grow tired and leave, she could.

I leaned in close one more time and thought I heard sniffling. And then a thumping noise, as though something had fallen over. Or broken.

The sniffling and coughing stopped.

I knocked again, harder and faster.

"Morgan?" I waited. "Morgan? Just let me know you're okay."

I knocked again and again, increasing the pace, feeling the vibration in my hand.

"Morgan?"

The door I'd knocked on earlier with no response came open. A middle-aged woman in workout clothes stuck her head out into the hallway, her brow furrowed. She looked at me, wondering who the boorish idiot disturbing the peace was.

"Everything okay?" she asked, although her voice told me she didn't think it was. "Is there a problem?"

"My friend," I said. "Did you hear anything from in there?"

"Maybe I'll call the front desk."

"Oh, well, maybe not that. I just—"

And then Morgan's door swung open. Her eyes were red, but otherwise she looked no worse for wear. She stayed back in the doorway, out of sight of her curious next-door neighbor.

"I'm sorry, honey," Morgan said, loud enough for the woman to hear. "I was in the shower."

I looked at the woman and shrugged. She gave me a suspicious glance from the corner of her eye and then slipped away. I followed Morgan back into her room.

Inside, she closed the door and bolted it again. Then she spoke to me in a low, harsh voice. "Are you trying to make a scene? That's the last thing I need. Somebody might call security. Or the police."

"I was worried. You didn't answer. And it sounded like you were crying or something."

"I'm fine, Sir Knight. You know, it's one thing for you to show up here. Uninvited. It's another for you to stir the pot like this."

Morgan walked over to the fridge and took out another beer, studying the label as though not sure what the bottle contained, and then she turned to me and asked for my opener.

I brought it to her and she popped the top with a soft hiss. Then she went past me and returned to her seat on the bed. I remained standing, uncertain of what I should do.

"I'm sorry you went through all that," I said.

"Thanks. It's life in the big, grown-up world, I guess."

"It sounds like a lousy work environment. But now you have enough experience to move on to something else."

Morgan remained silent, staring at a stain in the shape of Alaska on the carpet.

I wondered if she wanted me to leave. If I left the hotel, she could lick her wounds or clear her head. Or she could walk around campus while the changing leaves rustled overhead and feel like a college kid again. Whatever she'd planned for her trip, it didn't involve me.

Not in any way.

But I wasn't finished asking questions. And if she wanted me to go, she'd have to ask.

"If all of that happened the way you say it did, and I have no reason to think it didn't, why are you traveling this way? Under another name and keeping such a low profile?"

Her eyes remained fixed on the carpet stain, her face stony and unresponsive. She looked a little childish, like a kid who thought she could outlast any inquiry with a sufficient amount of stubbornness.

I scanned my mind, searching for something to say. The right thing, the one that would shake her loose.

But Morgan broke the spell herself.

"I'm not perfect, Joshua," she said, still looking at the floor. Her jaw was set, the muscles clenched. "Yes, I was treated poorly by my company, but I didn't handle myself well either."

I waited.

"I told you my mom is sick. She needed help, and I was so fed up with everything at work that I just quit. I walked away and decided to spend time with her in Nashville, trying to figure out what to do next." She paused. "But it didn't really help. I just thought about what happened more and more. I stewed. I didn't have much to distract me. I'd started to make some friends in Nashville, the people who are so worried about me on Facebook, but they weren't enough of a distraction without a job."

She reached up and scratched her cheek with a trembling hand.

"My mom needed money for a nurse or in-home care. And I kept getting notices in the mail about my student loan. I still owe about twenty thousand bucks. And the interest keeps growing and growing. I made a dent in it while I worked at TechGreen, but without a steady income, I couldn't keep it up." She looked at me. "Did you take out a loan for school?"

"No. My dad . . . He had enough money."

Her free hand, the one not holding the beer, rested on the ugly bedspread. Her long fingers drummed against the fabric.

She said one word. "Lucky."

"So, what did you do?" I asked. "About getting your mom help?"

"I tried to make an appointment to see my boss, the one who controlled the money, but he kept putting me off. So one night I just went to his house. I'd been there for a cocktail party once." She shifted her weight on the bed, uncrossing and then recrossing her legs. "It was just one of those moments when I felt really ballsy, really pushy. Like I didn't have anything to lose. I just went up and rang the doorbell and waited for him to answer."

"Did it work?" I asked.

"He opened the door and let me in." Then she spoke in a rush. "There's not much else to say, except nothing changed. He told me the company was in a cash crunch because they were opening an office in another state. He said he valued my work and even offered me my job back. He said a lot of other things too . . . but none of it amounted to anything. The whole trip was just a dead end. And then . . ."

"What?"

She shook her head, her cheeks flushed. "I hate to say it. I cried. Like a stupid idiot little girl, I lost my shit and broke down. I couldn't even keep it together long enough not to cry in front of him. I cried in his living room. I hate that. But everything had built up inside. My mom, the job, the money. I couldn't control it."

When she finished rushing her words out, she drank from her bottle.

But I knew that couldn't be the whole story.

And I think she knew it.

"There's got to be more," I said. "You still haven't told me why you used a fake name."

For a second, she acted again like I wasn't there. But then she quickly set the bottle down on the bedside table so hard it made a loud thunk. She went over to the luggage stand and undid the zipper on her carry-on bag. The one she'd held so close at the airport, the one she'd refused to leave behind when she went to the bathroom.

She rummaged around in the bag and then drew her hand out. Something small was clutched inside.

"This is the problem," she said. "This . . . complicates everything."

27

I squinted, trying to see the small object she held in her hand.

She stayed near the bag, seemingly reluctant to turn and hand the item over to me.

It took me a moment, but then I saw she was cupping a small bundle of red tissue paper, the kind you'd use to wrap a Christmas gift.

"Can I see it?" I asked.

She finally turned and extended her hand—which still shook—to me. I lifted the bundle of tissue paper, cradling it gently in my palm like a baby bird. Which it might have been for all I knew, since she'd been so protective and deliberate with it.

"Go ahead and unwrap it," she said.

So I did. I peeled back a couple of layers of the red paper, wondering if there was anything inside there at all. Then I wondered if I'd be shocked or disturbed by what I uncovered. Had she cut off her former boss's finger and spirited it away? Had my dad been correct? Was I about to unwrap a stolen human kidney?

My own fingers started to shake a little. But instead of an extracted organ or a severed human finger, I found an antique ring, one with a fairly large diamond in the middle and two smaller diamonds on either side. I knew next to nothing about such things and owed all my knowledge of the subject to Renee. We'd once gone to an antique fair where there were a few rings like the one in my hand. Renee said she'd love to have one like it someday, since her grandmother had worn something similar, and I knew a hint was being telegraphed in my direction. But the size of the diamonds we saw that day at the antique fair didn't compare to that of the ones I held in my hand.

I wasn't sure what to do next.

"I don't understand," I said. "It's someone's ring, obviously. Are you saying . . . Did this come from your boss?"

"It belongs to him, yes," Morgan said. "Or I guess I should say it belongs to his family."

I still didn't follow. My brain felt thick and sludgy, like I was permanently one step behind. "Did he propose? I thought you said there was nothing like that going on."

Morgan sighed to let me know I truly didn't understand anything.

"I stole it," she said, her voice sharp. "From his house. When he shut me down again, I took the damn ring. Impulsively. I just grabbed it. He went to the bathroom and left me alone and there was the ring. It belonged to his mother."

"Oh," I said, wrapping the ring back in the tissue paper and handing it over to Morgan. I didn't want to be the guy who lost it, dropping it onto the floor and kicking it under the bed, never to be found again.

She took the ring, cradling it in her hands and staring at it like it might explode.

"I assume his mother is deceased," I said.

"Within the last year." Morgan slid the ring back into her bag. Then she shuddered. "It was kind of weird, to be honest. He had an urn with his mother's ashes in the entryway. It was like a shrine, with a picture of her and a few odds and ends. A deck of cards because she liked bridge. The leash for her dog. It was all there, right on display on a shelf with a light shining on it." She scrunched her face. "A bright light. It was freaky weird. And the ring was there too. That was the only jewelry I saw."

"So, why did he have it just sitting out?"

She shook her head, as though trying to wipe the memory away. "He was close to her. I'd heard him make a couple of speeches around town. You know, to the Rotary Club or whatever. And he always talked about what a big influence his mom was on his career. I guess he wanted to honor her and remember her. I wish I'd kept my hands to myself, but I wanted to do something that would hurt him, something that would feel like a reward for my work."

"Were you planning to pawn it?" I asked. "That might be hard to do."

"I don't know. Once you have something like that, once it's done, you realize . . . well, you realize how stupid it is. What am I going to do with the damn ring? And then . . ."

I waited, but nothing else came. A horn honked once and then twice outside the window. I wondered if Sean had come after me, surrounding the building with a team of security guards in oversize suits, all chewing gum.

"And then?" I said, prompting her.

"And then there's my boss. There's . . ."

"What about him?"

"They're going to know I took it. They're going to know everything. And . . . look . . . I just know none of this is ever going to stop."

28

I paced back and forth in the room a few times while Morgan tracked me with her eyes. I felt confined, restless, like an animal in a cage. Yes, I'd come this far because I'd felt a connection with Morgan in the airport. And also because her behavior made her seem like a person who needed help.

But I couldn't deny what my dad had so eloquently explained to me on the phone.

I understand the temptations. The hotels and the bars and the late nights.

I'd be lying if I said I wasn't hoping, wishing, that she and I would follow through on that kiss once I reached her hotel room. Having watched Morgan sit on the bed, drinking her beer, her long legs folded under her body . . . Having felt our fingers brush when I handed her a beer . . .

Yes, I hoped for more than just pleasant conversation. I felt it in every cell in my body.

But I also wanted to help her, even if I didn't know how.

I tried, though.

"Okay," I said as I stopped my pacing and tried to sound practical. Strangely, I reminded myself of my dad in that kind of situation. He had always been able to remain calm in a crisis. "You made a mistake. You screwed up. You acted impulsively and took a valuable ring."

"Very valuable," she said.

"How valuable?" I asked.

"I don't know. Twenty thousand? Maybe more."

"Okay. Really? That much?"

"Have you ever priced rings like this?" Morgan asked.

"Someone I know wanted one."

"Really?" Her voice perked up. Curiosity? Jealousy?

"I didn't buy it, though, and I have no idea how much they cost."

"They're worth a lot. Hell, this is larceny I've committed."

"Grand larceny, probably."

She gasped. "Really?"

"Could be," I said, remembering my business law class. I went over to the bed where she sat and eased myself down next to her, the mattress sinking with my weight. Our thighs touched. Morgan didn't flinch or lean away from me. "Look, why don't you just go home? Take the thing back to your boss. Put it on his doorstep and ring the bell. Apologize and—"

"I won't apologize," she said, suddenly scooting back, moving her body away from mine. "I won't."

"Okay, don't apologize. But then . . . do you think he's going to press charges against you?"

"He clearly loved his mother," she said. "Hence the creepy shrine and the tributes to her in the speeches."

No surprise there. Most people loved their mothers. I loved mine, even though I hadn't seen her in years. I understood that when it came to parents, feelings were intense. So intense people might be capable of doing anything. I felt an intense bond with my dad thanks to the many years it had been just the two of us.

"Okay," I said. "I believe you."

Morgan turned to look at me straight on. "I mean, he *really* loved her. Really. When she died, he was a wreck. A total wreck. For weeks." She made a frustrated noise deep in her throat. "The guy falls apart when his elderly mother dies, and then treats the women who work for him like shit. Go figure." She blinked rapidly, but no tears popped out of her eyes. "He's going to take this very personally. Very. Like, Norman Bates personal."

"This is why you ran? Because you took a ring worth a lot of money, and you think this guy is really going to bring the hammer down on you with the police?"

She nodded, finished her beer, and stared at the empty bottle in her hand. "Maybe later, one of us—and by one of us I mean you— might have to go out and get us something else to drink."

"Will you be hungry?" I asked.

"Hungry? In a way." She put the bottle down on the floor, then reached over and placed her hand on my knee, just rested it there. Her touch hit me like a shock, one that traveled through my body with a crackling jolt. "It's good to finally tell someone about this. Finally. You know, it's not the police so much. And it's not me I'm worried about. It's my mom."

"Right. Cancer?"

"Yes. And I'm the only one who can take care of her. If anything happens to me . . . if I get in trouble . . ."

"Who's with her now?" I asked.

"She's being cared for. My mom and I . . . We've had a complicated relationship. But we're working on it now. I don't want that to slip away. But if I go back . . ."

"You might get in trouble."

"I *will* get in trouble. Or . . ."

"Or what?" I asked.

"There's something else."

"Okay, what is it?" I asked.

"After I took the ring and left the house . . . Well, my boss has this brother. I'd met him at a couple of work functions. You know, the office holiday party and stuff like that. He was kind of weird, like my boss, but so what. Right?"

"What does he have to do with this?"

"Yesterday, while I was out of town, the brother showed up at the hospice facility where my mom is staying. He was looking for me, I assume, but I wasn't there."

"Where were you?" I asked. "Why were you flying through Atlanta?"

She sighed, but she told me. "I have an aunt who lives in Norfolk. Virginia. My mom's sister. They've been estranged, but I flew there to tell her about how bad my mom's condition has become. And because I wanted her to come and help. To visit and sit with her as things, you know, get near the end. Since I might be in this trouble . . . I wanted to make sure Mom wouldn't be alone."

"Sounds like it didn't work."

"It didn't. Aunt Linda . . . Well, she's not budging."

"So, what about your boss's brother?" I asked.

"Okay. He came to the hospice, and he really wanted the ring. He told my mom how much it meant to him and to the family. That it belonged to his mother and I needed to give it back."

"If you'd been there, you could have done it right then," I said. "Just handed it to the brother."

Morgan turned to me quickly. "That's not helpful. If I'd been there . . . who knows what he would have done? The guy scares me. And my mother."

"Okay," I said. "I'll keep my retroactive suggestions to myself."

She calmed a little. "Sure, now I wish I'd been able to give it back. But I couldn't. And then . . . the brother told my mom if I didn't give the ring back and come clean, something bad would happen to me. And to her." She lifted her hand to her head as though she'd been struck by a piercing pain. The strain, the fear, was etched on her face.

"You didn't tell the police?" I asked. Then I figured it out before she spoke. "If you'd told the police, then you'd be admitting the crime. But if you don't tell the police, you worry your mom is in jeopardy."

"I *am* worried about her," she said. "That's why I'm here. The brother scared the hell out of me. The more I thought about it, the more I worried about what he might do. To me. Or to Mom."

"Aren't you worried he might try again?" I asked. "Go back to the hospice or whatever?"

"That's why . . . I'm trying to take care of things. I'm gambling that he won't go back. And that he'll have enough decency not to harass my dying mother." Morgan groaned, then shook her head. "It's a risk, sure. But she's getting round-the-clock care. It was a struggle getting her admitted in the first place. She only has weeks left. She may not last the month. The last few days have been hard; they've taken something out of her. I came to Wyckoff because I thought I could make it right."

"Make it right here?" I asked. "How?"

"I want to end it, once and for all."

"But I don't understand. . . . What's here?"

I looked down. Her hand had inched halfway up my thigh. I swallowed hard, my mind unable to think about much else.

I reached down, placed my hand on top of hers. She smiled at me, then adjusted her grip so our fingers intertwined.

"I think if you go home and come clean," I said, "then nothing too bad will happen. They're not going to send you to prison over this ring. Talk to a lawyer. Tell them about the stress and strain of caring for your mother. Say you need to help her. Plead for mercy."

Her grip tightened on my hand. "They have money. *He* does. And power. I just don't know if any of it can go the right way for me."

"It can. It will." I started to move away, reaching into my pocket for my phone. "You could call right now. Call the police or a lawyer and explain everything to them. You could go to the cops here in Wyckoff and start the process. They could tell you what to do—"

She shook her head. "No, no." She reached out and placed her long index finger over my lips. "Let's just . . . let's just not think about that tonight." She stopped shaking her head and her eyes bored in on mine. "Tomorrow, okay? It will be okay until tomorrow."

And then she leaned toward me. We moved closer to each other.

And then we were kissing again. It was as good as it had been in the airport bar. Better.

Our lips pressed, our tongues found each other. Our hands explored.

Tomorrow.

Morgan was right.

It could all wait until tomorrow.

29

Kimberly parked in front of the imposing brick house in Laurel Falls. She checked the clock on the dash before turning the car off: 7:43. She reminded herself not to think about what she could have been doing with Maria if the day had been normal. Going home early, cooking a good meal, talking about school over dinner . . .

Maria would do all of those things, and she'd have a perfectly pleasant evening. She would just do them with Peter instead of with her. And that was fine. Absolutely fine.

Kimberly told herself that over and over. She was still trying to convince herself when the phone rang before she could get out of the car. "Hello, Brandon. Aren't you supposed to be at home?"

"I'm on my way," he said. "But I wanted to give you an update on our mystery man, Joshua Fields."

"What about him?" she asked as she silently thanked the officers of the Nashville airport for taking down the man's information. The man who kissed and then followed Morgan Reynolds onto her flight to Tennessee.

"Nothing too exciting. Clean record. Twenty-six years old. Works in commercial real estate. His dad's company. He lives in Chicago, a neighborhood called Rogers Park. I guess he's a big-city boy."

"And you haven't been able to get hold of him?" Kimberly asked.

"Not yet."

"Anything on social media?" she asked.

"Nothing. No connection to Morgan Reynolds. No indication they knew each other."

"But this guy Fields travels a lot for work?"

"All over, it looks like."

"So they could have met," Kimberly said. "Somewhere. Otherwise why is this guy running around with her when she's missing?"

"You don't believe his story? That he just met her in the airport?"

"I don't know." The wheels turned in Kimberly's mind. "It's weird. You think Giles Caldwell and Morgan Reynolds could have been involved? A boss and an employee running off together? Older man, younger woman? It happens."

"Kind of gross. But, yes, it happens."

"He's not that old," Kimberly said. "Well, keep trying. Short of that, we'll keep talking to people they know. Thanks, Brandon. Now you really should head home."

"You don't need help with these interviews?"

"Only a few more left. Tell Marcie hello. And kiss the baby for me."

"You should come over and see him again. Anytime you want."

"As soon as things quiet down, I will. I promise."

She hung up and stepped into the cool evening air. The sun had disappeared, leaving the sky dark, the stars popping into view one by one. She heard the voices of kids from a distant yard, shouts and yelps as their games wound down for the night. Free-range kids playing something wild and unstructured, a rarity these days.

The neighborhood was certainly safe, a recently built subdivision for the upper middle class. No interlopers here, no obvious dangers. The yards were all uniformly neat, the bushes trimmed, the minivans and SUVs washed and waxed. No cops lived there, no firefighters or factory workers. Kimberly thought again of her career choices, couldn't imagine the job she'd need in order to land in one of these houses. She couldn't imagine the man she would have to marry to keep her there either. Peter was a lawyer, but he worked nonprofit. That meant he did okay, but not okay enough to buy into that neighborhood.

She walked up the drive and approached the front door. The house glowed from the inside. The lights were bright, the windows clean. She smelled fresh-cut grass and the lingering odor of grilled meat, which made her stomach rumble. She looked through the big window by the front door and, seeing no one, rang the bell. It chimed through the house, loud and long, needing the extra volume and length to reach all corners of what must have been close to four thousand square feet.

It didn't take long for a figure to emerge. Kimberly had called, asked if she could come by. The door swung inward, and a young, smiling face greeted her. Mid-twenties, pretty, blond hair pulled back. Her snug jeans were perfectly tucked into tall boots, the zipper on her hoodie expertly placed midchest to reveal the low-cut T-shirt underneath.

"Hi. Detective Givens?"

Kimberly flashed her badge. "Ashley Clarke?"

"Come on in."

Kimberly followed her into a high-ceilinged entryway. The chandelier above glowed like the sun. Kimberly looked around, saw no discarded shoes, no dropped jackets. All of that would be out of sight, in the garage or in a mudroom at the back of the house. People who lived like this had whole rooms for their junk and debris.

"Thanks for making time for me," Kimberly said. "I know it's getting late."

"I just put the baby down, and my husband will be home from work soon. He got held up. Again." She rolled her eyes. "So this is great."

Ashley sounded breathless, happy. Excited about everything. And why not? She was a stunning young woman with a wealthy husband and a new baby. Kimberly would arrest the kid if she weren't happy.

They left the foyer for a sitting room that looked unused. Ashley took a spot on the couch, and Kimberly settled into a love seat that felt stiff beneath her butt. She spotted a photo of Ashley with her baby and her husband on a small end table. He looked like the handsome star of a toothpaste ad. She'd dealt with so many losers and abusers and dead enders that she'd forgotten people like that even existed. People who shined. People for whom the road of life stretched ahead without so much as a pothole in the way.

"You wanted to know something about Morgan?" Ashley confidently held Kimberly's gaze as she asked the question, but after she spoke, her top teeth—straight and white—settled on her bottom lip and remained there, digging in. Nobody ever felt truly at ease when a cop showed up at their house.

"You're friends with her. Right?"

"Yes. Well, used to be, I guess."

"Used to be?"

"She moved away," Ashley said. "And Brianna is nine months old. She doesn't allow me time for much else."

"Ah, I remember those days. I have a daughter too."

Ashley's face relaxed. She stopped gnawing her lip. "How old is your daughter?"

"Twelve. She's a little more challenging than an infant."

"I bet. I remember the way I used to talk to my mom." She made an exaggerated frown. "I guess I need to prepare for that."

"Someday," Kimberly said, projecting a smile, glad to see Ashley relax a little. "So, Morgan Reynolds. You're not as close as you once were. But you were friends at one time?"

"Oh, yeah. We met a couple of years ago. We went to the same gym. This was before I got married, before the baby. We're the same age, so we started hanging out. We weren't superclose but there was a group of us who went out for drinks after work. Or we exercised together. I guess most of us have been getting married, and even having babies now." Ashley leaned forward, tilting her head down, a strand of hair swinging loose across her face. "Is what they're saying on Facebook true? Is she really missing?"

"We're trying to figure all that out. So tell me, did anything unusual happen before she moved away?"

Ashley shook her head. She sat back, brushed the loose strand away, and placed the tip of her index finger in her mouth as she thought about it. Kimberly waited patiently. And then she realized Ashley might be closer in age to Maria than to herself.

Ouch.

"Not really. I only saw her once right before she moved."

"How long ago was that?"

Ashley's face scrunched. "A few months at least. And we didn't talk long. I ran into her at the grocery store. I hadn't seen her in a while. And when I said she could come out to the house and see Brianna, she told me she was moving. She'd quit her job and was heading down to Nashville. She said her mom was sick."

Ashley's face remained scrunched.

"What is it?" Kimberly asked.

"She went to school at Henry Clay. I went to Centre College, over in Danville. I guess I don't know when or why her mom moved to Nashville. But maybe I'm not remembering that right. Morgan's from Wyckoff, right?"

"She is. Originally. Did she talk about her job at all? Why she was quitting?"

"No. She said she just needed a change. I thought she was doing really well there. She worked a lot, which is why I didn't see her much. And she was developing apps. I figured she had it all."

"Did she ever talk about her boss? Giles Caldwell?"

"Not that I can remember." Then recognition spread across Ashley's face. Her mouth formed a small, perfect O. "He's the guy who's missing, right? And Morgan . . . you think . . . ."

"I don't know if there's any connection yet. But Morgan never mentioned him?"

"I don't remember her saying anything about him."

"Did she ever talk about her boss's brother? Simon Caldwell?"

"I don't know that name either."

"Her coworkers?" Kimberly asked. "Anyone at the company?"

"Just in passing. That was it."

"A boyfriend? A girlfriend?"

"No one serious. Just, you know, guys. A date here or there."

"So, you say she never mentioned Giles Caldwell or a boyfriend," Kimberly said. "Was she the type to keep that private? If she was dating anyone?"

"She was a little private. But she talked about dates and stuff."

"But no mention of Giles Caldwell?"

"I don't think so." Ashley made a sour-lemon face. "You don't think they're a couple, do you?"

"I'm not sure. How about a man named Joshua Fields? Did she ever mention him?"

Ashley shook her head. "I don't think so. Is he a suspect?"

"Just a name right now. Would you say you knew Morgan well?" Kimberly asked.

Ashley gave the question a good amount of thought. While she did, a grandfather clock chimed in another room. It seemed out of place in the brand-new, shining house.

"Not terribly well. No. We weren't best friends or anything."

"Was anybody close to her?" Kimberly asked.

Ashley's brow furrowed. "She had lots of other friends."

"You're the fifth friend of hers I've talked with today. A couple on the phone and a couple in person. None of them have really stayed in touch with her. Why do you think that is?"

Ashley's brow remained furrowed, her face serious. "I guess she was kind of closed off. Like I said, I didn't think we had a whole lot in common. I was settling down, and she wasn't."

Kimberly waited. Ashley still seemed to be thinking. She stared at a spot in space just to the left of Kimberly's head.

Kimberly gave her time.

"She said once she had a rough childhood. That . . . I don't know. It just wasn't very pleasant."

"Any details?"

"No. I guess she implied her mom wasn't very stable and had some issues. She never seemed to want to open up about what happened, though. And I like to give people their privacy. Tony says I just want everybody to be happy." She shrugged, as if she was powerless to change her sunny outlook.

"It happens to some people," Kimberly said.

"What does?"

"Rough childhoods."

"Oh, yeah. Right. But that's why it was weird when she told me she was moving to Nashville to be close to her mother. She never mentioned her family, never went into any details about them. But then all of a sudden she was going to move to be close to her mom. I guess . . . well, I guess something changed."

Kimberly checked her watch. She didn't want to keep Ashley

from her life. She imagined her husband, the aforementioned Tony, strolling through the door at any moment, tie loosened, jacket jauntily slung over his shoulder. Would Ashley greet him with a kiss and a beer? Were they ready to start on kid number two?

"And that's pretty much it for you and Morgan?" Kimberly said.

"Until a few days ago."

Kimberly's head jerked forty-five degrees to the right. "What's that?"

"I saw her one more time. Just a few days ago."

"You saw her here? In Laurel Falls?"

Ashley nodded rapidly, her eyes wide. "Is that okay? Was I not supposed to see her?"

"Where was she?" Kimberly asked.

"It was in a gas station of all places. I was there the other night, on my way home from my yoga class downtown. Tony normally fills the tank, but I hadn't told him we were low, so that stupid light came on and flashed at me. I didn't want to run out. Not by myself when it was getting dark. And Bri had to go to the doctor the next morning, so I figured I could pump it myself. I used to, before I married Tony."

"And which day was this?" Kimberly asked.

Ashley's face scrunched again. "Bri went to the doctor the next day, and I was coming home from yoga." She snapped her perfectly manicured fingers and pointed at Kimberly. "It was Thursday. Five days ago. Right?"

"That's five days, yes."

"You see, Brianna gets up in the middle of the night sometimes, less now than she used to. But I have to sit there while I feed her, so I read." She bit her lip again. "I've been into romance novels.

Historical ones. I get them at the library. Tony was home with Bri, so I stopped to get a new stack after yoga. I'm kind of addicted. Then I'm there at the gas station, watching the pump run, and I look up and see Morgan."

"What did she say?" Kimberly asked, keeping her voice level.

"Nothing. I walked over to say hi, and she saw me coming. I know that. We locked eyes across the pumps. It was getting dark, and the bright lights were on. It was like standing on the moon, you know? All lit up and shiny? No way she didn't see me. But as I got closer and waved, she turned away and jumped in her car. She didn't say a word to me. And then she sped out of there, fast. The tires squealed a little when she went."

Kimberly leaned forward. "You're sure it was her? I mean, maybe it was someone who just looked like her."

"I'm not crazy, Detective. I recognized my friend." She shrugged. "Former friend, maybe." She lifted her finger back to her mouth. "Although I don't know what I did to offend her."

Morgan Reynolds had been back in Laurel Falls five days ago. And earlier that very morning she'd been on a plane to Nashville from Atlanta, where she was supposed to be living with her sick mother.

And on that plane she'd ignored a guy she'd kissed in the airport. Just like she'd ignored Ashley when she saw her at the gas station.

"Did she have friends or family in Atlanta?" Kimberly asked.

"I don't know."

The baby started crying in the other room.

"Oh, shoot," Ashley said. "Why is she awake?"

"She has her own mind."

"I have to . . . Is it okay?"

"It's fine," Kimberly said. "I think I've heard everything I need to right now. And I can show myself out."

"Thank you."

"If you hear from Morgan or see her again, will you call me? Right away."

"Of course." Ashley looked at the floor, her brow scrunched again. "Detective? Do you think I should have helped her? Should I have . . . I don't know, run after her? Maybe she's in trouble. Maybe someone was trying to hurt her."

"You did fine," Kimberly said. "We don't know what's happening with Morgan just yet. She's missing from Nashville, so the police down there are in the lead on that case. I'm investigating Giles Caldwell's disappearance. But they might be related since they're connected through work. So we have to check out everything."

Ashley shivered. "It creeps me out. I mean . . . what if she's . . . and I saw her . . ."

"I don't think she's dead, Ashley," Kimberly said.

"Oh, good." The baby's cries increased in volume, so Ashley started for the other room. But she stopped, turning back as Kimberly stood up. "Do you think it's normal, what happened with Morgan?"

"You mean disappearing? No—"

"I don't mean that," Ashley said. "I mean . . . Well, my mom is my best friend now, so I couldn't imagine living away from her. But some people do. Like Morgan. And she moved back to be close to her, so they must have figured things out or patched things up. Do you think that always happens? Do people work things like that out?"

Ashley's optimism burned brighter than the chandelier. Kimberly asked herself, *Who am I to burst her bubble? Does she really need a cold splash of reality before she goes to tend to her newborn?*

Some people, and maybe Ashley was one of them, managed to spend their lives wrapped in a safe cocoon of happiness and order.

"It certainly happens, Ashley," she said. "Yes, it does."

Ashley smiled, and the baby cried louder than Kimberly thought possible. She really didn't miss those days, not at all.

"Duty calls," Ashley said, shrugging in her hoodie.

And she slipped away as Kimberly turned to the door.

30

I woke up sometime during the night.

I didn't know where I was. I'd been dreaming about flying, about being on a plane, high in the air, but the flight never landed. We kept going on and on, and the pilot made the same announcement saying we still had five more hours to go. Always the same number—*five more hours*.

I looked at the other passengers, faces I didn't know, but the news didn't seem to bother them at all. They didn't see me looking at them. It was as if I was invisible.

When I woke up, I was naked and sweating. The sheets felt cool against my damp skin. Everything came back to me. The day-long quest to find Morgan, the drive to Wyckoff. Our night in the hotel. Two rounds of sex that knocked me out, sending me so deeply asleep I felt like I'd barely moved.

My bladder was full to bursting, so I stumbled through the dark and found the bathroom. I peed, washed my hands, made some attempt—I'm not sure why—to smooth down my hair, which went in every direction. When I came back to bed, I saw Morgan facing the wall, away from me, still naked. I slid back in bed and scooted my body next to hers. But when I did, she tensed, and I moved away as though shocked.

"I'm sorry," I said, thinking she wasn't awake, that I'd startled her from a deep sleep. "What's wrong?"

She kept quiet, but I heard her sniffle. I propped myself up on my elbow and looked at her face, my vision adjusting to the dark. Her tears glistened against her skin. She reached up and wiped them away, her eyes still staring at the wall, ignoring me.

"Can I do anything?" I asked.

"Go back to sleep. I'm fine."

"You're upset. Clearly."

"I'm not. I'm fine. You need to sleep."

"You're crying."

"I'm just . . . being here, I started thinking about my childhood here in Wyckoff." She sniffed. Above our heads, a mindless red light on the smoke detector blinked on and off. My body started to feel cool, so I reached for the sheet and pulled it over both of us. "Thanks."

"You're welcome."

She started talking a little more. "My mom used to take me to an amusement park near here. All the time. It was expensive to get in, but she always found a way to scrounge up the money."

"That's what parents do. Good ones anyway."

"I don't know about the good part."

"What do you mean?" I asked.

"My mom . . . Let's just say they served beer at the amusement park. Fantasy Farm, it was called. They provided something for the adults to drink while the kids rode the rides. My mom . . . She couldn't handle drinking so well. So when we went there . . . it could get ugly."

"I'm sorry."

She took my hand and squeezed it. "I remember the petting zoo. There were goats and sheep. You could bring them little pellets of food, and they'd eat out of your hand. I loved that."

"That sounds like a great memory." The ones of my own mother were scattered and few. Picking apples when I was about five. Petting a neighbor's dog when I was three or four, my mom standing nearby, watching me carefully.

"No, it isn't." She rolled onto her back, turning to face me. "We went there one summer when I was about nine. My mom was drinking. I went to the petting zoo to feed the animals, and I'm having a great time with the other kids. All of a sudden there's a commotion. Some people gasp, some rush to one place in the petting zoo. It's my mom. Down on the ground."

"She fell?"

"She passed out. Cold. They had to call security. The police came. It's a long story, more than I want to say."

"It sounds terrifying."

"The place is closed now," she said, wincing a little. "It closed about five years ago. It's kind of satisfying to drive by and see that part of my childhood boarded up and shut down. That memory of my mom . . . I wish I could forget."

"So why are you here if the memories are so bad?" I asked.

"I have other things to do, things to resolve."

"Should you go back to Laurel Falls?" I asked. "Turn in the ring? It's what—thirty minutes east of here? That's not far."

She nodded in the dark. Her hair was loose. Released from the ponytail, it fanned across her pillow.

"I mean it when I say I think it will be okay," I said.

"I know." She reached over and brushed her hand along my cheek. "You're sweet. But I think we both need to go back to sleep."

"Are you sure?" I asked. "You don't want to talk more?"

"No. I'm fine."

"I'll go with you to the police if you want. We can take my rental car."

"Really, let's just sleep on it."

I decided not to push. And she was right. We were both tired. From everything. I turned away, scooting back to my side of the bed. The glow from the streetlights and the garish hotel sign leaked through the curtains. The night was quiet, not a sound except the soft hum of the air-conditioning.

When I woke again, there was bright sunlight coming through the window. The real thing. I squinted. I felt like I hadn't eaten in months, and my head hurt. I needed food. And water.

The clock read 9:02. The combination of travel, Xanax, alcohol, and sex had made me sleep later than I ever did anymore. I felt like a man of leisure. It occurred to me I had no idea what I was going to do. Was I going to go back to work? Return the rental car and hop on the next plane to Tampa? Catch up with everything I'd let go?

Or would I go with Morgan? Help her return the ring and make all of that right? I liked the sound of that much more than I liked the sound of getting on a plane or going back to work. Just then my dream of endless flight came back to me, and it made me shiver.

I rolled over. Her side of the bed was empty. I looked around the room, listening.

I heard water running in the bathroom. The shower. For a moment, I thought about joining her but then decided to give her space.

I picked up my phone. There were a number of missed calls, all from numbers I didn't recognize. I had no idea why.

And a missed call from Renee. And a voice mail from her as well.

"Shit."

It irritated me. I'd told her what was going on. I'd told her almost everything. But I knew she'd worry, and that's why she was checking in.

I sent her a text without listening to the voice mail.

> Just got your message. I'm fine. In hotel. Will call later
> when I can. Everything fine.

I felt like a Grade A jerk writing those words. I wasn't really lying, but I wasn't exactly telling the truth either.

Renee's calls and texts served one purpose. They told me I had to make a decision, that I couldn't stay in limbo without making some kind of choice. Unlike my dream, I couldn't stay in the air forever, living in a bubble and not touching the ground. People were waiting for me. They expected things from me. It was possible the calls on my phone were work related, things I had to deal with. And soon.

I was still naked. I pulled on my boxers and T-shirt and walked over to the bathroom door. It stood ajar an inch or two, so I leaned my head down close without going in.

"Hey. Are you almost done in there?"

No response.

"I just want to know what you're thinking. I can go with you if you want."

Still nothing. The water ran and ran.

I took a step back.

"Morgan?"

I looked around the room. I hadn't seen it before because I hadn't been looking. But her bags were gone. Her clothes. Her shoes.

Everything. All of it.

I pushed open the bathroom door. The steamy mirror, the foggy space. I pushed the shower curtain aside.

Empty.

I went back out to the room and looked around. The night-stand, the dresser. Her pillow. I searched for a note. For anything.

But I knew it was a lost cause.

She was gone.

PART TWO

31

Morgan had left her room key sitting on the nightstand. I grabbed it, threw on clothes, and bolted out the door. I went down the stairs at the end of the hallway as quickly as I could, my momentum carrying the upper half of my body forward so I felt like I was about to fall over, my footsteps echoing off the concrete walls.

In the lobby, I saw no sign of Morgan. I approached the desk and asked if anyone had seen her.

The clerk was a college-aged woman with thick dark hair piled on top of her head. Her glasses rested on the tip of her nose, and she pushed them into place with the knuckle of her index finger. She stifled a yawn before answering me.

"What room was she in?" the clerk asked, her words slow and deliberate.

"Three oh six."

She typed something into the computer, then studied the screen. "She's due to leave today. Checkout time is noon."

"Did you see her come through the lobby this morning?" I asked. "With bags? Or anything?"

"I just came on a few minutes ago, sir. I work early on Wednesdays. And the closest exit for that room is on the west end of the building. Is something wrong?"

"No," I said, before abruptly dashing out the sliding doors and stopping under the front portico. It was a bright morning, the sky clear and blue, hurting my eyes. The sun picked up the dew on the grass that lined the parking lot, making it sparkle like diamonds. I immediately thought of the ring.

I went down to the west end of the building, expecting to see . . . what?

Morgan waiting for me?

She was gone. Intentionally so. And not waking me was intentional too.

I searched the parking lot. A number of cars remained. Sedans and minivans. Rentals for businesspeople like me. Vehicles that belonged to travelers. Plates from Kentucky and Tennessee but also Nevada, Ohio, California. I had no idea what Morgan drove.

Birds were chirping as I trudged back to the front of the hotel, mocking me with their cheery songs. What had I expected? If she'd wanted me to help her, she would have waited. Twice she'd ditched me. I thought about asking the desk clerk if I had a "Kick Me" sign on my back.

The doors slid open, and I went back in. The lobby smelled of brewing coffee, the sweet odor of cooking waffles. A few people sat eating, sipping from paper cups, their small plates full of pastries and fruit. They all looked up when I came in. A disheveled man walking through the door must be what passed for excitement at the Best Western so early in the day.

"Is everything okay, sir?" the clerk asked, pushing her glasses up again.

"It's fine. Thanks."

"Our complimentary breakfast goes until nine thirty," she said. "Yum."

I started across the lobby, heading back for the slow walk up the stairs. I needed to shower, and then I'd go down and eat their free food. What the hell? I could live it up on Morgan's dime. And then after that . . .

Who knew what I'd do next?

I went down the hall and entered the stairwell again. My steps felt heavy, my legs like they were full of lead. I was halfway to my floor when the door below me opened, its hinges creaking. I paused. I looked down but saw no one before continuing on my way, and when I reached my floor I pushed through the door and into my hallway. I took out the key card, and as I waved it in front of the lock and turned the handle, the door from the stairwell opened.

I froze, hope rising inside me.

Had Morgan returned? Had she seen me outside?

Had she always planned to come back?

Instead, I saw a man. Middle-aged and taller than me. He looked familiar. It came back to me like a dying lightbulb flickering to life. The guy from the lobby the night before, the one who seemed to be having some kind of dispute with the clerk.

Why was he there? The night before he'd gone in the opposite direction from Morgan's room, as though he was staying in the east end of the building. Had he moved? Did he like to wander the halls?

Or . . . ?

"Excuse me," he said, waving at me.

I stopped. Was he undercover hotel security? Was he Sean's mentor, wondering why I was using Morgan's room key? His hands were empty. No flashlight.

I waited as he approached me.

"Can I talk to you for a moment?" he asked.

Years of hotel stays had made me cautious. I'd heard all the cautionary tales about people being robbed, but if this guy was going to commit a crime, why would he do it in the middle of a bright morning? Farther down the hall, a cleaning crew pulled sheets and towels out of rooms and stuffed them into a laundry cart. We were hardly alone. I felt certain if I screamed, one of the maids would come and whack the man with a broom.

He wore a light jacket, a ball cap, rimless glasses, and a toothless smile. He looked to be in his mid-forties, trim and fit. His knuckles were large, his hands giant. He wore Timberland boots like he intended to hit the trail at any moment.

"Can I help you?" I asked.

"Yes, I think you can," he said.

I pulled the door almost shut, the key card still in my hand, and waited.

He nodded to the room. "Maybe we want to talk in there," he said. "It's more private."

"What do we need to talk about that's private?" I asked. "I don't even know you."

But I should have guessed.

He said simply, "Her."

32

The man followed me into the room. I stood as he looked around, almost like he expected to find someone else inside, waiting, and when he saw nothing, he sighed, his disappointment heavy in the small space.

"Do you want to sit?" he asked, as though it was his room and I was the interloper.

"No."

He shrugged, his face giving me a "suit yourself" look. "Mind if I do?"

Without waiting for my answer, he settled onto the bed closest to the bathroom, the one Morgan and I had slept in. The covers were still mussed, but that didn't seem to bother him. He sat with his knees spread, his giant hands resting on his thighs.

"Do you know where she went?" he asked, not exactly one for formalities.

I almost laughed at his audacity. "Hold it. I don't even know who you are."

He stood up and came closer, held out his huge hand. "Simon Caldwell."

He left me little choice. I reached out and we shook, his grip strong. "Joshua Fields."

"Nice to meet you, Joshua. And I'm sorry to barge in on you like this." He returned to the bed and sat, the springs squeaking under his weight. "Well, not really sorry. I think you can help me. And maybe I can help you. I sure hope so."

His voice was deep and commanding. He looked like a guy used to getting his way, the kind of kid in high school who would have perched at the back of the bus and lobbed gross things at the freshmen in front. He also looked certain of his right to be in my, or Morgan's, hotel room.

And he'd said the magic word: "Her."

"Well, now that that's out of the way," he said. "So. Morgan. Where is she? Did she leave town? Or what?"

"Hold on."

The man, Simon, wore an expectant look on his face, like he'd paid admission and I was there to provide him with whatever information he wanted. His smug entitlement irritated me, and I regretted letting him in the door, although I wasn't sure I would have been able to keep him out.

"What do you want with her?" I asked. "And how do you know her?"

Simon tilted his head. He looked surprised that *I* would ask questions. He must have assumed our conversation would be one-way. He'd ask, and I'd answer.

"You don't know what you're dealing with, do you?" Simon scratched the side of his face, then rubbed his chin. "I'm sure she told you quite a tale. How did you meet her anyway? Are you her boyfriend? It looks like . . ." His eyes traveled over the bed, the mussed covers. The second bed obviously hadn't been slept in. "Well, it looks like you two know each other pretty well." His face turned sour. "Oh, jeez, don't tell me you love her. Is that it?"

"Okay, I've had enough of this." I took out my phone. "I can call the front desk. Or the police. I want you out of here."

Simon waved his hand at me, signaling me to put the phone away. "Not that," he said, shaking his head. "Don't bother them. Not yet anyway. There will be a time for that."

I had to give him credit. He had a way of knowing how to re-direct me, to keep me curious.

"You've got to tell me something. You've got to tell me why you're looking for her. What do you want?"

"Okay. Okay." He spread his hands wide, a calming gesture that failed to put me at ease. "You want to know the truth, here we go. I'm sure she told you all about her job, right? About the app and the way she didn't get her bonus or whatever she thought she was entitled to."

Then the clouds started to part. I understood. She felt cheated by the company she worked for. She told me she'd confronted the owner of the company. And now this guy wanted to talk to her. For what purpose?

To reach an agreement?

To bring her back?

To apologize? To tell her to stay the hell away?

"You're her boss," I said. "You run the company."

"Nope."

So I waited, but he didn't add anything.

"So who are you?" I asked. "A lawyer? Someone here to pay her off?"

"My brother owned the company. He's the reason I'm here."

"Owned? He sold it?"

Simon paused, his eyes moving away while he took a deep breath. And then he looked at me again.

"Owned, as in my brother is missing. And I think Morgan knows where he is."

33

Kimberly entered the station on Wednesday morning carrying her bag, which was stuffed full of the reports and crime scene photographs she'd been studying the night before. She'd promised herself she wouldn't look at them once she went home, that she'd just bring them with her for safekeeping or in case some amazing brainstorm hit her in the middle of the night.

But she knew she'd lied to herself.

She'd opened the bag as soon as she walked in the door of the town house, taking advantage of the late-night quiet and using the papers to distract herself from the fact that Maria wasn't there.

She'd woken up on the couch with the papers spread around her, a string of drool on her chin. She'd showered quickly, missing the sounds of Maria's laborious morning routine, and left for work as quickly as she could, hair still wet, coffee steaming in her travel mug. The October morning was beautiful, the sun luminous, and she felt a little like a prisoner newly released, amazed by all the beauty in the world she'd been missing with her head buried in Giles Caldwell's disappearance.

A tired-looking Brandon stood by his desk. She guessed he'd been kept awake by an unhappy baby, and that brought Kimberly's mind back to Ashley Clarke. Kimberly wasn't sure where to fit the information Ashley had provided into the grand scheme of things. Two missing people—boss and former employee. And they'd both disappeared over the same weekend. Except one of them—*the employee*—had been seen back in Laurel Falls around the time of her boss's disappearance. And that had happened when she was supposed to be living an hour away in Nashville.

Maybe she was just passing through, stopping to get gas like anyone else.

So then why not talk to her friend? Why run off like John Dillinger?

"Rough night?" Kimberly asked.

Brandon looked her over, taking in the wet hair, the no-doubt dark bags under her eyes. "Speak for yourself."

"Touché."

Kimberly filled him in on what Ashley Clarke saw at the gas station.

"And Morgan just drove off?" Brandon asked. "Without saying anything?"

"Not a word. None of her other friends in town had a story like that to tell. They all said she moved away and hadn't been in close touch. It sounds like she was a bit of a loner. She just told them her mom was sick when she left, and that was that. They'd get the occasional text, check in with each other on social media. Some of them talked about getting together but never really did."

"So why was Morgan here?" Brandon asked, presumably knowing I had no answer to the question. "And this was Thursday night she was at the gas station?"

"Yup."

"And the last time Giles was seen at work was . . ."

"Thursday afternoon."

Brandon whistled. "Did this Ashley know of any, um, deeper connection between Morgan and Giles?"

"Nope. But I like the tactful way you expressed that."

Kimberly started to sit at her desk.

"Don't get settled in," Brandon said.

"Why? I'm desperate to settle in. I'm desperate to finish this coffee. And then have some more."

"Coffee you can have. But no settling. Steven Hatfield called. He's back in town and says you can go see him anytime. In fact, he's eager to talk. He even said he'd come here if we wanted."

"No, that's okay," she said, dropping her things on the desk. "I'm happy to go to the office again. You never know what else might come up there."

"Want me to tag along?" he asked.

"No, I'm good. What's happening around town?"

"We've got volunteers searching," Brandon said. "The State Bureau of Investigation is canvassing again. The Public Information Office is hammering the airwaves and the Internet with announcements about Giles, hoping someone saw something."

"Good."

"Have you heard anything more from the mayor?" Brandon asked.

"Not much. She only called me twice last night. The second time at ten fifteen. I feel like a chew toy, and she's the energetic puppy. We're coming up on forty-eight hours since Giles was reported missing." Kimberly made a quick inventory of what she needed. Coffee. For sure. To go. She nodded at Brandon. "Thanks, friend." She started to go but then stopped. "Hey. Is the baby okay?"

"Yes," he said, but he groaned. "They do start to sleep consistently at some point, right?"

"Eventually," she said, walking away. And she didn't feel quite so sad about missing a night with Maria. Instead she felt a spreading glow in her chest, the recollection of how fast the kid was growing up and how much fun most of it had been. And how many more memories were still to come. *I'm raising a woman,* she thought. *And a pretty decent one at that.*

And she was potty trained. And liked to sleep. Big pluses.

Kimberly went outside, enjoying the chance to have the sun on her face again. The city sedan she drove was comfortably warm, so much so she cracked the window, letting a rush of air inside, and drove the ten blocks to the TechGreen offices with the wind drying her hair. The company occupied the top floor of a new complex south of downtown, a modern structure with restaurants and coffee shops on the ground floor and a view of the city from the top. Tech-Green had started gaining national attention, occasionally getting written up as a tech company to watch. Who knew something like that could happen in Laurel Falls, Kentucky? Kimberly remembered a Steak 'n Shake opening in town when she was a teenager, and the line of people who'd shown up on the first night. How far the town had come . . .

Kimberly also knew a successful tech company couldn't maintain a sterling national reputation if the town seemed unsafe, if the cofounder of that company disappeared under mysterious circumstances. She could imagine Laurel Falls being featured on a future episode of *48 Hours. The little Kentucky town with the big secret . . .* The thought made her shiver.

She stepped off the elevator into an open-concept office. No walls separated the coworkers. No cubicles. She saw large computer monitors and lots of young people in horn-rimmed glasses wearing T-shirts and tight jeans perfectly rolled up above lace-up boots. She heard witty banter and music by bands she could never identify.

She introduced herself to the young man at the reception desk, and when she said her name, his eyebrows rose. She was apparently expected.

"I can take you right back to Steven," he said.

As they walked, he offered her a coffee. She held up her stainless steel travel mug in reply. "I'm covered."

"Oh, wow, look at that," the kid said, as though he'd never seen such a thing before.

Steven Hatfield stood up when Kimberly walked through his open door. She recognized him from the local news and the occasional coverage of TechGreen. His curly salt-and-pepper hair and loose sweater gave him the air of a college professor, someone you'd expect to be lecturing on the civil rights movement or American involvement in Vietnam. She pegged him at about the same age as Giles Caldwell, around fifty. He held out his hand, which felt smooth as Kimberly shook it, and his soft blue eyes caught the artificial light from above.

"Thanks for checking in, Mr. Hatfield," she said. "I'm glad we're going to get a chance to talk."

"I got back to town late last night," he said. "I thought I was needed here. Everyone is shaken."

"Do you mind?" Kimberly closed the office door without waiting for his answer, shutting out the noise. Despite what Steven said, no one in the large space seemed particularly perturbed over the unknown whereabouts of Giles Caldwell. She'd been in the office yesterday, conducting interviews before anyone really knew what was happening. The mood seemed the same. Life went on. Duty called.

Hatfield resumed his seat.

"Barbados? Isn't that where you were?" Kimberly asked.

"Right. With my family. A little getaway while my kids were on fall break. Then I got called about this. Is Giles really missing? Missing, as in no one knows where he is?"

"It looks that way," Kimberly said. "He didn't come into the office on Friday. But my understanding is that's not unusual for him, is it?"

"He doesn't come in every day, no."

"And he doesn't always tell people he's not going to show up. That's the sense I've gathered from your employees."

Hatfield nodded. "That's true. On a day-to-day basis, Giles doesn't need to be here. So he goes his own way sometimes. If he misses a couple of days, it isn't a big deal. Did something happen to alert you to his absence? How did the police get involved?"

"His brother contacted us on Monday. He hadn't been able to reach Giles over the weekend, and then he wasn't at work again. The brother called us, so we went to the house. No sign of a break-in. No blood or anything like that, but some things were out of place. The neighbors didn't see or hear anything, although it's a quiet neighborhood. No alarms went off, no nine-one-one calls."

"Oh, crap. Oh . . . just . . . I don't know what to say. I don't. Had he been robbed?"

"We're not sure that's a factor. Not much was missing."

"So you really think . . . I mean, this looks suspicious to you. Is that what you're telling me? It's not just . . . I don't know. A misunderstanding?"

"Do you think Mr. Caldwell would up and leave this way? And not tell anyone?"

Hatfield shook his head, his curls bouncing a little. "No. I haven't heard from him since I left. But he and I have an understanding. If one of us goes on vacation, the other handles everything. No need to bother someone unless it's an emergency."

"So you don't know where he is. And you haven't heard from him. Do you have any reason to think someone would harm him?"

Hatfield looked perplexed. He lifted his hands above the desk, then dropped them. He looked around the room, as if he could find an answer there. The creases in his brow grew deeper and deeper. Kimberly followed his eyes, checking out the space. Abstract art prints hung on the wall. A wire sculpture sat on a bookcase. No awards or plaques. They didn't fit the vibe of TechGreen. If something good happened, they'd just tweet about it. "I've got nothing."

"Disgruntled employees?"

"We always have those. But no one who would hurt him. I don't think."

"Competitors? Your company is doing pretty well."

"We have a lot of competitors. Not many in town. None who would . . . Are you thinking someone . . . I mean, could it be that someone . . ."

Steven Hatfield couldn't bring himself to say the awful words. His features trembled at the thought. *Murder. Death. Killing.*

"We're trying not to speculate. Do you think something else might be going on?"

"No, I don't." His hands rose and fell again. Kimberly wanted to give him a pen or a fidget spinner, something for the man to grab hold of. "Sometimes he talked about retiring. He mentioned selling and moving on. He wants to travel, do other things. He likes boats. He likes the water. But . . . just disappearing would be odd, even for Giles."

"Even for him?"

"He's an . . . unusual guy. With a sharp mind and his own way of doing things." Hatfield settled on clasping his hands together on the top of the table. Kimberly noticed he wore a Bulova watch and a titanium wedding band. "Anyone will tell you that I'm better with people, and Giles is better . . . behind the scenes. He can be short. He doesn't understand social cues. The give-and-take that the rest of us engage in. It's not natural to him."

Kimberly sipped her coffee and waited.

Hatfield went on. "If an employee made a mistake here, he'd tell them. Directly. Harshly. If someone got a haircut that didn't look good, he'd mention it. He just didn't take the time for the social niceties the rest of us agree to use."

"That's an easy way to piss people off, right?"

Hatfield remained silent, his lips pressed tight.

"Mr. Hatfield?"

"Okay, yes, he pissed people off, Giles did. He . . . I'm reluctant to talk about these things because they make Giles look so bad. But he hasn't committed a crime here, has he?"

"What things are you reluctant to talk about?" Kimberly asked.

Hatfield rubbed his hands together. "A couple of female employees have complained about Giles."

"Oh?"

"Not in that way. Not . . . sexual. They complained that Giles, when he got angry or frustrated with them, he could be aggressive."

"Aggressive how? Yelling?"

"That, yes. But more than that. Almost . . . almost physically abusive. Now, none of them ever said he hit them. But they feared for their safety to some extent. He seemed like he was almost out of control."

"What did the company do about it?"

"I talked to Giles," Hatfield said. "We tried to dial back his interactions with people, make him more hands-off. We didn't want to make a big deal and alarm the employees. Most don't know about it."

"That's all you did?"

Hatfield looked offended. "I said he never harmed anyone. He just didn't know how to act. His behavior hurt feelings more than anything else. Bruised them."

"Bruised them? How about Morgan Reynolds? Did she get bruised?"

"Oh, no." Hatfield leaned forward, letting his forehead rest in the palm of one of his hands. "I saw that on Facebook. And the news. I saw all of that, her being missing or whatever. Are you telling me . . . I mean, why are you bringing her up? Do you think there's a connection?"

"What was her departure from the company like?" Kimberly asked.

Hatfield looked pained. "I knew that would come up."

"What would?"

"Morgan. And her bonus."

"What bonus?" Kimberly asked.

"She thinks she wasn't paid what she should have been for her work on an app. It's not true."

"We've been talking to your other employees, but why don't you tell me all about it?"

Some of his professorial demeanor slipped. The businessman underneath that façade stepped forward. "She got paid the way she was supposed to be paid. Nothing more, nothing less."

"But no bonus? Did other employees receive bonuses when they did that kind of work?"

"Sometimes."

"Other employees who were men?" Kimberly asked.

"Okay, look, I don't like that. You're implying something there."

"I don't think I'm implying at all. You said Giles acted aggressively toward women. Did that extend to bonuses? Did men receive bonuses that Morgan Reynolds didn't?"

"Did someone say that?"

"Can you just answer me?"

"We're expanding now. . . . It's hard. It's about cash flow. We're a very fair company. We treat our . . . we treat everyone . . . The company's diverse. You can see that, can't you? You were here yesterday and talked to people? Look around."

Kimberly had. And she knew he was right—they did have a diverse workforce. She saw that when she looked around the room. Not much diversity in age, she guessed. Lots of twentysomethings, but that seemed inevitable in the tech world. Kimberly also knew being diverse wasn't the same as being fair.

"Back to Morgan," Kimberly said.

"Morgan. Right. She'll get it, the bonus—would have gotten it. Probably."

"But?"

"She quit. She had a family emergency, something back home. She left us. Months ago. As far as we knew, she wasn't even in the business anymore. And that was the end of our connection to her. I haven't seen or heard anything from her."

"Did she make any threats?" Kimberly asked.

"Morgan? No. Not to me."

"To others?"

"Not that I know of," he said. He scratched his curly head. "Damn."

"Morgan Reynolds called Giles three times in the last few weeks. And they exchanged some e-mails. She wanted to meet with him."

Kimberly withheld the information about Morgan being seen in town right before Giles disappeared. No need to color what the man thought too much.

"He didn't tell me."

"Now, why wouldn't he tell you?" Kimberly asked. "If you're the people person, wouldn't he want you to deal with an unhappy employee?"

"*Former* employee. And I don't know why he didn't tell me. Like I said, Giles has his own mind. Maybe he saw it as a business decision more than a people issue. . . ."

"Did he do that often?" she asked.

Hatfield looked confused, uncertain. "Not that I know of. It would be strange. Do you really think those two things might be related? The two of them disappearing?"

"What do you think? Were Giles and Morgan . . . involved in any way?"

Hatfield looked like he'd swallowed a bad oyster. "Oh, no. I can't imagine anything like that. It would be inappropriate."

"Not if she wasn't an employee anymore. Did you know everything about Giles's personal life? Or Morgan's?"

"Giles?" He shook his head. "He was divorced. For years. I never knew him to have a date. We didn't talk about such things. Morgan? Who knows? We have a lot of employees. So you think they're connected in some way? Even if it wasn't romantic?"

"Giles's brother thinks the two things are connected."

"Oh. Him." Hatfield slumped in his seat. His shoulders slackened, and his butt slid forward. "Simon. Oh, Simon."

"You know him?"

"Of course. Very well. And for many years."

"Is there something we should know about him?" Kimberly asked.

"There's so much to know about him. Where do you want me to start?"

34

When I was a kid, living with my dad, a bat got into the house through the attic. It flew around in spastic panic, bouncing off ceilings and walls while my dad pursued it with a pillowcase, trying to corral it.

My eight-year-old self watched my highly competent father with a mixture of fear and awe as he calmly approached the job of removing the invasive, careening animal from the house. I always felt safe and protected with him around.

In the hotel room with Simon, I felt like I'd been invaded again. By something I couldn't predict or fully understand.

"I think you better go," I said. "I have a plane to catch and—"

Simon wore a smug, self-satisfied look. Like a smart kid who knew all the answers even better than the teacher. "You don't want to hear this, do you?" he asked. "You're taken in by her. Hey, I get it. She's a pretty girl. If I were younger, a guy like you, I'd go for it."

"I'm calling the police if you don't go."

Simon wasn't put off. "You're not going to make that call." He pointed at me, punctuating his words. "You're not going to call, because you've been asking yourself all of these questions. What exactly is she up to, running around the country from flight to flight, town to town? Why would someone do that?"

"I know why."

"I do too." He pointed at me again, and waved his hand in the general direction of my phone. "You know she's missing?"

"I do."

My eyes trailed past him in the direction of the door. If I made a quick move, as sudden and darting as the bat from my childhood, I would stand a pretty good chance of getting out. Given his size and age, I had to be faster and more agile. But if he did grab hold of me, if it came to a struggle . . . Well, I just didn't know. Given his superior size. Given that I hadn't been in a fight since ninth grade. And I'd lost that one.

Besides . . . did I really want to turn tail and run?

I gave Simon credit for being right about something. He knew how much I wanted to know anything about Morgan. Anything and everything. And the list of unanswered questions kept growing.

"You know what?" he said. "Google my brother. Go ahead."

I didn't move. I hated being ordered around.

"What did she tell you about him?" Simon asked. "My brother, Giles? Did she say he refused to pay her bonus? That she got cheated out of money from that app she helped develop?"

"If you know, why are you asking me?"

"Go ahead and Google him. Giles Caldwell."

Again, I didn't move—except my hand twitched. I clutched the phone tight, and I wanted to raise it in front of my face and search. But a part of me feared what I might learn. Simon spoke with the confidence of a man holding all the aces from the deck, and his certainty held me back.

"Look, Joshua, my brother was a bastard." He pursed his lips and turned his head toward the window. He looked like a man contemplating a tough problem. "*Is* a bastard. I hope he still is a bastard." He gave his attention back to me. "How do you think he made all that money? How do you think he built that company? Not by being nice. And not by giving his money away when he didn't have to."

But something about his words stood out to me.

"Hold on," I said. "You said your brother is missing. Maybe Morgan had nothing to do with it. Maybe he's alive and well somewhere. Maybe he's on a fishing trip."

"Sure, I'm trying to be optimistic."

My thoughts raced. What had Morgan not told me? Was she involved with Giles Caldwell in some romantic way? Or were they united by something sinister?

Simon was grinning. It looked like the corners of his mouth were being forced to move with piano wire. "Google Giles. Please. It's important, Joshua. For both of us. After all, how do I know *you're* not involved in this? How do I know *you* didn't conspire with Morgan to harm my brother? And how do you know the police won't ask the same thing?"

He grinned again. It looked no more natural or comforting than it had before, like a grizzly bear trying to blend in to a kid's birthday party.

I brought my phone up where I could see it. I froze for a moment. I remembered the missed calls and messages from earlier. I needed to check them. Maybe it was work. Or maybe Morgan had called. But I couldn't check in front of Simon.

So I tapped in the name "Giles Caldwell" and waited for the results.

I watched Simon while Google did its thing. He met my eye, refusing to look away, the sick smile still in place.

When I looked down, I saw the results. All of them.

I clicked on the most recent news, a story from the *Laurel Falls Times*.

Simon was right.

Giles Caldwell hadn't been seen since Thursday evening.

35

"What about him?" Kimberly asked. "Simon."

Hatfield rubbed his forehead again. The gesture looked painful. If he rubbed any harder, his skin might start to come off.

"Do you know him?" Hatfield asked.

"He's come to the station," Kimberly said. "And he's called on the phone. Repeatedly."

"He came here yesterday when I was still away," Hatfield said. "Apparently he stopped a few employees in the parking lot and asked them about Giles. If I'd been here I would have asked him to tone it down."

"He's . . . intense. Understandable. He's worried about his brother. I get that it's distressing when a loved one is unaccounted for."

"Yeah. Simon in distress . . ." His words trailed off.

"What about it?" Kimberly asked. "What happens when he's in distress?"

Hatfield shook his head. He looked weary, and it seemed to be about more than just jet lag. "I met those guys in college. Simon and Giles. That's how long I've known them. We all went to Vanderbilt together. Giles is older by a year. And they're very different on the surface. You heard what I said about Giles. Well,

Simon isn't like that. He can be warm. Affable. That's the impression he can make on people. That's the guy I became friends with."

"But he's not part of the business."

"Oh, no. He wanted to be in on it when we founded the company. He was around, offering ideas. But his presence concerned me."

"Because?"

"Simon didn't seem like someone who would work well in a company like the one we envisioned. We were in college when the Gulf War started. The first one. He quit Vanderbilt and enlisted, got sent to Iraq for a year. He finished his degree later, but I had already graduated by then. He went on to law school, but he doesn't really practice anymore. He works for a financial firm now."

"You still haven't told me the problem with him. A Vanderbilt graduate who volunteered for the Gulf War? What's the issue?"

"Okay. In college, Simon had a girlfriend. Not even a very serious one. We went to a party one night, something off campus, and some guy we didn't know, some frat boy, started hitting on her. With Simon right there. It was really disrespectful. To him and to the young woman."

Kimberly assumed she knew where the story was going. She expected to hear about a fight, Simon Caldwell administering a beating to the poor sap who had the bad judgment to hit on his girlfriend at a party more than twenty-five years earlier. She'd seen the macho mating rituals. Like animals in a wildlife program on TV, men sometimes needed to butt their heads together and lock horns until someone rolled onto his back and offered up an unprotected throat.

But Hatfield surprised her with the rest of the tale. "Simon didn't do anything in the moment. He didn't even step in and steer the girl away from this guy. He acted like he didn't care. If she wanted to talk to the guy, then so be it. He was indifferent enough that she was mad at him. We all walked home together, and admittedly we were kind of drunk, but the young woman—I forget her name after all these years—laid into Simon pretty good, telling him she felt uncomfortable and he should have done something. I have to be honest, Detective, I agreed with her. I didn't get his behavior, but I didn't have the balls to say anything to Simon. But his date did."

"I'm guessing there's more to the story."

"There is." Hatfield tapped his thumb against the varnished tabletop. "About a month later, we hear through a mutual acquaintance that the guy, the one from the party who hit on Simon's girlfriend, had dropped out of school. In the middle of the semester, just dropped out of school. Someone had been harassing him. Slowly. Systematically. Flat tires on his car. A stolen bike. Things missing from his apartment."

"Did he report this to the police?"

"Of course. His home had been broken into, his property damaged. I heard from people who knew him that he became really anxious. Not sleeping. Struggling in classes. It was a huge stress for him. You can imagine."

Inwardly, Kimberly rolled her eyes. *Boys. Boys and their stupid games, their stupid desire to hurt other people . . .*

"What happened finally?" Kimberly asked, knowing there had to be a "finally."

"About six weeks after all this harassment started, the guy's stuff showed up on his doorstep one night. The bike, the items taken from the apartment. All of it. And . . . in the box with his stuff was a dead rat." His shoulders rose and fell with despair. "*That* was it for the guy. He didn't want to stay at Vanderbilt anymore, didn't want to remain in the state of Tennessee anymore. He withdrew, transferred to a school somewhere across the country, and that was it."

"And you think Simon did all of this?" Kimberly asked.

"I know he did."

"He admitted it?" Kimberly asked. "Or are you saying he was arrested?"

"Neither. But I mentioned the story to him one day. I told him about the guy leaving, told him about all of it—the harassment, the missing things, the dead rat. I wasn't going to accuse him. No way. But I wanted to see how he reacted."

"And?"

"Simon looked smug. He just . . . smiled. And he had a very self-satisfied air about him. And then he said something interesting. He said it sounded like justice."

Hatfield said nothing else. He let his story hang in the air of the cleanly appointed office like the dead rat the kid had found on his doorstep.

But Kimberly pressed for more. "Okay. So maybe Simon just wanted you to think he'd done it. Maybe he just wanted to show off, act like he was the big man. Some people like to do that."

"Maybe. But . . ."

"But what?"

"Either Simon carried out this slow, exacting, patient punishment for a relatively small grievance. Or . . ."

Kimberly saw where he was heading. "*Or* he's a guy who wants you to think he could enact that kind of slow, exacting, patient punishment for a . . . relatively minor grievance?"

"Right."

"And your point is . . . neither one sounds very appealing. Someone either commits a bizarre crime, or else they enjoy having a close friend *think* they committed a bizarre crime."

"Exactly, Detective. He and I were good friends. Why put on that show for me? None of it was healthy. Or normal. And you know what? I think Simon probably did the deed. And he *loved* getting credit in his own sly way."

"So one brother acts aggressively toward his female employees. The other acts aggressively toward . . . everyone?" Kimberly asked.

She hadn't eaten. The coffee made her jittery, and Hatfield's words settled like a stone in her gut. Everything he said about Simon Caldwell made sense. It fit with her impressions of the man.

"Does Simon know who Morgan is?" Kimberly asked.

"I have no idea."

"But it's possible that Giles told Simon about the issues with Morgan, right?"

"It's possible. And if that's true, then I think you should find Morgan, wherever she is."

"Because she might know where Giles is?" Kimberly asked.

"Because she might need your help if Simon is looking for her."

36

I scrolled through the information on my phone as fast as I could. The words went by in a blur. Giles Caldwell, owner and founder of TechGreen, had not been seen or heard from in five days. And police had declared him a missing person on Monday, two days earlier.

I continued to read the phone as I moved to the empty bed, letting the mattress take my weight. If it hadn't been there, I felt like I would have fallen through the floor and kept going, my arms flailing.

"You see what the issue is?" Simon asked.

I did. Clearly.

Morgan admitted to me she'd been to Giles Caldwell's house to talk about the bonus. And she'd admitted to stealing the ring from him. But the information online added a disturbing element—the man had disappeared. Without a trace. A grown man vanishing into thin air.

"This doesn't mean Morgan did it," I said. But my voice was low. I was unconvinced.

Simon laughed. Maybe he did so out of discomfort or misplaced anxiety, but it sounded more than a little strange when we were discussing the disappearance of his brother.

"Like I said, I don't know what kind of story she told you about Giles. What matters is she held a grudge against him. When bad things occur, you have to ask the question—who benefits from this? Who stands to gain? And who stands to gain from something happening to my brother?"

"Not Morgan," I said. "No bonus if he's dead."

"But she got no money before he disappeared either. Maybe frustration set in. Maybe anger. And rage."

When I first saw the headlines, a buzzing sound started in my head. A low thrumming, like faint static through a radio. As the news sank in, as my bearings gradually returned, the noise began to diminish. Some clarity slipped back into my mind.

"A grown man . . . How could Morgan have killed or kidnapped a grown man?" I asked.

"Where there's a will, there's a way."

"The police have no evidence. They don't mention Morgan as a suspect in any of these stories. You're grasping."

"I'm not. I went by my brother's office yesterday and chatted with a few employees. I know some of them, even though I've never worked in the company. It turns out Morgan was e-mailing and calling my brother in the days leading up to his disappearance. Asking about this bonus she thought he owed her. Hell, my brother hardly talked to anybody else. He didn't have enemies. He barely had friends. But this one person, Morgan, was hounding him about money she thought he owed her. *She* wanted to meet with him. And now they're both gone. Isn't that too neat?"

"Maybe it's just a coincidence."

"Yeah, right." Simon stood up. It felt like his shoulders filled the room. He walked back and forth, swinging his arms, even stopping once to slam his fisted right hand into the palm of his left. "I tried to tell them about all of this. I tried to tell the cops Morgan should be a suspect. But they're not returning my calls. They're afraid of saying the wrong thing or violating someone's rights. Giles is gone and then *she's* gone. What else can you conclude?"

He asked the question in a reasonable tone of voice, making it seem as if no normal person could fail to agree.

If Morgan had done something to this man, Giles Caldwell, if she was responsible for his disappearance—or worse—then it explained her secretive behavior. The rushing away and not wanting to talk or be followed.

Her taking off before I woke up without the benefit of a note.

It explained everything.

I tried to move my mind in a direction so the facts didn't all point me toward an inevitable conclusion. But no opening showed itself. I could see things only one way—Morgan had done something to Giles.

And Simon had reasoned himself down the same path.

He resumed his perch on the edge of the bed. His pacing seemed to have bled some of the nervous anger out of his body, which made me no more at ease in his presence. His face relaxed, became almost friendly. He forced another smile, which still didn't look natural. But he was trying.

"Look, I'm sure you're a nice, normal guy," he said. "Good job. Clean-cut. Now you got yourself wrapped up in something you didn't understand when it started. It happens. To everybody."

I wanted to say—*No, it doesn't. Not every guy finds himself with a strange man accusing the woman he just slept with of murder in a hotel in Wyckoff, Kentucky.*

Nope. I was likely the first. Which made me a trailblazer of some kind, right?

"I don't even care about this Morgan so much," Simon said. "The police, well, someone is going to find her, and they're going to arrest her. And she'll be taken care of the way she needs to be taken care of. You know what I mean?"

I fought off a shiver. He seemed gleeful when he said the phrase "taken care of the way she needs to be taken care of."

"There are other considerations," he said. "Now that the deed is done, that Giles is . . . Well, for all intents and purposes, what are the odds he's alive? Where else would he be if he isn't hurt or in danger?"

"There's no body or evidence of foul play. Maybe—"

Simon shook his head. "We both know the odds, okay? After a couple of days . . . forget about it."

"Isn't that just the case with little kids?" I asked. "Maybe he ran off? Maybe he owed someone else money?"

"No. No way." He adjusted his glasses, moving them up and then back down on his nose. "My mother, our mother, died about a year ago. And she left something very valuable behind, something meant for me that's been in the safekeeping of my brother. It's a certain family heirloom, something I want to see passed on to *my* daughter when she gets married. It has sentimental value as well as . . ." He raised his hand and wiggled it in the air. "As well as financial value."

My heart rate accelerated, and I itched all over, but I didn't move.

"It's a ring," he said. "My mother's ring. A ring she wore for fifty years. Until the day she died. A ring they removed from her hand in the funeral home before they closed the casket. *That* ring. It was supposed to come to me to be passed down to my child. But it didn't. You see, Giles and my mother were very tight. I think he convinced her to give him the ring before she died, to keep me from having it. Like he needed the damn money. My brother had that ring in his house. And I want it back. It's a family treasure. And it's supposed to be mine. Not his. Mine."

"How do you know your brother doesn't have it in a safe-deposit box? Or somewhere else—"

"He doesn't." Simon raised an index finger as he made his point. He looked like an angry god ready to call down the lightning. "He doesn't. I know where he kept it."

"How? You don't seem to be on the best of terms with him."

"We've had to meet and talk about the estate," he said. "I was just there a few days before he disappeared. I saw the ring in its place. He hadn't moved it since he got his greedy hands on it."

"Maybe you took it," I said.

"Don't be simple. It's gone. And I want it back." He shrugged. "Plus, I also want to know the location of my brother's mortal remains, assuming he's dead. I hate to think of him in a ditch somewhere, covered with blowflies and maggots. A crow pecking at his eyes. He deserves a proper rest, next to my mother. In the cemetery in Laurel Falls. That's what I want, even if he is a bastard and a shit heel."

I had to hand it to Simon. He possessed a rare gift. He managed to seem off-kilter and perfectly reasonable at the same time. His wishes concerning his family made complete sense. Who wouldn't want to give his loved one a proper burial? Who wouldn't want a missing family heirloom?

And something else turned over in my mind as I sat there listening to Simon. A new perspective on Morgan took shape. She'd lied to me more than once and she'd bolted on me more than once. Was I supposed to protect and defend someone who'd been so dishonest with me?

"It sounds to me," I said, adopting a reasonable tone, "like you need to let the police track her down. And if you want me to call them, or even go to the cops right here in Wyckoff, I will. I have no problem with that."

But Simon's head was shaking, his eyes closed. It looked like he couldn't stand to see my face as I spoke those words.

"The Laurel Falls cops are slow-witted," he said. "They didn't know where she was. I did."

"And how exactly did you find out she was here?" I asked, truly curious. "You were here last night. I saw you in the lobby. But you didn't say anything to Morgan."

Simon kept shaking his head, but this time he directed his disgust at himself. "Foolish, foolish. If I'd been just a few hours earlier, if I'd put it all together sooner . . ." Again he thumped one meaty fist into the other palm, the impact making a splat. He opened his eyes. "I talked to people in Laurel Falls, where she worked and still had some friends. Sometimes I got there right before the cops did. And I went down to Nashville too. A consensus emerged—if she was in trouble, she might retreat up here to Wyckoff. No one had any better guess, and I had to take a chance. It's where she grew up. Where she went to college at Henry Clay. I didn't know with certainty she'd be in this one-horse town. I hoped, though. A wild hope."

"So how did you choose the right hotel?" I asked.

"I didn't." He reached over and slapped me on the knee. Apparently we were becoming allies. I found it disconcerting. "I just checked into a hotel. This one. I'd been looking all over town since yesterday, and not finding a damn thing. I was going to leave this morning. I was ready to go, packed and everything. And then *you* came into the lobby. Like manna from heaven. There you were, asking the clerk about a woman, describing Morgan to the letter. Maybe, I thought. Maybe . . ."

"So you followed me up here?"

"I did. And what do you know? I was right. I found the very guy who was with her last." Again he looked overly satisfied, a shark with a taste of blood. "So it's on you now. Tell me where she went. Tell me why she isn't here. Did she see me? Did I spook her?"

"She didn't say anything about you," I said. "How well does she know you?" I asked.

"Oh, she knows who I am. In fact, I may have forced her hand back in Nashville with my nosing around. And I fear I may have pushed too hard. I can do that sometimes. So can Giles."

"Look, she didn't tell me where she was going," I said. "She left this morning without saying anything to me. No note. Nothing. I have as much clue as you do."

"Don't do that, Joshua. Don't block me because you think you like this girl."

"I don't know about that." He started to say something else, but I talked over him, cutting him off. "Look, all of this just landed on me. This is all new to me as of . . . right now, okay? I mean, my God, you're telling me I spent the night with a killer. That's what you want me to believe?"

Simon considered me. "Yes, that's what I believe."

"Let's call the police, and I'll tell them the whole tale. I passed a police station on my way here. It's right up on High Street. You can't miss it. Or just call them. Bring them here, and we can talk."

Simon looked pained. He lowered his head, his chin nearly touching his chest, his eyes closed again. He spoke without looking up. "I don't like these delays. You know the clock is ticking. She's getting farther and farther away."

"You don't really know that."

He looked up. "I don't know what?"

"That she's getting farther and farther away. You don't know where she is. And neither do I. But why would she come to Wyckoff if there wasn't a reason? You said yourself she's not here randomly. All you know is you're sitting in the one place she isn't."

"What are you driving at?" he asked.

"You should go look for her." I stood up, hoping he'd get the hint. "I need to shower. I need to put on clean clothes. And then . . . I don't know."

"I'll wait." He folded his arms.

"No," I said. "You don't need to wait for me. Do what you want."

Simon looked up, his eyes widening. "I want to wait for you."

"Why?"

"You're my best hope. So I'll wait."

I felt like I was dealing with a stubborn child. A large, stubborn child.

"Can't you wait down in the lobby? Look, I'm in the same boat you are. I'm trying to understand what's happening with Morgan." He continued to stare at me. "I slept with her last night. I followed her here from Atlanta. I almost got thrown off a plane. Do you think I don't want to know what's going on? You're the first person to make any sense about this whole thing."

Simon rocked a little, his arms still folded.

"Go down to the lobby," I said. "Think about calling the police. If you don't want to, we can decide what else we might do. But . . . can I please just get ready alone? Seriously, I don't know you."

Simon waited. And waited, rocking a little.

And then he stood up. He came close to me, so close I could see the hairs in his nose, the capillaries in his eyes. He took his index finger and poked me once—hard—in the chest, knocking me slightly off-balance.

"I'll be in the lobby, then." He pointed to his watch. "Twenty minutes." He went to the door but looked back once before he stepped through to the hallway. He pointed to his watch again. "Twenty."

37

Kimberly held her travel mug in her right hand, resting it on her knee. She lifted it and took a long drink of the warm liquid, then looked across Steven Hatfield's uncluttered desk. No papers, no notes. No pens or paper clips. How did people work in such a sterile, organized environment?

"You're telling me Simon is dangerous," she said. "A threat to Morgan Reynolds or whoever he thinks may have harmed his brother. That's why you told me the story about the dead rat."

"Yes."

"Do you have any reason to think that besides something that happened more than twenty years ago? Are the two brothers close?"

"Giles refused to go into business with Simon. When we were starting the company, Simon knew about it. Like I said, he was around for some of our initial discussions. I could tell he wanted in. I was willing to bring him on board because he was Giles's brother. I thought Giles would want him, so I was prepared to swallow my doubts."

"But you didn't."

"I brought it up with Giles once. Casually. About Simon. Giles got very angry. He wagged his finger at me and told me in no uncertain terms that Simon was to have nothing to do with the company, that the whole thing would be off if Simon got involved."

"Did he say why?"

"He said he didn't want that kind of volatility in the company. That was it for me. They knew each other better than anyone else. He was happy to have Simon on the outside, so I was too."

"Did that lead to bad feelings between the two of them?" Kimberly asked. "I mean, this company is doing well. So if Simon was cut out of the loop on that, he missed out on a nice amount of money. That can make someone angry, right?"

"I don't think they were ever very close. They didn't spend a lot of time together as far as I knew. Whether Simon resented being cut out of TechGreen, I don't know."

"Okay. Siblings sometimes get closer as they get older. Sometimes they drift apart. What happened with them? Did they have other problems?"

"Not that I'm aware of." Hatfield paused. He took a deep breath through his nostrils. "I sensed they didn't agree on everything when their mother died. Giles was very close to her, and he was the oldest. Simon was close to her too, but Giles . . . He was a little . . . I don't know. *Close* to his mother for a middle-aged guy. Too close? I suspected he might have gotten first crack at some things Simon wanted. It's just the two of them, and neither one is a shrinking violet."

"Was there a lot of money?"

"A decent amount, but, of course, I'm just guessing. But it put a strain on Giles when the estate was being settled. He became withdrawn, moodier than normal."

"But didn't say why?"

"Giles? Hell, no. He wouldn't discuss a personal problem. The day his mother died he came to work. Around three he casually mentions to me that he has to leave early because his mother died that morning. That's how he told me."

"And Giles doesn't have any kids?" Kimberly asked.

"No."

"So . . . who gets his share of all this if he's . . . if the worst happens?"

Hatfield looked surprised by the question. He rubbed his forehead. "I guess I don't know. I really don't. Simon?"

"Could be," Kimberly said. "No kids for Giles. No other siblings. Parents dead."

"Crap. You're not thinking . . . I mean, would he do that?"

"I don't know. But I do know somebody went in there and took the ring. And that's all they took."

"Okay. Sure. But that doesn't make sense. If Simon inherits from Giles, then he gets the ring. So why kill for it?"

"Maybe we made the wrong assumption. Maybe Simon doesn't inherit Giles's estate. Maybe someone else does. We'll have to get a copy of the will at some point. That requires a subpoena and could take days or even weeks."

"Why did Simon come in and push you to look for his brother if he killed him?" Hatfield asked.

"It would make a good diversion. You said yourself how crafty Simon is." Kimberly sipped her coffee. Something crossed her mind. "I'm just curious. You're expanding, right? Where?"

Hatfield looked cagey, like he didn't want to reveal his business plan to her, like she might leak it to his competitors. "We're thinking of a few places."

"Have you worked with a commercial real estate developer named Joshua Fields?"

"Joshua Fields?" He frowned in concentration. "I don't know him."

"Did Morgan ever mention that name?" she asked.

"Morgan? I said I don't know anything about her personal life."

"Fair enough." There didn't seem to be anything else to ask him, so she stood up and told Hatfield she'd be in touch if she needed to know anything else.

When she stepped outside his office, a few heads turned her way. When she noticed, they looked down, pretending to be back at work. But Kimberly saw something on the desk closest to where she stood.

"Landlines?" she asked Hatfield. "Is there one on every desk?"

"Pretty much." He rolled his eyes. "It's silly, but Giles insisted. He wanted to have phones that would work all the time. He only used a flip phone. After all these years running a tech company."

"Where did Morgan Reynolds sit?" Kimberly asked.

Hatfield looked perplexed. He leaned down and asked the woman at the desk closest to them the same question.

She pointed across the room. "Where Sasha sits now."

"Do you mind?" Kimberly asked but started walking that way before Hatfield could answer. He hustled along behind her as she moved among the desks, eyes lifting to her as she passed each workspace. Conversation slowed at last. She heard mostly the clacking of keyboards, the sound of unfamiliar music playing. Somewhere a Ping-Pong ball thwacked against a paddle.

She came alongside Sasha's space. "Excuse me."

Sasha looked up. She was young. Very young. She wore a tank top, and a butterfly tattoo ran up onto her neck. An image of Maria with a tattoo like that on her neck ran through Kimberly's mind. *Please don't. Please.* Sasha's dark eyes were pretty and clear, and the tips of her hair were dyed purple. "Hi."

Kimberly didn't remember her from the first round of interviews. "Did you know Morgan Reynolds?"

"No, I sure didn't." She spoke like some of Maria's friends, who turned even statements of fact into questions by letting their voices rise at the ends of sentences. "I started here after she left. That's how I got this desk."

"Does the phone number change when a new employee takes over the space?" Kimberly shifted her gaze from Sasha to Steven Hatfield. "See, where I work, if you change desks or offices, like if you get a promotion, you can take the number with you. They just reroute it. But if someone new starts, if you replace someone who leaves, then you get their old number. What happens here?"

"We do the same thing," Steven said. "Most of our employees don't even use the landlines. They text, e-mail, use cells."

Kimberly turned to Sasha. "Did you ever get any calls for Morgan Reynolds on this line? Anybody looking for her?"

Sasha reached up and started twirling her purple tips. She wore black everywhere else. Leggings, socks, shoes. Lipstick.

"A few calls came in for a while. People who didn't know she'd quit. I'd just tell them she didn't work here anymore. If it was about a project Morgan had started, I'd refer them to the right person. You know, other people here took over her work."

"Sure. And that's it? Anything lately?"

"No." Sasha continued to twirl. She looked past Kimberly, staring into her own memory banks. "Well, nothing about work. There was a wrong number a week or so ago."

"That's all?"

"Well, somebody called and asked for Morgan, but they gave a different last name. Morgan . . . I don't remember. Woodward? Woodhead? Something like that."

"And?"

"I told them they had the wrong number. I know Morgan's

last name is Reynolds. And anyway it had been so long since she'd quit."

"Why would you remember a random call like that?" Kimberly asked, hoping there was more. Begging inside for more.

"Well, I'm supposed to take this trip, with my boyfriend? We're supposed to go to Ireland? And I need to get a passport."

"So?" Hatfield said.

"It was the passport office calling. That's why I remember. The passport office was calling looking for this Morgan . . . whatever her name was."

38

I stood under the shower for as long as I could.

Twenty minutes.

I still felt the impact of Simon's index finger on my chest. I wouldn't be surprised if I ended up with a dime-size bruise right there.

Twenty minutes.

He seemed like a man who meant what he said. He'd tried to be affable, tried to be friendly, almost fatherly. But I didn't believe it. I'd seen his type before, mostly at work. A middle-aged man who appeared as normal as anyone else . . . until you tried to veer away from what he wanted.

I stepped out of the shower, glad to finally be clean. I wiped steam off the mirror with my hand, thought my skin looked pale and drawn.

While I combed my hair and brushed my teeth, I tried to sort through what Simon had told me. I knew only one thing for certain—Morgan was involved in something. She'd admitted to stealing the ring. Had she done more?

I almost couldn't contemplate it. . . . Had she killed a man?

Then I ran through the past twenty-four hours. If that was true, it meant I'd met, fallen for, pursued, and slept with a murderer.

That low humming, the white noise of mental overload, started buzzing through my brain again. And it grew louder and louder.

I left the bathroom and started getting dressed, pulling clean clothes out of my bag. I felt like I was washing and putting away the last remnants of Morgan as I did.

Simon made it all seem so easy. So certain. He'd laid out his case, and everything Morgan had done backed it up. But if it was all so easy, why not go to the local police? Simon knew Morgan had just been in Wyckoff. I'd seen her. If he simply wanted justice, then he should just let the authorities handle it.

But Simon seemed unable to wait for the slow grind of the wheels of justice. Was he just impatient? Or was there something else?

I wasn't sure, so I did what I sometimes do when I'm confused. I picked up my phone to call my dad. I ignored the seven missed calls for the moment and called Dad.

"Thank God," Dad said, sounding relieved. "Are you calling to tell me you got everything out of your system? You met your girl and . . . Well, you don't have to tell your old man about all of that."

"Dad, I need your help."

"Crap. What is it? Are you in more trouble?"

"Not exactly. I need you to look someone up for me."

"You mean on the Internet?"

"No. And I was hoping . . . I was kind of hoping you could ask your friend Jim Tuttle to do it."

A long pause. I knew Dad wouldn't like where I was going. "Jim Tuttle? Are you for real? You can't just ask a retired cop to use his connections to look somebody up for kicks, Joshua. What is going on?"

I checked the clock. I'd used thirteen of my allotted twenty minutes. If I didn't make it in twenty, I might get another poke in the chest, one that would leave me with a broken sternum.

"I can't explain," I said. "But I'm not in danger. I'm just working something out. For that friend of mine I mentioned. And Jim owes us a favor or two. You helped him find the location for his pet store when he retired, right? So he can do a little favor in return."

"Are you still in Kentucky?" he asked.

"I am. A little college town called Wyckoff, at the Best Western. I'll be here for a little while." I gave him Simon's name and a brief description. "Call me when you hear anything."

"Maybe I'll just call Tuttle and get him to have the cops come to that hotel and check on you." He cleared his throat. "You know . . . you're my only kid. If you're in deep here . . ."

"It's okay, Dad." I tried to sound more certain than I really was. "Look, if you don't hear from me in an hour, you can ask Tuttle to do that."

"How about thirty minutes?" he asked.

"Okay, thirty. Fine. So you'll give the name to Tuttle?"

"I'll call him. And you're right. He does owe me one. Or two. And I think opening that pet store was a dumb idea."

Before we hung up, I asked him to do one more thing.

"Can you have Jim look up someone else, Dad? Morgan Reynolds. Nashville. Formerly of Laurel Falls, Kentucky, formerly of Wyckoff, Kentucky."

39

Once I was off the phone, I gathered my things, zipping my carry-on and my computer bag. My movements remained precise despite the situation. I impressed myself by managing to maintain a semblance of calm.

I took a last look around the room to make sure I hadn't forgotten anything, and that's when I saw something on the floor, something that had fallen between the bed and the nightstand. In the process of getting undressed—or I should say *being undressed* by Morgan—the night before, my T-shirt ended up getting flung into that narrow space. I bent over and picked it up, and when I did, I saw something beneath it.

A receipt? A napkin? No. It was a photograph, a snapshot, the kind I almost never saw anymore. It felt funny in my hand, the corners sharp, the paper slick and flat. My dad kept boxes and boxes of old pictures in our attic, and after my mom left, I'd go up there from time to time, maybe once or twice a year, and look through them, fascinated by the images of my parents as young people.

The photos in our house showed my dad with longer hair, frequently running around without a shirt or shoes on. My mother was thin and lithe, her hair long and straight and parted down the middle with an exacting precision. Some of the photos were fading, yellowing due to the stuffy air in the attic and the passage of time. I never mentioned them to Dad, never told him I went up there. I suspected he knew—it would be natural for me to be curious—but he never brought it up. And I left the many questions I had about my mother unspoken, assuming that the subject was better left unopened.

The light through the curtains had grown brighter, and I used it to study the photograph Morgan had left behind. It showed a child, unmistakably her, probably about eight or nine years old. Her hair reached her shoulders, the bangs cut straight across her forehead. She wore a red top and denim shorts, white sneakers with Velcro straps. She looked at the camera, her eyes squinted against the sunlight.

Behind her stood a woman who looked to be about thirty. She had limp, overprocessed blond hair. She wore sunglasses and held a cigarette in one hand, a purse in the other. She looked almost as skinny as the child, her skin sallow. She appeared unhealthy, sickly even. In the corner of the image, on the lower right-hand side, I saw something else.

It took me a moment to understand what it was. It was ghostly white and slightly blurry, as though whatever it was had been moving when the shot was taken. In the middle of the splash of white was a small black object, almost like a marble amid the light background. I scratched my head, and then the image became clear. A goat. The young version of Morgan, her hand clutched into a fist, reached out toward the animal. I remembered the story she'd told me, brief though it was, as she cried during the night. The petting zoo in the amusement park, the place her mother used to take her.

I flipped the picture over. On the back, in a feminine script, someone had written *Morgan (7) and me at Fantasy Farm. 7/13/01.*

Her mother. Her dying mother, the one she'd moved near when

her job in Laurel Falls went south. The photo had likely fallen out of her bag the night before, probably before I arrived, and she'd been in such a rush to leave that morning—*to leave me*—she hadn't bothered to look under my discarded T-shirt. Who would? Even something so precious—a photo of her dying mother she'd taken the time to carry with her all the way to Wyckoff—could get left behind in a hotel room.

Or had it even been an accident?

She'd spoken about the amusement park in the middle of the night, telling me some precise details about it and sharing the pain of the memories associated with her mother. And then she just happened to leave the photograph behind when she took off?

Someone thumped on the door. It was so loud it sounded like the police.

I checked the clock. My time was up with Simon, but I clung to the faint hope that it was the housekeeping staff. As far as I knew, the "Do Not Disturb" sign remained on the door, and I suspected they were unlikely to violate that sacred symbol unless it was right at checkout time.

And no housekeeper knocked like that.

It must be Simon, and he appeared to take punctuality very seriously. Had he even gone down to the lobby? Had he waited in the hallway to see how quickly I left the room?

Or if I would try to slip away? And suddenly that sounded like a good idea.

"Come on," he said, his voice muffled by the heavy door. "Joshua?"

He knocked again, even louder. And then he knocked again.

I went over and looked through the peephole. Simon's frame filled the space, distorted and warped by the fish-eye view. He moved closer, pressing his head against the wood.

"Joshua?"

"I need another minute."

"Come on. You're not helping her. Or anybody. Certainly not me or my brother."

"Can you just hold on? I'm packing."

I stepped back, holding my phone. But before I could make a decision about calling for help, it rang.

I almost jumped.

It was my dad. I moved farther away from the door and answered.

"What the hell is going on up there?" Dad asked.

"Did you get that information from Jim already?"

"Jim? No, I haven't called him yet. Hell, I didn't have to."

"You didn't have to?"

"No. The cops called me right after I hung up with you. A cop named Reichert from some place called Laurel Falls, Kentucky. He's looking to talk to you. They've been trying to call you. Why haven't you answered them? Joshua, this woman you've been spending time with is a missing person. And she's wanted for questioning in another case. They wouldn't give me a lot of details. But reading between the lines of what they said, it seems like you're in hot water here. Really. This isn't like you. What's going on?"

Simon banged on the door again.

"Dad, what did you tell them?"

"I told them all I knew. You're in Wyckoff, Kentucky. Apparently with a young lady named Morgan Reynolds."

"You told them that?"

"It's true, isn't it? And let me tell you, that piece of news sure got their attention. I'd say you should be expecting a visit from the police soon. Now, I'm going to call Rich Baxter. You know, that lawyer with an office down the block from the grocery store. He's supposed to be good—"

"Dad, I'm going to have to call you back." I hung up.

Simon pounded on the door again, even louder.

When he stopped, he called my name.

"Joshua?"

40

Kimberly inhaled the familiar scent of burning coffee, which hovered over the squad room like the odor of overheated tar. She glanced in the direction of Brandon's desk, which was empty. He'd said something about going to court, so she went to talk to her boss, Lieutenant Larry Willard.

Before she got there, Brandon stuck his head out of Willard's door and waved her over.

"I was just about to call you," he said.

"I thought you were in court."

"Continuance. Again. Come on. You need to hear this."

She followed him in, happy to be able to shut the door and staunch the oppressive odor of the seared coffee.

Willard sat behind his desk, his big gut squeezed against its wooden edge. His broad shoulders and wide chest seemed too big for the space. Kimberly had never said it out loud, but she thought of him as the Buddha of the Laurel Falls Police Department, dispensing wisdom without ever showing much emotion. He wore a short-sleeved white shirt and a navy blue tie, and Kimberly knew he was counting the days until his retirement in a few months. And Kimberly wanted his job.

She very much wanted it.

Three years earlier, they both—she and Willard—had gone up for that same job, and he'd beat her out. She hated to admit he'd been the right choice, but it was her turn now. She tried not to be greedy and demanding, but she really believed she'd earned it.

"Kimberly, Brandon was just about to share some good news," he said, pointing to the two empty chairs across the desk from him. "He promises me we'll all be happy for a change."

They sat like obedient children. She noticed Brandon's grip tightening on the armrests and knew he grew nervous around Willard. Poor Brandon, she thought. Such a good boy.

"So?" Willard asked when Brandon was slow to speak. Even Buddha had a limit. "What did you want to share with the class?"

"Well, we've got a really good lead on Morgan Reynolds," he said. "This guy Joshua Fields, the one who saw her on the plane and followed her? We've been trying to reach him on his cell because he's traveling, but he hasn't answered. This morning he called his father and told him he was in a hotel over in Wyckoff with Morgan, that they'd spent the night together."

"I never told my dad anything like that," Kimberly said.

"They work together," Brandon said. "Him and his dad. They're close, I suppose. And he didn't want his dad to worry. I guess Fields skipped out on a big meeting and changed all his plans to run off with Morgan Reynolds."

"And this guy, this Fields, decided to do all that after meeting her in the airport?" Willard asked.

"That's right," Brandon said.

"So, he's there. And she's there," Kimberly said. "Did we—?"

"We're on it," Willard said. "We called Wyckoff PD. They're heading to the hotel right now."

"Good," Kimberly said.

"This old dog still knows how to do his job," Willard said. "We'll hear from them soon."

"Good. Do we *know* Morgan Reynolds and Joshua Fields just met in the airport?" Kimberly asked. "And as far as we know they haven't been friendly before? Not online or anywhere else? People can meet all sorts of ways these days."

"We haven't found any connections," Brandon said. "Online or elsewhere. But that doesn't mean they haven't connected some way. Or met in person during Fields's travels."

"What else did the father say?" Willard asked.

"It took a while to get this information out of him. The guy was cagey at first. You could tell he didn't want to get his son in any deeper."

"Understandable," Willard said.

"So I laid it on thick. I told him he needed to tell us everything so we could *protect* his son. Which is true, of course."

"And that got through to him?" Willard asked.

"Yeah. It's obvious the guy loves his kid. Anyway, here's the big news. Fields called his dad, asking him to have a cop friend look into *two* people for him. One was Morgan Reynolds, who he was with. The other name he gave his dad?" Brandon paused, adding his own dramatic touch. "Simon Caldwell."

Kimberly felt a burst of energy travel up her spine and hit the base of her skull. "He's right there, then. Thirty minutes away from here, in Wyckoff."

"My alma mater," Brandon said. "Henry Clay."

"Mine too," Willard said.

"He's there. He has to be."

Willard raised a cautioning hand. "We don't know that for sure."

"Why else would this Fields guy be asking to have the police check on him?" Kimberly asked.

"It's possible," Willard said. "Of course."

"Think about it. We haven't seen Simon in almost forty-eight hours," she said. "When Giles was first reported missing, he was all over us. I called him back yesterday, and he didn't return my call."

"Yeah, you're getting warmer," Willard said. "But maybe he's laying low because we learned about the two assaults on his record."

"Not to mention the one in college Steven Hatfield just told me about."

"Assault?" Willard asked.

"Intimidation, maybe?" Kimberly said. "Harassment? It's close. But there's more."

Brandon and Willard both edged forward in their seats.

"It turns out Giles had some issues with his temper." She told them about the run-ins with two female employees, the ones she'd heard about from Steven Hatfield. "We know Morgan Reynolds and Giles Caldwell had a beef over money. Could it have blown up into something more?"

"We don't know," Willard said. "But it's a theory."

"But we do know Fields and Reynolds are together in Wyckoff," Brandon said. "At least they were as of last night."

"And Morgan grew up in Wyckoff?" Kimberly asked.

"Yup," Brandon said. "She also went to Henry Clay. Like us."

Willard shifted his weight. He turned his head from one side to the other, grimacing. He looked like he had a crick in his neck. "So, we have a missing person here, Giles Caldwell. Meanwhile, that man's brother, his former employee, and a random complete stranger may all be together in beautiful Wyckoff, Kentucky, where the former employee—"

"And . . . can we call her a person of interest yet?" Kimberly asked.

"We're getting there. And that's where she grew up and went to college. And the stranger is trying to get his dad to call in favors with the police to dig up dirt on the other two. What a wonderful world we live in."

"I just got back from TechGreen," Kimberly said. "Hatfield didn't have any insights about Morgan Reynolds, except he didn't think the company did anything wrong in not paying her the bonus."

"It's in her contract," Brandon said. "Whatever they develop becomes the intellectual property of the company."

"That's in everyone's contract," Kimberly said. Her words snapped out like a beat on a snare drum. She took a breath. "But everyone else who made an app got a bonus. Just not her. Some people don't always get what they deserve at work."

Willard nodded, seemingly unaware of her irony. "But it's a big leap from disappointment to murder."

"What else do people kill for?" Kimberly asked. "Love and money. Right?"

"We need a body, though," Willard said directly to Kimberly. "Or some kind of evidence. Is that all?"

"No, it's not," Kimberly said. "I learned something about our brothers. Apparently Simon feels like he got the shaft when their mother died, that certain things went to Giles in a way that wasn't fair. If you're looking for a motive, that's money right there."

"But to kill his brother over it?" Willard asked. "He came in here pitching a fit, saying we weren't doing enough."

"That's a big risk," Kimberly said.

"This guy doesn't seem like one for the safe bet," Willard said. "He's over in Wyckoff chasing down leads on his own. He's not shy. Or completely stable. Was that it at TechGreen?"

Kimberly shook her head. "Get this: TechGreen still has land-lines. On every desk."

Willard pointed to his phone. "They come in handy. What if the grid goes out?"

"Right. Turns out the desk where Morgan Reynolds used to work still gets the occasional call for her. And one of them was from the passport office just a few days ago. Except they didn't ask for Morgan Reynolds. They asked for Morgan something else. But the woman who has Morgan's desk now couldn't remember the name. Thought it began with a 'W.'"

"Maybe it was a wrong number," Brandon said.

"But what are the odds?" Kimberly asked. "She used another name on the plane. She probably used another one for the passport."

"Why give her work number to the passport office?" Brandon asked. "Why not home or a cell?"

"Maybe she gave them both," Kimberly said. "They tried one, and when they didn't get an answer, they called the other."

"Whatever the reason, it's all starting to sound like premeditation," Willard said. "Maybe she planned to do something to Giles and then leave the country."

"Exactly," Kimberly said. She thought about all the angles, all the moving parts. "And she's right over in Wyckoff."

"Actually," Willard said, "I wanted to talk to you about that for a minute."

"You mean you want me to take a little road trip?"

41

It turned out to be one of those rare hotels with windows that actually opened, and I managed to slide the pane over, creating a three-inch space, big enough for a six-year-old. Unless I could lose fifty pounds in two minutes, I wasn't going out that way. Not to mention that I was on the third floor, about twenty feet above the parking lot. I could jump, sure, but I'd likely end up with two broken legs. Or worse.

But then I saw something useful.

Simon banged again. If Simon's goal was to attract the attention of every housekeeper and guest on the floor, he was likely succeeding. I bounded across the room and said, "Give me one more minute. I have to use the bathroom."

"You better not be screwing with me," Simon said.

I cracked the door, leaving the security latch in place. Simon's big head filled the small opening like a hungry dog's.

"Can't you just wait for me in the lobby?" I said. "Can't a man use the bathroom in peace?"

"You said twenty minutes."

"No, *you* said twenty minutes. Do you mind?"

"Let me wait in the room."

"Look, Simon, I'll be down soon. Just let me go to the bathroom."

"You better—"

"Simon. I could have called the cops by now, and I didn't. Will you be chill?"

I shut the door in his face, realizing I might have missed my chance at the window. I rushed back across the room, and the pleasant morning air blew in, a nice change from the artificial, musty atmosphere of the hotel.

I looked down and saw Billy, the garbage boy, pushing a cart full of what I hoped was clean laundry across the parking lot. Thanks to Simon, I'd almost missed him. Billy was just reaching the back entrance of the hotel, his hair mussed, his shoulders slumped. Whatever he'd done with his girlfriend after work the previous night had left him worn-out and not quite ready to face the new day.

I gave a soft whistle, hoping Simon had left the other side of the door and couldn't hear me.

Billy looked up. He squinted for a moment, his face uncertain and confused. He probably thought he was being summoned from on high, my whistle from the third floor of a two-star hotel the modern equivalent of a burning bush.

"Oh," he said, recognizing me.

I dug in my wallet and pulled out a twenty. It fluttered in the breeze two stories above Billy's head. "I need your help. Bring that cart to my room. Three oh six. Right now."

Billy blinked a few times. I could see a scattering of acne on his cheeks. "But my manager—"

I pulled out another twenty. "There's more. Just get up here. Fast."

"Is this illegal?" he asked.

"Not at all. Is Sean working?"

"No."

"All the better. Come on."

Billy pushed the cart into the building without committing one way or the other. I went over to the door and looked through the peephole. No sign of Simon. Maybe I'd put him off just long enough.

And then I waited.

I'd like to say I waited calmly on the edge of the bed, making plans for what I was going to do once—*if*—I made it past Simon and out of the hotel. But I didn't.

Instead I paced. Like a caged lion. Back and forth, back and forth.

I quickly concluded that Billy must have flaked out, that he'd run into his boss or Sean the security guard, who'd decided to show up on his day off just to make sure nothing unseemly was transpiring in the hotel. Or maybe Billy just figured my money wasn't worth the possibility of getting fired.

As far as my plan B . . . it didn't exist. I could call the cops and risk never seeing Morgan again, but the abandoned photograph made me think she wanted me to find her. Or I could talk to Simon and tell him what he wanted to know, which meant he might track Morgan down. But neither of those options was appealing. . . .

A gentle knock sounded. I went over, hopeful. Through the peephole I saw Billy, hair still mussed, laundry cart by his side. I undid the chain and the security bar and pulled the door open. I looked past Billy, up and down the hall in each direction. Not only did I not see Simon, but I didn't see anyone else at the moment. No housekeepers, no guests. No man with the giant eagle tattoo and the Fu Manchu mustache.

"Do you know what I want you to do?" I asked.

"I'm guessing you don't need a bunch of clean towels."

I grabbed my bags and came back to the door. Billy was already moving some of the laundry aside, making space for me. Before I got in, I handed him three twenties, a big raise from the night before. A trip in the laundry cart past a maniac seemed like a more expensive job.

"There's a man in the lobby. Big guy, light jacket, edgy."

"I saw him. He looked at me like he wanted to choke me."

"He wants to choke me, I think. For sure he wants to choke the woman I was looking for last night. He can't see me. My car's on the north side of the building. A black Charger. Just get me there."

"We'll have to go right past him. The elevator comes out into the lobby. If he's down there, he'll see me."

"Don't look at him," I said. "Roll me past and then we're done."

Billy stared at me, no doubt contemplating his life choices. No doubt he hadn't expected this when he applied for a part-time job to help him pay for college.

"You're crazy, man."

"Think of the story you can tell your friends. Or your girl."

He nodded. I knew when a sale was closed.

"Okay, I'm feeling you," he said, pointing at the cart. "Get in."

42

Kimberly felt like a coward. She could have called Maria directly but opted for reaching out to Peter first. She knew Maria would be at a game-day soccer practice, and she hoped Peter would lift the burden of breaking the bad news to their daughter. She listened to the phone ring while the tires of her city-issued sedan hummed against the two-lane state highway, heading west to Wyckoff.

"What's up?" Peter asked.

"Everything."

He sounded instantly concerned. "Is something wrong?"

"No, no. Nothing's wrong. Not really." Kimberly regretted alarming him. No one needed more stress added to their lives. "It's just . . . it's work. Something's come up. I'm not going to make the soccer game tonight."

"Oh, okay. I'm going. No worries."

"I know you're going. With Jennifer."

"Yeah. So?"

"It's not you I'm concerned about. We have a touchy, judgmental preteen to deal with."

"Yes, her," Peter said with a sigh. "But she'll have to deal. It's nothing you can get out of, is it? Oh, is it about Giles Caldwell? Is that it?"

"You know I can't really say."

"Oh, come on. You used to give me all the good dirt. Even after we split up, you'd tell me. I can keep a secret."

"Okay, you win. Who else could it be but Giles Caldwell? He's taking over my life. Or at least the people who knew him are. And the mayor."

"Did you find him?" Peter asked, not trying to hide his interest in any potentially macabre details. She could tell by his tone he was expecting to hear about a body stuffed in a trunk or a finger mailed to the police as part of a ransom demand. And she had to admit she liked hearing his voice that way. While she could find no single atom of desire inside her body to be with Peter again, she liked the sense of familiarity, the easy give-and-take they could fall into. Only people who knew each other a long time—and well—could so quickly settle into that rhythm. And they certainly knew each other well. They'd been through a lot together—marriage, childbirth, divorce. They'd lost their virginity to each other senior year of high school. Jennifer couldn't say that. All things considered, Peter was her friend. And it was nice to be able to talk to a friend. "Or . . . did you find any part of him?"

"No, nothing that concrete. We have good leads on a couple of interesting people, so I'm driving out to Wyckoff right now. Willard is sending me to check on it all in person."

"It's a nice drive out there," he said. "Always makes me think of taking Maria to Fantasy Farm when she was little. Remember that?"

"Of course I do."

"You must have a good lead if you're going in person."

"You forget, Giles Caldwell is a prominent citizen in our little burg. He employs people, pays a lot of taxes. Gives a lot to charity. And . . ."

"And what?"

"He and the mayor are friends. Of course the mayor wants this to be a high priority. She wants it wiped away as soon as possible, so Laurel Falls can go back to touting itself as the nicest small town in America."

"I guess they can't claim that title when someone has gone missing. Maybe they can revise it to Nicest Small Town in America with a Potentially Murdered Business Owner."

"It has a nice ring to it." Kimberly saw an oasis of fast food restaurants, and her stomach rumbled. She'd had only coffee that morning. In fact, that's all she'd had all day. Not a good plan. She felt wired, edgy. And her hunger exacerbated her frustration over missing the soccer game after promising three times she'd attend. "Sometimes I hate my job."

"Well, let me ask you something," Peter said.

She recognized his tone. He was going to launch into something completely reasonable and logical, something that shifted her frame of reference so she saw the situation in a new light. Isn't that what friends do for each other? Yes, it is.

"Go ahead, ex-husband," she said.

"If you were the lieutenant—*when* you are the lieutenant—would you have sent you out to Wyckoff to check on . . . whatever it is you're checking on up there? These so-called interesting people or whatever?"

Kimberly considered her reply. She kept two hands on the wheel, Peter's voice coming through the hands-free system, the talk show she'd been listening to silenced so she could make the phone call. She gave the matter serious thought, considered all the facts, the same ones Willard knew.

"Of course," she said. "But that doesn't mean I'd like it."

"Isn't that what it means to be an adult?" Peter asked. "Doing stuff you don't want to do just because you know it's right?"

"Like I said, that doesn't mean I like it."

"Do you want me to break it to Maria?" Peter asked. "And then after the game we'll take her for pizza. That usually soothes her preteen angst."

"Yes, and tell her I'll call her when I get the chance."

"Isn't it good for her to learn she's not the center of the world?" Peter asked. "Sometimes work comes first, right?"

"Right. And it is kind of important to find a missing person."

"Exactly."

Kimberly sighed. "I was looking forward to the game even though I know nothing about soccer."

"Match," Peter said.

"Whatever. I'll keep you in the loop about when I'm coming back. Maybe we'll learn something big in Wyckoff and wrap this up. I'm trying to look for positive things."

"Be safe," Peter said.

"I will. And you be safe too."

"At the soccer match?"

"With Jennifer. How old is she? Twenty-five?"

Peter made a scoffing noise, then laughed. "Twenty-eight, if you must know."

"Pace yourself, guy. Pace yourself."

She hung up and continued driving with a small smile on her face.

43

The laundry was warm. And it smelled fresh and clean, better than anything else in the hotel.

If I hadn't needed to sneak past a man who seemed mildly unhinged, I would have welcomed the trip in Billy's cart.

Neither one of us spoke once I was inside. The ride was smooth as we went to the elevator, the carpet cushioning any shock and making for a flat, easy track. I jostled around a little as Billy pushed the cart into the elevator, and then I felt the slight downward lurch as we descended to the lobby.

The combination of warm laundry and frazzled nerves made me sweat. When I heard the elevator ding and the doors slide open, I took a quick swipe at my forehead with my right hand, brushing away a few beads of liquid. I knew I couldn't move again.

We exited the elevator onto the lobby's tiled floor. The cart rumbled and rattled, shaking me with every movement. It was like we were traveling through a bombed-out city. I squeezed my eyes shut and waited, hoping for a quick trip.

Then the cart stopped. I tried to guess how far we'd gone. Halfway through the lobby?

I heard a sharp voice, muffled by the towels.

"Where are you going?" a voice asked. It didn't sound like Simon.

"I have to take this outside."

"I thought you did that already."

"Not yet."

A long pause. I hoped Billy had a good poker face. If not, I wondered if I could contract my body to the size of a pea.

"They need those on four," the voice said.

"I'll go right up there after this," Billy said.

We started moving again but stopped almost immediately.

A familiar voice spoke. I could almost see the smug look on his face. "What floor were you on?" Simon asked.

Billy seemed stuck for an answer. An eternity passed. "I was outside," he said finally.

"You were upstairs," Simon said. "You just got off the elevator. What floor were you on?"

Another long pause. Billy either froze when under stress or had no future as a poker player.

"Five," he said.

Had Simon been watching the numbers move?

"Five?"

And then my phone started ringing.

I had a choice—scramble to silence it, which meant Simon might see me moving around under the laundry. Or let it ring and hope Billy got me out of there.

I remained still, wishing for the best. The phone kept ringing. Rotten phones. Rotten technology.

Billy's hand started scrambling around in the towels. "Let me shut this off," he said.

I used Billy's movements as a screen and contorted my body so I could reach into my pocket. I silenced the call with my thumb.

"There," Billy said, withdrawing his hand. "Well, I've got to get going."

"You didn't see anyone up there?" Simon asked.

"Up where?"

"Up in the hotel," Simon said.

"No, sir."

I heard Billy say something else, and then the cart started moving again, rumbling over the tiles. We hit a large bump, one that required Billy to jostle the cart as he guided it along. Then I sensed a change in the light. We were outside, and the parking lot asphalt was rough but not as rough as the tiles in the lobby. I breathed a little easier.

We finally stopped, and Billy said, "Okay, it's clear." He flipped the towels off me and reached in to help me out. It wasn't easy, but I swung one leg and then the other over the side of the cart, grabbing my bags in the process. I'd already paid Billy, so I shook his hand, threw my stuff in the backseat, and opened the driver's door of the rental car.

"The guy you told me about, the big one, he started talking to me," Billy said.

"I heard."

"You should have silenced your phone before you got in the cart," he said.

"Next time I will. Where did the guy go when you left?"

"I think he went upstairs. He seemed pissed."

"Stay away from him," I said. "And don't tell him anything else."

"Got it."

"Hey, you ever hear of a place called Fantasy Farm?" I asked.

"Fantasy what?"

"Fantasy Farm." He might have thought I was looking for a strip club. "You know, the old amusement park? It's closed now."

"I've never heard of it," Billy said.

How quickly the past disappears, I thought. I shook his hand again. Both of our palms were sweaty.

"Okay." I looked at the hotel, the closed front door. "Thanks, Billy. Be safe."

I started the car and drove off.

44

Kimberly reached Wyckoff around noon, her body slightly stiff from sitting in the car. Her stomach rumbled, which made her mind fuzzy, and she wished she could jump out of the car and go for a run, even just around the block. Anything to get her blood pumping, to make her feel alive.

But there was no time.

She headed straight to the police station. Willard had already spoken to the Wyckoff PD twice, letting them know one of his detectives was coming into town, but still, as a courtesy, she went there first and showed her face, holding off on going by the hotel in question. No police department liked having cops from other jurisdictions just showing up and nosing around without them knowing about it.

The Wyckoff PD occupied a new building just a block off High Street downtown. The brick looked clean, the landscaping tidy and trimmed. She hated to think of the hassles they dealt with on a regular basis in a college town. Laurel Falls had over fifty thousand more residents than Wyckoff, but Kimberly, despite the disappearance of Giles Caldwell, thought she had it better. How many citations for underage drinking did the Wyckoff PD hand out? How many fights did they break up between entitled frat boys? How many times did they face back talk from a rich kid?

Before Kimberly pulled open the front door of the station, a woman in her thirties wearing a well-cut business suit, her slightly graying hair pulled back in a ponytail, stepped out.

"Detective Givens?"

"That's me."

"I'm Alicia Hughes. That hotel we told your lieutenant about? There's been a disturbance there. I think you'll want to check it out."

"I think I do," she said.

"I'll drive," Hughes said. "I can fill you in on the way."

They climbed into another dark sedan, almost a twin of the one Kimberly had driven over from Laurel Falls. The interior felt hot, the temperature elevated by the sun through the windshield. Hughes flipped the air on as she backed out of the parking space and started talking.

"When Willard called we sent an officer over to the hotel, hoping we could catch one of these folks, but none of them were around. That was a couple of hours ago."

"Did you sit on the place?" Kimberly asked.

"We tried. But we're a small department, limited manpower. The officer had to assist on a domestic violence call and left. By the way, I've met Willard before. He's a good cop."

"He's retiring."

"That's what he said. Anyway, after our officer was gone, something else went down—we just got a call about a disturbance. Not sure it's related to the folks you want to find, but . . ."

"You don't believe in coincidences."

"I don't," Hughes said.

"Neither do I."

Kimberly felt tense as they drove, hoping this wasn't merely a coincidence. Could the Best Western have another problem and have it be unrelated to Simon and Morgan and Joshua? She distracted herself by trying to pay attention to the passing scenery, to the Georgian buildings on campus, the young, attractive kids strolling by in apparent bliss. The sun slid behind the trees, its light filtered by the changing leaves. She pictured Maria visiting colleges in a few years, mulling over what she hoped would be many options, and then making a choice. Kimberly hated the thought of her going away even though it was exactly what she wanted for her. Did all parents live with that intense contradiction? She could use the promotion and raise to pay her tuition, but would the regular hours leave her sitting at home alone once Maria was gone?

"We rarely get this level of excitement here," Hughes said.

"I think we all crave excitement, and then when it comes . . ."

"Yeah. It can be horrible." They drove in silence for a moment. "But at least we're helping people. Or trying to."

"You're right, of course. Most of the time we manage to get it right."

They came in sight of the hotel. Actually two hotels side by side with a squad car in front of one, the parking lot mostly empty of other vehicles. Hughes guided her sedan with one hand and pulled to a stop near the cruiser. They jumped out, the sliding doors whooshed open as they approached, and a small cluster of people greeted them—a uniformed officer and a handful of hotel employees. The staff looked excited, talking over one another as the officer, a young woman who looked like she should be in high school, tried to sort through everything they were saying. The officer looked relieved to see Hughes.

"What have you got, Williams?" Hughes asked.

"Ballard is in the office with the victim," she said. "It's an assault. Basic, really. One of the guests roughed up a hotel employee pretty good. But . . ."

"But?" Hughes asked.

"He's telling a pretty wild story along with it," Williams said.

Hughes nodded, and she and Kimberly went behind the counter and back to the small, cluttered office. A kid, college age by the looks of him, sat in a desk chair with an ice pack on the back of his neck and another one pressed to his lip. His eyes were half-closed, and he grimaced like someone was slowly working a knitting needle into his side.

Ballard, the other uniformed officer, nodded and shook Kimberly's hand when introduced. "This is Billy Newcomb. He's a maintenance worker here. Why don't you tell them what happened?"

Billy shook his head slowly. He kept the ice pack pressed against his lip where Kimberly saw swelling. She felt a rush of maternal affection for him. If Hughes and Ballard hadn't been there, if the circumstances had been different, she would have gone over to Billy and placed her arm around him, pulled him close. But professional decorum prevented her from doing that, and Billy didn't look in the mood to be comforted.

"I just want to get to class," he said, his voice a groan. "I have one this afternoon, and I've already missed it four times. And I haven't eaten."

"You should see a doctor," Kimberly said. "You might have a concussion."

"I called an ambulance," Ballard said. "It's coming."

"Shit," Billy said. "How much will that cost me? I've got a student loan."

"What happened?" Hughes asked. "Who did this to you and why?"

Under his breath Billy grumbled a few words that Kimberly

didn't understand. Then he started talking with more clarity about a guy who showed up at the hotel the previous evening, looking for a woman he said he knew. Except he didn't know which room she was staying in or how to contact her. Billy closed his eyes as he admitted that he took the guy's money and asked the desk clerk if she'd seen the woman.

"The clerk remembered her because she was crying as she checked in," Billy said. "It was obvious something was wrong."

"So you revealed her location to this guy?" Kimberly asked. "What if he'd wanted to hurt her?"

"No, no, it was nothing like that. He liked her, I could tell. When he described her, he had that kind of look in his eye that said he really cared about her. I swear."

"So this guy went to look for this woman, and that was as far as it went?" Hughes asked.

"He was still here this morning. I don't know what happened to the woman. I never saw her again."

Billy then told a whole story about the guy asking to be wheeled out of the hotel in a laundry cart, so that he wouldn't be seen leaving the hotel.

"And who did he want to avoid?" Kimberly asked, but then she went on. "Let me guess. . . ."

"Yeah, he's the one who did this to me."

"And why did he do that?" Kimberly asked.

"He wanted to know where the guy went. The first guy. Or where the woman went. Either one, I guess. When I pushed the laundry cart out to the parking lot, he went upstairs. I don't know where he went after that. I didn't see him for a little while. I was busy and thought he'd checked out. But he came back out of the blue."

"And he just jumped you here?" Hughes asked. "At work?"

"Out back. When I was dumping a mop bucket. About half an hour ago."

"Do you know where this first guy went?" Kimberly asked. "The one you . . . the one you pushed out in a laundry cart?"

"Dude, I have no clue."

It was a shot in the dark. Kimberly looked at Hughes, who nodded at her. The whining of the ambulance reached them in the small office. Just in time. Billy leaned back, his eyelids closed. The ice pack slid off his neck and splatted against the floor.

"I have no clue. Did I tell you? I have no clue."

He was clearly concussed. Repeating himself.

The paramedics came into the lobby, wheeling a gurney. Kimberly started to move out of the way.

But Billy mumbled again, something about a farm, so she stayed put.

"What did he say?" Kimberly asked.

"Fantasy Farm," Billy said again.

"What is he talking about?" Kimberly asked Hughes.

"Did he say Fantasy Farm?" Hughes asked. She held up her hand, stopping the paramedics from coming into the office. "Billy, what about Fantasy Farm?"

"The guy . . . He asked . . . laundry guy . . ."

"He did. Why?"

"About Fantasy Farm . . ."

"We heard that. Why?"

His eyelids fluttered. "He asked me . . . I told the guy. The crazy guy. I told him laundry guy asked me that. I didn't want my ass kicked, but he did it anyway."

"You told the older guy, the one who beat you up, that Mr. Laundry Cart was interested in Fantasy Farm?" Hughes asked.

"Mmm . . . yeah . . . hmm . . ." His eyelids closed.

Kimberly and Hughes walked out, letting the paramedics in as they moved past the cluster of hotel employees.

"Is he talking about the old amusement park?" Kimberly asked.

"Fantasy Farm. Yeah, but it's abandoned. About thirty minutes outside of town."

"I've taken my kid there. It's been years."

"I don't know," Hughes said. "Like I said, it's closed. There's nothing there anymore. I don't even think you can get in. And if you did . . . what would be the point?"

"Looks like he got thumped pretty hard," Kimberly said. "He could be spouting nonsense. But it might be worth checking out."

45

I ate first, as soon as I drove away from the Best Western, fast food from a drive-through window. I ingested it in the car, crumbs from the hamburger and salt crystals from the fries tumbling down the front of my shirt. I felt a lot better after eating, lack of nutrition be damned. I'd barely eaten the day before, but I'd had plenty to drink and two Xanax. I needed food of some kind.

Stomach full, I considered my options.

Then I remembered the missed calls from that morning. The ringing phone while I was in the laundry cart. Who had been calling and why?

I listened to the first of several voice mails. Two were from a cop named Reichert. He sounded like he was my age and was unfailingly polite as he told me the police in Laurel Falls, Kentucky, wanted to speak to me.

Laurel Falls? Where Morgan worked at the tech company.

Where her boss disappeared from, according to my stalker, Simon.

Then a female detective named Givens left me a series of messages, saying the same thing. Until the last one, in which she informed me she knew I was in Wyckoff, and would I be able to talk to her there? She was coming to town to look for Morgan Reynolds. . . .

"Damn," I said.

But I called her right back. When she answered, she sounded happy to hear from me, which immediately made me think I was in deep trouble. Why would a cop act happy to talk to you unless they were out to get you?

"Mr. Fields? You're a tough man to get ahold of."

"I'm traveling. And my phone was off for a while."

"Are you still in Wyckoff?"

"How did you know I was here?" I asked.

"You told your father. Word gets around. So. Are you?"

"I was thinking of leaving actually."

"Was it the ride in the laundry cart? Too bumpy?"

She knew about that too? Was she going to tell me my underwear size and the name of my best friend from kindergarten next? Before I could answer she continued talking.

"Is Morgan Reynolds with you?" she asked.

"No, she isn't. I haven't seen her since . . . well, since the middle of the night."

"Do you know where she is?" she asked.

"I don't. She took off without saying anything or leaving a note."

"You spent the night together, then?"

"We did."

"I guess you became fast friends. Or did you already know each other?"

"What? No, we met yesterday. At the airport."

"In Atlanta?"

"Yes."

"You know, Mr. Fields, these phones are so impersonal. And

you never know when the signal will go out in these little towns. What do you say we meet in person? We could use a room at the Wyckoff Police Department. Or if you feel more comfortable, somewhere else. A coffee shop? A park? See, I'm worried you've gotten in over your head here, and the longer you stay out there, the deeper you get. It could start to look suspicious."

"Suspicious?"

"Or maybe dangerous. I know you had to run away from Simon Caldwell this morning. I don't know where he is either."

"He's not with me."

"When can we meet, Mr. Fields? I'm eager to hear your side of the story."

I didn't like the suspicion being cast on me. And I didn't know who to believe—Simon or Morgan. Or neither.

"Detective, do you think Morgan Reynolds harmed her boss?" I asked.

"I'm trying to figure that out. Did she say anything to you?"

"No, she didn't. But I don't think she hurt anyone. I guess I can't believe that."

"Where can I meet you? I can come to you if you'd like."

I watched people coming and going at the fast-food restaurant. Elderly couples. Mothers with children. A few college students. Their lives looked good. And safe. Perfectly safe and predictable.

Did I want to be one of them? Wasn't I already?

"Give me some time, Detective. Morgan, she's . . . skittish. I think if I can talk to her . . ."

"You're not a police officer. You're in no position to do that. Let us handle it, Mr. Fields."

"Can I talk to you after I look for her? She might already be gone, out of town. She probably is. Long gone. But if she isn't, if I can find her and talk to her . . . I'll meet with you then."

"That isn't wise, Mr. Fields. The longer you avoid us, the worse it looks for you."

"You've looked me up already, haven't you? The cops in the Nashville airport did, so you must have too. And what did you find? Nothing. There's nothing to find. Not on me."

"Sir—"

"Give me a few hours," I said. "Just a few hours to look. And then I promise I'll call."

I hung up, cutting off any reply she might make.

And my hands were shaking.

46

After I hung up with Detective Givens, I almost called her back immediately.

I'd never disrespected authority in that way in my life. And she clearly held some suspicions about me. How deep was I digging the hole for myself?

And I faced the prospect of looking for a human-size needle in a small-college-town haystack. A human-size needle who'd run out on me, leaving me to face her pursuer.

I checked my phone again. There were plenty of flights from Nashville back to Chicago, so I'd have no problem getting home and away from everything that had happened over the past day. My real life waited for me there. Predictable. Boring. Safe.

No cops. No Simon.

It sounded better than it had in months. Maybe years.

And then I remembered Renee.

I texted her.

> Just wanted you to know I'm leaving Kentucky today.
> Coming home. We can talk when I get there. If you want.

My thumb hovered over the "Send" button. I waited. Then waited some more. Then I hit SEND. I looked out the window.

Students passed by, men and women younger than me. They all looked happy. They all seemed to be smiling. I knew their lives weren't as blissful as they appeared, but I let myself think they were. If I could go back, if someone invented a time machine, I'd spend less time with my nose to the grindstone, less time marching in lockstep, my eyes on the horizon ahead.

Renee wrote back instantly.

Sure, let's talk. Are you safe?

I wrote back. Perfectly.

I didn't like the word. Or the sentiment. *Perfectly safe.* Is that all I wanted out of life—to be perfectly safe? But it seemed to have summed up everything in my life.

Safe. I was playing it safe.

Why?

I put the phone down, watched the crowds for a few more minutes, thought about the gap between them and me. The five years that had passed so quickly and had turned into a lockstep march toward . . . what? A mortgage and kids and a minivan?

I couldn't just go, not without looking around town a little bit.

I decided not to call Detective Givens back. She and I wanted the same thing—to find Morgan and convince her to turn herself in. I'd tried to get her to do that the night before. Admit she stole the ring, make an excuse, face the music. It wouldn't be too bad, would it?

And who was going to have a better chance of convincing her to turn herself in? Me? Or a cop?

Well, I wasn't really sure. She'd run from me that morning. She'd probably run from a cop. But I really wanted to try. And I meant what I told Detective Givens—I'd look for a little while and then give up. If I saw no sign of Morgan, I'd call Givens and then head to the airport when she was finished with me. So I started looking, hoping Simon kept off my trail.

A little bit of looking ended up taking hours. I drove systematically through town, starting on the south side, where I ate, and working my way north, past the edge of campus until I pretty much ran out of town to look through. As the day passed, I grew more and more frustrated and tired, feeling very much like a man on a pointless mission. It seemed highly unlikely I'd see Morgan again— in the town or anywhere else. And if I did find her and couldn't convince her to go to the police . . . what then?

Another night in the hotel? Another Houdini-like exit, leaving me with the key card and a trip through the breakfast buffet?

I remembered the flight times I'd looked at earlier. It was getting close to five o'clock, and if I started driving toward Nashville and the airport I could make the one at seven thirty or eight. I was ready to throw in the towel and call Givens when my phone rang.

I expected it to be the police calling me.

Or maybe Renee. Or my dad.

But the number on the car's display was unknown to me. From an area code I didn't recognize.

My hand shook a little as I reached out and pushed the button on the console that answered the call, placing it on speakerphone.

"Don't hang up," Morgan said. Her voice sounded tinged with emotion, with a nervous edge. But was it because she was talking to me—the guy she slept with and ran out on—or because she was on the run from the police and a crazy man?

"Oh, I won't," I said, shaking my head even though she couldn't see me. My frustration came out more than I intended. I'd stuffed a lot of emotion away as I drove around that day, and it was ready to emerge. "I have a ninety-minute drive to the airport, and I forgot to bring an audiobook. You should provide plenty of entertainment as I go. I like mysteries and thrillers, the crazier the better. I'm sure you've come up with something good."

"Don't be such a baby," she said. "You know I had to leave. You know I have to keep moving."

"Yeah, I guess so. You're Lucy, and I'm Charlie Brown. And I keep missing that football."

"I'm guessing you managed to get away from Simon," she said. "You sound unblemished."

"Did you know he was in the hotel?" I asked.

"I saw him this morning. When I left." She made a low, whistling noise. "I'm lucky he didn't see me. You won't believe it, but I was already having regrets. I thought about coming back and saying good-bye to you the right way. But when I saw him, then I knew I had to go. And go fast."

"You could have called. Clearly you had my number. And how did you get that, by the way?"

"I got it off your phone while you were asleep. And, yes, I thought about calling you and warning you. But, to be honest, I knew if Simon was occupied with you, then I'd be able to get away. I've had other things to do in town while I was here. They took longer than I thought. I don't know how long I can be here . . . or if I'll ever get to come back."

On either side of the road, corn grew taller than the car. In the distance, a farmer rode a combine, knocking the stalks down. The leaves would change soon. The bleak Chicago winter would close in on me.

"You're still in Wyckoff?" I asked.

"Kind of," she said. "You said you have a ninety-minute drive to the airport. Does that mean . . . ? Are you still in Wyckoff?"

"I'm just leaving. But I'm going to call the police first. They're interested in talking to me. Very interested. They want to talk to you too."

She didn't say anything else. I worried the call had dropped, since I was moving out into the middle of nowhere.

"Hello?"

"I'm here," she said. "Are you going to the police?"

"Soon."

"Well, I want you to do something for me. I know I don't have a leg to stand on."

"That's true. Especially since you left me to the whims of a crazy man with the temperament of a teething pit bull."

I heard faint breathing sounds, but that was it. "This is all very complicated."

"What is it?"

"Since you haven't left and you haven't turned me in to the police yet, I want you to meet me somewhere. I want to do something, to show you something. Then . . . then you'll see why I'm here and maybe you can help me end all of this."

"And this is why you came to Wyckoff in the first place?" I asked.

"Mostly. It will explain everything anyway. It's the only thing that can, I guess."

I gritted my teeth. I looked ahead, saw the horizon. The sun was going down, the sky transforming to reds and oranges. I flipped on the headlights. Nothing lay ahead but a long stretch of road and yet another airport.

"What do you think?" she asked. "I need your help. And, for better or worse, you're the only person I can trust right now. And after that, if you want to call the police, you can. I might call them. See, I think it will all make sense if you come and meet me."

"Where are you?"

"I think I left something in the hotel room. Did you find it?"

I tapped the breast pocket of my shirt. The photo.

"Why did you leave that there? Did you want me to find it and guess where you are?"

"Not really. I had the picture out . . . just to think about things. When I drove away, I realized I'd left it. Maybe, on some level, I wanted you to find it. I don't know. Things got crazy last night, didn't they?"

"They did."

"So . . . do you have it?"

"I do," I said. "You want it? Why do you want a photo of a place where you have horrible memories?"

"They're not all horrible."

I thought about my perfectly safe life again.

A long, perfectly safe Chicago winter with Renee. Deiced planes and dirty snow in the gutters. Making money with Dad.

"Is that where you are?" I asked. "Fantasy Farm? Why?"

Before she answered, I was already turning the car around.

47

Kimberly spent the afternoon in Wyckoff, using a desk at the police station. She called and spoke to Willard about what she'd learned at the Best Western. Then she took a nearly hour-long phone call from the mayor, who expressed her disappointment at what she called Kimberly's "inability to find these people." Kimberly hung up, shaking her head. Hughes came by and offered a sympathetic look, then said, "Bureaucrats."

Hughes also told her that she'd asked the county to send an officer to Fantasy Farm to see if anyone had shown up there.

"And?" Kimberly asked.

"He didn't see anything. It seems unlikely someone would go there. It's out of the way and abandoned. Private property technically, even though it isn't being used."

"No one ever goes there?"

Hughes thought about it. "I guess high school kids might go there to drink. But we haven't had any problems. It's kind of a dump."

"It wasn't anything fancy when it was open. My daughter liked the animals. My ex-husband liked that they served beer to the adults. I thought the place was a little run-down."

"Its heyday was when my parents were growing up. Before Six Flags and Kings Island and all those places."

"Makes sense."

Kimberly turned back to her laptop and started checking Morgan Reynolds's Facebook page again, looking for friends or acquaintances of hers who might still live in Wyckoff. She used people-finder software to find their phone numbers. A few people didn't answer, but then she reached one of Morgan's friends from college. Jamie Cassel had no idea Morgan had disappeared and hadn't spoken to her since the day they graduated.

"I kept meaning to call her, but I never did."

"Was she close to anyone else in college? Who were her best friends?"

Jamie provided four names and even a couple of up-to-date phone numbers, but the two women Kimberly reached told a similar story. They'd moved away from little Wyckoff years ago and had maintained only sporadic contact with their college friends, including Morgan.

Kimberly felt hungry again, and the carpal tunnel syndrome in her wrist hurt from using a chair that sat too low. The whole afternoon had slipped away with little to show for it. She had stood up to stretch, contemplating heading back to Laurel Falls and writing the trip off as a bust, when Hughes knocked gently and then opened the door.

"What's up?" Kimberly asked.

"I asked the county cops to keep an eye on Fantasy Farm, maybe cruise by again if they had the chance."

"And?"

"There's a car at a side entrance. It wasn't there before. A rental car. They're reaching out to the company to see who rented it, but we might want to check it out if you're game."

"How far away is it?"

"About twenty minutes."

"Let's go."

On their way out of Wyckoff, Kimberly's phone rang with Maria's ringtone. She asked Hughes if she minded, and Hughes said no. So Kimberly took the call, bracing herself for a short conversation with a disappointed child.

"Hey, baby."

"Hi, Mom."

"So? How was it? I would have called, but I'm in the middle of everything here."

Maria's voice brightened. "We won. Two to nothing."

"Oh, that's great. Really, I'm happy for you." Apparently being on the right side of the scoreboard tempered her disappointment over Kimberly's absence.

Kimberly breathed easier, listening while Maria gave a brief blow-by-blow of the game, including the spectacular save she made in the match's final minutes.

"And we're on our way to get pizza now," she said. A slight pause, then she whispered, "And Jennifer can't go. Bonus."

"I'm glad you're having a good time," Kimberly said, wishing she wasn't as happy as she was that Peter's new girlfriend was missing out on pizza and time with Maria.

"How long will you be away?" Maria asked. Her voice sounded small, childlike. During moments like that, she slipped back out of being a preteen and became a kid again. It sounded like she actually missed her mother.

"I'm not sure," Kimberly said. "But we're on our way to something we hope is important."

Please, Kimberly thought, *be important.*

There was a long pause. Kimberly listened for clues. She thought she heard music playing in the background. Then Maria said, "Well . . . you can go to my next match, right? Or the one after that?"

"I fully intend to."

"And then *we* can go out for pizza?"

"Do you like soccer or pizza more? Which is it?"

Maria laughed. "Do I have to pick?"

"I guess not."

Kimberly's phone beeped. Another call coming in. She checked the screen. *Brandon.*

"Shoot," she said.

"What's wrong?"

"Nothing. I'll call them back."

"If you have to go, Mom, it's fine. We're almost at the restaurant. And I know you have a job. And it's important."

"Okay. I'll call you tomorrow."

"Okay. Good night. I love you."

"I love you too."

Kimberly's phone beeped again. Kimberly pushed a button, hoping for an undefeated soccer season, anything to bring peace in her time.

"Kimberly? Sorry to bother you," Brandon said.

"That's okay. What is it?"

"I found out that . . ."

But the call dropped. It sounded like Brandon fell down a well without benefit of a splash.

"Brandon? Hello?"

She tried calling back, but the call dropped again.

"No service out here," Hughes said. "Country life."

"One of my colleagues," Kimberly said. "He said he found something out." She hit the "Call" button several times, and each time a "No Service" message mocked her from the screen. "Damn it."

"Do you want me to turn around?" Hughes asked. "If we head back to town, service will pick up."

"Yeah . . . but what about this amusement park?"

"Up to you," Hughes said. "It could be nothing."

Kimberly thought about it, her mind processing the choices. She trusted her gut, played the hunch. Whatever Brandon knew could wait.

"No," she said, "let's keep going. I want to check out this place right now."

48

I took the state road, heading east. The sun was sliding down the sky behind me, so as I drove the sky began to darken, the first faint stars popping up ahead of me along with a bright half-moon.

I'd lived in Chicago so long, I'd forgotten what it was like to be out in the middle of nowhere at nightfall. The trees and farmland pressed close to the road. I went miles and miles without seeing another car or even a house or a gas station. And the darkness felt heavy, like a physical presence descending on top of me as I drove. Reflectors on the berm flashed in my headlights. The beams occasionally caught the eyes of scurrying animals, a raccoon or an opossum that heard the car and dashed away.

As I drove, I thought about Morgan. I could have ended the whole thing by calling the police and letting them know where Morgan was and headed on my way, never looking back. As I'd told her, it might have been the best thing for her, to give the ring back and be protected from Simon.

But then what would become of her? She'd face charges for the theft. She'd have to deal with that during her mother's final days. She'd told me she quit her job.

And then there was the fact that I'd likely never see her again.

She'd promised some kind of answers at Fantasy Farm.

So I went to get them.

The GPS told me I was getting closer, that the site of the abandoned amusement park was coming up in less than ten minutes. I'd seen nothing for several miles, just trees and more trees. I thought the computer might be wrong. I seemed to be nowhere close to anything that might once have been civilization. But before I knew it, I saw a billboard-size sign, battered but standing, announcing the entrance to the park. It appeared as a dark shape against the darker night, and only as I came closer and the headlights picked it up did I see I was in the right place.

FANTASY FARM, the sign still read. FAMILY FUN FOR EVERYONE.

I turned left into the entrance to the park and came face-to-face with a low, padlocked gate. In the high beams, I saw it wasn't tall, would be easy enough for an adult or a child to climb over, and the chain securing it in place looked loose, meaning that with a little effort it could be pried apart so someone could slip through.

Another car sat at the entrance already, a gray sedan with Kentucky plates that I parked alongside. I assumed it was Morgan's rental, although I hadn't yet seen the vehicle she was driving. Before I turned the engine off, the headlights sliced through the gate and down the midway. I stared for a moment, looking for Morgan, looking for sign of her, but I saw only a series of squat buildings on either side of the midway, weeds and grasses growing through the cracked pavement. Empty beer bottles and soda cans littered the ground.

I turned the car off and climbed out. The ground was gravelly, and my shoes scraped against the small rocks, every noise amplified in the quiet air. The only other sound came from crickets and night birds. There was no traffic. No human sounds.

I went over to the gray vehicle. I wished I'd brought a flashlight, then remembered the app on my phone. I turned it on and waved my phone over the car, trying to see if there was anyone inside. There wasn't. Just some papers, a fast food wrapper, an empty soda can. Morgan could have just opened up the window and tossed all of the junk inside the park, where it would have had plenty of company. Or Billy could have come up from the hotel and had plenty of work to do, hauling it away.

I looked around the area and saw no one. I'd expected Morgan to wait for me, to tell me where to go or what to do since I'd never been to the place, and it was getting darker and darker. I thought about calling her name, hoping to summon her out of the night, but that seemed unwise. I wasn't sure why, but I didn't think I should call attention to myself out in the middle of nowhere.

I hesitated there, before the gate to Fantasy Farm. I could easily turn around and go back to town. Or I could call for help.

I checked my phone, intending to call Morgan back and ask her where she was, but there was no service. I walked in a circle, even going out into the road, hoping to catch a signal but couldn't.

A slight chill had descended with the darkness. And something rustled in the brush—a bird, a small animal.

I'd come that far. . . .

Once I'd made up my mind, I covered the short distance to the gate, quickly pulled it apart, and with a little effort squeezed my body through. I stood alone on the midway. I started walking, looking for Morgan.

49

My eyes adjusted to the dark.

I moved slowly down the midway. I wasn't sure what I expected to happen as I walked. Did I think a killer clown with a knife would leap out from behind a bush? Did I think I'd encounter the ghosts of long-forgotten park employees?

If anything, the remnants of the park brought back my own memories. On both sides of the midway I saw small, empty booths that once held games: a shooting gallery, a ring toss, an automated horse race that patrons could place bets on. All of them had either been torn out and removed or were in such disrepair as to be almost unrecognizable. Graffiti, little of it clever or interesting, covered every surface.

I felt a stirring of nostalgia in my chest, a fluttering as light as the wind that stirred the trees arching overhead. I remembered my dad taking me to the county fair every fall. He showed enormous patience then, walking by my side and handing me dollar bills as I tried my luck at games just like the ones I passed. After my mother left, we went back, both of us wandering through our lives a little like survivors of a bombing. I'm not sure he knew how to talk to me about what had happened, so going to the fair was his way of trying to cheer me up. I felt grateful for his patient efforts, and the last thing I wanted to do was get myself into some kind of trouble I couldn't get out of, to make my father face the prospect of losing me after everything he'd already been through.

The games and booths gave way to empty and abandoned rides. I saw what was left of a carousel, the horses long gone, and then a circular conveyance called Down to the Sea, where kids had pretended to steer tiny boats in about a foot of water. There were bumper cars, the skeletal remains of a tiny roller coaster, a series of stanchions that once held a Ferris wheel. I listened intently as I walked, looking from side to side. But I saw no sign of other people and heard little beyond the incessant chattering of crickets, the lone hoot of an owl. A car passed on the road far behind me, its engine a low hum as it went by.

I came to a crossroads of sorts where the main midway intersected another path. It took me a moment in the dark, but then I saw a signpost on the right, indicating with arrows where the park's other attractions lay, to guide the overwhelmed and confused parents who were shepherding their kids along. Most of the surface area of the signs had been graffitied, but I was able to tell through the sloppy spray paint that if I turned left, I'd end up at the water slide and swimming pool. If I turned right, I'd be heading toward the petting zoo.

I remembered Morgan crying in the night, her troubled memories of her mother specifically about the petting zoo. And the photo showed the same thing, so I turned that way.

I passed a padlocked bathroom and a former snack bar that someone had set on fire, leaving the sides scorched black, the comical image of a child eating an ice cream cone obliterated except for the smiling face.

Ahead I saw the outline of a rail fence and a small barn. Years had clearly passed since the park was last open, so maybe it was just my imagination playing tricks on me, but I would have sworn I smelled the sweet scent of hay and the ripe stench of farm animals reaching me as I moved closer. That was when a tall, slender figure emerged from the shadows of the barn. She walked over to the fence and waited for me until I got there.

"For a minute there I wondered if you'd remember where to find me." She leaned against the top of the weathered, decaying fence, looking as natural as if we were just hanging out at the ranch, preparing to exercise the horses. "But then I knew that was foolish to wonder. You seem like the kind of guy who listens and pays attention."

I came closer and leaned against the fence next to her. I looked past Morgan and peered into the darkness of the barn. "Yeah, I don't know if that's a good thing or not. Sometimes it's better not to hear everything."

"I'm glad you did," Morgan said. She reached out and placed her hand on my arm.

I wanted to pull back but didn't. Still my body tensed, something Morgan registered, her face showing surprise at my edginess.

"What did you think?" I asked. "Did you think I'd show up and . . . what? I'd be happy to see you?"

"Okay, I guess I can see that now."

"You should have seen it when you ran out on me. Hell, you've run off several times. The only reason I'm here is because you promised to clear everything up once and for all. You said you'd explain why you were in Wyckoff in the first place. So . . . let's get to it. It's dark, and there's a crazy man and the police looking for both of us. So this better be good. Really good."

Morgan glanced down at the ground, almost as though she wanted to rest her head against the top rail. I waited until she looked up again.

"Do you want to climb over the fence and have a look in the barn?"

"Why would I do that?" I asked. "Are we going to re-create your childhood?"

She leaned back. Even in the dark, I could see the hurt on her face. I hadn't meant to send my words out like a slap, but I was more frustrated than I realized.

"Okay," I said. "What's in there? Why am I going in the barn?"

She stepped back. "You wanted answers. They're here."

What choice did I really have?

So I took a step up, placing my foot on the lowest rail, and swung my body over, hoping the fence would hold. Once on the other side, I followed Morgan to the barn.

50

When we reached the opening to the barn, the two big doors stood wide and appeared on the verge of falling off their hinges. Morgan stopped. She looked into the darkness and then back at me. She dug around in the pocket of her hoodie and came out with the tissue-wrapped object, the one I'd seen back in the hotel room.

"The ring?" I said.

She nodded. "I wish I'd planned better, but everything has been a little chaotic." Her voice was somber, quivering slightly. In the darkness, the whites of her eyes were prominent, like a scared animal's. "I'm glad you're here. I really don't want to go in there alone."

"Why not?"

"It sounds crazy, I know. Because I've been in there already."

"You mean when you were a kid?" I asked. "Or . . ." I felt like I was one step behind, trying to keep up with someone who knew much more than I did. "Why exactly do you have the ring here? You said this was going to explain everything."

"In there. It explains everything."

"Then let's go in." I tapped my phone, activating the flashlight. I knew I sounded more confident than I felt. Sure, it was just an empty barn in an abandoned amusement park on a pleasant early

October night. But Morgan's anxiety had infected me. She knew why we were here, but she didn't want to go in.

Did I have something to be afraid of? And if so, what?

There was no other way to know. . . .

I stepped past her, holding the light in front of us. It cast a glowing cone over the barn floor, picking up decaying hay, dirt, a beer bottle. Off to the right, I saw a used condom, limp and tangled in the bright beam, and some small scattered droppings, likely from mice or rats. Something scurried off to the left, and I jerked the phone over that way, my heart rate accelerating, but the creature moved so fast the light couldn't catch it.

"Easy," Morgan said behind me.

"Easy?"

"Near the back there," she said. "On the left. That's where we're going."

"And do you mind telling me what we're going to see?" I asked. "Is there a giant monster waiting to eat me?"

"Not quite—"

She stopped speaking and spun around, facing the entrance to the barn.

I froze in place and whispered, "What is it?"

She held up her index finger.

We both stood there, like kids playing statues.

Just when I thought there was nothing going on, that we'd be able to continue toward whatever she wanted to show me in the back of the barn, I heard the noise. Footsteps. Heavy and not at all subtle. In the flashlight glow, Morgan's eyes widened farther than seemed possible.

I thought it was the police. Or maybe some kids hoping to have a good time, only to find adults there ruining their fun. There was no way the light hadn't been visible through the rickety wooden slats of the barn. I shut it off, but it was obvious we were inside.

I moved past Morgan, back toward the open doors.

She placed her hand on my arm, trying to stop me. "Wait," she said. "You don't know who it is."

"We're trapped in here anyway," I said. "What else can we do?"

I went over to the door, stepping carefully over the garbage, making sure not to kick anything. When I reached the entrance, I peeked out, moving my head slowly.

In the dim light, I saw a figure, a *large* figure, leaning against the top of the fence. He looked like a rancher in an old movie, the corrupt cattle baron who would do anything to see that his empire survived.

I wished I'd stayed inside the barn. I wished there were another way out.

But there wasn't. We were all face-to-face.

"Well, well," he said.

"Hello, Simon," I said.

51

With surprising ease and deftness for a man his size, Simon swung his leg up onto the fence rail and came over it, landing on both feet like a gymnast. He straightened and moved toward us, his jacket lifting away from his body in the light breeze.

I put my hand out instinctively, placing it in front of Morgan and moving her behind me. As though that would make any great difference.

He stopped a few feet away from me, looming before us like a giant tree. He smiled without showing his teeth.

"What do you know? This worked out better than I could have imagined."

Morgan moved forward, her body pressing against my hand. I pushed harder, keeping her back.

"What do you want?" I asked.

He stared at me for a moment like I was something he'd discovered under a microscope. "The laundry cart, right? You went out in the laundry cart, didn't you?"

"I preferred it to dealing with you."

He wagged his finger at me. "You should have worked with me. You could have told me what I wanted to know, and then you would have been done with it all. Now you're tied up with her. And whatever happens to her might happen to you."

"Maybe the police are on their way," I said, trying a bluff.

"How would the police even know where we are? I bet they're not coming by anytime soon." He looked to either side of me. "Judging from the shape of this place, they don't really care what goes on out here, so long as no one gets too crazy. And if things get crazy, we can hope it isn't too loud, so no one will hear."

"Why don't we all just head back to town?" I said. "We can talk in public. It's getting late and dark out here. We can barely see."

But Simon's attention left me. He looked past me, over my left shoulder, at Morgan. His eyes zeroed in on her as if there was nothing else in the world to look at.

"You know what I want," he said directly to her. "I made it clear in Nashville. There can be no doubt you understand what this is about."

The words almost sprung out of my mouth: *Give him the damn ring*. But I held back. Even though I found myself standing between the two of them, and even though it was painfully clear I was in as much jeopardy as Morgan was, it wasn't my choice to make. And, no, I didn't trust the guy. He didn't seem to be the kind of person who would keep his word or be satisfied with just getting one thing handed back to him. He seemed like the kind of guy who wanted it all, who wouldn't be content until he'd crushed everyone into dirt under his shoes.

Morgan must have read my mind.

"I don't believe you," she said. "I don't believe you'd ever leave me alone. You threatened me. You threatened my mother."

"And you killed my brother," he said. "Which is worse?"

"It's a big leap to say she's a murder suspect," I said.

"Oh, really? Hell, you're probably a suspect too. You're running around with her. Do you think that doesn't look bad?"

"Let him go, okay?" Morgan said.

"What?" I asked, looking over my shoulder at her. "No."

"Just let him go," she said. "He didn't have anything to do with this. He wasn't involved . . . except that he followed me here. But not because he knows what I've done. Let him go, just let him walk away, and then you and I can settle things."

Simon looked surprised. And then he shook his head. "How are we going to settle things out here?" he asked. "We're so far from where we started, there's no way we can end this. Not easily."

Then Morgan thrust her hand out. Simon jerked his head back, then furrowed his brow as he studied what she held.

I looked too. And I understood. The red tissue paper. The little package.

Simon snatched it out of her hand and started to unwrap it.

52

Kimberly quickly became disoriented as they headed down the dark state road. The sun was long gone, and the stars popped out like white dots against the black night. She wanted Hughes to drive faster, but she seemed to be going as quickly as was reasonably safe. The road wound and dipped, and Kimberly's stomach rose and fell with each hill.

"If it's really her there," Hughes said, "I hope we don't miss her."

"If it's her, I hope she's not alone. I'd like to talk to that dope Fields who's been chasing her around."

"You think he's involved?"

"I don't know what to think about him. But he's hitched his wagon to her for some reason."

Kimberly's phone rang again. It was Brandon. "He's trying again."

"Go ahead. Maybe we caught a tower."

She answered. "What's up, Brandon?" Kimberly asked. "This call may drop."

Kimberly thought she heard a baby squealing in the background. He was calling from home, working late hours. She hated to think of it, hated to think of the case cutting into everybody's time with family.

"I just heard from one of Giles's former employees, someone I called yesterday. A woman named Megan Bright. She worked for Giles for about eighteen months and then quit. She's in Memphis now."

"Yeah, yeah. What did she have to say?" Kimberly asked.

"Apparently, those two women Hatfield told us about weren't the only ones to have run-ins with Giles Caldwell."

Kimberly sat up straighter in her seat. She clenched her hand around the phone, squeezing it so hard it almost popped out of her grip. "Yeah?"

"Yeah. This woman felt the same kind of threat from Giles. But this time he actually put his hands on her."

53

Simon fumbled with the paper, moving so quickly I thought he was going to drop it in the dirt. But he held on, casting each layer of paper aside as he pulled it off. His eyes opened wide, a look of glee shining out of his face like a spotlight.

Finally, he held the ring in his giant hands, muttering to himself. He looked like a man who had no idea anyone else was nearby.

"Yes, yes, yes, yes," he said over and over, his voice low, the sound prayerlike.

I managed to slip past him while he was distracted. I looked down the midway. There was nothing between me and my car. If I simply ran—and I again assumed I could outrun Simon—I'd be out of the park and back to my car in a matter of minutes. I could drive off and call the police for help.

But I'd be leaving Morgan in Simon's hands. And I suspected the ring wasn't going to distract him for long.

I looked at the ground. An object caught the faint light from the moon and stars. A beer bottle.

"Okay, okay," Simon said.

I sensed movement behind me. I turned and saw Simon step closer to Morgan.

"What about the rest?" he asked.

"What rest?" Morgan asked.

"My brother," he said. "Where is he? I want the body. I want to bury him next to our mother. That's what they'd both want. Just tell me where he is. In the woods somewhere back home? In a ditch? Did you grind him up in a wood chipper? Or are you going to stand here and try to convince me that he's alive?"

"How can you talk about your own brother that way?" Morgan asked.

Simon lunged for her, reaching out and grabbing her arm and shouting one word in her face.

"Where?"

Morgan tried to pull away, tried to free her arm from his grasp, but couldn't.

"Where?"

I picked up the bottle.

I turned and, with one motion, brought it down on the back of Simon's head.

I'd never hit anyone with a bottle before. In the movies, the glass always shatters, and the guy on the receiving end of the blow is immediately knocked unconscious and slumps to the ground, incapacitated. But Simon must have had a stronger constitution than any of those movie characters because the bottle remained intact, flying out of my hand when it made contact with his head. Simon remained on his feet while letting go of Morgan.

He reached back and rubbed his head where I had struck him. Then he turned to face me. His initial movements were slow, but when he turned, he shifted into a higher gear. He came right at me, both hands out, clutching at my throat. His momentum carried him into me, and I fell backward, his body landing on top of mine and crushing the air out of my lungs.

His hands flailed. He gave up on trying to grab my throat and started swinging his fists, making as much contact with me as he did with the air. I bucked beneath him, trying to get away. But he was too heavy, so I started to fight back. I worked my right hand loose and swung at his head, making solid contact a few times and slowing down his onslaught.

Simon repositioned himself, shifting his weight to pin my right arm under his knee. He did, taking away my ability to punch at him. But he could still swing at me. And he did. Over and over.

He brought his right hand down against the side of my head once and then twice. I started to see the helplessness of my situation, that there was no way for me to escape. I was going to lie there, pinned like a bug, while a crazy man loomed over me, bashing me in the head until my brains started leaking out of my ears.

I squeezed my eyes closed, strangely detached as I contemplated what an odd place this was to die.

But then the punching stopped.

I thought for a moment Simon might be winding up for one big, final blow. But it never came. Instead I heard a thumping, like the sound of a baseball making good contact with a wooden bat. I opened my eyes.

Simon still loomed over me, but his arms went limp at his sides. His eyes fixed not on me but on some point in the dirt above my head.

And then he fell. Like a giant oak, he slowly tipped over and landed across my body.

That's when I saw Morgan. She stood there, her silhouette out-lined in the dark, holding the still-unbroken beer bottle.

For once she hadn't run off. For once she'd stayed.

She'd even saved me.

54

Brandon's call dropped. Again. He disappeared down the voice well.

"Shit. Brandon?"

"We're coming up on it," Hughes said.

"I lost the call."

Hughes slowed the car as they came around a bend. Kimberly squinted into the night, her eyes trying to make out the entrance to the park through the gloom. Then she saw it. A small driveway, a gate. Two civilian cars plus a police cruiser.

"This *is* in the middle of nowhere," Kimberly said.

"Pretty much everything out here is in the middle of nowhere. That's why your call dropped."

"Did you call for backup?"

"I let the county boys know we'd be out here. They must have sent someone. Slow night in the sticks, I'm sure."

Hughes parked next to the cruiser. A uniformed officer stood by the two civilian cars, a flashlight in his hand. He swept the beam back and forth around the vehicles, looking for something . . . anything.

Kimberly tried not to dwell on the dropped call. Brandon had something to tell her, something about Giles Caldwell putting his hands on an employee. A female employee. But since they were at the amusement park, it was time to concentrate on the task at hand.

They climbed out of Hughes's car. When they did, the uniformed officer came over, his flashlight pointing at the ground.

"What have you got?" Hughes asked.

"I found the first car at an entrance about a quarter mile away. Then I came over here and saw these two." The officer reached into his breast pocket and brought out a small spiral notebook. He flipped to the proper page. "The one at the other entrance is a rental, and so is this one. This other vehicle here is registered to a Simon Caldwell. Laurel Falls, Kentucky."

Hughes looked at Kimberly. "Your boy Fields is probably in one of the rentals."

"Morgan Reynolds would be in the other one."

Hughes turned to the officer. "Did you go in?"

"I haven't yet. And I haven't heard anything. It's a big place. Lots of spots to hide."

The officer sounded a little uncertain about the task of searching Fantasy Farm in the dark. Kimberly understood. It felt like they were the only three people left on planet earth.

"You ever been in there, Officer?" Hughes asked the uniformed cop.

"Not since I was five."

"Me either," Hughes said. "Okay, you ready, Detective?"

"Sure am," Kimberly said.

Hughes pointed to the officer. "Call county for a little more help. We might need it."

The officer followed instructions, using his lapel mike to call. When he was finished, they all squeezed through the gate and started down the midway.

55

I pushed out from under Simon and to my feet.

As I did, Morgan reached out and took my arm, helping me. When I got up on two legs, I wobbled briefly as my equilibrium came back. My hands went to my face, probing. I worked my jaw from side to side, checking for blood. I didn't see any on my hands, and all the moving parts seemed to be working. The longer I stood, the steadier I felt. The world remained still and untilted.

"Are you okay?" Morgan asked.

"I think so."

"Thank God," she said. "I thought he was going to kill you. And me."

"How is he?" I asked.

I looked down at the ground. Simon lay there like a felled oak. He was on his side, his face in a clump of hay. He was still. Very, very still.

I bent down, kneeling next to Simon. I took his arm, running my hand down it until I was able to slip my fingers under the cuff of his jacket and shirt. I pressed against his wrist.

I waited. And waited.

Nothing.

So I moved up to his neck. I placed my fingers against his throat, the way I was taught in the first aid class I took in high school. I remembered how easy it was to find a pulse. On a living person.

I pressed harder against Simon's skin, feeling his stubble against my fingertips.

"What is it?" Morgan asked.

"I don't think he's breathing."

"No, you can't say that."

"Morgan, I think he's dead." I pressed even harder, but I still felt nothing. "Whatever's going on, we have to call for help. We have to get an ambulance."

"Our phones don't work out here."

I stood up. "Then one of us has to go back to the road and get in the car and drive until they do work. Go. You do it. I'll wait here. Just go. Time is wasting. He might die. Or he might already be dead."

But she refused to move. She just stood there in the dark, shaking her head.

"I can't," she said.

"Bullshit." I dropped back down to my knees and pounded on Simon's chest a couple of times. "He needs help. I don't care if he is a piece of shit, we can't just let him die. Go get the police."

"I can't," she said.

"What do you mean you can't? You must have a car, right? Get help."

"I can't." She made a vague gesture in the direction of the barn. "I've done some things I can't come back from, Joshua. Bad things."

"You took a ring. Get the cops to help this man."

"It's not just the ring," she said. Then, quickly, she took a step closer to me. "And I'm about to do another bad thing."

I didn't see the bottle. I only saw her arm make a sweeping

motion toward my head. And then I felt it. The bottle. It made the same baseball-bat *thwump*.

Before I understood, I felt wobbly on my knees next to Simon, shaking my head.

I tried to get up. But then she swung again.

56

I tried to open my eyes.

They felt like they were glued shut. And weighed down by lead.

I opened my mouth to speak, my throat dry and cracked. I couldn't produce a sound. My heart raced. But I couldn't speak.

Someone spoke to me. Someone said my name. The words sounded distant and muffled, like they were coming from far away, down a long tunnel.

I had no idea what was going on.

Had hours passed? Days?

Someone said my name again. But I still couldn't move. I made no noise.

The voice saying my name sounded closer.

It sounded like a woman's. I tried to respond, thought I made a sound. But I couldn't open my eyes.

Suddenly I felt colder.

Someone came and wrapped a blanket around my body.

I made a noise.

"Mor . . ."

When my eyes opened, everything was bright.

Too bright.

I closed them again. It felt painful to squeeze the lids shut. The action put pressure on my brain and made my head hurt.

It didn't just hurt. It throbbed. Like a giant bass drum.

I felt nauseated, like I'd been traveling on rough seas.

A presence came close to me and said my name. "Mr. Fields?"

I groaned, keeping my eyes shut.

"Mr. Fields? Do you know where you are?"

"Hell."

Undeterred, she asked again. "Do you know where you are? Do you know why you're here?"

I chanced it, opening my eyes ever so slightly. The light came rushing in, but I fought it off. I saw a curtain attached to the ceiling. A woman wearing a colorful shirt, something so intense it hurt my eyes, leaned close to me. It wasn't hard to figure out where I was.

"Hospital," I said. "Emergency room."

"That's right," she said, drawing her words out like I was a kindergartner. "And do you know why?"

I almost said, *Head went boom*, but she might not appreciate that. And, truth be told, the events leading up to my hospitalization were still hazy.

"Someone hit me," I said.

"Yes, they did," she said, encouraging me.

"Am I okay?" I asked.

"The X-ray was negative."

"I had an X-ray?"

"On your head. You slept right through it," she said. "The doctor will be by in a minute. We're going to keep watching you closely."

"How long . . . ?"

"You've been here since Wednesday evening," she said. "It's Thursday morning now. Very early Thursday."

My eyes adjusted. I opened them more but didn't like the starkness of the room and promptly shut them again.

"Do you want to rest some more?" she asked.

"Yes."

"You won't be able to for long," she said. "There's someone who wants to see you."

I didn't know who she meant. Did she mean Morgan? Or someone else? I drifted back to sleep until the nurse came in again and told me I had to wake up. That's when the detective came in. That's when I started talking.

57

I lost track of time. I just poured the story out, welcoming the distraction from the throbbing in my head. It felt good to have someone to listen to everything that had happened. The detective mostly listened, interjecting with questions only when she had to.

I thought I'd reached a stopping point.

"What time is it?" I asked. "I don't even know."

"It's getting near daylight," she said.

She sat in the chair next to my bed. She looked patient, if a little tired. Dirt stained her flat shoes, and I imagined she'd been wandering around in the amusement park, kicking up dust, trying to make sense of everything that had happened out there.

"That's quite a couple of days," she said.

"More than I bargained for."

"So . . . do you know where she went, Mr. Fields?" the detective asked.

She didn't use a notebook to take down my words. She didn't hold a recorder.

I hoped she had a good memory. My mind still felt fuzzy.

"You mean after she hit me on the head with an empty bottle?" I asked. "Do I know where she went after that? No, I don't. I have no idea."

I looked over at the little table next to the bed. A water pitcher, its sides beaded with condensation, sat just out of reach. My lips were cracked and dry. I suddenly wanted water more than I'd ever wanted it before.

I scooted over a couple of inches and reached for the pitcher. My hand shook.

Detective Givens stood up. "Here. Let me." She filled the plastic cup that sat next to the pitcher and handed it to me. "Can you get that? Do you need to sit up more?"

"I'm good."

I guzzled the water. It was sweet relief. The cold swept through my body. When I'd emptied the contents of the cup, Detective Givens poured more, which I also swallowed with greed.

"Thank you," I said. "That helps."

Givens remained standing close by the side of the bed. I saw her hands were empty of jewelry. No wedding ring, just a functional digital watch.

"So you have no idea where she might go?" Givens asked. "She didn't mention anything? No places she wanted to travel to?"

I strained my mind. "No. She apparently doesn't like to tell me much."

The detective nodded at my scraped-up knuckles. "A pretty good struggle out there, wasn't it?"

"Yeah, I'm not a skilled fighter." I tried to read her face. She kept it blank. My stomach turned over, and something cold seized my bowels. More details came back to me. I remembered kneeling over the man, pumping his chest. "Is he okay? Simon? He wasn't . . . I wasn't sure he was okay."

The detective studied me. She knew what she was doing. She wanted to make me wait. I wanted to shout *Just tell me!* But I didn't. My head still thumped. I couldn't yell even though I wanted to.

"Mr. Caldwell took a pretty good knock on the head," she said, her face still revealing little.

"And?"

"You're worried about him?" she asked.

"I am. I hit him. And then . . . then she did too. I thought . . . he looked like he might be pretty bad. Can you just tell me?"

She waited a long time. It felt like hours. "He's alive, if that's what you're wondering. He got it worse than you. Last I heard, he hadn't regained consciousness yet. That's all I know."

A trickle of relief flowed through me. He wasn't dead. Simon wasn't dead, and Morgan hadn't killed him.

But it didn't sound like he was doing well either. I guess I didn't know what Morgan had done after I was incapacitated. Had she smacked him again?

I flexed my hand, felt the ache in my knuckles.

"Will you let me know when you get an update?" I asked.

Givens nodded. "Do you know what else we found out there? In the amusement park?"

Why did it always feel like a trick when a cop asked a question?

I tried to think of the correct answer, but I came up empty.

"What?" I asked.

"What was Simon looking for?"

"The ring? You found that ring?"

Givens nodded. "We did. And do you know where we found it?"

Again, I tried to think of the answer. Who had the ring last? Simon did. But he couldn't have held on to it while we were fighting. His hands were free as he swung at me.

Could he have slipped it into his pocket before he came after me? Before I hit him?

"Did Simon have it?" I asked. "Look, Morgan wanted to give it back. She said she brought me out there to resolve everything, to put an end to it."

"And how did she intend to do that? What did she mean?"

"I don't know," I said. "We started fighting before any of that happened."

"So you don't know where we found the ring?"

"I don't."

Again, the blank look. The cool consideration of my words.

I felt like a piece of art she wanted to buy.

"You don't seem to know much, do you, Mr. Fields? Either you've been kept in the dark, or you're lying to me."

"I don't know where you found the ring. You found me, and I was out cold. Right?"

She showed nothing as she thought about that.

Then she said, "We found it in the barn. It was sitting on top of a shallow grave. The one where Giles Caldwell's body was buried."

58

Kimberly watched Joshua Fields's face as she delivered the news. The man was already green around the gills from the blow to the head and the concussion he was suffering from. But when she told him about the discovery of Giles Caldwell's body, he looked even sicker.

He closed his eyes and gritted his teeth. He lifted his hand and placed it against his forehead. He said nothing.

"Mr. Fields?" Kimberly asked. "Did you know the body was there?"

"No."

"How did you end up out there?"

"Like I told you, she told me to meet her there. She said she could explain everything if I went."

"What did she explain?"

He kept the hand on his forehead. "I feel sick."

"What did she explain?"

"Can you call the nurse?"

As if she'd been listening outside, the nurse appeared. She didn't look at Kimberly, but she said, "I think he needs his rest."

The nurse picked up an emesis basin and placed it under Joshua

Fields's chin. Kimberly left the room. She'd heard enough for the time being.

Later that morning, Kimberly found the woman at the Spring Street Elementary School. She worked as a teacher's aide and agreed to meet Kimberly before the school day started.

Kimberly checked in at the front desk, showing her badge to the receptionist. She hadn't slept all night, and her eyes burned with exhaustion. She fought off a yawn. After she'd waited a few minutes—and caught a whiff of the familiar smell of simmering cafeteria food—Elaine Adams came into the lobby, a young, pretty, slender woman who wore her curly red hair pulled back. Kimberly supposed that gave the children less to grab on to.

They shook hands and stepped through a set of double doors, then settled on a bench just outside the main entrance of the school. Elaine wore tall boots and an oversize sweater. She blinked a lot. Nerves? Who wouldn't be unnerved by an out-of-town detective showing up at their place of work?

"I saw the news about Morgan on Facebook," Elaine said. Blink. Blink. "Is there any new information? Do you know what happened?"

"Have you seen or heard from her?" Kimberly asked.

"Not since high school, really. We were friends then, but I went away to college, and she went here to Henry Clay. We saw each other sometimes during the summer. Then I moved back here two years ago, but she was over in Laurel Falls then, so we didn't see much of each other."

"So you haven't seen or heard from Morgan recently?"

"No. We're friends on Facebook. I wish her happy birthday and all that. She seemed to have a good job. Better than being a teacher's aide here."

"So you knew her in high school?"

"And junior high."

"We've heard she had a rough childhood. Is that true?"

Elaine nodded eagerly. She looked like she'd been waiting to tell someone about Morgan's childhood for years. "Her mom had a lot of problems when we were growing up. Her parents got divorced when Morgan was young, before I knew her. And her mom . . . I got the feeling she never got her head on straight after the divorce. She was an irresponsible parent."

"How so?"

"She drank. Then drugs. She wasn't abusive so much. I wouldn't say that." Elaine lifted her hand to her mouth and drew her index finger over her lips as if considering what to say next.

"Was she neglectful?"

"Yeah, that's it. That's the word for it. Just . . . neglectful. That might be worse in a way. Who knows?"

"What form did the neglect take?" Kimberly asked.

"Just . . . she'd be out with a bad crowd of people, and Morgan would be home alone. She'd have to wake up and get herself off to school because her mom was sleeping it off. My parents used to have Morgan over for dinner when they could, and then my mom would send her home with leftovers. That kind of thing."

"She must have been grateful for that."

Elaine shook her head, but she smiled as she did. "You don't know Morgan very well. You don't know how prideful she is. See, all that time, while we were really good friends and all of this was going on, she never talked about it. I almost never went inside her house either. I almost never saw her mom. Morgan always said everything was fine. I could tell it wasn't, but I respected that she didn't want to talk about it."

"But you knew?"

"My aunt worked at the school we went to. South High. I heard things." Elaine raised her arms, gesturing to everything around them. "You know what a town like Wyckoff is like. It's small. It's tough to hide things here. When Morgan went into foster care, we all heard about it."

The wind kicked up, scattering some fallen leaves across their feet and under the bench. A muffled announcement came over the PA, the words lost to the two of them outside. "She went into foster care? When was that?"

"You didn't know that?" Elaine asked. "You're the police."

Kimberly wanted to explain how tough it is to know everything about everyone, but she held her tongue. "We're just starting to learn about Morgan. We've been looking for her and looking for her boss. You know about that, right?"

"Right. I heard." She looked sad as she thought about all of it. "Well, this was in high school. When we were about fifteen. And then . . . maybe another time, when we were seventeen. It wasn't long. Morgan was gone for three months or so the first time. And then the second time . . . maybe it was more like six or seven months. The second time she came back and seemed pretty happy about her experience. She raved about her foster mother, about how caring and protective she was. She told me it had been a long time since someone paid so much attention to her, and she was sad that she couldn't stay with her permanently. I guess compared to her own mother, the foster care families must have looked amazing. Living in a house where you're practically neglected makes the grass greener everywhere else."

"It's all relative, right?"

"Right."

"So you knew her mother then?" Kimberly asked.

"Better when we were younger. Like I said, once the big problems started, she became withdrawn. I mean, she'd be holed up in the house. Drunk. Or who knows what else." Elaine rubbed her hands together. Her nails were short and unpainted. "It's a shame. She was nice to me when we were younger. I liked talking to her. You know how you can kind of enjoy talking to someone who isn't your parent more than your own mom?"

"I do, yes."

"Morgan's mom was like that for me. She just . . . Well, my parents were so boring, and she seemed so full of life. At least back then. Ava. Ava Reynolds."

"What about other friends from growing up? Are many of them in touch with Morgan?"

"Probably a few. But our friends . . . they didn't go to college. They married young, had kids. It wasn't my scene. Or Morgan's. She overcame whatever went on with her mom and went to college. I was so happy to see her succeeding," Elaine said. "I moved back, but I've made some different friends. And I'm not sure I'm going to stay here. I don't want to be a teacher's aide in Wyckoff all my life."

Kimberly turned to the parking lot. A few cars pulled in, parents eager to drop off their charges and get to work. Elaine checked her watch.

"Back to the grind?" Kimberly asked.

Elaine sighed, her shoulders rising and falling inside the sweater. "I do like the kids. Most days. Most of the time. And I want to have my own someday."

"It's the best roller coaster you'll ever ride," Kimberly said as they both stood up. "For what it's worth, Morgan and her mother seem to have patched things up recently."

Elaine remained still, staring back at Kimberly like she'd started speaking in tongues. A cloud drifted in front of the sun, casting a faint shadow over the front of the school.

"What did I say?" Kimberly asked, noticing the confusion on Elaine's face.

"That's not possible."

"What's not?" Kimberly asked.

"It's not possible. About Ava. About Morgan's mother."

"Why not? Morgan moved to Nashville to live near her."

Elaine shook her head. "That's just not possible. Not Morgan's mom. Not Ava. That just can't be."

59

They kept me a whole day for observation. They said I had a concussion, and something on the X-ray concerned the neurologist, a
middle-aged man with an untrimmed goatee. He ordered a CAT
scan, which made me nervous but not as nervous as if I'd had to go
inside a closed-in MRI machine. The results were normal—no
bleeding in my brain—but he wanted to observe me more closely,
so I spent the day lounging around my room, watching bad daytime TV and passing in and out of sleep.

As darkness fell, I realized I'd never spent the night in a hospital before. Not since my birth. I had stitches once when I was in the
third grade. That was about it.

I had no idea what a lonely place a hospital could be.

And on the few occasions when I dozed off, I slept fitfully.

Nurses came in and out, checking my vital signs. My roommate, a man who had suffered a neck injury in a construction accident, moaned and groaned throughout the day but never woke up
or spoke. No one came to visit him.

When I did manage to sleep, I dreamed about the events in the
amusement park. I dreamed about my hands on Simon's body,
swinging at him, bashing him. Or I dreamed about being chased
through the dark, prey to some unknown predator.

When I woke, I stared at the ceiling, listening to the ambient noises of the hospital. Beeping machines, wheeling carts. The low voices of nurses and orderlies in the hallway. My roommate's agonized grunts.

Morgan.

Why was that body in the park? Why did she lead me there?

Around eight thirty that evening, Friday, Detective Givens came back and grilled me about Morgan all over again. She asked the same questions several times. *Where did she go? Did she say anything about where she might be heading?*

Over and over, I said I didn't know.

Givens nodded a few times. She became quiet, but I knew she had more to say. So I waited.

Finally, she said, "You said Morgan told you her mother was sick, right?"

"She did."

"And that's why she moved to Nashville?"

"Yes, to take care of her. After she quit her job."

"Did she say what was wrong with her mom?" Givens asked.

I tried to remember. "I think so. Cancer? She gave the impression it was terminal."

Givens reached into her jacket pocket and brought out a folded sheet of paper. She unfolded it, looked it over, and then passed it to me.

I read it once and then again. It was an obituary, printed from a newspaper Web site. My brain must have still been moving slowly, because it took a moment for the name to register. Then it clicked.

"Ava Reynolds," I said.

"Do you know who that is?" Givens asked.

I scanned the paper again. I saw one relative mentioned as a survivor. Morgan Reynolds, loving daughter.

"This is from when?" I asked.

"See the date?"

I found it. Three years earlier. Morgan's mother had been dead three years.

My head immediately started to throb again. Even worse than earlier.

Had Morgan told me a single thing that was true?

"Is this supposed to make me feel better?" I asked.

"I thought if you knew the truth, you might remember more details," she said.

I handed the paper to her. "It's not like that. I'm not holding anything back."

"Fair enough. Maybe you should rest."

But I finally asked a few questions of my own.

"Do you think Morgan killed Giles Caldwell?"

Givens stared down at me in my hospital bed. She looked sympathetic, kind even. She spoke in a calm way and seemed willing to wait for information to come to her in its own time. But her apparent lack of judgment concerning my actions had another effect. It made me feel like a sap, a sucker who had stumbled into something bigger and more complicated than he could handle. And now I had to sit back and let the grown-ups straighten it all out.

"We're not jumping to any conclusions," she said. "We're going to examine the crime scene. We're going to do an autopsy. We hope there will be more information when we do those things."

"I know, Detective. I know. But . . . did she kill him?"

She studied me again. "You don't want the public relations answer, do you?"

"No."

She cleared her throat, checked her watch. "You tell me, Joshua. *She* knew where the body was. *She* brought you to the body, saying it would explain everything. *She* took off before the police arrived. She placed the ring on the body. It was a place she knew of from growing up here. She loved it so much she told you about it."

The detective lifted her hands and held them out in front of her body as if to say *What more do you need to know?*

I shrank down into the pillows. I felt small. Like that eight-year-old getting stitches under the emergency room lights.

"How did he die?" I asked.

"We can't tell yet."

"Can you tell anything?" I asked.

She nodded. "We suspect foul play."

I wished I could sink further, but there was nowhere else to go.

Givens leaned closer to the bed. Her phone beeped twice, but she ignored it.

"If you want some free advice, I'll offer you some," she said. "You're not out of the woods on this yourself, Mr. Fields. You were with her. You were at the scene where the body was found. You say you just met in the Atlanta airport, but we intend to make sure of that."

"You think I'm lying?"

"I think everybody is lying until I know they aren't. And I have an unsolved death on my hands and a woman who keeps running away."

I felt sick again. Not like yesterday morning when I vomited into the emesis basin and then onto the floor, an effect of the concussion. I felt real fear. Had Morgan left me holding the bag? Would I face an investigation, an arrest, maybe more, over the death of this man I didn't know?

"Do I need a lawyer?" I asked. Then I thought, *If you have to ask that question of a cop, you probably do.*

"You can head on home when they clear you to travel," Givens said. "But stay in touch. We've notified Chicago PD about you. They'll be keeping an eye. And don't leave Chicago without letting us know."

"I have a job."

"We know. We'll be keeping an eye on the places you travel if you do. And we've got the word out about Morgan, and she'll probably be brought in soon. If not, she's going to spend the rest of her life on the run. You want to stay away from that, or it's going to get even deeper even faster."

I knew she was right. I just hated giving her the satisfaction of saying so.

I nodded the tiniest bit, accepting the truth in my silent way.

"But what about . . . Simon?"

"You mean are you going to be charged with anything?"

"Yes."

"Like I said, head on home, and we'll be in touch."

And that's exactly what I did, flying back to Chicago and my regular life the next afternoon.

PART THREE

60

Kimberly hung up the phone, ending her call with the medical examiner's office in Louisville. She'd been back in Laurel Falls for two days, following every path possible to find Morgan Reynolds, officially a "person of interest" in the death of Giles Caldwell. So far, they'd found nothing worthwhile. A few false alarms trickling in, people claiming to have seen her at various points around the country. But none of it panned out. She'd pulled a complete Houdini act after she smacked Joshua Fields over the head with an empty beer bottle at Fantasy Farm.

When she ended her call Brandon came across the room and plopped down in the empty chair next to her desk. He wore a polo shirt and dark pants. His cheeks looked rosy, his eyes fresh.

"Sleeping better?" she asked.

"A miracle has occurred," he said. "The baby has slept through the night twice in a row."

"Party time."

"I know. I almost didn't want to tell you because I'm afraid I'll jinx it. But then again, I'm so well-rested and happy, I want to tell the world."

"Enjoy it while you can," she said.

Kimberly was happy too. She'd found time to take Maria out to dinner the night before, just the two of them. And it had been exactly the distraction Kimberly needed. Maria talked about soccer and school and friends, and even let slip the name of a boy she had a crush on. Kimberly played it cool, absorbing the information without comment, and then went on to discuss horror movies they might watch later in October. The night felt chilly, the wind blowing, and Kimberly sensed the seasons turning, the world moving on. Would they have Morgan Reynolds in custody before Halloween? Thanksgiving? Christmas? Or would they ever find her?

"Was that Louisville with our autopsy results?" Brandon asked.

"It was." Kimberly looked down at her notes, even though she didn't need them. "Our first impressions were correct. Official cause of death on Mr. Giles Caldwell—manual strangulation."

Brandon whistled. "Wow."

"No other significant injuries. Some marks on the backs of his legs and torso, likely from being dragged out of the house and thrown in a car. Then being dumped on the ground at Fantasy Farm."

"Good thing the petting zoo is closed. I'd hate for the kids to find a corpse among the chickens and goats."

"Right. He wasn't intoxicated at the time of his death either. Apparently, though, Giles's heart was in shit shape. Mostly clogged arteries and some fluid in the lungs. He was cruising for a heart attack. In fact, that might have made it easier to strangle him. He didn't have the cardiovascular capacity to hold out very long."

"Could make it easier for a woman to do the deed."

"Exactly. Not much else to report. The time of death matches what we know from Morgan Reynolds's whereabouts. He likely died last Thursday night, had been in the well-fertilized ground at Fantasy Farm since shortly after his death. They took hair and fiber samples, so we can match them to samples from Morgan Reynolds's home and car. . . . And to her, if she ever resurfaces."

"And I guess there's no other real news?"

"Nope." Kimberly flipped her notebook shut and pushed it aside. "I'm going to have to tell Simon Caldwell his brother's official cause of death. He's supposed to be home today. Apparently, Morgan Reynolds hit him much harder than she hit Joshua Fields. Simon's concussion was pretty severe, and he's had some short-term memory loss. He may need therapy, but he's being discharged."

"He's probably in a great mood."

"I'm sure." She paused, thinking over the last couple of days. "It's possible he just feels like crap, but it's weird that he hasn't been bugging us at all. Maybe the bottle knocked some sense into him. Or maybe he's just happy no one's pressing assault charges against him."

"Not even the kid at the hotel?"

"He doesn't want to bother. So Simon's in the clear right now. There's a case to be made for intimidation, I guess, but given what everyone's been through . . ."

Brandon nodded. He placed his thumbnail between his two front teeth. He appeared to be thinking of something.

"What?" Kimberly asked.

"What are we thinking about him as a suspect in Giles's death?"

"Who? Simon?"

Brandon nodded, and Kimberly took her time answering. After talking to Steven Hatfield and getting an earful about Simon, she seriously considered him a suspect in his brother's death. He had the temper and the track record. Even if the will cut him out, he could contest it. At the same time, so much of what had transpired over the past few days and so much of what they'd learned pointed toward Morgan Reynolds.

Kimberly wasn't willing to entirely let go of anything yet. Not until the case was signed, sealed, delivered.

"I'm keeping my options open," she said.

"Lots of unlikable people aren't killers."

"Yeah. And lots of unlikable people get killed."

"You mean people like Giles Caldwell?" he asked.

"Yeah. Dudes who threaten women. I'm going to ask Simon about his brother's employees, especially Megan Bright, the one you found. Giles actually laid hands on her, grabbed her by the arm hard enough to leave a bruise when they argued at work. I don't like any of that. Hatfield's clammed up, started referring us to the company lawyer. I guess he's worried about the word getting out or someone getting sued."

"It's bad PR to be associated with a guy who roughs up women. Is that why the mayor has backed off?"

"What a strange coincidence, right? So I'll go see what Simon knows. If anything."

"Do you really think Simon is going to tell you something useful? Or anything at all?"

Kimberly laughed. "Will anyone ever tell us anything useful? I try to keep my expectations low. That way I'm pleasantly surprised when good things happen."

61

Simon Caldwell opened the door of his town house and blinked against the midday sun. The air remained cool, the wind crisp. Simon's neighbors already had two pumpkins and a bale of hay decorating their stoop, while his own displayed two discolored newspapers and an old phone book.

Simon stepped back, out of the light. Either his concussion was making him more sensitive to brightness, or he was just sick and tired of talking to cops.

"Can I come in?" Kimberly asked, stepping forward.

"A personal visit? You never returned my calls before."

"I returned as many as I could. Can I come in and talk to you?"

Simon just grunted, and she took that as assent.

Inside, the blinds were drawn, the surfaces cluttered by empty glasses and dirty dishes and stacks of mail. He wasn't a tidy man. No way all of it had accumulated in the time since his brother disappeared. They went into the living room and sat on opposite ends of an overstuffed sofa. Simon wore sweatpants, white socks, and a loose, oversize sweatshirt advertising his support for the Kentucky Wildcats.

Simon kept his head down. Kimberly saw no bandages or other signs of injury until she glanced at his knuckles. They were scabbed, healing from his battle at Fantasy Farm, just like Joshua Fields's knuckles in the emergency room. *Boys being boys.* How many of the crimes she investigated came down to that? *Boys being boys.*

But then it was also possible Morgan Reynolds was the person who'd committed murder.

Kimberly told Simon about his brother's cause of death, as well as the information about his bad heart. Simon listened without looking at her, and she wondered if he was hearing her at all, or if the effects of the concussion were causing him to completely zone out and miss what she was saying. She paused, giving him a chance to speak.

Finally, he said, "He ate a lousy diet. I knew that."

"It looks that way."

"But that doesn't mitigate the cause of death. She killed him. It's murder."

"I'm not ruling that out," Kimberly said.

Simon looked up at her then, their eyes meeting for a moment, and he seemed to be seeing her for the first time not as an adversary but as an ally. Kimberly knew the feeling might not last, but it was there. She tried to take advantage of it.

"I was hoping you were up for a couple of questions," she said. "Specifically, I wanted to know if your brother ever mentioned an employee of his named Megan Bright."

Simon stared at her, his cheeks dotted with gray stubble. The skin around his jowls hung slack and loose, and he seemed to have aged a decade since she'd last seen him.

He shook his head from side to side.

"You don't know her at all?"

"No, I don't. Why? Is she missing too?"

"No, it's not that. She worked for Giles a couple of years ago. Apparently they had a disagreement over some additional work she had done. She says he'd promised to pay her but refused once the work was complete."

Simon grunted.

Kimberly tried to determine if the grunt was because his head hurt or because he was tired of answering questions about his brother's treatment of his employees.

"You don't know anything about this?" Kimberly asked.

"My brother kept me at arm's length from his business affairs. A long arm's length."

"So you don't know about this woman's claims?"

"I don't."

Kimberly waited. The man across from her looked too miserable to be hiding anything. And what Steven Hatfield told her lined up with what Simon was saying—his brother kept him away from the business.

"She says Giles grew aggressive," Kimberly said. "Physically aggressive. He grabbed her by the arm, and she had to pull away. And flee. This happened after hours one night in the office, when everyone else had gone home. She resigned from the company the next day and never went back."

"But she never filed a lawsuit or anything?" Simon asked. "A harassment claim?"

"She didn't. She says she was scared. Had he ever been violent with women?"

"I don't know."

"You don't know? Do you think he was capable of something like that?"

Simon reached up and rubbed his temple. Then he gently probed around on the back of his head, grimacing slightly as he did so. "I don't know what you want me to say. I suppose you're trying to make a case that this Morgan Reynolds killed my brother in self-defense."

"I'm not making any case at this point," she said. "I'm exploring all avenues."

"Well, you'll have to explore that avenue without me." He rubbed his temple again.

Kimberly felt a measure of sympathy for the man. He'd lost his brother. He'd been attacked in the amusement park. But she also couldn't dismiss his single-minded pursuit of Morgan Reynolds, a pursuit that led to an innocent college student getting beaten up.

"Okay, Mr. Caldwell," Kimberly said, "I'll let you rest. We may need to talk again as the investigation proceeds. I'm sure you understand that."

"You haven't found that woman yet?" he asked. "I was hoping she'd be brought in quickly and all of this would be over."

"Sometimes it's slow. Especially when someone doesn't want to be found."

Kimberly stood up, ready to go. Simon stayed on the sofa.

"I figured you were here to read me my rights or something," he said. "I was about to call my lawyer."

"I told you the guy in the hotel isn't pressing charges. And neither is Mr. Fields. Given the circumstances of your brother's death . . . and everything you've been through . . ." He continued to rub his temple. She thought he looked paler than when she'd first come in the door. Kimberly feared he was about to pass out. She leaned down and asked, "Do you need help, Mr. Caldwell? Can I call somebody for you?"

"I'm fine," he said. "I have pills. Pain pills. I'll take a few of those and go back to sleep."

"Then don't bother getting up," she said. "I'll let myself out."

"And . . . thanks. I know . . . I know I didn't make your life any easier over in Wyckoff. Thanks for working out the charges or whatever."

"Just feel better, Mr. Caldwell."

"I suppose the Nashville Police will want to talk to me about the other thing," he said before Kimberly left the room.

"What other thing?" she asked, turning.

Simon stopped rubbing. "The Nashville thing? The thing with Morgan Reynolds's mother?"

Kimberly came back and sat down on the sofa again. "What about her mother?"

"Remember? She says I went down there and threatened her? The mother?"

"Yes, I remember. But her mother is dead. Has been for three years. How could we charge you with threatening a dead woman?" Kimberly had never asked such a question before. "Is there something I don't understand? I figured Morgan Reynolds was lying, trying to make Joshua Fields feel sorry for her. What are you saying?"

He picked at a loose thread on his shirt. "Well, maybe I'll regret being honest about this. . . . Look, I didn't threaten the woman. I went by Giles's office that Monday after he disappeared. Somebody told me he and Morgan Reynolds were having a dispute over money." He pointed at Kimberly. "I called you. Five times. But you didn't answer or call back. Five times. I could sue you all for neglect. Or dereliction. You just brushed me off."

"Somehow you ended up talking to this woman you say is her mother."

"It was a Monday afternoon. Look, I didn't know the woman was so sick. If I'd understood that . . . Well, I have my limits too. But I did talk to her. I asked her the questions I wanted to have answered. But I never threatened anyone. Certainly not a woman who was so frail."

"Did you hear me clearly, Mr. Caldwell?" She wondered if the blow to his head had scrambled his brains. "Morgan's mother is dead. You must have talked to someone else in Nashville."

"Her . . . mother . . ." He reached up to his head again, but this time he appeared to be confused instead of in pain. "No, not her mother." He stared into space for a moment.

Kimberly remained quiet, letting him think, even though she wanted to shake the answer out of him.

"Her foster mother," he said. "That's who it was. Her foster mother. The woman didn't really understand what I was talking about. Not very much of it."

Her foster mother?

Kimberly went back to the conversation with Ashley Clarke. The comments about a rough patch in Morgan's childhood. And then Elaine Adams had reported the same thing. Foster care. During high school.

And how much she liked one of the families she stayed with.

Had she reconnected with that woman?

"How did you find this woman?" Kimberly asked. "How did you know about her?"

Simon shook his head. Slowly. Carefully.

"I didn't find her," he said. "She found me. She called me up on Monday afternoon and said she wanted to talk to me about her daughter. When I got there, I didn't learn a damn thing."

62

Kimberly recalibrated. Instead of merely showing up to inform Simon Caldwell about his brother's cause of death, she was suddenly learning new information.

"Her foster mother called you?" she asked. "Why?"

Simon leaned back, easing his body against the large sofa cushions. For a moment, his imperious demeanor returned. Except for his ragged, sickly appearance, he looked like an emperor preparing to make a pronouncement.

"You'd like me to tell you these things," he said. "You'd like me to admit to all kinds of stuff, wouldn't you? Are you rethinking? Trying to get me for intimidation or obstruction or something?"

Kimberly hid her frustration. So often questioning witnesses felt like the days of Maria's Terrible Twos, when even the simplest task—putting on clothes, pouring juice—turned into an epic battle of wills with an utterly illogical individual. She'd grown to temper her expectations for adults, knowing they could be as recalcitrant and stubborn as children. And just like with Maria, no matter how much she wanted to reach out and slap the smugness off Simon Caldwell's face, she knew she couldn't.

"Mr. Caldwell, anything you tell us about Morgan Reynolds or any circumstances concerning Morgan Reynolds will only help us solve the case sooner. Don't you want that? A suspect in your brother's death brought in and questioned fully?"

"I had other things in mind," he said.

"I'll pretend I didn't hear that," Kimberly said. "Your ham-handed approach to people connected to this case isn't my highest priority right now. So why don't you do us all a favor and tell me about this call from Morgan's foster mother?"

Simon remained reclined, his lips drawn wide in a smirk. But then something passed across his face, a weariness or resignation similar to what Kimberly had seen when she first came in.

"Okay," he said, flipping his hand in the air as though shaking water off of it. "If it helps you nail that bitch." He took in a deep breath and went on. "Fine. Her mother or whoever she is called me because I'd been down to Nashville on that first Monday when you didn't call me back, trying to find Morgan. Asking her friends and anyone else I could find where she was. And, yes, I was . . . How did you put it? Ham-handed? I can't help it. That's the way I approach the world. I guess I do think of myself as a hammer, and every problem as a nail."

"And word got back to the mother that you were looking for her?"

"Yes. And that woman got my number from someone so she could tell me to knock it off. I almost laughed. A grown woman being defended by her mother? Are you serious?"

"You're surprised a mother would be protective?" Kimberly asked.

Again, Simon flicked his hand. "Here's the thing I want you to understand. I didn't know she was dying. She calls me and tells me off a little bit and then hangs up. But her number comes up on my caller ID. So I look up the address and find out it's a hospice facility. River Glen in Nashville. I figured the woman was a nurse, not a patient."

"So, what did you do with that information?" Kimberly asked.

"I went down there. Only when I arrived did I find out she's a patient. And she was pretty coherent at first. She told me how Morgan came to live with her when she was in high school. I guess her birth mother was having trouble. Drugs? Booze?" Simon shook his head. "Something like that. So Morgan goes into foster care. And really gets along with this woman in hospice. The woman says they just clicked, that she felt like Morgan was her own child, even though she'd just met her. Valerie Woodward. That's her name. But, of course, when the real mom gets her act straightened out, what happens to the kid?"

"She has to go back."

"Exactly. Courts always want that, right?"

"For the most part," Kimberly said.

"Fast-forward a few years. The real mom dies. Liver failure, from what I can gather. So I guess Morgan feels like she wants to have a relationship with the foster mom. Maybe she feels freer to do that once her real mom is dead and can't be jealous. Maybe she just wants a mother figure in her life. Who knows?"

Simon paused. Something showed in his eyes, a glistening hint of real emotion. Kimberly held her tongue, waited for him to go on.

"It stinks," he said. "Now the foster mom is sick too. I know what that's like, to lose your mom."

"And a brother," Kimberly said.

He looked at her a moment before he said, "Yes, a brother too."

"Why did she say you threatened her?" Kimberly asked.

Simon gave a half-hearted shrug. "Let's just say . . . maybe I was a little overzealous. To be honest, she slipped away while I was there. She started out clear, but then she lost her focus. The pain, I guess. And the medication. By the end of the conversation, I didn't know what she was talking about. So I left. She must have remembered, because at some point she told her daughter I'd been there."

His face brightened, as though an idea had just come to mind. "Hell, I can just claim she was delirious. Who would believe anything a dying, delusional woman would say?"

"I'm really glad you figured that out," Kimberly said.

"Hey," he said, leaning forward. "I told you all of this. Okay? I came clean. I listened. I want this over with as much as anyone else."

Kimberly agreed. She wholeheartedly agreed.

63

I expected to feel relieved when I walked through the door of my apartment in Chicago for the first time in a week. And for a moment I did.

I welcomed the familiar sights and smells. The spot on the couch shaped to my body. The window I sat by with my computer and coffee.

But I pretty quickly found myself looking at the place with a different set of eyes. Maybe it was everything I'd been through. Maybe it was giving voice to my concerns about my life to Morgan. Maybe it was coming face-to-face with a snarling, living, breathing madman who wanted to bash the life out of me.

Maybe it was all of the above.

I picked up my stack of mail, mostly junk and bills and magazines I never read. I opened my refrigerator to a few bottles of beer, a jar of pickles, and some Chinese takeout that had gone bad weeks earlier. I saw the unmade double bed. A gust of wind rattled the windows, reminding me that time was passing, that the dark, cold Chicago winter would set in soon and stretch ahead of me seemingly forever.

I called Morgan a few times.

Since she'd called me when I was in Wyckoff, it was easy

enough to call her back. But she never answered. The phone rang and rang and rang. And I had no idea what I'd say if she did answer. *So, you really were a murderer. . . . Imagine that! And you lied about your mother!*

I checked in with Renee the first night back. I'll be honest—I simply didn't want to be alone. She answered, her voice laced with cold caution. I told her I was home and hinted at the insane experiences I'd had in Kentucky.

Renee wasn't impressed. "You're just calling me because you're lonely. You just want me to come over so you can have a warm body in your bed."

She was right. So I said nothing.

"You want me to fall in next to you tonight. And then what, Joshua?"

"I don't know," I said. "I think I want to quit my job."

"Then do it," she said. "You've been talking about it for years. I think you've stayed at that job as much for me as for your dad. At some point, just do what you want to do and quit talking about it."

I knew she was right. About everything. And I told her so.

When I invited her over, she came. We fell into bed pretty quickly and didn't waste any time discussing my adventures. When I tried to bring them up, Renee placed her finger over my lips, shutting me up. It sounds like a cliché, but the sex was amazing. It felt like the exorcising of a need more than anything else, but I think we both enjoyed the release of tension that had built up between us.

When I came out of the bathroom, Renee was sitting on the edge of the bed, pulling on her clothes. She went about the task with a businesslike efficiency, not even bothering to look up.

"What's going on?" I asked.

"I'm not spending the night," she said, pulling on her boots. "I agreed to come over because I wanted to do that. And only that. I don't want to wake up here tomorrow."

She stood up and came over to where I leaned against the door-jamb. Still naked. I wished I had a towel or a shirt or a washcloth to cover up. I felt exposed. But Renee acted nonchalant as she grabbed her purse and pecked me on the cheek on her way by.

"I don't know if we'll do this again," she said, "but it was fun tonight. Maybe if you get your act together and figure out what you want, we can do it more. Or try to . . . I don't know. We can attempt to be something again."

Then she was gone, and the apartment felt even emptier than it had before she arrived.

But I didn't have long to think about that.

Half an hour after Renee left, Dad called. It was good to hear his voice, and I was happy to listen to him go on about how glad he was that I'd made it home safe. I told him I agreed. Then he asked me about my health and the status of my head.

"It's better. Pretty much back to normal."

"Are you sure? Really?"

"I feel good, Dad."

"Good, good. No lying, I was worried about you," he said. "To have my kid in a hospital in another state. I was ready to get on a plane and come up there when they said you could go home."

"I know. I'm sorry if I scared you."

"It's okay," he said. "You got caught up in something. It happens. I know who you are. I know you're true-blue. Maybe you just need to move on? Get back to your real life?"

"Probably."

"Good call. Look, I need you to do something for me. I need you to head down to Tampa. That deal there, the one we've been working on with those guys, Lutz and Newberry, it's unraveling a bit. I need you to smooth their feathers. They really want to meet you. I think it will seal things if they see your face. It's just one night. Down there and then back."

I felt the emptiness return inside me upon hearing his request. It sounded to my ears like an order to go to the dentist or the tax office. I heard the merry-go-round music starting up in the back of my head. Another flight. More Xanax.

"Okay," I said. "Middle of the week?"

"Monday. It has to be."

"Really?"

"Strike while the iron's hot," he said. "You know you're the only one I can count on to do this. I'd go myself, but I need to be in Minneapolis at the same time. Plus, they've been dying to see you. They wanted to meet you the other day, but . . . well, you were wherever you were."

"Kentucky," I said. "I was in Kentucky, Dad."

"I know. Head down there, take care of business, then come back and take a few days off. Hell, take a week. I don't care. You've earned it."

As much as I dreaded the flight and another night in a hotel, staring at the cable TV offerings and eating a room service hamburger, I didn't have anything keeping me at home.

"Okay," I said. "I'll do it."

64

I loathed going into the airport on Monday.

But I went.

I arrived at the last minute and sweated through the long security line, worried I'd miss my flight. But I made it with time to spare and managed to swallow my Xanax so it would have the desired effect. I avoided the bars and instead found a quiet, out-of-the-way spot where I could read before my flight boarded. I'd brought the novel I'd purchased in Atlanta, the one with the grizzled loner who kills in order to forget the pain of losing his wife and child. I'd reached the part of the book where the hero develops a drinking problem and then exchanges flirty banter with a female FBI agent. It interested me enough to keep reading, so I did.

Then Detective Givens called. When I saw her name on my screen, I couldn't answer fast enough, even though I wasn't sure I wanted to hear whatever she had to tell me. But I couldn't help wanting to know something. *Anything.*

She sounded friendly when she asked if it was a good time to talk. I told her I was in the airport, waiting for a flight. A slight pause followed, as I'm sure we both thought immediately about how I'd met Morgan.

Detective Givens, for her part, refused to let the moment pass.

"That's why I'm calling, Mr. Fields. I need to check in and make sure you haven't seen any sign of Ms. Reynolds."

"No, I haven't."

"No contact of any kind? Nothing you need to tell me?"

I thought about my attempts to call her. The phone ringing and ringing. Endlessly ringing. That didn't count as contact, did it? "Nothing."

"And nothing else has come to mind about where she might be? Any thoughts, no matter how crazy?"

"I really can't think of anything," I said. "I really don't know that much about her. Has there been any kind of break in the case?" I asked, still holding out hope.

"The investigation is ongoing," she said, her voice switching to businesslike efficiency. "We've kept as close an eye as we can on places she might go, but there's been nothing. We'll keep looking as long as we have to."

"I see. What about the . . . you know, the murder investigation? I mean, is there anything going on with the Caldwells?" I wasn't really sure what I was asking. I was just curious, I guess.

"Mr. Caldwell's body has been released to the family. They're having a private memorial for him tomorrow. And he's being buried in the family plot, just like his brother wanted. That part of their struggle is over. I'm hoping we bring them justice one of these days."

I wasn't sure how to respond, since I knew bringing them justice meant arresting Morgan. I hadn't yet been able to reconcile the idea that the Morgan I knew might be a murderer. I couldn't force my mind to bend completely in that direction.

"Is that all, then?" I asked as an announcement came over the speaker right above my head.

"Since I have you on the phone, did Morgan Reynolds have anything else to say about her mother?"

"Her dead mother."

"She told you she moved to Nashville to be near her because she was sick. Dying, really. Was there anything else?"

I wondered about the line of questioning. Was it meant just to humiliate me? "She didn't tell me that whole story about her mom being sick in Nashville was fictitious. I don't know what else I could know."

"Did she say anything about being in foster care?"

"Morgan? In foster care? No, she didn't mention that. She just told me her mom was a drunk who had some embarrassing moments when Morgan was a child."

"Did she ever mention the name Valerie Woodward?"

"No. Who's she?" I asked.

Givens explained to me that Morgan had a foster mother, a woman she lived with for a time during high school. And that woman was currently in a hospice facility in Nashville. "We think that's who she meant when she said Simon Caldwell threatened her mother. Simon Caldwell did visit the woman and utilized his . . . unique, delicate powers of persuasion. This woman has a different last name than Morgan Reynolds. She goes by Valerie Woodward. But we're starting to wonder if Morgan wasn't using the last name Woodward some of the time."

I'd been holding my thumb between the pages of the novel, marking my place. But when I heard the news, the book slid off the end of my hand and onto the empty seat next to me. "So what does that mean? She wasn't lying about her mother?"

"This gives us a plausible explanation for why she told you what she did," Givens said. "It doesn't change the way we feel about anything else, but she probably wasn't lying about her mother. Her foster mother, I should say."

I let the information sink in. But what did it really mean? That she hadn't lied about that one thing? One piece of the puzzle made some kind of sense? It didn't change everything else.

"So her mother," I asked, "or foster mother, is in hospice in Nashville?"

"She is. The police down there have been watching it, making sure Morgan Reynolds hasn't been by to visit her. If she shows up, she'll be arrested."

"I see." I bent down and picked up the book. "And that's it?" I asked.

"That's the latest," she said. "How have you been doing, Mr. Fields?"

"I'm good. Fine. I'm back to my routine."

"Do let me know if you hear or see anything," she said. "Any helpful information you can provide to us going forward will allow us to look more favorably on you."

"I understand. Sure."

When we hung up, it was time for me to board. And I read my book all the way to Tampa.

65

I took care of everything in Tampa that Monday. I met with the investors. We went to a nice meal, capped off by drinks at the bar. I made jokes and laughed at theirs, and by the time the night ended, by the time I walked bleary-eyed back to the hotel elevator to return to my room, I felt certain the deal was saved. The alcohol and the travel—and, let's be honest, the Xanax—made me feel wiped, but before I fell asleep I texted Dad and told him.

Mission accomplished.

The next morning I was back in the airport, following my old routine. Gift shop, Xanax, breakfast. I had to remind myself which city I was in and where I was headed. The thought of returning home brought little joy.

The restaurant I chose didn't help. While it wasn't the Keg 'n Craft, it might as well have been. All those airport restaurants and bars blurred together in my mind, and while I sat there in Tampa, eating my tepid oatmeal and slightly blackened toast, I thought of Morgan and the first conversation we'd had.

Had she been right about the airport? That it was a neutral space, the kind of place where you could say anything without consequence? If that was true, then I was following that dictum to the letter. I apparently must not have meant anything I'd said to her that day, because I hadn't changed a damn thing in my life since then.

When I finished eating, I wandered onto the concourse, thinking of what Detective Givens had told me the day before. Morgan's mother—or mother figure, perhaps—really was alive and maybe in fear for her life in Nashville. It sounded like the police were keeping an eye on her, both to protect her and just in case Morgan came by.

I remembered how distraught Morgan was at the thought that something might happen to her mother. How she'd left town to find help from her aunt and learned that Simon had been by. Her fear suggested a deep bond, the kind I would expect between mother and daughter.

Who was likely to know more about Morgan than her mother?

I could go home and continue with the routine I'd come to despise, or I could finally make the change I wanted to make. My own future was currently without direction, so I found myself at the gate, changing my destination once again.

Instead of returning home to Chicago, I was going to board a flight for Nashville.

66

Kimberly ordered a coffee and took it to a table near the back of the café. It was midmorning, half of the space filled with senior citizens slowly sipping drinks and the other half with hipsters tapping away at laptops. Kimberly watched the front door and waved when Trooper John Mattingly of the Gordon County Sheriff's Department came in and caught her eye. He saw Kimberly and returned the wave, then pointed to the counter, where he ordered a drink. He carried his paper cup over and sat across from Kimberly, removing the Smokey Bear hat from his closely shaved head.

"I think I'm a few minutes late," he said.

"Not at all. And I'm always late. I appreciate you taking the time to meet."

"I had to be here in Laurel Falls for something else anyway. It's nice to get out of Wyckoff and come to the big city." Mattingly sipped the coffee, which sent steam curling past his youthful face. "And I could use the break. I missed my coffee this morning."

"Then I'm glad I could help one of you Gordon County boys," Kimberly said. She'd met Mattingly a few times before, worked on cases with him when the Laurel Falls and Gordon County police departments cooperated. She'd found him to be a reliable, by-the-book cop, thorough if unspectacular. "Did you have a chance to review your notes?"

"I did." He nodded his big head. His scalp showed through the fine hair. "And it came back to me once I looked everything over. What can I tell you about it?"

"You got called to a dispute between Valerie Woodward and Blaine Fant. At his house, right?"

"That's right."

"And this was . . . four years ago?"

"That's right."

"What was going on?" Kimberly asked.

"He called us. Said his girlfriend was getting violent with him, and he didn't feel safe. I was the closest officer on duty, so I responded first."

"And what did you find?"

"They were in a little house, a prefab-looking job out on Spring Mill Road. Out near Morgan Township. I don't know if you're familiar with the area, but there's not much out there, not even farms anymore. He answered the door, Fant. About fifty, sleepy eyes. Wearing a T-shirt and shorts. No shoes. As soon as he saw me, he started trying to get rid of me."

"Saying he didn't mean to call?" Kimberly asked.

"Exactly. It was all a misunderstanding. He loved his girlfriend, they'd had a disagreement, but they'd worked it out. I could go on my way because everything was fine. I, of course, told him I couldn't do that. I said I had to make sure no one inside the residence was injured. He argued a little longer, and then he called back into the house to Mrs. Woodward and said a cop was coming in."

"Did you see any injuries on Fant?"

"He looked fine," Mattingly said. "He wasn't hurt or bleeding or anything. I just wanted to see her, make sure she was okay."

"And you did?"

Mattingly nodded. "I went out to the kitchen, and she was sitting at the table. She was smoking, had a glass of wine next to her. I asked her if she was all right, if she felt she was in any danger or needed any assistance. She told me no on all counts. Again, I didn't see any sign of injury, so I figured I'd leave it at that."

"Not much you could do at that point," Kimberly said.

"No reason to do anything else," Mattingly said. "Until I turned to go, and I saw a .38 on the counter. It was underneath a kitchen towel. Just the barrel peeking out. I asked them about it, and Mrs. Woodward told me she was licensed and registered. I asked to see the paperwork, and she produced it. It all checked out. I ran them both through the system too."

"And?"

"He'd been arrested for DUI once. She was clean. Nothing outstanding, so I left. That was that."

"Until . . ."

"Right. Until the thing with her daughter."

67

When I got off the plane in Nashville, I still didn't know where Morgan's mom was. Waiting for my flight in Tampa, I'd started calling hospice facilities in Nashville, once again looking for the needle in the haystack. All I knew was her foster mother's name, which had been given to me by Detective Givens.

Valerie Woodward.

I'd called six facilities before my flight boarded, asking if they had a patient by that name. They all told me no.

As the flight was called and I shuffled toward the jet bridge, I started to wonder if it was worth it. Was I going to travel to Nashville and strike out, never finding her mother?

And even if I did find her, what did I expect to learn?

But I couldn't stop. And, I told myself, Nashville was on the way home to Chicago.

Once off the plane, I called four more places with no good results. On my phone it looked like there were about thirty facilities in the metro area. More if I included the sprawling suburbs. I might be spending the rest of my life on the phone.

But then I caught a break. The next number I dialed went to the offices of a group of hospice facilities. The receptionist could check their patient list for me, and that covered five locations on the west side of town.

I waited while she put me on hold. And then she came back on and informed me that Valerie Woodward was a patient at a place called River Glen. She even gave me the address, which I wrote down inside the back cover of the paperback novel I still carried.

When I hung up, I rented a car and started on my way.

River Glen sat off the road in an upper-middle-class Nashville neighborhood full of new-construction homes, wine shops, and organic grocery stores. From the outside it looked like a high-end doctor's office. The covered entryway allowed visitors to pull up and walk in without getting wet during rainstorms. An American flag on a tall pole fluttered and then fell with the breeze. Across the front of the building, a series of large windows caught the early-afternoon light. The landscaping was impeccable, the grass perfectly trimmed, the edges fine and clean.

The lobby was filled with comfortable leather furniture. On one side was a Halloween-themed display—hay bales, pumpkins, paper skeletons, and cornstalks. It made me think of autumn. Death. The decorator either didn't mind the connection or hadn't thought of it. But I did. Patients came to River Glen for only one thing.

On the other side of a reception desk a woman looked up and smiled at me as the sliding door whooshed shut at my back. Soft, soothing music played over hidden speakers. I asked her which room Valerie Woodward was in.

She checked a list on the desk in front of her and told me room 4, down the hall and to my left. Then she asked me to sign in, which I did. I gave the names above mine a quick scan, hoping to see Morgan's, but the sheet was new. Mine was only the fourth name on the list. I thanked her and moved along.

The hallways were wide and spacious. Art prints showed delicate flowers and forest scenes. I heard nothing from behind the closed doors of the patients' rooms. No televisions, no conversations. I wondered how many people were on the brink of their mortal end at that very moment as I walked by, how many family members squeezed the hands of a loved one, eyes filled with tears. I came to room 4 and knocked gently. I waited but heard nothing. So I knocked again. When I still received no response, I tried the handle, which turned easily, so I pushed the door open and went in.

The room was large and spacious. A window, one of the large ones I'd seen when I pulled into the lot, allowed sunlight to stream through and across the floor. I saw a couch and two chairs, an end table covered with flowers and magazines, a coffee maker and a minifridge. A heck of a nice place to stay except . . .

In the middle of the room sat a hospital bed with, I presumed, Valerie Woodward under its covers. I closed the door softly and walked across the laminate hardwood. It must have been new or expertly installed, because my body didn't create one squeak before I stopped by the side of her bed, my back to the large window.

Valerie's eyes were closed, her hands on top of the blanket. A single long gray braid stretched across the pillow next to her head. Her chest rose and fell peacefully.

"Valerie?" I whispered, my voice so low I almost couldn't hear it. She kept on breathing, eyes closed. She looked thin, her skin pallid, but not like a dying person's. But what did I know? Had I ever seen a dying person before? I hadn't. The closest I'd come was Simon Caldwell after Morgan beaned him in the Fantasy Farm petting zoo, and he'd managed to survive. "Valerie?" I said louder. "Mrs. Woodward?"

I waited for a nurse or aide to come in behind me, to shoo me away for bothering the sickest of patients. But no one did. I assumed Valerie was doped to the gills, given the gift of blissful sleep by the pain medication. It crossed my mind that I might never be able to wake her, that maybe no one could.

"Valerie?" My voice sounded like a shout that time, and I regretted it. But her eyelids fluttered, her head shifting from side to side.

She swallowed and worked her cracked lips. Her hands moved on top of the covers, the index finger stained by nicotine, the nails thin and brittle. I noticed a slight discoloration on her left elbow, the remnant of a fading bruise.

Her eyes came all the way open and settled on me. "Are you another social worker?" she asked.

"No, ma'am. My name's Joshua Fields."

She pointed at something, her hand lifting and making a gesture in a direction near my right elbow. She worked her lips some more but seemed unable to find the words she wanted. I looked around and saw a large plastic tumbler of water.

"You want some?" I asked.

"Please."

I held it near her face so her mouth could find the straw. She took several long pulls, and I remembered being in the emergency room just a few days earlier while Detective Givens helped me drink. Was that what people who wanted information from someone did? Help them, get their guard down, and then go in for the kill by asking questions? Was I any different from the cops who offered the suspect a cigarette in the interrogation room on a TV show?

When she was finished drinking, I put the cup down. Valerie looked content, as though the water had brought her some major relief. She closed her eyes again, and I thought she was going to slip away.

But then she asked, eyes still closed, "Who did you say you were?"

"Joshua Fields." And then I wondered—how exactly would I explain who I was? I took my best shot. "I'm a friend of Morgan's."

"Oh." Her eyelids came open again. It seemed to take her a moment to focus on me that time, but she did. Her eyes were blue, lined with red. Dark circles of exhaustion and pain smudged the skin beneath them. "How do you know her?"

"I haven't known her long," I said. "We met a few days ago."

Her eyelids fluttered and then once again came fully open. "Oh . . ."

"Do you need something? More water?"

"You met her . . . where?"

I felt silly saying it. Almost as silly as I felt being in a hospice facility talking to a dying woman I didn't know. But I had to learn whatever I could about Morgan, so I had to tell the truth.

"We met in the Atlanta airport, while we were both waiting for our flights. And then we met again after that. It's all very complicated and strange, I guess."

"I know. . . ." Her eyelids fluttered again. She turned her head away from me, showing me the back of her neck, the skin blotchy and red. "She's such a sweet girl, Morgan. I love her."

I thought she'd fallen asleep, as her breathing became slow and regular.

But then she shifted again, turning her head toward me again, her eyes still closed.

"I know who you are. . . ." She smiled slightly, her cracked lips turning up. But then she seemed to fade away again.

"How do you know who I am, Valerie? Hello? Are you awake?"

She remained perfectly still, except for the rising and falling of her chest.

"Valerie?" I asked one more time.

Her eyelids came wide open. "You're the boy Morgan was telling me about this morning."

68

Kimberly finished her coffee. She felt the pleasant buzz of caffeine working through her body, bringing every nerve ending to life. She felt smarter, sharper, more alive. And she wished she could bottle that feeling, uncork it, and tap into it whenever a challenging problem vexed her.

Then she told herself she actually could. *Coffee.* Brew, swallow, repeat.

If only it were that easy. If only . . .

"So," she said, "this other thing, the one with her daughter."

"Foster daughter," Mattingly said. "Mrs. Woodward initially said 'daughter.' Then the daughter herself clarified and said 'foster daughter.' But then she added that they were really very close despite that."

"Right. Go on."

Mattingly shrugged, sipped his own drink. "This was about a year after the thing with Fant and the gun. We got called there again. Same house. I was the second officer to arrive. Mrs. Woodward had a new boyfriend, some guy named Rick Yates."

"And, according to the report, this Yates got into it with the foster daughter."

"Right. First he got into it with Valerie Woodward. They were arguing. The daughter, Morgan Reynolds, who was just visiting, tried to intervene. And Yates got in her face, threatened her."

"And that's when Valerie Woodward reached into her trusty bag of tricks."

"She got out the .38, the same one from my first visit. So Yates called nine-one-one, and we showed up. Almost an instant replay, except the daughter was there."

"And this time the boyfriend wanted to press charges."

"Right. He did. So we brought Mrs. Woodward in and booked her. Charged her with assault. She said she didn't care what we did to her, that she'd do anything to protect her child. Yates didn't waver, so she pled out. She managed to avoid jail time but received probation. An unpleasant experience for her, but she had a clean record. It could have been worse."

"It would have been worse if the first guy had pressed charges."

"Exactly." Mattingly looked flushed with pride at having important information about a big case. "When you found that body at Fantasy Farm and named Morgan Reynolds a person of interest, it all came back to me."

"I'm glad it did," Kimberly said.

"I hope it helps. I wish I could tell you more."

"This is very helpful," Kimberly said. She couldn't expect a trooper to remember the specific details of every call he'd ever responded to. She knew what they dealt with on a daily basis. The domestic disturbances and disputes, the petty squabbles over property and family. Someone waving a gun at someone in Gordon County might barely register with an experienced cop unless something else made it stand out. "As you know, we do want to know everything we can about Morgan Reynolds. Anything else about her?"

Mattingly shook his head. He looked frustrated with his limited ability to remember. "Nothing I can think of. She seemed educated and smart. Pretty. Tall. She was very concerned about Mrs. Woodward. Said her health hadn't been great, that she'd recently been diagnosed with cancer, and she worried the stress of being arrested could make her take a turn for the worse." He shrugged again. "She acted the way a daughter would if she was deeply concerned about her mother. She seemed emotional, very worried about the strain on Valerie."

"So no real trouble?"

"She was polite. Not threatening in any way." Mattingly cleared his throat. "I'm sure you've already thought of this, but—"

"We're trying to find Yates now," Kimberly said. "But it's a long shot, isn't it? Why would he be tangled up in this after all this time? He's the one who pressed charges."

"You're right. I'm grasping there."

"No, I had the same thought," Kimberly said. "I want to talk to everybody."

And she wanted to know about that gun. She'd wondered for days how Morgan Reynolds, a tall woman but still a woman, would have been able to overpower Giles Caldwell, an older man with health problems, yes, but still a man. Had she taken the gun from her mother? Had she used it to force her way into Giles Caldwell's house?

Had she taken a page from her mother's playbook and then things had gone horribly, horribly wrong, leading to Giles Caldwell's death?

69

I leaned in closer to the bed, closer to Valerie Woodward. A sickly odor came off of her, like that of something decaying. I knew it was the scent of death wafting over me, but I didn't step back.

"Morgan was here?" I asked. "She was here this morning?"

"Morgan . . ."

Again her head lolled around on the pillow, from one side to the other. Her eyes closed and then opened a few times, but it was nearly impossible to tell if she was in any way aware of what was going on around her.

My eyes scanned the room. They settled on the water cup again. I picked it up and held it out to Valerie. I wasn't sure why. I was grasping at anything I could to keep her with me.

"Here," I said, angling the straw near her mouth. "Have some of this."

But she turned her head away. I kept the cup there a moment longer, but she refused to turn toward it, so I put it back down on the bedside table.

I decided to try a more direct approach.

"Valerie? Did you say Morgan was here? This morning? Was she really here this morning?"

"Morgan . . ." Her head stopped moving. The braid lay along-side her face. "She was here. She's so protective. She worries about me. About falling. About my arm getting hurt."

"Your arm? What happened?"

"She thinks *I'm* protective. . . . She told me about you." She coughed a few times and cleared her throat. "She told me about Joshua."

"She mentioned me? By name?"

She didn't answer.

"Where is she now?" I asked.

Valerie muttered something, but I couldn't make it out. She said the same word a second time. I leaned even closer, breathing through my mouth to avoid the smell of decay.

"What did you say?" I asked.

"Shelly," she said. "Shelly was here. . . ."

"Who is Shelly? Is she a friend of yours? Or of Morgan's?"

"Shelly was here. And Bud."

"Bud?"

"Bud was here too. . . . He came to visit."

"Who's Bud?" I asked.

The door to the room swung open then. I straightened up and turned to look. A quick, sudden thought flashed through my mind—maybe it was Morgan.

But it was just a nurse. A woman only a few years older than me, wearing a sky-blue smock and white pants and white shoes that made no sound as she came across the room toward us.

She smiled, her face warm. "Hello," she said. "I just need to check Valerie's chart. You can continue with your visit."

"Oh, okay." But I didn't want to keep pressing Valerie with a nurse in the room. In fact, the nurse's appearance served to break whatever ridiculous spell I'd been under, badgering a dying woman about her recollections of people who had visited her in hospice. "We weren't talking about anything important."

The nurse studied some information on a stapled packet of papers she'd removed from a drawer, looked up and smiled at me again, then put the papers away.

"Any company is good," she said, looking at me like she was ready to go. She placed her hand on Valerie's arm and gave it a gentle squeeze, then turned away from the bed.

"Excuse me," I said, causing the nurse to pause. I looked back at Valerie, who appeared to be sleeping. Her head remained still, and she was no longer muttering. I walked to the foot of the bed where the nurse had stopped and spoke to her in a low voice. "Has Valerie had a lot of visitors?"

"She's had some. Not an excessive amount. Like I said, any visitor who brings comfort is a good visitor."

"Of course. She mentioned her daughter, Morgan. Has Morgan been here to see her?"

The nurse smiled like she knew some secret information. "We all know one thing about Valerie. She has a lot of children. Apparently she took more than one in through the foster care system. She was very dedicated to them." She considered me through eyes that remained warm. "Maybe you're one of them? One of her children?"

"No, I'm not. Just a family friend. A friend of her daughter Morgan. That's why I was wondering if she'd been here. Valerie said her name."

The nurse tipped her head toward the door, indicating that I should follow her, so I did. We didn't leave the room, but we stood as far from Valerie's bed as we could get.

"You know about Morgan, right?" she asked. "The police have been here asking about her."

I nodded. "Yes, I know that."

"I haven't seen her." Some of the warmth went out of her eyes. "And we'd call the police if we did."

"Right. Of course."

"*You* haven't seen her, have you?" the nurse asked.

"No. Not lately."

"It sounds like that's for the best," she said.

"Maybe," I said, glancing over at Valerie's sleeping form. "She mentioned a couple of other names too. Shelly and Bud? Do you know who they are? I guess what I'm wondering . . . Is she . . . co-herent when she says things?"

"Someone in her condition can be in and out of lucidity," the nurse said. "And it can change from moment to moment. People think a hospice patient is on the brink of dying any moment, and that's not true. We have some patients for months, even up to a year. Sometimes they rally and look like they're getting better. And their condition can change quickly. Very quickly."

"I guess I don't have much experience with this," I said. "Do you know who Shelly and Bud are?"

The nurse's brow furrowed. "Shelly? She told me about Shelly." She snapped her fingers. "That's Valerie's sister. Oh, you see? She told me Shelly passed away several years ago. That happens some-times with someone in this condition. They may see people who aren't there. Despite all of our medical advances, dying remains something of a mystery."

"Yeah," I said, my inarticulate response unable to bring any greater clarity to the situation. "Thanks."

"If you want to help Valerie," the nurse said, "and if you're a friend of Morgan's, then maybe the best thing to do would be to sit with her. Just visit . . . so she's not alone."

I looked across the room again. Valerie looked small beneath the covers, dwarfed by the surroundings. What the nurse said made sense. And I had nowhere to be. . . .

When the nurse left, I went back to the chair by the side of Valerie's bed and sat down. Valerie turned toward me, her eyes still closed, and muttered something I didn't understand. And I gave up trying to make sense of it.

If I ended up alone someday, dying in a hospice facility, would it matter to me if I knew the person who sat with me and gave me water? Was there such a thing as the wrong kind of comfort?

I decided there wasn't. And if Morgan couldn't be there, then I would step in.

I stayed the rest of the afternoon.

70

Kimberly arrived at River Glen just before ten in the morning. The day had gradually grown overcast as she'd driven down the interstate, and by the time she reached the outskirts of Nashville, light rain was pelting the windshield of her sedan. She parked near the front and hustled inside without an umbrella. She'd called the day before and arranged the visit after talking to Mattingly, and then she'd let Nashville PD know she'd be poking around in the city. On the phone, the administrator of River Glen had suggested she arrive in the morning if she wanted a better chance of finding Valerie Woodward coherent.

The receptionist seemed nervous once Kimberly introduced herself. The more innocent and law-abiding the citizen, the more unnerved they were by the presence of a cop. And when one showed up at work . . . Kimberly knew her appearance gave everyone the heebie-jeebies. She asked for the administrator, Brooke Boyle, explaining they'd talked the day before.

"She's in a meeting right now," the receptionist said. She wore a name tag that read TAMMY and seemed to be choosing her words carefully. "But you can wait."

Kimberly looked over the items on top of the desk. A calendar, a jar of pens, a massive phone with more than a dozen buttons, and a blue three-ring binder. She tapped the binder with her index finger.

"What's this?" she asked, although she knew.

"That?" Tammy asked, as though she'd never seen it before. "That's where visitors sign in."

Kimberly didn't ask permission. She picked it up, flipped it open, and started paging through.

"I'm not . . ." Tammy's voice rose higher. "Can you . . ."

"You didn't ask me to sign in," Kimberly said without looking up. "Should I?"

"Well, since you're a . . . I mean, we don't ask the police to sign in," Tammy said.

"Do the police come here a lot?"

"No, they don't."

"I see," Kimberly said. She studied the pages more closely. The log went back only a few days. Lined sheets of white paper where visitors wrote their name, the name of the patient being visited, and the time in and out. If she'd come across the name "Morgan Reynolds," she would have fallen over. If Morgan Reynolds had taken the chance of slipping in and visiting her foster mother, she wouldn't have used her real name. She knew the police were looking for her, and she had to have guessed they'd told the River Glen staff to be on the lookout. Kimberly flipped a page and scanned through the day before. That was when she saw a name that made her eyes lock on the page. She read it twice. "Well, hello."

"Is something wrong?" Tammy asked.

"Were you working yesterday? Around twelve fifteen?"

"Yesterday? Yesterday. Yes, I was."

"Did you see this man?" Kimberly spun the book around and tapped a name with her index finger. "Joshua Fields? Did you see him?"

Tammy stared at the book, her eyes widening. "Oh, yes. Him. He came in yesterday."

"You talked to him?"

"Briefly."

"What about?"

Tammy took a big breath, her shoulders rising and falling. "Not much. He told the nurse he was a friend of the family. That was about it."

"Was he alone?" Kimberly asked.

"Yes, he was."

"Did anyone drop him off or wait for him?"

"I don't know. I only saw him in here."

"Did you see him in Mrs. Woodward's room?" Kimberly asked.

"I don't go down there. I usually just stay in reception."

"So you don't know what they talked about?" Kimberly asked.

"No, I'm sorry, I don't. That's about it."

"Did any other nurses or doctors talk to him?"

Tammy started to speak and then stopped. She looked around and then back at Kimberly. "Maybe you should talk to Brooke about this."

"I will." Kimberly closed the book but didn't put it down. She held it against her body like a precious object. *Joshua Fields.* Joshua Fields had come to River Glen to see Valerie Woodward. He might not have said much to Tammy, but Kimberly intended to talk to him about his little excursion to Nashville. She'd definitely do that. "And where is Brooke? Is she done with her meeting?"

"You know what?" Tammy said, picking up the phone on her desk. "I'll just remind her that you're here."

71

Brooke showed up not long after that.

She breezed through the lobby, carrying a small stack of manila folders under one arm and holding a cell phone in the other hand. But she kept her eyes on Tammy as she approached, acting as if Kimberly wasn't standing there with the visitor log in her hands. Brooke sounded out of breath and slightly irritated when she spoke to Tammy.

"You're going to have to tell Byron I'm running late," she said. "I was supposed to meet with him twenty minutes ago, but I have to speak to the detective first."

Tammy nodded and picked up the phone on her desk again. She punched numbers like her life depended on it.

Brooke turned to face Kimberly. "I'm sorry, Detective. It's been a crazy morning."

She didn't sound sorry, but Kimberly smiled anyway. "I'll try not to take too much of your time."

Brooke led her to a small office, where she sat at a desk littered with papers, leaving Kimberly to take an empty chair adjacent to the desk. Brooke checked her phone, tapped on the keypad a few times, and then set it aside. She glanced at her computer screen, while Kimberly waited patiently until Brooke finally turned to her and said, "Now, what can I help you with, Detective?"

"I was looking over the visitor log. . . ." Kimberly held it in her lap.

Brooke saw it and her face blanched with disapproval. "Do you have a warrant to look at that?"

"It was sitting out on the desk," Kimberly said. "Anyone who comes in can page through it."

Brooke didn't appear mollified, but she remained silent.

So Kimberly went on. "I see that a man named Joshua Fields visited Mrs. Woodward yesterday. Did you talk to him?"

"I didn't. I don't spend a great deal of time in the patients' rooms." She brushed a stray hair off her forehead. "He did speak to one of the nurses, who reported the conversation to me."

"What did he say?"

"Just that he was a family friend." She cleared her throat. "And he asked about this Morgan Reynolds woman you're looking for. He wanted to know if she'd been by, and the nurse told him no. Then she encouraged him to stay and visit."

"Did he?"

Brooke nodded, some of her disapproval fading. "He did. The nurse told me he sat by Valerie's bedside for several hours. It was in the afternoon, so Valerie was in and out."

"And that's all he did? Sat by her bed?"

"He gave her water when she was thirsty. He bought himself a candy bar out of the vending machine. That's what the nurse on duty told me."

Kimberly tapped her fingers against the binder. Joshua Fields never failed to surprise. Not only did he track down Valerie Woodward in hospice, but he sat with her like she was his own relative. Did he just want to feel closer to Morgan?

"And there's been no sign of Morgan Reynolds?" Kimberly

asked. "She's not in the log book, but I assume she wouldn't sign in under her real name."

"No sign of her besides that thing a couple of days ago."

Kimberly tightened her grip on the binder. "What thing?"

Some of Brooke's exasperation returned. "The Nashville cops didn't tell you?"

"Apparently not."

"I don't think it's a big deal," Brooke said. "Maybe I shouldn't have mentioned it."

"No, I'm glad you did. What happened?"

Brooke looked like she wished she'd never opened her mouth. She brushed her hair back again, let her eyes take a quick glance at the computer, then turned back to Kimberly.

"One of our desk clerks, someone who works in the evening, was coming in for her shift. She'd seen the notices about Ms. Reynolds, the ones we posted for the staff here and the ones on the news. We've all seen them. Anyway, she saw a woman in the parking lot, sitting in a car, who looked like her. She wasn't sure, so to err on the side of caution, she called the police. They came, they looked around."

"But the woman was gone?"

"Yes. And then the clerk, the one who saw her, backpedaled a little, said maybe she was wrong, maybe she overreacted." Brooke shrugged. "That was it. I just assumed they told you."

Kimberly would've assumed the same thing. But she knew she couldn't count on everything going the way she wanted it to go. "And there was nothing else? No other sightings or disturbances or anything?"

"Nothing."

"Well, thanks for telling me." She decided to try a different tactic with Brooke. She got out her metaphorical butter knife and began spreading it on thick. She figured that would work with a stressed-out and edgy administrator. "I know how much you have on your plate here and how difficult the work must be. Emotionally. Spiritually. I know it can't help to have the police adding to your stress. I can only imagine."

Brooke nodded, almost smiled. "Well, we understand how important it is. But you're right—things here are usually stressful. And emotional."

"Of course."

"Even as an administrator, I feel it."

"I'm sure you do."

They sat in silence for a moment. Brooke's phone beeped once, but she ignored it.

Kimberly said, "So, how is Mrs. Woodward? What's her condition?"

Brooke looked like she didn't know what to say. "She's in hospice care. Her condition is only moving in one direction."

"Sure. But are we talking . . . sooner? Or later?"

"That's privileged information," Brooke said. "I can't discuss a patient's medical condition. Not without authorization from the family."

"Sure, I understand."

Brooke took a deep breath and said in a low voice, "I guess . . . if by 'later' you mean a month or so, then I would say sooner. Her condition has improved slightly since she's been here. When her daughter brought her in, she'd had a fall. Bruised her arm. She was very tired and weak. I wouldn't have thought she'd last more than a day or so. But she's stabilized a little in here. She's been getting good rest."

Kimberly nodded. "Is she coherent? Able to talk or respond?"

"Sometimes. That's why I said to come earlier in the day. Patients tend to be more alert after a good night's sleep."

"Thanks for helping me with that. I'll get out of your way, then." She handed the blue binder over to Brooke, who took it with a smile. "If it's okay with you, I'm going to go down and poke my head in the door of her room. Just to see how she's doing."

"That's fine. If you have any questions, there should be a nurse nearby."

Kimberly stood up, and so did Brooke. They shook hands. "Oh, and if anything like that happens again, someone thinking Morgan Reynolds is around, would you mind letting me know too? Even if it seems like a false alarm?"

"I will. For sure."

"Thanks."

Kimberly started down the hall to Valerie's room, wondering what she'd find.

72

Kimberly stepped inside the room, expecting the worst. She'd last been in a hospice facility when her uncle Jim was dying eight years earlier, and she'd vowed then never to go back. She'd seen her uncle wasting away, his body reduced to almost nothing, the smell of illness thick in the room. She couldn't bear to see the look of aching, searing pain on her uncle's face and so she left, prompting her dad to ask her later how she dealt with the things she had to see as a cop.

It's all easier than that, she told him. *I don't* know *the people I see at work.*

But once she was inside, she saw that Valerie Woodward looked . . . okay. Her eyes were open, her hair clean. She was propped up in bed, supported by several pillows, and the TV in the corner played a game show with the volume low. The faint sound of applause reached Kimberly as if the televised audience was thrilled to see her enter.

"Hello, Mrs. Woodward." The woman showed no reaction. "I'm Kimberly Givens. I'm with the Laurel Falls Police Department."

She thought Valerie nodded slightly, but she couldn't be sure, so she walked across the room, moving closer to the bed. Valerie's eyes didn't track her. Maybe she wasn't in as good a shape as she'd first appeared.

"Can you hear me, Mrs. Woodward?"

Valerie, her eyes slightly glassy, finally turned her head toward Kimberly. "Yes." Her voice came out as a hoarse whisper.

"Do you know why I'm here?" Kimberly asked.

"Last rites?"

It took Kimberly a moment to process that the woman was making a joke. Kimberly let out a little laugh, hoping it meant she might get some valuable information out of the woman. "No, that's not my department."

Valerie looked away, her eyes wandering to the TV, where a contestant in a floral shirt spun a giant wheel. Big dreams. Big money. Sometimes a big game-show payout sounded better than working for a living, trying to sort through the broken pieces of people's lives.

"You know what I want, right?" Kimberly asked. She saw the bruise on the woman's arm, remembered Brooke mentioning a fall.

"She's not here," Valerie said.

"I figured that. Has she been by at all?"

Valerie started fumbling with the covers.

Kimberly craned her head. "Are you looking for the remote?" she asked.

"I want that off."

Kimberly went around to the other side of the bed and found the remote. She clicked the TV off. "Better?"

But Valerie had let her eyes close, and Kimberly feared she'd fallen asleep. There was only so far she wanted to push a cancer patient, but then Valerie's eyes popped open a moment later, and she fixed her gaze on Kimberly.

"What do you want?" she asked.

"Morgan. Has she been here?"

"I'm tired. I'm dying."

"Do you know where she is?" Kimberly asked.

"If I did, I wouldn't tell you."

"Where might she go? Does she have friends or family anywhere else?"

"I'm her family," Valerie said.

"That must mean she came to see you. Or told you where she was going."

Valerie started fumbling around again. She reached for the bedside table, where Kimberly spotted a call button on a cord that she knew could be used to summon the nurse. Valerie couldn't quite get ahold of it, so Kimberly picked it up, holding it just out of reach.

"What did Joshua Fields want?" she asked.

"Who?"

"Your visitor yesterday."

"I don't know who that is," she said, irritated. "Give me that."

Kimberly handed it over. She didn't want to be accused of tormenting a dying woman.

But Valerie held the device without calling the nurse. She kept it in her hand, running her thumb over the button without pressing.

"Do you want to tell me something, Valerie?" Kimberly asked. "I came all the way from Laurel Falls."

"I left Kentucky behind. Wyckoff. All of it."

"Can you tell me anything about your gun? You know, the one you use to threaten men? Where is it now?"

Valerie closed her eyes. She looked like she'd been hit by a wave of pain. But it seemed to pass quickly, and she opened her eyes again, wider than ever. She pursed her lips with disdain.

"You cops always think you know everything, don't you?"

"I'll be the first to admit how little I know," Kimberly said.

"I'm ready for my lunch now. They come in and spoon broth or gruel into my mouth every day, whether I want it or not."

"If you care about Morgan, if you want to protect her, then you should tell me where she is. If we can get to her, it will make things go better."

Valerie's eyelids closed a little. "Promises, promises. I've heard it all."

"Okay," Kimberly said. "I'll leave you alone." She took a step away from the bed. "That seems like what you want anyway."

"It is." Valerie raised the call button, preparing to push.

But she didn't.

"If I see Morgan," Kimberly said, as she backed up to the door, "I'll tell her you said hi. Of course, I'll be arresting her at the same time."

Her hand rested on the door handle, but Valerie still hadn't pushed the call button.

"You sure you want me to go?" Kimberly asked.

Valerie stared at her, her face displaying a trace of desperation. Kimberly couldn't be certain, but it looked like she shook her head no.

"Okay," Valerie said. "Stay. If you really want to know what happened . . ."

73

TWO WEEKS LATER

I went through my usual routine in the Atlanta airport.

But everything seemed different. I'd probably never again be able to visit the Atlanta airport without thinking of Morgan, without reliving our first encounter.

I felt a greater sense of anxiety as I went through the security line, fumbling with my belt, almost falling over as I took off my shoes. My hands trembled ever so slightly as I gathered my belongings from the plastic bin once I reached the other side, where a single airport cop stood, watching me, watching everything, his thumbs hooked into the thick gun belt he wore around his waist.

Cops. I knew they'd be everywhere.

When my shoes were tied, I went to the gift shop closest to my gate. I did everything I normally did. I purchased a pack of gum, grabbed another paperback. This one promised twists and turns galore as an alcoholic ex-cop helped his former army buddy find his missing daughter. The army buddy was an alcoholic too. I felt their pain. I needed something to calm my nerves as well.

I went into the bathroom and used the facilities, then washed my hands. I reached into my pocket and took out the Xanax. I needed it then. More than ever. I stared at the little orange pill resting in the palm of my hand. People came and went around me. I probably looked like a junkie, wrestling with some inner demon over whether to pop that pill.

I decided I wouldn't take it.

Not because I didn't want it, but because I needed to be sharp. When I'd boarded any one of the thousands of flights I'd taken in the course of working for my dad, I hadn't worried about being clear. I didn't need to be. The work became routine. I felt like I could do it in my sleep. A little Xanax haze made no difference.

But a lot was at stake that day.

I wanted to remember everything that was about to happen.

I went into the concourse, looking both ways when I emerged from the bathroom, scanning the faces around me, searching for any that might be familiar. I saw the usual blur of anonymity, people rushing here and there, none of them making eye contact, none of them noticing me.

I crossed the stream of people and entered a bar called Brew-Flyers. It was the first time I'd been back in that airport since I'd met Morgan three weeks earlier. I walked around to the back, to the far side of the bar away from the concourse. It wasn't as nice as the Keg 'n Craft, not even close, but it would have to do. Five bleary-eyed travelers were scattered around the place, most of them sipping coffee and eating breakfast. One man, wearing a polo shirt and khaki pants, drank a large beer while he tapped away on an iPad. Wherever he was heading, he felt no need to remain sharp.

I hopped onto a barstool, dropping my carry-on to the floor next to me and looking up at the inane morning show playing on the TV. The volume was off, but the closed captions told me all I needed to know. Two talking heads were discussing disciplining children and whether spanking caused permanent psychological damage.

I thought of my dad. He'd never laid a hand on me. He'd never done anything but support me. And yet I'd recently told him I didn't want to work for his company anymore. That he'd be on his own going forward. I'd been trying very hard to suppress my guilt, to remind myself that it was my life to do with as I wanted.

I told myself he'd be fine. He'd adjust. He'd hire someone else. But I didn't quite feel better yet. . . .

And I wondered when—or if—I'd see him again, depending on how my time in the airport went.

The TV program shifted to a commercial, an advertisement for a Caribbean vacation. Just as I found myself getting sucked in by the images of palm trees and blue-green water, someone slid onto the stool next to mine.

I waited a moment before I looked, even though the anticipation flooded my bloodstream like boiling oil.

When a sufficient number of seconds had ticked away, I turned my head.

She'd cut her hair a few inches shorter and dyed it a different color. A dark, subtle shade of red. Again she wore dark glasses, but not the same ones she wore in the Keg 'n Craft. These were bigger, rounder, seemed to cover half of her face. She wore a knit cap that hugged her skull, and she carried just one bag, which she plopped on the floor next to mine.

Our hands rested next to each other on the bar top. My left and her right. The polish on her nails was chipped. I wanted to slide my hand over, place it on hers, and squeeze. But I didn't. I couldn't be that demonstrative, could I? Not yet.

The bartender approached us from across the way and asked us what we wanted.

I ordered a bourbon on the rocks, then turned to my left to watch her.

She kept the sunglasses on but ordered in the same voice I remembered from that first day.

"Bloody Mary," Morgan said.

And it was all under way.

74

We didn't say anything to each other as we waited for the drinks.

My heart thrummed along at what felt like twice its normal rate, fluttering like a trapped bird inside my rib cage, the adrenaline pumping through every cell in my body, lighting each up with a vibrant, surging energy.

I needed the alcohol to help me mellow out, and when the bartender set our drinks in front of us, I reached for mine right away, like a child grabbing at candy. Once the first couple of sips were down, a measure of calmness worked through me, tamping down the heat of the adrenaline. From the corner of my eye, I saw Morgan take long pulls through her straw, the red liquid of the Bloody Mary drawing up into her mouth like a transfusion.

"I'm sorry about your mom," I said as I turned to face her. "About Valerie."

"Thank you."

"I saw the obituary online," I said. "But I guess you know that."

"I know. Or you wouldn't be here. It's been exactly a week. . . ."

"That was the plan," I said. My mind raced along, full of a swirl of questions. "There are so many things I've wanted to ask you, so many things I've been trying to piece together. Questions you wouldn't answer that day—"

"Like what?"

"Like the name. You started using her last name. That's why you didn't show up on the passenger list the first time we met."

"You guessed. Or someone told you. The police, I'd imagine." She nodded. "You really want me to explain this stuff? Now?"

"I do."

"Okay, I'll try. I started the process to change my name right before I moved back to Nashville. But it takes a few months at least. So I kept using Reynolds until it became official, which was about a month before I met you. I'd always felt something special for Valerie, so I went with it. New life, new name. My own mom left something to be desired. And she was gone. . . . And, yes, it came in handy when I needed to travel under the radar. I used my new name on the plane. I'm using it now."

"But you told me Reynolds in the airport that first day. Why?"

"I didn't want you to find me. I really meant to never see you again. It was all too complicated. And I was right—it was. But you looked and found me anyway. I hadn't changed my name on Facebook yet, so the trail was right there for you."

I swallowed more of my bourbon, the ice rattling in the glass. "Did you get to see her? I mean, before she died?"

Morgan nodded. "I got in there a couple of times. Once just a few days before she died. There was one clerk, a woman who worked a lot of nights. I told you this, didn't I? I knew when she slipped out to smoke. She drank a lot of coffee and went to the bathroom over and over. When I got in that last time . . . Valerie . . . Mom . . . wasn't doing well. I don't even think she knew I was there. But I saw her. I squeezed her hand. I kissed her cheek. If she was still with it at all, then she knew."

I told her what I thought she wanted to hear. After all, I didn't know the answers to those questions better than anyone else. "I'm sure she knew you were there."

Morgan held my gaze for a second, then turned away, taking another long sip of her drink and staring at the bar top. She stayed that way for a moment before she reached up, swiping her index finger under the edge of her sunglasses.

"I guess you couldn't go to the funeral," I said.

She shook her head. "She really didn't have one. Just a small memorial. But I stayed away. I figured that's where the police would expect me to be, that's where they'd look for me. . . . Anyway, I'd already said good-bye."

"Sure, sure. That makes sense."

Then she seemed to get it together. She sniffled a couple times before taking another drink. "I went back to Wyckoff. I obviously had to leave in a hurry that night we were at Fantasy Farm."

Involuntarily I reached up and touched the back of my head, letting my fingers run over the spot where she'd hit me with the bottle. It was fully healed, didn't even hurt anymore. Morgan offered no comment about my injury or the fact that she was the one who'd inflicted it. So I asked.

"Why did you bring me out there to Fantasy Farm and then whack me with the bottle? What good did that do?"

"You have a lot of questions, don't you?" she asked.

"Yes, I do. And time is short, so could you answer them?"

"I know time is short," she said. "Our flight for LA boards in forty minutes. We'll be on the plane for four hours."

"I'd like to talk about some things now."

She sighed. "Okay. I got scared. I panicked when Simon showed up," she said. "I brought you there because . . . you'd been telling me to come clean, and I wanted to. I wanted to leave the ring there, with the body, and make a phone call to the police. They could find everything there and give it back to Simon. Then it would be over. And I could leave when Valerie died. But I was too scared to do it alone. I got panicky. When I went into that barn and came close to that body . . . it all hit me. Everything that had happened, how big it all was. I thought having you there would help. That you'd understand and support me. And someone else could go through it with me. No one else knew what I was going through except Valerie. But Simon blew the whole thing when he arrived. I freaked out. I couldn't deal with you and everything else."

"You could have just told me."

"I'm sorry. I am."

"Okay. What have you been doing?" I asked.

"I went back to Wyckoff last week," she said. "I visited my mom's grave. My biological mom. I hadn't seen it in a little while, and I figured I'm not going back there for a long, long time. Likely not ever. So I wanted to take one last look. I wanted to remember."

"That was probably a good idea."

"We can talk about all of this later," Morgan said. "Once we're on the plane and once we're away."

"Sure we can," I said. "But there's something you need to know." I hesitated, wondering what her response would be. "Did you hear the latest about the case? About Giles?"

"No, obviously I've been lying low."

I left my drink in front of me on the bar and swiveled on my stool so that I faced Morgan. She kept the sunglasses on, and I didn't bother to ask her to take them off.

"Several women who worked for Giles over the years reported feeling threatened by him. Several. They had disputes with him, problems at work over pay or bonuses or promotions, and he became physically aggressive toward them."

"I heard some rumors like that when I worked there, but none of it seemed conclusive."

"How about Megan Bright? Do you remember her?"

"I remember her. Barely. But, yeah, I remember her."

"She went on record and told the police that Giles grabbed her by the arm when they had a dispute at work. She feared for her safety—she thought he might hit her. And she eventually quit her job at the company and moved away. She didn't want to be around him, didn't want to deal with him. And, apparently, the company just overlooked these things or made them go away. No one really knew."

Morgan's lower lip dropped. She nodded a couple of times but didn't say anything.

"You see where I'm going with this?" I asked. "These women have said they felt threatened by Giles. In danger. So maybe *you* felt threatened by Giles. Maybe that's why everything that happened in his house that night happened. Maybe it was all an act of self-defense. Is that it? Is that what went down that night?"

"That's what you're hoping, isn't it?" she asked.

"I'm kind of hoping for the truth more than anything else," I said.

She reached over and put her hand on mine and gave it a squeeze.

"That's not exactly what happened, Joshua," she said. She paused, considering her words carefully. "That's not what happened at all."

And then my phone rang. Insistently.

I knew who it was.

75

The phone rang and rang.

Kimberly muttered under her breath. . . .

"Come on. Come on. Answer."

"Nothing?" Brandon asked.

Kimberly looked around at the uniformed airport cops, at Brandon. They were all looking to her, seeking her guidance and leadership.

Her wisdom, if she had any.

She ended the call when it went to voice mail and then immediately hit REDIAL.

The phone started its endless, annoying ringing again.

Kimberly replayed everything with Joshua Fields. . . .

They trusted him. They made a deal with him. He was supposed to be at the Keg 'n Craft in Concourse B. He was supposed to call and let them know once he met her.

But he hadn't called. . . .

And now no answer . . . Was he backing out?

Would they be able to find him in the giant Atlanta airport?

The phone kept ringing.

"Come on," she said. "Come on."

76

The phone stopped ringing. Then it started again. It insisted on being answered.

"I have to take this," I said.

She looked at me over her sunglasses, her eyes clouded by suspicion.

"Who is it?" she asked.

"I just have to take it."

"Is it your dad? Or that girl who was texting you?"

"I'll be right back."

I took the phone out to the concourse before she could say anything else. People streamed past in both directions. I dodged between them, looking back once to make sure Morgan wasn't following me. I took the call.

"Mr. Fields?" Detective Givens said. "I thought you were going to be in Concourse B. You were going to call us when you found her."

"I did say that, yes. But you need to give me a minute."

"Where are you? Really?" Givens asked. "More importantly, where is *she*? We took a big risk letting this happen this way. Now you have to give us something. We agreed to that."

A tour group went by, fifteen teenage kids wearing matching

T-shirts advertising their church. They laughed and playfully shoved one another.

"I need time to talk to her," I said. "You promised me that."

"Where are you?"

"I'm in a bar."

"Which one? The Keg 'n Craft?"

"A bar," I said. "They all look alike."

"Which concourse? B?"

I hung up.

It felt bold. A little crazy. But Morgan had that effect on me.

And the cops could wait just a little longer.

I took a deep breath and went back, cutting across the foot traffic in the concourse again. When I arrived, Morgan held her drink to her mouth, but she didn't take any. She held it in the air.

"What's going on?" she asked. "Who was that?"

I sat and faced her. She'd pushed the sunglasses back up on her nose, but her lips were parted in a way that said she was nervous. Uneasy.

"We don't have much time."

"Why?" Then recognition spread across her face. "Who was on the phone? Tell me."

"Not my travel agent."

"Who?" She studied my face. "Joshua? Is it the police?"

I took a moment to answer, her laser glare boring in on me.

"They came to me," I said. "After I got back from Nashville. They came by more than once."

She put her drink down, the glass clunking against the bar top. "What's wrong with you? Why are you doing this?"

"Hold on," I said. "*They* told me about these women who Giles was rough with. They don't know what happened in his house that night. I got the feeling from that Laurel Falls detective, Kimberly Givens, that they really don't have much to go on." I leaned forward. "They wanted me to wear a wire, to get you to spill everything when we met here. But I refused. I simply refused." I put my hand on her knee, felt the soft denim against my fingers. "I wouldn't do that to you. It's too dirty, too underhanded."

"They're bastards. They're—"

Before she went on, I stopped her, but her hand moved on top of mine.

"I wouldn't do that to you," I said.

She reached for her glass and took a drink. She studied me again, her eyes moving over my chest. "You're really not wearing one?"

"Of course not. Do you want to check?"

Her eyes roamed over my body again, studying my shirt for any bump that would give things away. There was nothing there, nothing to see.

"Okay, fine."

I checked my watch. I didn't know how far away the police were, but they would be coming. Soon enough they'd be coming.

"Listen, the cops told me something Valerie said."

Despite the sunglasses, I saw the change that passed over her when I mentioned Valerie and the police. Her cheeks flushed, and the muscles along her jaw tightened as though she was clenching her teeth.

"What is it?" she asked, the words slipping out through her pressed lips.

"If it's true, if what Valerie said to the police is true, then maybe . . . maybe it can help you out as well."

"What exactly did she say?"

I paused, not exactly sure how to say it out loud. "Valerie said she's the one who killed Giles Caldwell. She said she took it upon herself to go see him when you needed the money, to stick up for you and defend you, and when he wouldn't come around to her way of thinking, she killed him. She said *she* took the ring and hid the body."

Morgan let go of my hand and turned away. She swiveled on her stool and bent over her glass, gripping the straw and taking a long drink. Her throat bobbed as she swallowed.

"I know that sounds kind of crazy," I said. "A sick woman doing that. The cops seemed pretty skeptical of that story. But they have no way to prove or disprove it. And they have no way to prove or disprove whether Giles tried to hurt you."

The TV had shifted to a morning program in which the host stood behind a stove while the guest flipped a pancake in the air and caught it with a skillet. An announcement came over the PA system, summoning someone to Baggage Claim C.

Morgan let go of the straw and reached up with both hands, rubbing at her temples. She continued to rub them as she spoke to me. "So what you're saying is I have a couple of options here, right? I can claim self-defense because Giles has a documented history of threatening or even grabbing women and making them feel unsafe. Or I can back my mother's claim that she did it. That she's the one who went to Laurel Falls and killed Giles. Since she's gone now, they can't do anything to her. She's out of their reach completely."

"She is, yes. She was even when she confessed to Detective Givens. After all, they weren't likely to arrest and jail a woman who was in hospice taking her last breaths."

"I guess that's one benefit of dying," Morgan said.

"Maybe the only one."

She turned to face me again. "And what is your interest in all of this now?" Her words carried an undercurrent of anger, her cheeks flushing a deeper red. "You're here. And the police are here too? In the airport?"

"They are. I told them we were meeting here, but I didn't tell them the truth about where. I gave them the wrong concourse and the wrong bar. If I had told them where we were really meeting, they would have snatched you right away. I put them off. But they're going to be looking everywhere eventually, so we have to talk fast."

As if on cue, my phone rang again. Givens. I silenced it.

"I don't want to have to relive what happened in Giles's house that night."

"But you lied to me," I said. "Or at least you didn't tell the whole truth. You said you went there to demand your bonus, and when he balked you took the ring. But you knew exactly where his body was. You led me right to it. So if you didn't have anything to do with his death, how did you know where the body was? In a park near where you grew up?"

"You shouldn't worry about this," she said, shaking her head but not looking at me.

"The cops aren't going to let it go. So I am worried. We can't move ahead if we can't trust each other."

She stared into the distance before heaving a deep sigh. "Okay," she said. "Okay. What do you want to know? Just ask me, and I'll tell you what you want to know. I thought this could wait until later, but you might as well fire away now. And then we're never talking about it again."

77

"What about the CCTV?" Kimberly asked. "Can they see anything?"

The airport cop shook his head. "It's not that easy. There are thousands of people here. They could be in a bathroom. A gift shop. We don't cover everything with the cameras."

"Shit," Kimberly said. "Shit, shit, shit. If they get on a plane . . . or if they leave the airport . . ."

78

I hesitated before I spoke. Once, when I was a kid, I saw a bird's nest in a tall pine tree in our backyard. I wanted to know what was inside—eggs? chicks?—so I climbed up to the branch it was on, about twenty feet off the ground. Then I had to shinny out along the limb in order to get close enough to peek into the nest. It all seemed like a good idea until I got there.

The farther I edged out, the farther away the ground appeared. And I started to wonder how I'd come that far without thinking it all through.

But did I just want to go back to the safety of the ground without learning the answer? After all that effort?

I felt the same way in BrewFlyers that day. I'd come so far. . . . I needed to hear it all, but . . .

"Valerie had a gun," I said. "The police know that. And she used it to protect herself, even to protect you, before."

Morgan looked disappointed. Her shoulders slumped. "So you really *have* been talking to the police. And believing everything they tell you."

"No, they've been talking to me. At me."

"Whichever it is, they've told you a lot."

"See, I've been wondering—how did you get into Giles's house?

And once you were in there, how did you get him to sit and listen to what you had to say? He could have called the police. He could have made you leave. He could have just dragged you out. But if you had something to control him, something to keep him frozen in place . . . something like a gun . . ."

"You want to know if I took my mom's gun up there to threaten Giles?"

"Did you?"

"No."

"Did your mom?"

She leaned forward and spoke in a low voice. "Why do you want to know all of this? And in such detail?" She leaned even closer, until her face was about six inches from mine. "When we ran into each other that day at River Glen, you didn't have any of these questions. I was so moved by the fact you were visiting Valerie. And then when we talked in the car, and we made these plans to go away once . . . once she was gone. I thought we'd figured it all out. Why do you need to know all of this now? Are you having second thoughts? If you are, you can just leave. We can go our own ways now."

"I'm asking *because* we're going away together," I said. "We didn't talk very long at River Glen. We couldn't afford to. They were after you then and they're looking for you now. They're going to be looking everywhere in this airport. And I'm in it too. But if we're going to do this, if we're going to start over together somewhere, then I need to know what happened that night. We need to trust each other. I quit my job, Morgan. I'm giving everything up. We need to begin on the right foot. No secrets. Nothing hidden."

"And that's what you want to know?" Morgan asked. "If it was my mother or if it was me who killed Giles?"

"Yes. Because I guess I find it a little hard to believe that a woman who was dying of cancer would be able to drive an hour from Nashville to Laurel Falls and still have the strength to kill a man. Gun or no gun."

Morgan smiled a little. She looked like someone remembering something mildly amusing and strange. "You're underestimating her, Joshua. You don't know how strong she was, how fiercely protective of her children. That's what she lived for, her kids. Her foster kids. Yes, she did go there," she said. "She had the strength to make that drive, and she went there to confront Giles. But that's not all of it."

79

Kimberly and Brandon walked down Concourse B with a uniformed officer on either side of them. The word had gone out to the police and security throughout the airport along with photographs and descriptions of Joshua Fields and Morgan Reynolds, aka Morgan Woodward.

Passengers gawked at them as they walked by, but they also moved out of the way, parting and stepping to the far sides of the concourse to allow the officers to march through. Kimberly had been out of uniform for so long she'd forgotten the way most citizens backed away when a decked-out officer came by.

They checked every restaurant, every store. But the airport was massive, almost like a small city unto itself. They might be in the wrong concourse, might be a twenty-minute walk from Fields and Reynolds. Maybe farther.

Just get to them before they get on a damn plane.

She'd held off on using her last resort—a complete lockdown of the airport. Nobody wanted that. Nobody wanted to deal with the hassles and delays that would create. The headlines, the angry tweets, the explanations to her superiors.

But if they had to . . .

"Can we search every concourse here?" Brandon asked. "This place is endless."

"They're looking everywhere," Kimberly said. "But *I* want to find them. I want to ask Fields what's wrong with him. Why isn't he doing what we asked him to do?"

"We asked him to get the story if he could," Brandon said. "Maybe that's what he's doing."

"Maybe. Or maybe they're on their way to Belize or Timbuktu."

"We knew it was a risk, letting them meet, letting them go this far. . . ."

"I know, Brandon," she said.

She tried not to think of any mistakes she might have made. She tried not to think of the promotion she'd just earned days before. The one she might lose if things in the airport went sideways.

And Maria. She wanted to make her proud. Wanted to prove for her daughter what she could do.

Kimberly tried to focus on the task at hand—finding Joshua Fields and Morgan Reynolds.

80

"Valerie went there to defend me," Morgan said. "She knew I wasn't getting the money I deserved, and she knew Giles wasn't budging."

"And you needed the money," I said. "She was sick, and you hadn't been working."

"Yes, we needed the money. She had doctors' bills piling up. Prescriptions and tests all the time. Plus she wanted to leave something behind for me. When she was gone. But even with insurance it was getting way too expensive. She had a little house in Nashville, but she thought she might lose it because of the bills."

"How did she manage that, though?" I asked. "I mean, she was so sick she went into hospice. . . . She must have gone into hospice right after she went up there to Laurel Falls."

Morgan looked into her glass. There was melted ice tinged with red in the bottom, and a lonely celery stalk next to her straw. She picked up her glass and rattled it, then put it down like she was disappointed.

"Valerie had her moments when she was really, really doing well," Morgan said. "Even when she was getting sicker, she'd have some days when it seemed like she was perfectly fine. She'd get out of bed. She'd cook. She'd shower and put on makeup. Those days were fewer and farther between that last month . . . and they were kind of cruel. Because on those days I would forget how sick she was, how inevitable the end that was coming."

"That seems so strange," I said. "That she could have those kinds of days."

"I've talked to other people with relatives who had cancer. It happens. Someone can appear to be as healthy as anything one day and then be out of it the next. They can be that way just days before they die. Sometimes they can even seem well on the day they die."

"Fascinating," I said. I remembered the words of the hospice nurse when I went to see Valerie: *Dying remains something of a mystery.* "So I'm guessing she was having one of these good days when she decided to go see Giles. With her gun."

"She'd been talking about it, saying things like she was going to go and set things straight with Giles before it was too late. I didn't take her that seriously, although now I realize I should have. That day she got in her car and drove off, I was out of the house running an errand. I was out meeting with the hospice people, ironically, because I knew that was getting close. And then I came home and couldn't find her. She didn't answer her phone. There was no note. Then I checked her bedside table and saw her gun was gone. I immediately remembered all her talk about going to see Giles. I put it together, but I didn't know how long she'd been gone. I didn't know what to do, so I jumped in my car and drove off after her."

"And you caught up with her?"

"You know, I was more worried about her health than anything else," Morgan said. "I thought I might come across her on the road. Her car in a ditch or maybe find her pulled over because she felt sick."

"But she made it to Laurel Falls? Right?" I asked. "That's what happened?"

"She did make it. And when I got there and rang the bell, Giles let me in."

"He was still alive?"

"Yes. Very much alive. He looked almost happy to see me. I'm sure Valerie had told him who she was, and he hoped I was there to straighten everything out. That I would get the crazy lady out of his house so he could get back to his normal, entitled life."

I started to feel a dull ache growing in the center of my chest. I looked at my empty glass, suddenly wishing for more bourbon. If Giles Caldwell was alive and well when Morgan showed up . . .

"What happened then?" I asked. "What went wrong?"

She scratched her cheek absently, the nails moving slowly across her clear skin. Skin I'd touched that night in the hotel. Skin I'd touched and kissed and wanted to feel again . . .

"Giles had taken the gun away from her. It was just sitting there on an end table. Valerie was in a chair in the living room. She looked . . . unwell, totally tired and spent. Driving up there and saying whatever she'd said to Giles must have taken a lot out of her. And it scared me seeing her like that. I think it scared Giles too. I thought we were going to have to call an ambulance. That's really how I thought it was going to go. And if we did, how was I or anyone else going to explain what we were doing there in Giles's house? The two of us had each driven an hour in separate cars to confront a guy over money I couldn't really prove I was owed. And Valerie had brought her gun to do it. How did that sound?"

"Why didn't you just leave?" I asked. "You could have put your mom in the car, apologized, and left."

Morgan flared. Her cheeks and the tips of her ears flushed even redder than before. "Apologize? To him?" She shook her head from side to side. "Never. I was never going to do that."

"Valerie could have. She was the one who brought the gun."

"No. Never. I'd take her out of there, but I wouldn't apologize. And I wouldn't let her either."

"So then what happened?" I asked. I didn't say it out loud, but it was there between us. At some point, Giles ended up dead.

The pain in my chest increased, spreading through my torso. If I'd been older or in poor health, I would have worried I was having a heart attack. But I knew the pain wasn't physical. It was emotional. I braced myself as though waiting for a physical blow.

81

Morgan looked away, out toward the concourse and then up at the TV, which played a commercial for a roasting pan. She puffed her cheeks out, and her hands were clenched into tight fists.

She turned back to me but didn't say anything.

I said, "I'm not going to go away and uproot my whole life unless I know what happened in that house. That's the only way I can do it."

"I told you in the hotel that night. In Wyckoff."

"No, you didn't," I said. "You didn't tell me how a woman with cancer, a woman who had collapsed in a chair, could strangle a grown man."

"He was out of shape—"

"And you also didn't tell me how that body got out of the house and from Laurel Falls out to Wyckoff. And ended up buried in the middle of Fantasy Farm. If it was Valerie, then tell me. We can all be done with this. Or if you thought your life was in danger. If he tried to hurt you . . . I'm sorry, but I have to know."

She shifted on the stool a little. She looked at her watch and let out a deep breath. "Is that what you want to hear?" she asked. "You want to hear that I did it all? Would that make you feel better right before we leave together?"

"At least I'd know what I was getting into," I said. "You haven't exactly been predictable, Morgan. Hell, I'm kind of surprised you showed up here at all. You've left me hanging more than once."

I could tell she was hurt, even with her eyes covered. "You know why I did what I did those other times. And I promised to be here today. We both did."

I had promised that. And I couldn't believe I was about to ask the question I needed to ask. But I had to do it.

"Who killed him? Who strangled him?"

Morgan stood up from her stool and took a couple of steps away, toward the concourse, and then she came back. She bent down to pick up her bag but stopped. She just waited there, hands on hips, obviously trying to figure out what to do next.

I let her think.

She eventually sat down again and turned to face me. She studied me for a long time, and then resumed her story.

"Did you see Valerie's arm?" she asked, her voice as level as the bar I rested my hand on.

I thought about it. The bruise. Valerie had said something about falling, about Morgan worrying.

She thinks I'm *protective.*

"What happened?" I asked.

I held her gaze and waited for answers. My face felt numb. I expected my jaw to drop, but I kept it in place through force of will.

"I was going to take Valerie out of there. Just get her up and in the car and away. And hope nothing else came of it."

"Okay."

She shook her head from side to side, so slowly it was almost imperceptible. She didn't look sad or angry. She looked tired. "Valerie . . . Mom . . . she couldn't leave well enough alone. She couldn't concede we'd lost. She tried to get the gun. She pushed herself out of the chair, just barely, and reached for the gun. When she did, Giles grabbed her by the arm. He held her and then pushed her back into the chair. Hard."

"Did that hurt her?" I asked. "Did she try to get up again and get the gun?"

"It was a breaking point for me. I just got so sick of it. I got so sick of being told no. Of . . . of Giles's absolute certainty that he could do anything or say no to me and get away with it. That he could shut me out and shut me down. Or try to hurt her. I had a sick mom, and we needed money. And he wanted to say no and not give an inch. He could just push someone around, literally and figuratively. It ended up being too much for me to take." She laid her hand flat on the bar. "Joshua, he saw my mom. He saw what Valerie looked like and how desperate she was . . . and still he said no. Just like that. One word over and over. *No.*"

"And you just . . ." My words came out low. I almost couldn't hear myself over the din of the airport.

"He took . . . I think, but I'm not sure—I think he took a step toward her, toward where she sat in the chair," she said. "I was behind him, and he was watching Mom, so I got the advantage on him. I'm taller than he is—was—by a little, so I could get leverage. And it was like a choke hold, and I squeezed and I held on. And on. Valerie tried to stop me. I remember that. She told me to stop, to let go. But I felt like I was outside of my body, looking down on the scene, looking down on myself choking the life out of this man. And I couldn't stop. I didn't want to stop. I just didn't want to."

I suddenly felt cold, like my core temperature had plunged twenty degrees, and if there'd been a winter coat or a blanket nearby, I would have wrapped myself in it. I sat there facing Morgan, letting everything she'd said to me sink in.

"It's not like in a movie," she said. "It took some time."

A heavy silence fell between us, broken only by the never-ending noises of the airport. The announcements, the conversation, the ringing phones, and the low rumble of the planes.

It took me a moment to come back to myself, to remember that there was still more to the story, more that needed to be told.

"And you took the body . . . out to Fantasy Farm."

"I took the ring, and I messed the place up a little so it looked like a robbery. I just wanted to get rid of him, to never have to see him again."

"You drove thirty minutes with a dead man in your trunk?"

"I sure as hell obeyed the speed limit. I had to stop and get gas on my way out of town. My car was on empty. I ran right into an old friend. . . . Every mile felt like it was loaded with land mines."

"Why that park? Why not . . . a field? The woods?"

"I didn't plan to go to Fantasy Farm. I was scared as hell, and I just wanted to get rid of him. Somewhere. Anywhere. I went outside of town to the Hawke River. I'd been kayaking there a lot growing up, and it was quiet and deserted. And this was late at night. I was just going to throw him in. But . . ."

"But?"

"I turned off the main road onto the smaller one that led down to the kayak put-in. And there was a cop back there. I don't know why, but he flashed his headlights at me so I'd pull over." She looked pale, sickened, as she relived the moment. "I thought I was done. Arrested and gone forever. He asked me what I was doing there, and I just stammered through something, saying I was out for a drive, clearing my head. He looked suspicious. And he ran my license, and when he saw I was clean, he told me to go home."

"But you didn't?"

"I had a dead man in my trunk," she said. "I had to get out of there, so I did. And my mind scrambled for someplace else to take him. I thought of a cornfield, but they were all being harvested right then. If I put him there, he'd be found almost immediately. I tried to think of the last place someone would look for a body, a place that no one would associate with death or crime. A place nobody went anymore."

"An abandoned amusement park."

"I could only remember my mom passing out there. That's the most powerful memory I had. Why not dump a body there? Why not bury another shitty memory in that place? Every kid in the county went there. Every family for fifty years. They couldn't connect it to me."

"That must have been a scary drive."

"It was."

"Morgan," I said, "this sounds insane."

"It was. Valerie left for home when I left with Giles. She made it okay . . . but something went out of her that night. She wasn't the same. When I came back from Wyckoff, she was out of it, slipping. That was late on Thursday night, early on Friday morning. I was scared, but I couldn't keep up with caring for her. She was in pain, tired. I told hospice she fell—that's why her arm was bruised. And I told them I was worried she would fall again. They didn't question any of it. She went in on Friday around noon. They had a bed open, and she went right in."

"You must have been terrified you'd be caught."

"I was. More than you can know. Mom told me to leave. She said I could just leave the state, the country. I had my passport and ID with the different name. I could go, but I didn't want to. She'd die alone in that hospice room. It was Mom's idea to send me to Virginia, to talk to Aunt Linda. I made a deal with Mom. If Aunt Linda agreed to come and stay until the end, I would leave. I wouldn't even come back to Nashville. But Aunt Linda didn't go along, and that was when you saw me in the airport flying back that first Tuesday morning."

"People thought you'd disappeared. Didn't they try to reach you in Virginia?"

"They did. I got texts and calls. But I ignored them all. You see, when I first got there, it looked like Aunt Linda was going to go to Nashville to sit with Mom. And then I would leave. For good. So I didn't respond to anyone reaching out to me. I'd let them all go in my mind. And I was afraid someone would tell the police where I was. When the police asked Mom where I was, she said she didn't know. That's when they all reported me missing. But I should never have gone to Virginia. . . ."

"Because?"

"That's when Simon came and threatened her. He came to Nashville on Monday and started asking about me. He'd heard about me from someone at TechGreen. He figured I was his best lead. Maybe his only one. Word got back to Mom from a friend of mine that he was asking about me, and she called him, telling him to knock it off. But he went to River Glen on Monday evening and confronted her. Threatened her. And me. I found out about it that day we met. When I went to the bathroom at the airport, my mom called. When Simon threatened her, I felt such enormous pressure. I wanted to make it right . . . if I could. That's why I went to back to Wyckoff."

"What were you going to do there? Leave the ring with the body . . . and what?"

"Call the police once Valerie was gone. Call the police and let them know where everything was. I'd be gone, and so would she. But you know what happened."

Indeed I did.

I finally turned away from her and looked at my glass, but it was empty. I looked for something, anything, I could do with my hands, anything to distract me.

But there was nothing. Just the two of us. With all the truth laid bare between us.

Nowhere to hide. Nothing to hide behind.

"We should go," Morgan said, looking at her watch. "We should head to our gate. It's time. We were cutting it close already."

I didn't say anything.

"I mean, if you still want to go," she said. "Do you?"

I still didn't respond. I couldn't. Everything she had just told me swirled in my head.

"Joshua?"

I shook my head.

"I don't know if I can do it, Morgan," I said. "I just don't know."

82

Kimberly's radio crackled.

"I think we have eyes on them," the voice said.

Her heart jumped out of her chest.

"Where?"

"Concourse A. Some bar. BrewFlyers. Back by the window."

"Concourse A is one over," Brandon said. "Let's go. Fast."

They started running.

"Keep an eye on them," she said.

Please, please, please . . .

83

Morgan slid off her stool and picked up her bag. She slung it over her shoulder.

"What are you saying?" she asked. "We need to go."

"I just wanted to know the truth," I said. "And I thought . . . I hoped the truth would be different from what you just told me. I really did."

"I'm not lying to you, Joshua," she said. "I told you exactly what happened that night in Giles's house."

"I know," I said. "That's the problem. Your mom threatened him with a gun. Can you blame him for grabbing her? For defending himself? Maybe he was a shit heel to those other women, but in this case . . ."

"Did you want me to lie?"

"No, I didn't. You had a lifeline. Self-defense or Valerie's confession, but neither of those is true," I said. I felt frozen. Stunned. "Go now. Maybe you can make it to the gate. Maybe you can get on the plane to California. I won't tell them anything else until after you're gone."

She looked at me, confused. Then realization spread across her face.

"You're not going to come, are you? You're really not going to come."

"I wanted to prove to the cops you didn't kill Giles. I wanted to prove it to myself. I really had myself convinced until this conversation. I wanted to get away clean with you, to have a clean slate and leave the past in the past."

She continued to stare at me. Then she took a step forward, her face showing a mixture of hurt and affection.

"You really can't do it, can you?"

"I'm sorry."

She lowered her head, her shoulders slack and loose. It took her a moment to look back up, and when she did I saw one tear on her cheek.

"Don't be," she said. "I wouldn't want you to go with me if you didn't want to. Even if in the end it means I can't have you."

She leaned in and pressed her lips against mine. For an eternal but fleeting moment, we kissed, our tongues touching, my hands on her back, her hands in my hair.

And just as quickly it was over.

She pulled back from me, letting her hand trail along my arm and squeeze my hand before she left.

"Good-bye."

Morgan turned and started for the concourse, walking quickly. She almost bumped into a waiter who carried a tray of food, and he bobbled everything for a moment but managed to keep it all from falling.

I paused a moment, and then I jumped off the stool, leaving my bag behind, and followed her. I also brushed past the frazzled waiter, almost knocking him over, drawing stares from the other patrons, shocking them out of their airport-induced stupor.

Morgan turned right out of the bar and onto the concourse, walking fast at first and then breaking into a run. I hustled along behind her, dodging passengers and employees. The airport had become more crowded, filling as the clock ticked toward noon.

"Morgan!"

I lost sight of her in the crowd.

I ran faster, bumping and brushing against more bodies. A woman cursed at me when I stepped on her foot. A man pushed me, saying, "Slow down."

I ignored them and kept going.

And then the crowd thinned for a moment. Or maybe it parted. I couldn't be sure which.

Morgan stood in the middle of the concourse twenty feet ahead of me. She clutched her bag as she turned to face me.

I froze. There was no one between us. No one obstructing my view.

She looked so beautiful and so, so sad. And I didn't know what to do.

She raised her right hand, palm up. Empty.

"It's okay," she said. "It's over."

"I know," I said.

She looked past me. I heard rushing footsteps behind me.

Cops?

"It's fine," she said. "I'll tell them everything."

And I really didn't know what else to do.

Detective Givens came up behind Morgan. With three uniformed airport cops. And two more cops appeared from behind me, heading for Morgan.

They closed in on her, engulfing her.

Let her go, I thought.

But I was telling myself more than I was telling them.

She disappeared from my sight again.

For good.

84

It took a few hours to sort everything out.

I spent most of the time sitting in a room outside the airport police station. Waiting.

Eventually Detective Givens came out and sat in the chair next to mine. She looked worn-out—her hair was pulled back and her clothes were wrinkled—but also relieved, as if a burden she'd been carrying for weeks had been lifted from her back and shoulders.

"You're a lucky man, Mr. Fields," she said.

"I am?"

"You are. Morgan is telling us everything. And from what I can tell, she told you everything in that bar. I think she's relieved to get it out in the open."

"How does that make me lucky?" I asked.

"She's saying you had nothing to do with any of it. Not the murder, not the cover-up. I've had my doubts about you, considering the way you've behaved. And especially considering the fact you jerked us around a little here, telling us the wrong concourse and the wrong bar where you were going to meet. We could charge you." She raised a finger for each charge she ticked off. "Obstruction. Aiding and abetting. Conspiracy."

"Conspiracy?"

She remained silent for an uncomfortable amount of time, staring me down. She wanted me to squirm. She wanted me to panic and sweat.

I didn't have much left to feel. Morgan's story in the bar and her arrest in the concourse had pretty much drained me. It was over, and I didn't really care about the threats from the police. If they wanted to make my life miserable, they could.

I kind of expected it.

"Can I see her?" I asked.

"No. You're not going to see her for a while," she said. "Maybe you should feel relieved too?"

I thought about my answer. Then I said, "Yeah, in some ways. But also . . . It's complicated."

"Most things are," she said. "You know, we all took a huge risk letting this play out this way. Letting you come to the airport to meet her, letting you have one last conversation with her. We figured this was the best chance of finding Morgan and getting the truth out of her. But if she hadn't shown up today . . ." She lifted her hands and then let them fall back into her lap. "I don't know where we'd be. I'm not sure where you would be either."

"I understand. I thought there was a little more than a fifty-fifty chance she'd show up."

"I think she showed up for you, as much as anything else. She wanted to see you again. I really believe she wanted to go away with you. And I know you wanted to hear a different version of events. But at least we all know the truth now."

I felt so much at once. A stabbing regret in my chest, the ache of knowing the truth. And along with it a surge of emotion. She did want to see me. I fixed on the image of her in the middle of the concourse as the cops closed in.

Defiant to the end, refusing to apologize for killing a man who cheated her out of money.

I didn't like it, but I knew the truth.

And I remembered the kiss. I'd never forget that.

"I need to get back in there," Detective Givens said. "I think the officers have all the information we need from you for now. But we'll be in touch when we need to be. And can I offer you some advice?"

"Sure."

"Just get back to your regular life. And don't look back."

And the swirl of emotions grew more chaotic then. A vibration traveled through my body, one that moved from my fingertips to the center of my chest. The pain I'd recently felt there faded, replaced by a buzzing, humming quiver.

I was sitting in an airport with no job. But I had plenty of money and plenty of frequent flier miles.

I had nowhere to be and nothing to do. I'd quit my job, broken up with Renee once and for all.

I could go anywhere. Do anything.

I was free.

And the thought scared the hell out of me.

"Good-bye, Mr. Fields," Givens said.

85

I walked out into the concourse, unsure of where to go.

For so long, I'd thought being free of my job and any obligation would liberate me. But I quickly learned how scary liberation felt.

I stopped in front of a departure board. The cities rolled by— big ones, medium ones. East Coast, West Coast. So many options . . .

I don't know how long I had been lost in my thoughts, contemplating all of my options, when I heard my name being called by the PA announcer.

I was being told to head to the nearest white courtesy telephone.

The police. It had to be the police.

But I also flashed back to the time in Nashville, the time when I picked up the white phone and heard Morgan on the other end of the line.

Could she be calling me?

I went to the phone and picked it up.

"How are you, champ?"

My dad's distinctive, gravelly voice coming through the line surprised me like nothing else. He might as well have been calling me from the moon.

"Dad? What's going on?" I asked. "Why didn't you call my phone?"

"I tried. You're not answering."

Then I remembered. Ever polite, I'd turned it off when the cops were questioning me. "Sorry about that."

"Where are you?" he asked.

How did I explain it? How did I explain any of it?

"I'm in Atlanta," I said.

"I know that," he said. "I'm here too. I mean, where are you in the airport?"

"You're here?" I asked. "What are you doing here?"

"You booked your flight using the company account," he said. "I got a notice saying you were traveling to Atlanta. And I asked myself, 'Why would my son who just quit his job be heading off to Atlanta? Could it have anything to do with this girl he's been chasing? With the cops hounding him? Might he need moral support if it doesn't work out?'"

I didn't know what to say. I felt some of the weight lift from my shoulders. Someone else understood. . . .

"Thanks, Dad," I said.

And then I told him which terminal I was in.

I waited for him, and he showed up with his beat-up carry-on over his shoulder. He came right over to me and gave me a hug, a rarity, and I welcomed being folded up in his arms. He smelled the same as when I was a kid—of cologne and shaving cream. A hint of the cigars he occasionally smoked.

We sat down next to each other.

He dug around in his pants pocket and brought something out. "I stopped in the gift shop and bought some Life Savers. You always loved these when you were little."

I took the roll from him. "Thanks."

"You're welcome."

"I thought after I'd quit you'd be so busy, so overwhelmed. . . ."

"Nah." He waved my words away like a pesky fly. He considered me for a moment, and he clearly had something to say. "So, I'm guessing things didn't work out so well here, did they? With the girl?"

My thoughts were scattered, like leaves caught up in a high wind. I tried to sort them out and get them straight. "No, not exactly."

I gave him a quick rundown of the events, all the way up to and including Detective Givens's threats and advice to get on with my life.

"You thought this Morgan would be innocent?"

"Yeah. I couldn't accept that I'd have these kinds of feelings for someone who had done something so awful. I thought it would turn out differently. And I'm still processing all of that. I'm going to be processing it for a long time. I feel sick about her going to jail and everything."

"Let me tell you, kiddo, relationships don't always work out the way we want. I know that. Believe me." His eyes shone in the harsh fluorescent lights. "Hell, maybe I'm to blame. Your mom and I didn't set the best example. Or maybe I made you work too hard or expected too much of you."

"It's not that. Not you." I swallowed hard before I went on. "I've been holding things close to the vest in every part of my life, playing it safe. The job, the relationship with Renee. But then I let my guard down with Morgan. Because she was different. She was . . . just not like anyone else I knew. Maybe there's a lesson there. Maybe it's good I stepped off the merry-go-round."

Dad nodded. He looked pleased. I wasn't sure I deserved the look, but I took it.

"You know," he said, "I was thinking about it, and I realized I never took you to Disney World when you were a kid. And maybe that was a deficiency in your life."

"Do you think that's why I fell for Morgan?" I asked.

"Who knows?" He shrugged. "Do you want to go?"

"No, thanks. I have no desire to go back to Florida."

"Neither do I. I've been there so much lately, I could run for governor. Somewhere else, then? I rearranged things, so I have the time. But maybe you just want to be on your own. If you're interested in doing your own thing, I could catch a flight and do some work—"

"No, that's okay," I said. "It might be nice to just get away for fun."

He looked relieved. Happy.

And I liked seeing him that way.

"So where, then?" he asked. "You know, I was just thinking. . . . I've been to Arizona a dozen times for work, but I've never been to the Grand Canyon."

"Me neither."

"And Monument Valley is right near there. We could see that too."

"I'd love to."

He smacked me on the knee and stood up. "Great. Let's go check the big board for a flight."

But I remained in my seat. He looked down at me, his face creased with concern. He looked older. The lines deeper around his eyes, his hair thinner and grayer.

"What's wrong?" he asked. "Are you still . . . I mean, are you waiting for something from her?"

"It's not that, Dad. It's just . . ."

"What?"

"I don't want to fly. I'm not sure I want to fly ever again. Can we rent a car?"

Dad adjusted the strap of the carry-on. His brow furrowed. "Drive all the way to Arizona?" he asked, thinking out loud.

"We'd see a lot of the country," I said. "More than we've ever seen from the air."

He started nodding, warming to the idea. "A cross-country road trip. Sounds kind of crazy."

I stood up. "So you'll do it?"

"I'll miss more work," he said, scratching his chin. "But what the heck. I mean . . . how many more times can we do this?"

I clapped him on the shoulder. "As many as we want, Dad. As many as we want."

Acknowledgments

Thanks again to the highly creative Kara Thurmond for her Web design.

Thanks again to the tireless Ann-Marie Nieves and Get Red PR.

Thanks again to all the amazing folks at Berkley/Penguin.

Thanks again to the brilliant marketing team of Jin Yu and Bridget O'Toole.

Thanks again to my fantastic publicist, Loren Jaggers.

Thanks again to my wise and wonderful editor, Danielle Perez.

Thanks again to my stupendous agent, Laney Katz Becker.

Thanks again to all my family and friends, especially Craig Williams for his knowledge of airports and air travel.

And unending thanks to Molly McCaffrey for all things.